Deep Midnight

Deep Midnight

SHANNON DRAKE

ZEBRA BOOKS
KENSINGTON PUBLISHING CORP.
http://www.zebrabooks.com

ZEBRA BOOKS are published by

Kensington Publishing Corp.
850 Third Avenue
New York, NY 10022

All Kensington titles, imprints and distributed lines are available at special quantity discounts for bulk purchases for sales promotion, premiums, fund-raising, educational or institutional use.

ISBN 0-7394-1949-8

Dedicated with deep thanks to the folks at Max Art Shop, a wonderful stop in Venice.

To Antonia Sautter, Marie Lo Cueto, Nicole De Leo, Chiara Scomazzon, Tomaso Satta, Francesco Cavaliere, Teresa Lucente, Isabella Pachera, Clivia Muechler, Stefano Dardi, Franca Krippner, Katia Del Neri, Simonetta Perri, and especially to Sandra Poletto, who tries so hard and so patiently to help me with my Italian.

Also, to the Danieli, truly one of the most beautiful hotels in the world, and to the staff there, who are wonderful.

And, with love and appreciation to the incredible friends we met in Venice—Robin and Michelle Archer, David and Janet G.-W., Natacha Marro, Beatrix Ost, and Ludwig Kuttner.

PROLOGUE

The moon was full. Huge in the sky, a brilliant, iridescent orb that seemed to stare down mockingly at the earth.

Though his night vision was excellent, it helped him to see.

From the Campanile, he had chosen to survey the city. He looked out at the dazzle of the evening; at the people milling about, at the clear beauty of the dark sky far above, and he felt his tension and awareness increase.

Carnevale.

Venice.

The first true night of celebration. The first night of the grand balls . . .

Fat Tuesday.

The delirium of it all.

Tonight. They would strike tonight.

For far below, crowding the streets, alleyways, and canals, were all manner of masqueraders. Musicians, entertainers, stilt-walkers, rich and poor, all were out for a night of pretense, playacting, charades. The world here now was shadow, despite the lights that spilled forth in the city, despite the lanterns so many of the players carried.

Fat Tuesday . . .

The feast before Lent.

Yes, they would seek to feast tonight. And they would do so. Glut themselves . . .

Unless . . .

Silently, with the grace and skill of the natural born predator, he left his perch.

And entered the city.

Jordan Riley threw open the shutters at the window in her room at the Hotel Danieli, looking out at the loud and festive world around her. From her vantage point, she could see the waters of the Canale di San Marco, and down toward the Grand Canal; she could see the vaporettos, gondolas, and streams of people coming and going from the docks. Across the water was the magnificent dome of the church of Santa Maria della Salute. And, stretching her body out the open window, she could see, to her right, the beginnings of St. Mark's Square, the site of unbelievable revelry. The night was wild with the sounds of laugher and music, and everywhere there was camaraderie, joviality. The pre-Lent celebration might be well known and loved in other great cities as well, but Jordan didn't think that anyone else, anywhere, knew how to celebrate Carnevale quite the way the Venetians did.

No matter how strange, they were elegant as well.

"Jordan, ready?"

She turned around. Her cousin Jared was standing in her doorway, though, if she hadn't known it was Jared, she wouldn't have had the least idea that it was he. He'd come as the dottore, a popular costume here. Plagues had once consumed Venice, so the dottore wore a mask with a huge nose, usually beaked—reminiscent of the covering doctors had worn to combat the fetid vapors. The masks were elaborate, frightening. Jared wore a voluminous, hooded cloak as well; he hadn't been inclined to dress in anything as foppish as a Renaissance costume. The cloak and mask were easily donned; maybe that was why the costume was so popular.

"Ready? Yes! I can't wait. It's incredible out there!" She'd been to Venice several times before, but never for Carnevale. This year Jared and his wife, Cindy, had talked her into accompanying them to the festival. She felt a little awkward, being with the two of them but on her own at tonight's costume ball—unescorted. She felt just a bit like a fifth wheel. She spoke enough Italian to order room service and find her way around, but though it was true that many Venetians spoke English, she was afraid she'd find herself seated next to strangers with whom she couldn't begin to converse. Still, the excitement of the trip had outweighed the fear.

"Thank God! I thought you were going to try to weasel out tonight!" he told her.

"Me? Weasel out? Not on your life!" Of course, she was lying. She'd been thinking of doing exactly that until darkness had fallen, the music had begun, and the sheer vibrance of the evening had awakened a spirit of total devil-may-care adventure in her. Surely, there would be someone with whom she could talk, dance, and while away the hours.

"You're smashing, by the way," he told her.

She walked from the window and dipped a curtsy to him. "Thanks."

She'd rented her costume at the last minute, but it was spectacular. Renaissance—a popular era here—and festooned with sequins, faux jewels, and an overlay of lace. The gown had been available because Jordan happened to be petite—five three, standing very straight—and an even hundred pounds. The dress had been made for a young woman who'd had to cancel about a month ago, and no one the right size had arrived since.

"Smashing—and you look taller."

"It's the shoes," she told him, showing him the period shoes she wore. She wondered, however, if they'd really worn such wretched heels in times gone by. Surely, this kind of heel was a modern nod to women's vanity.

"Let's hope you don't shrink like Granny Jay. You'll be down to nothing."

"Go ahead. Be cruel because you got all the 'tall' genes," she told him. Strange. He was so tall; she was so petite. But they had both inherited very deep green eyes from their Granny Jay. That, and her penchant for new places, people, and cities such as Venice, with its truly unique character.

"Down to nothing," he repeated with a teasing sigh. She thought that he was grinning behind his mask. "Can you walk in those?"

"Um. I practice in heels a lot," she assured him. "It's the only way to see over counters, and manage to climb up on a bar stool, when necessary."

"Hey! You two, let's get going—it's late!"

Cindy, dressed in black Victorian mourning, came to the doorway. Like Jared, she was tall.

"Jordan! Great shoes. Maybe people won't think you're my child tonight!"

Jordan groaned. "Cindy! You're going to torture me, too?"

"Torture *you*. I'm only five years older—and people ask me if I'm the mother!" She shuddered.

"You're both smashing!" Jared said. "Two of the greatest beauties . . . there. That's said and done. Now, shall we go?"

A few minutes later, they passed through the centuries-old lobby of the gracious hotel. Even the bellmen carried masks, and everyone greeted everyone. It was a night for compliments, fun, and eternal smiles.

They left the hotel and came out on the walk before the canal. The pavement was thronged. People jostled people, and apologies were given in dozens of different languages. Jared, tall as he was, craned his neck to see over the people. Water taxis, vaporettos and gondolas all used the docks in front of the Danieli, and the place was simply packed.

"Girls, wait here just a minute. Our launch might be around the other side," Jared told them.

With a sweep of his cape, he walked away.

Jordan and Cindy moved toward the canal, away from the stream of pedestrian traffic, and waited while Jared went off to find the private launch which was to bring them to the ball. An annual event, the ball was always held in an historical palazzo, and was always one of the most prestigious events of the night. Jared's surname was Riley, just as Jordan's, but his mother had been a Genovese. Loving all things Italian, he had become the Venetian rep for a major American travel firm. He spent almost as much time in Italy now as he did in the States. His Italian was excellent.

Jordan wished hers was better. A man jostled her, paused, tipped his hat, and went into a long apology. Having no idea what he was saying, she smiled and nodded and told him, "Prego, prego!" Literally *I pray you* in English, it was, in Italian, a catchall for almost anything. He smiled, tipped his hat again, and went on.

"I'm going to have to keep a good eye on you all night!" Cindy told her. "That rat was trying to pick you up!"

"Cindy, that was mean. How do you know he was a rat?"

Cindy laughed, shaking back her long blond hair— very different tonight from its usual sleek cascade down her back, since she was wearing it in tight little ringlets. "He was dressed as a rat, Jordan, weren't you paying attention?"

"Oh!" Jordan murmured. "No, I saw the tail and the gray felt on his shoulders, but . . ."

"Rat," Cindy warned. "Renaissance rat, but a rat just the same. We'd best be careful. I imagine that there are a lot of rats out tonight. And wolves. And you look like prime bait."

"Girls!" Jared said, hurrying back over to them. "We've got to move down by St. Mark's Square—our fellow is way in back in the launch line, and he thinks he can get us easier ahead."

"Um, we need to move. The rats and wolves and basic slime-buckets are after Little Red, here."

"Little Red?" Jared demanded. This time, Jordan thought that he was frowning with confusion as he looked at her, but he was still wearing his mask, so she really couldn't tell. "Her hair is as black as pitch, what's little 'red' about her?"

"Never mind—he's no sense at all for fantasy," Cindy told Jordan, shaking her head with rueful affection. "We simply need to take care of your cousin, dear. She's far too delectable looking this evening."

"I guess," Jared murmured, and she knew he was staring at her. "Maybe you're right. Jordan, are those boobs all yours?"

"Jared, how rude!" Cindy protested.

Jordan laughed, her hands on her hips. "Yes, Jared, they are. How about you? What's behind that cod-piece?"

"Thank God we're in Italy and everyone on the street isn't understanding the two of you!" Cindy exclaimed. "Can we get going?"

They made their way through the crowd. Jordan was glad that Jared had such a firm hold on her arm; she could look around, stare, enjoy the sights and sounds.

The weather was crisp and cool, the city was wonderfully alive. Lights dazzled on the water, and each reflection caught in the shimmering canal was more beautiful, more colorful, and more fantastic.

Even the absurd was stunningly beautiful. The costumes ranged from elaborate period outfits, to fantasy, to animal. Birds strutted incredible plumage, cats were sleek and bejewelled. Newscasters from around the world interviewed people here and there; cameras whirred, music blared from the Square, voices and laughter rose above it all. They might celebrate in other places, Jordan thought again, but Venice was unique in its love of the sheer sophistication of dress-up; natives and visitors alike vied to be gorgeous.

Jared led them to the landings directly in front of St. Mark's Square. Jordan turned, feeling as if someone were watching her. She looked up. The Lion of Venice sat atop his high marble pillar, staring down at her. She looked around, at St. Mark's Basilica and the Doge's Palace. By night, shadows seemed to dance, as if they were real entities, hiding behind gargoyles, proud equine statues, and other fantasy creatures set upon splendid architecture by some of the greatest artists who had ever lived.

A church bell tolled in the evening.

A dozen church bells tolled. Jared gripped her arm, leading her over the dock to their vaporetto, and soon they were shooting through waters as heavily laden with revelers as the streets of the city.

Ah, there, ahead—our palace!''

She tried to remember everything she had heard about the event tonight. The ball was given by Nari Contessa della Trieste, a woman with a heredity as rich as that of the city itself. She was very wealthy, having married well—several times. Her first love, however, was the arts, and the Palazzo Trieste, far more of a palace than a castle, featuring the archways, architecture, stone and marble work of a building planned as a residence rather than a fortress from the very beginning. Beautiful, wrought iron gates allowed entry from the canals; there were elaborate, semicircular steps at the entry, where costumed footmen came to help the ladies and gentlemen from their conveyances.

Within the grand foyer, with its white marble staircase, they were greeted by their hostess. Of medium height and surely, a *medium* age, she was stunningly beautiful, dressed all in white, with huge white feathers sweeping the hem of her gown, an elaborate and very regal collar made of the same, and a mask of even longer feathers. She wielded her mask with experience, comfort and composure, nodding to the guests at her side, smiling, turning to greet the new arrivals. Jared, benvenuto! Cindy, ciao, bella!"

She drifted across the floor, greeting them with kisses on both cheeks. Then she took both of Jordan's hands, stretching away to survey her. "Oh, la, the cousin, Jared! Bella, bella, bella, cara mia! You speak Italian, a little? Poco, eh? Grazie, grazie, bella, for coming to my little soiree, eh? Grazie."

"Grazieanche ei" Jordan told her. "Mille grazie."

"You do speak Italian!"

"No," Jordan replied. "A very, very little, I'm afraid."

"Ah, still, dance, be merry. Most here speak English, but then, sometimes it's much, much better when a man *cannot* be understood, eh?" She grinned, expressive dark eyes sliding over Cindy and Jared. Jordan felt the strangest sensation of unease, wondering if their hostess weren't more familiar with her cousin than he had ever suggested. She quickly dismissed the thought; Jared and Cindy were very much in love, the perfect couple.

"The buffet is upstairs, the champagne is here!" the contessa said, reaching out for glasses from a passing waiter. "And the dancing, the dancing is everywhere."

As they moved on, Jared excused himself to her. "Jordan, I won't leave you alone for dinner, I promise. There are a few business associates I have to see . . ."

"He doesn't mind deserting me—just you," Cindy teased.

"You know people here."

"Does anyone really know people here?" Cindy queried, as they walked to the buffet table, looking around. The costumes here were even more brilliant than on the street—elegant and extravagant, costing thousands to tens of thousands of dollars, Jordan imagined. She began to feel underdressed in her sequins, faux jewels, and velvet. Too many women were wearing real gems. On one medieval gown, Jordan was certain she could see the sparkle of dozens of real emeralds.

"Jordan, sorry, that peacock with the chubby butt and big fan is Mrs. Meroni. I must say hi to her quickly. Come with me—"

"I'll wander," Jordan assured her. "Go talk."

"But—"

"I'll be fine."

"Watch out for the rats."

"If I go for any wolves, I'll make sure they're very wealthy," Jordan assured her.

"And young," Cindy advised. "Or else, old enough to keel off immediately and leave you filthy rich in your own right."

"I'll keep that in mind."

Cindy walked away from her.

He saw her walking idly to the buffet table.

She was small and perfect. A petite woman with dark, wavy hair curling over her shoulders, and drawn back from her forehead with a pair of slender braids in concession to the Renaissance style of the deep crimson gown she wore. Others might be more richly dressed; none wore a costume with such natural elegance.

As many here, she carried her mask, a silver and gold creation, on a wand. She pulled it away from her eyes, sipped her champagne, and studied a certain problem in regard to the buffet table—how to hold the drink, the mask and a tiny shrimp.

He left the balcony, and came down the stairs, studying her all the while. He joined her at the table, addressing her in Italian at first, but when her eyes immediately hit his with a certain confusion, he switched to English. "Good evening. Excuse me for being so impertinent—" he paused, lowering his voice—"I believe one is supposed to have an introduction here, but as you seemed to be in some difficulty, I thought I would be of assistance." He reached out a hand, offering to rescue the champagne glass, the mask, or both.

She looked up at him, green eyes that rivaled any gem here, alight with a sparkle, a slow smile of rueful amusement curling her lips.

She spoke softly, too. "I'm not so sure I can accept your assistance. I've just assured my cousin in law that I will watch out for rats and wolves and all predators of the night, I believe."

"Ah, unless they should be filthy rich," he murmured.

She laughed, the sound a bit guilty as she looked around, the slightest touch of a frown furrowing her brow.

"Well," she murmured, looking him up and down once again. "You are a wolf."

"A wolf?" he said with mock distress.

She indicated his costume. His mask was leather, with

carved nose and teeth. He wore a black cape, but beneath it were worn strips of fur.

"But perhaps I'm a young, very wealthy—filthy rich—wolf. Take a chance. Dance with me. Well," he amended thoughtfully, "have a shrimp, finish your champagne, and then dance with me."

"Ah, but—"

"Live recklessly. This is Venice. Carnevale."

Her smile deepened. She handed him her mask, quickly finished a shrimp, swallowed her champagne, and nodded. "I will do my best."

In a minute, they were out on the dance floor in the rear, a terrace that looked over another section of a canal. The moonlight captured on the water reflected the dancers. They played a waltz; she had warned him she was an American and frightfully behind in the etiquette of dance, but she seemed to waltz as if she had been following his lead for years. She glided, she laughed, she stumbled, and grimaced. "You're a bit too tall," she told him.

"You're a bit too small. But we shall manage."

"You're not Italian?" she told him.

"A wolf—and not even Italian," he admitted.

"But you're not American."

"A citizen of the world," he told her. "But you are, of course, American."

"I might have been English," she told him.

"Not in the least."

"Ah, but perhaps I'm Canadian."

"You've the clear mark of an American," he assured her.

"Oh, do I?" It was true; everyone always seemed to recognize Americans immediately. Before they spoke. It was as if they wore the word American tattooed on their foreheads. "From Charleston, South Carolina," she admitted. "And you?"

"Italy is my home away from home. At the moment. There are few in the world as warm and welcoming as the Italians."

"But you were born . . . where?" she inquired, curious green eyes bright on his.

He smiled, deciding not to tell her. There was little reason to do so. After tonight . . .

He shouldn't have danced with her. He shouldn't have spoken with her. The mayhem was coming. But she had caught his eye; she had awakened his senses, perhaps his instincts. Then, it seemed, she was capable as well of charming the mind.

And the soul?

Sir? Excuse me—Sir Wolf? Where are you from?"

"Far, far away," he said lightly, sweeping her in a circle. Then he paused at a tap on his shoulder. "Signore, per piacere . . ."

A Victorian gentleman, clearly English, broke in on him.

He acquiesced, bowing low. "Care Americana," he told her. "Ciao, bella. Ciao, bella."

She smiled at him, regret in her eyes, he thought. Or was it only that he could not help but hope?

He watched her dance away.

Her feet hurt—she had practiced in heels, but these were high. And the night was far from boring. First— the wolf. The enigmatic, very tall, oh-so-charming wolf. She hadn't the faintest idea of what he really looked like. He wore his mask. And yet, his height was hard to hide. Would she recognize him again? She would know his scent, she thought. Certainly. Very nice. An aftershave that was clean and woodsy but . . . with a very sensual, musky undertone.

After the wolf—the Englishman.

Then a harlequin, or joker.

He complimented her gown, then her eyes and her hair. Then the length of her neck.

She laughed, kept her distance. "You are too effusive, sir."

"Ah, never. Such lovely white flesh. The way your pulse . . . beats."

Just when she was beginning to feel uncomfortable, a Grim Reaper in brown leather and silk broke in on her. He was a Spaniard, tall, attractive. He commented on her wonderful energy, the ray of light that seemed to flow from her.

She thanked him. His features were colored with gray makeup, but his eyes were very dark and intense. *Sexy,* she thought.

Cindy, you're right, there are wolves everywhere. Tempting wolves . . .

As they spoke, a mummer in crimson tights and jacket came up on the terrace, ringing a bell, followed by a midget, clapping paddles together.

He spoke in Italian, at first, but translated for himself as well, to benefit all the guests at the ball. "Hear ye, hear ye, the masque begins! In days long, long gone, Odo, Conte of the Castello, had no son, but brought forth to the earth a daughter so glorious that the greatest of the nobility thought him rich. But Odo decried his lack of an heir, seizing his wife—"

He grabbed a middle-aged woman in a twelfth-century headdress, inquiring softly if she would play. She nodded, laughing, all for the game.

"Seizing his wife, he shook the poor wretched creature!" He pretended to shake her. "And gave her the kiss of death!"

It appeared that he whispered to the woman; she went limp, he set her down.

"So!" the crimson-clad mummer went on. "He married anew! But this wife, also, failed to give him a son!" From the growing crowd around him, he found another matron who eagerly nodded her assent to act out the part of the Conte's wife. He whispered to her; she went limp. He carefully let her fall to the floor.

"And again, he took a wife!"

He seized another woman, who was giggling and nodding before he could ask. She went the way of the first two women.

"Alas, he went through more wives than Bluebeard!" The mummer waltzed about the room, taking woman after woman.

Then he paused, dramatically shaking his head.

"But still, no woman gave him a son! So! He offered up his glorious, glorious daughter!"

The mummer came walking through the crowd. He, too, was tall and powerful, Jordan thought, muscles straining the form-hugging clothing.

He was walking toward her, she realized. She backed away. "American!" she said softly.

"No matter!" he told her. He reached out a hand to her. She started shaking her head, but he had her already. She was a guest; she didn't want to be rude.

"So he offered his soul to the very devil to find the man who would be his daughter's husband, and take on the family name! Ah! And where was the devil?"

As the mummer walked around the room, looking for the devil, guests laughed and moved about.

And then Jordan saw the crimson spill coming from beneath the head of the first woman who had fallen to the floor.

Blood.

She gasped, drawing a hand to her mouth, and began to scream.

The mummer saw her reaction, and snatched her up. She shrieked, trying to fight him off. He was stronger than she had imagined. And then, to her horror, she saw that the room suddenly seemed to be full of . . .

Beasts. Demons. She was seeing things. Surely. Men clad in furs, capes, coats . . . women suddenly let out shrieking cries, displaying . . . fangs.

"Let go!"

She fought wildly, kicking, screaming. She found herself dragged to the far end of the terrace by the mummer.

His crimson coloring as dark as the blood that had spilled . . .

Suddenly, the mummer was wrenched away from her, and she looked into the eyes of the wolf.

The mummer snarled, hurling out vindictive words in a language she didn't know. The wolf responded. The mummer struck at the wolf; the wolf ducked and fought back.

Jordan began to scream again and again as the force of the blow sent the mummer's head dangling to the side of his body, his neck broken.

All hell seemed to be breaking loose within the elegant palazzo.

Jordan stepped back, dazed.

Beasts were spilling from the house. *Beasts! Creatures*

in all manner of costume! Animals, with huge long teeth now, with blood dripping from those . . . fangs.

Then she started to scream again because the wolf reached for her. She ducked low, but he was incredibly powerful.

He bounded from the terrace . . .

Into fog! Sheer fog. A mist that had formed in the night, so rich, so thick, they seemed to jump into a black hole, into eternity . . .

His feet thumped down hard upon something. A launch. It rocked wildly with the impact of their weight. Jordan screamed with delayed terror; she could have fallen upon stone, upon marble, she could have broken her neck . . .

She could have just fallen forever and ever, into the mist, into hell.

He set her down in the small launch, then looked up at the startled oarsman.

"Row!" he thundered. "Row, row, now!"

The fellow sprang to life.

Then the wolf sprang from the launch to the pavement.

And turned.

And was swallowed into the mist.

CHAPTER 1

Morning.

Bright light.

No swirl of fog, no whisper of evil. Only the clear blue of an amazingly beautiful winter's day and the clink of cutlery, the chatter of many tongues, and the universal sound of laughter.

"I think," Jared said, his tone very soft, "that this is all because of Steven. I am so sorry to bring this up, and I have tried very hard not to, but Jordan, you are going on and on, after everything that has been explained. No matter how kind and patient people have been, you will not understand that it was all part of the party, a good taunting jest, and no more!"

Jordan stiffened at her cousin's tone. She looked down at her hands, counting to ten. Steven had been dead for over a year. She had accepted the fact. She was not psychotic. At his death, she had been devastated, and she had grieved, and she had been *angry,* but she had never been paranoid.

She stared at Jared icily. "This has nothing to do with Steven. Nothing at all. It has to do with last night. Historically, there *have* been monsters, *human* monsters," Jordan said. "And many of them very rich and exceedingly well positioned."

Jared let out a snort of aggravation. He leaned toward her.

"Jordan, get it straight. You were tricked, fooled. I understood at first; you were scared, worried sick, but you've been told that the whole thing was a masquerade, an entertainment. If you persist with this, you're going to destroy my relationship with the contessa, and ruin my entire livelihood," he said, his words beginning with a tone of impatience, and finishing with a ring bordering on anger. "Trust me—the contessa is an important, worldly and responsible woman. She gives huge sums of money to charities, and she enjoys entertainment, even scary entertainment. She is *not* any kind of a cultist."

The last word stung like a slap, as did the edge in his voice. Jordan chose to ignore his tone.

To herself, she admitted that this morning, seated in the rooftop restaurant of the Danieli, with their attentive waiters polite and cheerful and very *normal* in their uniforms, she should have been able to let it go.

It had all been explained to her.

Yet, she had kept on trying to explain what she had seen the night before!

Even the police had been angry with her at the end of last night. Still, as a book reviewer lucky enough to have earned a large syndicated audience, she'd brought work with her on this vacation. In the pile of advanced reading copies and galleys to be reviewed—including volumes of fiction and nonfiction—she'd happened to have a new book written by a Hollywood producer. The writer had been responsible for some of the most popular horror fiction seen at the movies in the past decade. It was a good book, and it went way beyond the movies, tracing the facts beyond the legends and myths that had sprung up through time throughout the world.

Jordan had listened to the explanations, the patience, the laughter, the anger. She'd witnessed a show they told her. *A show!* A damned perverse show, and if that had been the contessa's idea of entertainment, *she* hadn't been in the least amused. Jared, so convinced that his relationship with the contessa was his key to the movers and shakers of Venice, wouldn't even consider the possibility that *something* evil might have occurred at the palazzo, even without the contessa's knowledge or cooperation. Nor would he support Jordan in her anger that the contessa should never have hired such sick entertainment.

"Jared, you're wrong. Very wrong. I am not letting my imagination get the best of me, I do not believe in ghosts, goblins or spirits, but I do *know* that bad things happen. And beyond just the bad, there are people out there who believe that they themselves are something supernatural. Listen to this, pay attention, and remember, this is just one of dozens of documented cases involving real people. Antoine Leger, a French mass murderer, was a cannibal—and he drank blood," she informed him evenly, her finger on the page as she stared at her cousin. "He went to the guillotine in 1824, a truly horrible man who deserved his fate. His crime? He hid out in the woods, waiting for his prey like a viper. Then he would strike out at young girls, rape them, kill them, drink their blood, and dine on their hearts."

Cindy, who had been sitting quietly with them at the table, looked at Jordan with dismay. With an infinite patience now lacking in her husband, she reached over and gently touched Jordan's hand. "You're reading a book. It's just *stories.*"

"This is not fiction!" Jordan protested. "I explained that this man was real—"

Jared set his cup of coffee down with an impatience that threatened to break crockery. "It's a book of stories, fiction, a work on vampires in film and legend," Jared said with exasperation.

"It's a book about vampires in films, books and *history,*" Jordan corrected, trying not to raise her voice.

She and Jared were both only children. They had been raised together, and usually, they were as close as if they had been born brother and sister. She understood that he loved this city, and that it was important for him to befriend people such as the contessa, yet it was still very hard for her to accept what she had seen as *entertainment.*

"Jordan—"

"Jared, I just can't believe you won't even consider the possibility that *something* did happen last night!"

She knew that she was pushing it, but despite all the assurances that been given to her after the ball, and despite the beautiful, cool, sunlit Venetian morning, and her cousin's current discomfort, she couldn't let it go.

Near her, people drank their espresso and café con latte, laughed, chatted, and read their papers with utter normalcy. The world was light now, bright with sunshine, filled with talk, a multitude of languages, even the very down-to-earth cry of a baby. But no matter what explanations had been given to her, her hours of sleep had been punctuated by vivid, grotesque dreams of the 'show' she had witnessed the previous night.

It had all happened so fast . . .

She had somehow gotten the startled oarsman to understand her desire to get to a police station, despite the fact that in her horror and fear, she had forgotten every single word of Italian she had known. Luckily, police and *polizia* were close enough for the man to understand, and she had found herself taken to a station of the local *carabinieri*. There, she had found a kindly officer who spoke English, and he had assured her that the situation would be investigated immediately, even though he seemed doubtful when she told him she had been at the palazzo of the Contessa della Trieste. Babbling and close to hysteria at first—deeply frantic then for Jared and Cindy—she had told him about the story telling and playacting that had ended in real blood and real death, and that there had been a roomful of costumed people turning into monsters who had attacked the others even as they had stood and watched and laughed. Café latte laced strongly with brandy helped calm her. She finally spoke with enough reason and conviction to send the officers off en masse, despite the fact that it was Fat Tuesday and all kinds of charades and masquerades were going on, and she was speaking about the palazzo of a very well-known woman.

The carabinieri had returned with Jared and Cindy—and the contessa. They had all come in worried, but the contessa had also been amused from the beginning, even though she seemed to be apologizing—she hadn't expected such gullibility from such a lovely and sophisticated American girl. Actually, she had been damned condescending. At that point, however, Jared had acted like her older brother, showing his deep concern for her panic and fear, holding her, eyes worried as they probed hers, his tone very gentle as he explained she had been caught in a bit of elaborate theater, scary Carnevale fun, and that there had been nothing *really* violent or gruesome in what she had seen, and certainly, nothing *murderous* had taken place.

He hadn't known about that particular piece of scary fun the contessa had planned, and the contessa hadn't known about *Steven*. It was probably even natural that Jordan had been so terrified at what had really been no more than a haunted house display. But now that she knew . . .

Jordan had persisted then. She tried to convince the contessa that some of her guests had been madmen, and that perhaps she'd had no idea of what had been happening at her own party, but murders had taken place. The contessa shook her beautiful head with sorrow and regret. The kindly English-speaking officer cleared his throat, and told Jordan that they had searched the palazzo. All they had found were costumed guests, a few still wearing their fake blood, all contrite that they had frightened her so badly.

"But I'm telling you, I saw people *die,*" she said. "Go back—they've cleaned it up. I don't know much about police procedure, but perhaps if you were to use Luminal—"

It was then, Jordan was certain that the contessa got angry, for she began speaking rapidly in Italian to the officers, inhaling deeply for patience, then speaking to Jordan again. "My dear, as you are Jared's cousin, I will forgive this terrible affront, but you must simply forget all the silly movies you Americans see and accept the fact that we, too, have a sense of fun and the macabre. And," she added quietly, "what happened to your fiancé. Jared has explained to me, of course, about your past, and so, dear child, I do understand, and my heart goes out to you. My palazzo remains open to you. You are dear to me, as the cousin of Jared, and you must come anytime and see that the festivities and the amusements are over, and that we did nothing but provide a party *and* a charade. Dear, dear, Jordan, poor dear. I am so sorry, but please! You must be sane and rational about this!"

"Yes, and we must let the contessa go home," Jared said firmly, and before she could protest longer, the police were apologizing to the contessa and ushering them out to the street. The contessa had kissed Jordan's cheek with cold lips, urging her again to come by at any time. Despite their growing impatience, the police had remained kind to her throughout, far kinder than Jared when—after the contessa had departed in her private launch—she had kept trying to explain that she had seen real blood, nearly perished herself, and been rescued by a man in wolf's clothing.

"Where is this man?" Jared had demanded.

"He leaped with me from the balcony, then . . . disappeared into the fog."

They stared at her as if she had entirely lost her mind. Yes, poor Jordan. God knew, maybe she needed to be committed to the closest facility for the insane.

Back at the hotel, Cindy had managed to find a concierge who made Jordan tea, and then offered to

sleep in her room. Jared's sigh of impatience had
caused her to decline. But alone in her handsome,
antiques-laden room in what she truly considered to
be one of the most beautiful hotels in the world, she
still had not been able to sleep. It had been the words
of the contessa that had caused her to dig into her
pile of work, and find the book written by the movie
producer. She tried to read before realizing that Cindy
had slipped a Valium into her tea. She had fallen
asleep with the book in her hand, but the Valium
hadn't stopped her dreams. She had witnessed the
events time and time again; she dreamed that she
awoke, that a huge silver wolf guarded her window.
He was framed in the shutters that opened to the
pedestrian walk and canal where just hours before,
the last sounds of laughter and revelry had faded into
the darkness and shadows of the moonlit night.

Okay, so the party and the Valium had caused her
some serious nightmares. That didn't stop her belief
that maybe . . .

She broke off her own thought painfully, then continued with it.

Yes, maybe some *cultists* or some wretched cold-
blooded murderers had been at work.

Jared leaned toward her, at the rooftop restaurant
of the Danieli, all attempts at patience suddenly lost.
"Jordan, please, I am begging you—you've got to stop.
These are people I work with. The contessa is incredibly important to my job, my position here in Italy, to
my career, my *life!* If you keep up with this, you will
destroy me. Can't you understand? A party, masks,
costumes, a haunted house, special effects, elaborate, yes! The contessa likes to have the best ball,
the most talked-about. Leave it—leave it alone. All

of Venice will be talking as it is. You will destroy *me*, don't you understand?"

"Jared, I'm telling you—"

"And the police have told *you*. And the contessa left her party to come to you, because you were so frightened. Everyone has bent over backward to explain what went on to you, and you refuse to accept it!"

"Jared, you weren't there—"

He got up, throwing his napkin on the table. "I have to go. Jordan, get a fucking grip before you ruin my life!"

"Jared!" Cindy protested, speaking out again at last. "Jordan is your cousin, your flesh and blood—"

"Which she seems to have forgotten. You sit here and listen to her make up wild stories and convince herself that monsters exist." He stared hard at Jordan, placing his hands on the table to look into her eyes. "I'm sorry, so sorry about what happened to Steve. We've tried to be with you. To support you. And you've been good, Jordan. *Sane*. But Carnevale has apparently touched off something inside you. Again, I'm sorry, but I've had it. I'm tired—and guess what? I have a lot of bridges to mend today. I have to see a lot of people and apologize for my cousin behaving so insanely."

He turned and left, striding angrily from the terrace. Cindy, standing awkwardly, stared down at Jordan where she was sitting. "I know he doesn't mean to be so . . ."

"Cindy, you don't need to apologize to me for Jared," Jordan murmured.

Wrong thing to say. Cindy instantly became defensive. She sat again and stared at Jordan.

"Jordan, you've got to realize that you are risking his job, that he's friends with these people, that the contessa is very important to his work." Cindy sighed. "Honestly, Jordan, I know that you were really scared, and we should be there for you, but it's true, it was all explained to you. With concern, care, and a great deal of empathy. And you have this foolish book with you, making it all the worse."

"Signorina, more coffee?"

Jordan looked up. Even their kindly waiter was staring at her sympathetically. Had he heard all about the crazy American who had gone bananas last night at the contessa's macabre party, inviting the police to a bit of sport? Maybe she was being an idiot and she should see it all Jared's way. Entertainment. Damned bloody entertainment, but then, the contessa had been right about one thing—the gore had been no worse than what she should be accustomed to from American movies. Although, she might have countered, Italian filmmakers, such as Mario Brava, were surely just as gruesome.

She resolved not to try to convince Cindy anymore that there were monsters loose in Venice. Maybe she was overreacting. Perhaps she had been reading too much, too long. The sun was shining. It was a beautiful morning, especially for a winter's day.

She smiled for the waiter. There was no sense in trying to convince any of them—they hadn't been there, they hadn't seen. Who had? A group of masked strangers she would never recognize again. Enough coffee. She needed to move.

To be alone.

"No, basta, grazie, signore," she murmured. She

stood, ready to walk away. Cindy looked at her with sudden panic.

"Jordan—"

"Signora?" the waiter said, questioning Cindy. Surely, someone wanted more coffee.

"No, grazie, basta. It conto, per favore," Cindy said quickly. She started to rise as well. "Jordan, wait, where are you going?"

"Don't worry. I'm not off to the police again. I'm just going for a walk around the Square."

The waiter had gone to get the check as Cindy had asked. Jordan had tried to sign most of the bills to her room as a thank-you for all that Cindy and Jared had done for her here. This morning, Cindy could sign. Jared had been a horse's ass.

"I don't think you should go out alone—" Cindy said, frowning in protest.

"Why? You just told me there are no monsters out there. It's all in my mind. Entertainment."

"But you're upset—"

"And apparently, I have to get over it."

"Jordan, wherever you're going, I'll go with you—"

"I just need to walk, Cindy. Alone."

"Jordan, please . . ."

Cindy looked so upset that Jordan forgot some of her fear as well as irritation with Jared. She paused, touching Cindy's cheek. "I'm okay, honestly. I'm going to walk around the Square and look into some of the jewelry store windows."

"But you can get better deals off the Square. You'll find nothing but tourist prices. I'll take you to some more moderate places—"

"Cindy, you're a sweetheart. I love you, honest to

God, and I'm not in the least upset with you. See you later."

"Don't forget that we're going to the artist's ball tonight—"

"I won't," Jordan said, and determined, she shoved the vampire book into her large carryall bag and started out of the restaurant. She didn't wait for the elevator, but started down the steps of the hotel, noting none of the beautiful decor which usually held her so enthralled. On the ground floor, she encountered a bevy of activity. The parties in Venice would last the week. A costume shop had been opened behind the concierge desk, and people were milling about, renting costumes, returning them, talking about various parties and events. The registration desk was busy as well, with travelers coming and going, and the bar and salon seemed equally busy. Making her way through the crowd, she suddenly felt as if she was being watched. She turned, irritated with herself, hoping she wouldn't have this feeling of everyone looking at her all day.

She wasn't being absurd—she *was* being watched. Openly. An attractive young woman was staring straight at her while whispering to a stocky, older man standing by her. She saw Jordan look at her. She didn't blush, look away or pretend in any way that she hadn't been talking about her.

The woman approached Jordan. Frowning, Jordan waited. As the woman neared her, Jordan realized that she wasn't as young as she had first thought. From a distance, she might have been in her mid-twenties. At closer range, she was closer to forty, extremely trim and shapely, her hair cut stylishly short and highlighted to a silvery blond. Smiling, she extended a slim hand heavy with rings. "Hello, Miss Riley. I'm Tiff Henley, a fellow American."

Jordan accepted the hand that had been offered her. "Hello, how are you? Yes, I'm Jordan Riley, but . . ."

"We never met last night, but I was at the ball. I'm so glad that you seem to be doing well. You caused quite a stir last evening."

Jordan felt a flush covering her cheeks. "I'm sorry, I didn't see you—"

"I believe you wound up on the second floor during the entertainment, while most of us were dining and dancing on the ground floor. I didn't see the show, but you know, the contessa is known for her extravagance, so I'm sure it must have been simply *wicked*. I'm not that familiar with the contessa, but I've heard that she *never* leaves a party with guests still in attendance, so she must care for you very much. You are all right?"

So this manicured socialite had been at the ball as well. And she had been whispering about Jordan. Jordan Riley, the American woman who had called the police in on one of the most notable women in Venetian society. Great. Maybe everyone in the city had heard about her, and was whispering.

In the bright light of the elegant hotel, with dozens of people near, Jordan did suddenly feel somewhat foolish. Had the entertainment been so excellent and professional, the special effects so good, that she had let her imagination take flight?

"I suppose I did create quite a stir. I'm afraid it all seemed very real," Jordan said. The woman was still sizing her up. For Jared's sake—even if he was being a horse's ass—she was going to appear sane.

"You're a writer?" Tiff Henley queried.

Tiff? Was that short for Tiffany? The woman looked like a Tiffany—all decked out in diamonds, hair a mix of champagne and silver, her long wool dress and jacket stylishly cut to the perfection of her figure.

"Book critic," Jordan said. "If I could write, I would. I'm afraid my talent is in finding treasures put out by others. And you . . . ?" She queried politely.

Tiff smiled ruefully. "I'm simply filthy rich," she said. "But *not* well known in the best circles of society. Well, there, that admitted, would you like to have coffee sometime?" The woman was openly friendly, brash, and had probably become filthy rich in some scandalous way.

"Sure, I'd love to," Jordan said.

"Maybe tomorrow?"

Why not? Jordan thought. "Sounds great. Are you staying here?"

Tiff shook her champagne-toned head. "No, I'm here with a friend, Mack over there—" she pointed out the stout man—"who needs a costume for the artist's ball tonight. Are you going?"

"Yes, I believe we are."

"You'll enjoy it. The tickets are cheap, the food is so-so. The artist's ball celebrates the often talented and more often broke creative element in Venice for Carnevale. And, when all else fails, the drinks are usually strong."

"I'll see you there then," Jordan told her.

"You're not supposed to actually *see* me—I'll be costumed, of course. But we'll find one another. And make arrangements for coffee. I've rented a villa, next island over. It's a fabulous old place, owned by the family of a doge long past. If you like, you can come there. Great history, ghosts, scandal, and all. I'll tell you some of the tales I've been told. Oh! Sorry. I mean, I don't want to scare you or anything—"

"I'm really not scared that easily," Jordan assured her.

"Good!" She smiled and started away. Then she paused, coming back. "Don't let it bother you if people whisper about you today. They whisper about me all the time, and I've survived!"

Before Jordan could say more, Tiff had walked back to her friend. Jordan was surprised to realize that she felt much better after her conversation with the very blunt woman. She smiled, starting out of the hotel again. She mused over the woman's reassurance without really having to wonder why people would whisper about Tiff. Surely, it had something to do with her lifestyle.

Outside the hotel, vendors displayed their goods. The usual T-shirts were for sale, as were dolls and masks by the hundreds. By day, many people were in street clothes, as she was, but even by sunlight, many people were costumed. Walking in broad daylight, Jordan saw the masked and elaborately dressed strollers for what they were—revelers enjoying the beauty and make-believe of the immense party which was Venice at Carnevale. The air was cool, the day was bright, the sky was blue. Crossing the bridge outside the Danieli, she paused, looking down the canal to the Bridge of Sighs, connecting the Doge's Palace and the old prisoners to the new, where many a poor man had passed to his imprisonment, or his doom. That had been the past. This morning, a gondolier with a young couple in his sleek black gondola was singing an Italian love song. As he then came through the canal and glanced up at Jordan, he broke into English verse. "When the moon hits your eye like a big piece of pie, that's amore!" He winked. Jordan lifted a brow with a half smile and waved to the happy couple.

The gondolier stopped rowing, drifting slowly as he passed beneath her. "Buon giorno, signorina!" he called to her. "Care for a ride?"

"You have passengers!" she told him.

"Ah, but they are in love. I am alone."

"Ah, well, such is life," she teased. "Your gondola is occupied."

"Then you must ride another time. I'm Sal. Salvatore D'Onofrio. The best. The most fun, the most handsome."

"And the most modest!" she supplied.

He grinned and shrugged. "No, not the most modest. But you look for me, some other time, eh?"

"If I decide on a gondola ride, I will definitely look for you," she promised.

The girl in the back of the gondola, huddled to a young man who couldn't be much more than twenty, called out to Jordan, her accent French. "He is the best!"

Jordan laughed. "Thanks! Enjoy!"

As the gondola drifted beneath the bridge, Jordan moved on.

St. Mark's Square was crowded with people. Passing the entrance to the basilica, Jordan looked over the heads of the ever-moving horde to see that a costume parade was going on by the makeshift bandstand at the opposite end of the Square. A rock band was playing, and a jester was introducing the contestants in English and Italian, throwing in a few words of French here and there. Those in the most fetching and extravagant costumes posed at the columns around the

Square for tourists who snapped endless photos. With their masks, most of the elaborately dressed people were wholly anonymous—it was impossible to tell a person's nationality, color, or even sex.

Anonymous . . . there is the key, she thought. It's so easy to come here, don a mask, slip into the crowd, and . . .

The thought brought back a strange sense of unease. In truth, she wouldn't know anyone she had seen at the ball last night. Except for the contessa, of course. They had met face to face. But the others who had been there . . . they might be in the Square with her now, and she would not know.

She walked through the crowd, suddenly anxious to reach the streets beyond the Square where she would not be quite so tightly packed in by the throngs. An excellent Napoleon—followed by his court—was at her side. He stopped, bowed low, and indicated that she should precede them. She thanked him quickly and walked on by.

Passing by a plate glass window that displayed mannequins in various costumes, she suddenly went dead still, staring into glass.

For a moment . . .

No. It was just a mannequin. This one with a male form, with a short cut, sable brown wig. For a moment, she thought she had seen Steven's face on the mannequin. Serious hazel eyes, lean features, firm chin. But she was looking at a plastic mold, expressionless features. No hat and no mask adorned the dummy; it was just a well-painted figure in the typical cape. Still, her heart raced, and she mistrusted her own judgment more than ever. *Maybe Jared was right.* Steven had been dead only a year. He had died chasing down deadly game players. *Cultists*—with a yen for murder, for sacrifices to their cruel beliefs. She studied the mannequin again, forcing herself to think logically.

Yes, she could see why she'd had the momentary vision.

The lean features were similar to Steven's. The eyes had been painted hazel; the hair was his color as well. The size was about right.

A surge of sorrow swept through her. A year wasn't such a long time.

He had come suddenly into her life, and she had found herself suddenly responding. He had been charming, intelligent, impressive . . . *noble.*

He shouldn't have been a cop, she thought. He had been too trusting. He had hated violence, but had come on the force in homicide—a man who had believed in rehabilitation, who was completely against the death penalty, and was determined that suspects must be taken alive.

Taking suspects alive had cost him his own life.

She had known what had happened when she heard the sirens in the night, when she looked out her door and saw the cop car, and the officer coming down her walk. She had known what he did; she shouldn't have been shocked. That hadn't stopped her from being horrified, devastated. She had gone through the stages of grief: denial, anger, pain. *But she had remained sane.*

She had come to the stage of acceptance. She hadn't lost her reason or her mind in any way.

Maybe she had, she mocked herself, if she was seeing his face in the features of a store-window dummy.

Steven was gone. She still felt the sorrow, but she was living her life. He had died under cruel circumstances, and she would be a fool to forget that horrible things did happen.

A breeze whispered. Soft, cool, beautiful. She forced the past to the back of her mind. She loved Italy, adored Venice, and was not going to let the contessa ruin that simple fact.

She looked away and kept walking. She was *not* to blame in this. If it had all been a charade, it had been a deplorable one. Jared had no right to be so callous, and she had every right to be furious.

Beyond the Square, she came to streets filled with cafés and shops. Glancing through the window of a restaurant specializing in fish, she noted that many people had doffed their masks for the singular pleasure of eating. They all looked so . . . normal. A chubby little businessman had his cape thrown over his shoulder while his dottore mask lay on the chair by his side. A half moon mask and a large plumed hat lay on the table by the side of his companion, an equally chubby woman with a charming laugh that rang all the way to the streets. *Americans,* Jordan thought. Vacationers, like herself, loving this fantasy.

Looking into the restaurant had made her smile. Yet even as she watched, smiling back at the woman who had seen her, she felt an eerie feeling creep up her spine.

Stop! she commanded herself.

But the feeling persisted.

And it had nothing to do with memories of Steven. She had been smiling at a plump and friendly looking American woman when the strange sensation began a trek along her spine.

She felt again that she was being *watched.*

Whispers seemed to sweep by her, snatches spoken

in the wind, there and then gone. Whispers, swift, staccato, like an evil, raspy breeze, just touching her ears, her nape. For a moment, the street seemed to go dark. Reflected in the glass of the restaurant window, darkness seemed to descend, like huge wings sweeping over the daylight.

The woman seated inside the restaurant was still laughing. The darkness disappeared as swiftly as if it had flown away on wings of light. And still . . .

That feeling.

Something . . . someone . . . right beside her. A cold, fetid, whisper of menace . . .

Jordan swung around, feeling as if bony fingers of sheer ice touched upon her shoulder.

Gino Meroni did not at all dislike his work.

Years ago, when he was a boy, his parents had immigrated to America. He went to high school in New York City, but had neither the money nor the inclination to go any further with his schooling. By the time he was eighteen, his mother and father were still producing more offspring, and so he found himself on his own, trying to make a go of it. He was expected to work, to help with the family, but he couldn't stand the crying of babies, and his mother's prayers and insistence on church every Sunday, or the sorrowful darkness in her eyes each time she warned him that he was running with the wrong crowd. He liked his friends.

They knew the cheapest bars. And where to get money when they were broke. They knew which subway routes were poorly policed. They were excellent at removing the burdens of purses, briefcases, and backpacks from those who were surely weary of car-

rying them. Once, when plying his trade along Fifth
Avenue late at night, he made the mistake of mugging
an undercover officer.

He did a stint in jail. He called home. His father
refused to bail him out. He never went to prison; his
attorney managed to plea bargain a sentence of time
served and community service. Community service led
him to work in Central Park, a fine place to master
the art of surprise and attack.

One night, the thump on the head he gave to an
old geezer who had picked up the wrong prostitute
killed the man. He didn't know it at first; he read
about it in the paper the next morning. He wasn't
afraid of being caught; he had learned to wear gloves,
to strike, and to run. He hadn't been seen. The branch
with which he had killed the fellow lay on the walk by
him and bore no prints. The prostitute, who had lain
screaming and begging for her life, hadn't seen his
face or heard him speak. She had run faster than Gino
had after he attacked the old man.

His lack of fear at being caught was somewhat sur-
prising to him. More so was his total lack of remorse.
The guy had been old. The whack on the head he
had bestowed on him had merely put the geezer out
of any future misery.

But that wasn't it. Gino had liked the look of fear
on the guy's face. He had liked the feel of wielding
the broken branch with so much power that it shuddered in his hands as it struck gray hair, flesh, and
bone.

Robbing the unwary, however, wasn't enough. He
had to get work—a day job. The only work he could
find where he wasn't asked too many questions was
nonunion, back-breaking labor at the docks. There,

the bosses liked to use men who didn't have references. They didn't believe in bonuses. Overtime was overlooked. He had a strong, burly build. When he worked, he worked hard. His English was perfect, unaccented, though he could slip into the role of a struggling new immigrant when he found it necessary or convenient.

In a bar one night, he met a stranger who gave him some veiled hints on how to improve his income.

He agreed to meet the stranger again.

The man opened up a new world to him.

First, there were the drugs. What a difference they made after a long day of hard labor. Gino was a good-looking man. The stranger provided not just drugs, but women as well. They liked him. They liked the accent he could affect at will. Every night, when he chose, there was something. Some sweet reward.

He knew, of course, that nothing in life was free. He expected to be asked favors in return. They were usually easy. Because of his work habits by day, he was trusted. His powerful friends asked only that certain shipments at certain times go by without inspection, that certain crates be guarded and never opened. He was more than happy to oblige. He had a new car, a decent apartment. There were days when he stayed in some of the finest hotels despite his own pleasant lodgings. So little to pay, so much to be gained.

Then, late one summer afternoon, when he was about to call it quits for the day, two inspectors arrived at the docks. The *Star of Sheba*, registered to a Middle Eastern country, was about to leave port. There were a number of crates aboard that had been slipped onto the ship illegally. They were important; that had been emphasized to Gino. Crewmen, suspecting something was up, mysteriously disappeared. Gino found himself alone with the two men from the government.

One of them had put down a crowbar. Gino decided to use it.

He stowed the two dead men behind the crates. The *Star of Sheba* sailed as planned. But the bodies were found, and this time, he had forgotten to get rid of the crowbar, and there were those who had seen him with the government men. The good thing was that the crates reached their destination undisturbed. The bad was that Gino was arrested and charged with murder,

His friends, naturally, provided him with an attorney, an extremely attractive woman. When he tried to flirt with her and make light of his situation, he found out that she was very intelligent. Sharp as a tack, hard as a nail. He was immediately put in his place as she explained the gravity of the situation.

Jail was bad, his attorney told him. Prison was much worse. There were lots of guys in there much bigger than he was. All those things he had done to others could be done to him. And looking over the physical evidence . . . well, she could plea bargain, but he might find himself being a pincushion and more for men who were truly the dregs of society. As they talked, he came to realize that the best thing to do was what she suggested: escape and leave the country. She had a place in Italy; he could go back to his real home. He had come from Bari; her home was in Venice. No matter. There was plenty he could do for her. False papers could be arranged, and the actual escape seemed of little difficulty for his powerful friends. The idea appealed to him far more than being buggered by a bunch of apes. Filthy, toothless, animals, hardly human.

They arranged the escape for a day he was scheduled to be transferred to another facility. The driver of his car was apparently with his friends; the police escort was stopped by another police car. His escort simply disappeared; he never asked how.

At a hotel outside the airport he was given new clothing and a passport with a new identity. He reached Venice via Paris. At first, he had little to do; very little to do. He was warned that he must lie low, that he needn't seek income in any other way than his work for his friends. For a few years, he wasn't sure what his real worth was—he worked for an important woman, but he was a delivery man, a courier, and captain of the launch. His employer had been away for many years; she was just now reestablishing herself in her family home, yet she was very often gone: a woman of her stature and means had many social obligations in other countries.

Nor were women such as she bound by the rules of others.

In time, he discovered what his true talents were to be for his employer.

He didn't mind.

He didn't dislike his work. He didn't mind the cold, the sharp breeze that blew around him, nor the rocking of the boat in winter. The . . . *messiness* of his work didn't bother him, either. Thinking in American terms, his was a job *right up his own alley*.

Then he made a sudden realization, and he was afraid.

His employer was wonderful. But she wasn't to be crossed.

In the middle of his work, filling and weighting the barrels he would sink to the bottom of the Adriatic Sea, he was suddenly very aware of a cold breeze.

He dumped all the barrels he had filled, frantically looking around, counting, piecing together, counting again.

Ice filled him, colder than the sea.

He was missing a piece of cargo.

CHAPTER 2

Nothing.

Still standing in front of the restaurant, Jordan turned around slowly once again, puzzling over the strange sounds of whispering and the impression of winged shadows that had teased her senses. Scanning the street around her, she hoped for a moment to see if the outgoing and brassy Tiff had perhaps followed her route, and was watching her, ready to approach her again.

But as she looked around, there was no one in the busy street who appeared to be the least interested in her. Groups of people laughed and joked together. She heard bits of different languages—English, Italian, German, French—but she didn't feel even the faintest hint of a cold breeze touching her nape or hissing in her ear.

Then, suddenly, she heard her name called.

"Jordan! Jordan!" She spun in the opposite direction as her name was repeated in a loud and friendly
summons. Lynn Mallory, an American artist working
at the Venetian shop where she had acquired her
costume the evening before, was hailing her from the
door of the shop. Jordan hadn't realized that she had
walked quite so far, that she was right across from
the Arte della Anna Maria, named for the impressive
Venetian woman who had formed the co-op store for
rising and talented young entrepreneurs.

"Lynn!" she called back, starting over, then ducking
back as the same Napoleon and his courtiers came
rollicking along. Once again, Napoleon stopped, bowing low to her. "Oh, wait, wait! Please, wait!" someone
pleaded. A camera flashed. Napoleon smiled regally,
then swept his arm again. Jordan hurried by, and he
moved on with appropriate hauteur and arrogance.

"Jordan!" Lynn said, greeting her typically with a
kiss on both cheeks. Her eyes were merry and bright.
"Where is your costume? In true style, you know, you
should dress even to wander through the streets."

"I'm afraid I was in a far more casual mood this
morning," Jordan said lightly. Lynn was about Jordan's
age with close cropped dark hair and smoky gray eyes.
Jordan, speaking such poor Italian, had found a bond
with the American girl the moment she stepped into
the shop for the first time two days ago. Lynn's mother
was an Italian-American who had taught her daughter
her native language as a child; as an adult, Lynn admitted, she simply loved all things Italian. A semester of
college in Florence had convinced her that she wanted
to spend a few years, at the least, living in Italy. Anna
Maria's co-op had been the perfect place for her to

sell her creations—wooden marionettes dressed in detailed and exquisite costumes.

"Ah," Lynn murmured, eyes clouded with concern as she watched Jordan.

Jordan grimaced. "So you heard—"

"Some of our customers attended the ball." Lynn pulled a pack of cigarettes from the pocket of her jacket, shook one out, lit up, inhaled deeply, and exhaled a long plume of smoke. "It's been busy . . . my first cigarette in hours." She grimaced. "We still smoke everywhere, here in Italy, not like the States. But you can't light up in the shop, not with so many people and things, costumes, fabric, paint, and art! We could burn a hole in a costume, you know? Or go up like a tinderbox." Lynn was speaking casually, but she studied Jordan all the while. "You're okay now?"

"I'm fine. But the contessa's concept of fun is macabre. It was very real," Jordan said. She realized she sounded defensive.

"Yes, well, the contessa would have entertainment that included the best special effects." Lynn brightened suddenly. "Well, you needn't fear when you attend our ball." She grinned, seeing the confusion in Jordan's eyes. "Tonight, the artist's ball—naturally, most of us will be in attendance. Friday night is Anna Maria's Venetian Waltz. We have a palazzo as well, you know. Rented for the occasion, not owned by any of us, unfortunately. But we won't scare you half to death. We entertain with music, tarot card readers, jesters . . . a pleasure palace, but no monsters."

"Well, I assume that Jared has had tickets for us from the beginning, but are you sure you want me to come?" Jordan asked.

Lynn laughed. "Of course. Yes, Jared has had tickets

for months. Surely he told you that the Friday ball is ours."

"I just knew there was a round of parties," Jordan said. "I'm glad, delighted, that one of them is yours. I'm afraid that Jared only explained the contessa's party, and it seems the contessa is very important to his business."

"Ah, so Jared felt that *hers* was the most important party."

"I didn't mean to say that—"

Lynn shrugged philosophically. "The contessa . . . is nobility. She is rich. Her party is definitely for the truly elite—invitation only. It's a big deal to be invited. Come to think of it, none of us at the shop are ever invited to her events. We must be poor peasants in her eyes."

"I wish I'd been a peasant in her eyes. Everywhere I've been today, people stare at me. I'm the idiot American who panicked at a party and brought in the police."

Lynn's smile deepened. "Well, I'm afraid the story has traveled, but . . . you know, there are people who *don't* like her as well. Quite frankly, she's a snot. She breezes down the street as if she's got a stick up her ass."

"Lynn!"

Anna Maria, tall, slim, a beautiful woman in her early forties, had emerged from the shop just as Lynn spoke. A native Venetian, she had a striking bone structure, long brown hair touched with natural gold highlights, and a sense of energy and purpose. Her English was nearly perfect; her accent was charming.

Lynn choked, having been inhaling her cigarette when Anna spoke. Anna Maria had her hands on her hips, but a glitter in her eyes belied the stern way in which she had spoken.

"Sorry, the contessa is charming, just charming."

"Lynn! Such words you are using. It is sour grapes; I believe that is the saying," Anna Maria chastised. "We are not invited, so the contessa is a snob. Forgive us, Jordan."

Jordan laughed. "Actually, don't tell Jared I said so, but I think Lynn's description is rather apt."

"The contessa is beautiful. And she has done a great deal for Venice."

"Um, and she's a snot—*you've* done a lot for Venice and she ignores you!" Lynn defended.

"Lynn, Jordan is a visitor; we mustn't air muddy laundry—"

"Dirty laundry," Lynn corrected.

"Dirty laundry," Anna Maria agreed, shaking her head. "Lynn, do I make fun of your Italian?"

"Upon occasion, yes!" Lynn said.

"Jordan, you must not listen to us. Lynn, give me one of your American cigarettes." Anna Maria took a cigarette and lit up, exhaling with a little sigh of pleasure.

"The way I'm feeling this morning, Anna Maria, I hate to admit it, but I'm delighted to hear something bad about the contessa," Jordan said. "If it was all a charade, it was a horrible thing to plan to do to people."

"*If* it was a charade?" Lynn asked softly.

Jordan shrugged. "Everyone keeps telling me so. The police were angry, my cousin is still angry, and the contessa . . ." She paused, staring at Lynn ruefully. "Well, she acted as if she had a stick up her butt!"

"The streets sometimes have ears," Anna Maria

murmured. "Yet, I'm so sorry. I adore my city. And Carnevale. You should have all *good* impressions of the city and the gaiety."

"I love Venice," Jordan said quickly. "The contessa's party did not change that."

"But, poor dear!" Anna Maria said. "The rumor is that you were absolutely terrified. Again, I'm so sorry to hear that, but . . ." Her voice trailed off, and then she laughed and spoke very softly. "I like to imagine the contessa running through the streets in the middle of the night to the police station. That's what she gets for her great dramas, always promising something more spectacular than anyone else can offer. Her party might be more exclusive, but you're right. Such entertainment is sick. I promise you, the artist's ball tonight is wonderful, but our party will be the most fun. So. What are you wearing?"

"Being a visitor and a novice at Carnevale, I've only the one outfit—"

"Ah, that will not be enough. Come in, come in, we'll find more costuming in petite!" Anna Maria dropped her cigarette and stepped on it. "Now . . . we'll go in and find something fun for the artist's ball tonight and our party on Friday."

"It's really not necessary—"

"Ah, but it is!" Anna Maria corrected. "It is Venice, and it is Carnevale, and you must enjoy the splendor of it all." She glanced sternly at Lynn once again. "In a way that is not snobby, snotty, or stick up the *ass-y* in any way at all."

"No, look, it's all right, the store is crowded, you're so busy—"

"Never too busy," Anna Maria said. "Andiamo. We go in to the costume section. Many things are already

rented, but . . . we never run out of masquerades in
Venice, eh, Lynn?''

"Never," Lynn agreed.

"And if something does not quite fit, Lynn is an
extraordinary seamstress.''

Lynn groaned. "No rest for the weary!''

"Or the naughty," Anna Maria said sternly.

"I'm sure I can make my own adjustments—'' Jordan offered.

"No, no," Anna Maria protested. "Lynn wishes to
outdo the contessa, even down to your costume. We
shall all three see that it is so." She indicated the door.
"Come along, and we'll get busy.''

Jordan hesitated, thinking that perhaps she should
return to the hotel, but it felt good to be with people
who sympathized without thinking her totally insane.
It felt good to be here, and it would be fun to wear a
new costume.

She shrugged, and preceded Lynn and Anna Maria
into the shop.

Jared liked to take public transportation in Venice,
slipping onto the vaporettos with crowds of tourists
and natives, studying the islands of Venice as the boat
came to stop after stop. He knew how to get around
the city, and loved the architecture of it.

Today, however, he took a private launch. Arriving
at the palazzo, he was greeted by the contessa's aide,
a tall, skeletal woman with iron-gray hair and a forbid-
dingly gaunt face. Her disapproval of him was obvious
today, though she was always cold and silent.

He was led to the contessa's palatial bedchamber,
a room as large as many a full house. There was some-

thing exquisitely Renaissance about her decor, from the carvings on the great draped and canopied bed to the scenes on the lush Persian rugs. A sitting area flanked the fireplace; the mantel was marble carved in detail with two grinning gargoyles on either side, as if the pair guarded the flames which might be a gateway straight to hell.

The contessa, dressed in an elegant white silk robe, was seated in a crimson daybed before the fire. A tea service was before her; she had been reading the morning paper. She was one of those women who awoke beautifully: her hair was brushed out, long and sleek; her ageless face showed no signs of slept-in makeup, crinkles at the eyes, or the least of shadows beneath them. She glared at Jared with cool, controlled anger as he entered.

"Contessa . . ." he began softly.

"I have done everything for you," she countered. A small taunting smile curved her lips. "Everything. And you could not keep that silly girl with you at my party?"

"I don't know how she wandered—"

"That is not acceptable."

The contessa had not asked him to sit. Jared stood awkwardly for a moment, then came closer to where her impossibly graceful form was arrayed on the daybed. Her eyes met his; he lowered himself to a knee, humbly lowering his head. It occurred to him that he was behaving like a sycophant, but here, with the contessa, it was to be expected. She had that kind of power, and she didn't expect humbling reverence, she demanded it.

"I beg your pardon. Truly, I beg your pardon."

She thrust the local paper toward him. The front

page. A reporter had gotten wind of the trouble; the details were sketchy, the story was slanted in favor of the contessa, and written with a touch of humor. But though the contessa was mentioned by name, Jordan was cited as the naive American tourist.

"I am so sorry," he said.

"You will see that she ceases this nonsense," the contessa said.

"I've spoken with her firmly."

The contessa broke into laughter. "You've spoken to her *firmly.*" Her laughter rose shrilly. The sound of it caused a shiver deep in his heart. "Caro mio, you've spoken *firmly?* Well, we shall see. If I am forced to take matters into my own hands . . ."

"I can control Jordan."

"See that you do."

"*You* told me to bring her!"

"But I expected you to control her!"

He remained on his knee, his head down.

"You come here, you thrive here . . . you have everything, because of me."

He nodded. Something left of his pride twitched in his throat. He swallowed.

"You're in disgrace."

"I'll . . . I'll leave you now."

She touched his hair, her movement little more than a whisper against him. Somehow repellent. Still . . . seductively entrapping.

"No," she said after a moment. "You may stay. You may stay awhile because I am bored this morning. I will let you have . . . tea with me. You would like that, wouldn't you?"

He looked up at last. Her eyes were on his.

"I would die to have tea with you, Contessa," he said.

At last she smiled with a shrug. "Yes, you would, wouldn't you?"

The contessa rose. With a single shimmering drift of white silk, she stood in smooth perfection before the fire.

"Yes, dear boy, you would die for me."

"See? You wear it so!" Raphael Gambi placed the beaded hat atop his head. It fell over his forehead in a perfect swirl. He posed; body swayed in a seductive arch, lips in a pout, thumb and forefinger upon his chin. Jordan laughed. Raphael's antics had managed to make her almost completely forget the contessa and the ball. Costume was his life. He knew fabrics and styles, the traditional and the totally off-the-wall. Before she tried on any costume, hat or mask, he had told her about how it was worn, the period when it had been worn, and who had been the fashion plate of that particular day. As he showed her what he considered the proper way to wear the cap for a colorful jester's costume, he proceeded to move about dramatically, slipping a mask from a stand to cover his eyes and pirouette before her.

"It's lovely—lovely on you. I'm not sure if it's me," Jordan told him regretfully. Raphael was of medium height with bright blue eyes that continually glittered as he smiled, full of mischief even when the overload of tourists in the shop caused him a few moments of disgruntlement. Everyone at the Arte della Anna Maria shop had a specific job and Raphael headed the costume department. With his absolute flair for high style and his love of clothing, he was a natural, but today, while they were still in the midst of a round of parties, he was also under a great deal of pressure. When Anna Maria had come to him, saying they must try everything in the world on Jordan, he had not sighed under another workload, but eyed Jordan up and down, noting her good qualities—and the fact that she was so tiny. He'd gone through a rapid exchange in Italian with Anna Maria, then proceeded to sail through the rows of costumes with astonishing speed, providing Jordan with a wealth of choices that barely fit into the dressing room with her. She had tried on vinyl futuristic—supplied by one of their favorite contemporary English designers—Roman, Egyptian, Renaissance, Edwardian, Victorian, and more. Through it all, she had heard customers come and go; she had crashed into others while coming out to survey the costumes in the large full-length mirror, and even heard Raphael sigh with regret when he could not please a very beautiful Israeli woman. Despite the busyness of the shop, Raphael had managed to fully assess her in each of the various styles; he moved with the speed of light, always acting out the proper way of handling a parasol, a mask, a bustle, or whatever accessory or affectation might go with each mode of dress. Throughout it all, Anna Maria and Lynn found time to survey her in costume, as had others in the shop, among them a pretty young girl called Angelina, a native Venetian creator of masks, and Gina, an Austrian native who had made Venice her home for the last decade, and who could slip into any one of seven languages fluently to help whomever might come into the shop.

"Allora! Well, it's true," Raphael said, stepping

back. "Though it is petite, you are wasted in the clothing of the harlequin, the jester! Puff here, puff there—personally, I like the vinyl! Sexy, eh? Voilà, follows your little form with seductive precision!"

"The vinyl?" Jordan murmured. She'd never worn vinyl before—she didn't even own anything in leather, other than shoes or bags. Such form-fitting clothing always seemed right on blondes with long legs and lithe figures. "On me?"

"Ooh, si, si!" Raphael said. He placed a hand on his hip, sweeping off the jester's cap. "Not for *our* ball. No, no, no, you must be far more *elegante* for that! But for the artist's ball tonight? Yes, yes. Outrageous, daring, bold, sassy—brash! You will stand out entirely!"

"I'm not so sure I want to stand out," Jordan murmured.

"After last night!" Raphael said sorrowfully. "Allora, I have heard. That dreadful woman!"

Jordan arched a brow. Raphael shrugged. "She is too good for our shop! She thinks she is queen of Venice, eh, while Anna Maria was working hard for the city long before she came home and decided that she would rule! Ah, well. She makes this dreadful dance of death, and you are so frightened, and she is distraught that her party might be ruined." He let out a snort entirely out of character for his usual grace in speech and manner. Blue eyes sparkled with evil intent. "Trust me, in vinyl, you will outdo her. And you will wear the sci-fi boots by Justine, our French friend you will meet later, and you will be taller, and it will be perfect. Don't forget—you'll have a mask."

"I don't know; I'll think about the vinyl," Jordan said. "Now, as for the Arte shop ball . . ."

"No question. The fairy tale fantasy gown," Raphael said with firm determination.

The costume to which he referred was white, silver and gold. The style was somewhere between Renaissance and Revolution, managing to cinch in the waist and expose plenty of cleavage. The accompanying headdress was a tiara with a feather and silk drape to fall behind.

"You think?" Jordan said.

"I know," Raphael assured her.

Anna Maria appeared at the top of the curving staircase that led to the dressing rooms. "I'm so sorry. Roberto Capo is here. He says you arranged something for him for this evening?"

"Si, si, allora, si!" Raphael clapped his hands. He grinned. "A friend—he and I went to school together—a man who works most of Carnevale, but has found out he has tonight off. He loves the artist's ball. I'll be but a few minutes."

"Please, please, Rafael," Jordan told him. "Go ahead, and take good care of your friend. I've taken up way too much of your time."

"Come for an espresso with Lynn and me," Anna Maria said. "Then come back and make your choices."

"Her choices are made," Raphael said flippantly. "But you must come back and admit that I am right. And the vinyl . . . you should take that now. It is such a zoo here, it may take time to get the costumes to your hotel."

Raphael hurried down the stairs. "You'll come for an espresso, cappuccino?" Anna Maria said.

"I should go back. I rather ran out on my cousin-in-law this morning."

Anna Maria shrugged philosophically. "Cindy is a

dear. I will call her; tell her you're here, getting costumes."

"Then I'll come. I'll just hurry out of this . . ." She indicated the jester's costume she had thought a possibility.

Anna Maria nodded. "We'll be on the street—puffing away," she said.

Jordan changed back into her day clothes. When she came down the stairs, she saw that Raphael was talking to a moderately tall, dark-haired man. When the man turned around, she realized she had met him. He had been one of the cops at the station last night; he had come in with the contessa when she arrived with Jared and Cindy. He had done little talking to her, not being the officer who spoke such flawless English. He smiled now, somewhat gravely. "Buon giorno, Signorina Riley," he said pleasantly. His name was Capo, she remembered, Roberto Capo.

She felt her cheeks flood with color; all of the police had been aggravated with her by the end of last night. This man had watched her with deep, searing dark eyes throughout most of her babbling and the other man's questioning.

She saw him struggle for a moment; he had the kind of knowledge of English that she had of Italian—every word had to be recalled and thought out.

"Today . . . you are fine?"

"Yes, thank you, grazie. But . . ." She lifted her hands. "It was very real." She had said those words so many times.

He nodded. "It is . . . understand."

"Understandable," Raphael corrected.

The handsome young officer flushed. "Understand-able. Charades . . . masquerades . . . they get . . ." His voice trailed off and he looked at Raphael.

"Carried away," Raphael supplied.

Capo nodded. "In Venice . . . it is beautiful. We try not to—to throw up too much, you know? Not like your New Orleans."

Jordan wanted to defend New Orleans, a city she loved, but before she could do so, Capo was speaking quickly again. "New Orleans is a good city. Carnevale is—different. Here . . . the masks, the gowns . . . it is a show. Sometimes, the show is too much. There is bad that happens. The contessa should not play at murder and blood."

Jordan smiled at him. "Thank you," she murmured.

"Sono—I am Roberto—"

"Roberto Capo, I remember."

"Roberto, please."

"Roberto. Thank you."

"Prego. Please. I am sorry for your trouble."

"Again, thank you, Roberto. Well. I'll let you get to your costuming."

She started out, but Roberto stopped her, calling to her, striding to touch her shoulder, then blushing slightly again. He was very good-looking, she noted, with his endlessly dark eyes, classic features, and a taut build.

"If you are ever afraid, please, come to me. I will not . . ." He gave up and spoke quickly to Raphael in Italian.

"He will not laugh at you, or be angry with you," Raphael said.

Roberto spoke again quickly, and Raphael translated.

"It's always better to investigate; please don't hesitate to go to him, and if he ever thinks that you might help him, he hopes he may come to you,"

She arched a brow to Raphael, surprised, then looked at Roberto. "I would gladly help him at any time. Except that the police did go to the palazzo. It was a charade. Right?"

Roberto Capo had understood her. "A charade, of course. And still . . ."

She smiled, nodding at him. "Thank you. I'll remember to ask for you if I have any trouble at all while I'm in Venice. And if you wish to ask me anything, you know that I'm at the Danieli."

Roberto nodded gravely. "I would like to know more . . . how you came to the stazione."

"Boat," Jordan reminded him with a shrug.

"You ran from the palazzo."

"A wolf—" she hesitated, realizing that there was a language barrier and she was to insist that a wolf had leaped with her from a balcony. "A guest, dressed like a wolf, brought me to the boat," she said.

"Who was the guest?" Roberto quizzed her. "You have not thought if you know him, he offered you no name?"

She shook her head. "I'm afraid not."

Last night, it seemed that those words had made them all stare at one another, certain that she had truly given way to madness or—too much champagne. But today, this particular officer seemed to believe her.

"If you see this man, if you find him, I'd like to speak with him. You must tell me."

"I'm afraid that if I saw him, I'd never know him. He was wearing a mask."

"But you knew his voice."

"If I hear his voice in the street, I will be delighted to let you know," Jordan assured him. She bid him and Raphael a quick good-bye, and slipped out on the street.

"Ah, you are here!" Anna Maria said.

"I'm sorry to have been so long—"

"Thank you for being so long!" Lynn protested "It's a longer break from that madness."

"This way, down the street, you'll get the best to drink and eat at the cheapest price."

Anna Maria led the way past the popular shops to an alleyway Jordan wouldn't have explored on her own. They passed a few workers and a woman sweeping the tiles in front of her shop, and Anna Maria greeted them all.

For a moment, it seemed that a cloud swept over the sun. Jordan felt a chill; she pulled the collar of her wool coat closer around her throat. When the light faded, it was as if great black wings of shadow swept through the alleys, swallowing up the brightness like a great ravenous bird.

"Ah, here we are on break, and there goes the sun!" Lynn muttered, annoyed, and seeing nothing at all eerie in the natural conditions of the earth.

Jordan intended to shake off the chill immediately; instead, she found herself pausing. Listening.

Wondering if a strange sense of whispers hoarsely spoken on the wind would descend upon her again.

No sound . . .

"Jordan?"

Lynn had turned back.

"Sorry," she said, quickly stepping along, and feeling like a fool.

To her surprise, the tiny café deep in the alley was full. She was about to suggest some place else, thinking they'd never get what they wanted in the customary time for a break. But the two girls behind the counter made espresso, cappuccino, poured wine and aperitif with a skill that would have left any American bartender in the dust. Anna Maria called over the crowd huddled at the bar; in a moment, three espressos had been passed over to them. They found space at a counter against the wall, and stood, sipping their drinks.

"The city seems huge, eh, with all these people?" Anna Maria said, waving a hand. "But it is not so big really. We know one another, often. You mustn't worry about having offended the contessa, even if Jared is upset."

"Worry if you offend Anna Maria," Lynn said, grinning. Anna Maria made a face at her. "Well, it's true," Lynn continued. "The contessa hasn't really been back all that long. And Carnevale, as it is now, was really brought back by some American businessmen twenty years ago or so, and from the beginning, Anna Maria was asked for help. And that's true. The world hasn't really changed so much, especially in Europe. The contessa has money and a title. Anna Maria has talent and class."

Anna Maria shook her head with impatience and modesty. "You're going to confuse Jordan. Carnevale began here centuries ago. Years ago, American businessmen—European-Americans among them, cer-

tainly—became interested in Venice, invested not just
to make money, but to make people aware of the world
treasure that is Venice, in saving historical buildings.
It is difficult here; the sea is our beauty, and it is also
our destruction. I became friends with many of these
people working so hard for Venice. I have always loved
pageantry, costumes, parties . . . and so, I have been
somewhat involved."

"Somewhat involved?" Lynn exclaimed. "Whenever big producers from the world over wish to film
scenes in Venice, they come to Anna Maria."

"And to many other people," Anna Maria corrected.

"I can see why they would come to you," Jordan
told Anna Maria, smiling, and finishing her espresso.

"Don't go thinking so much of me," Anna Maria
said firmly. "What Lynn is trying to say is that you
must not be worried at all about last night's party. The
contessa may think she can damage your cousin's work
in Venice, and she can be nasty as a cat, but most of
the people who love the city and are involved are not
titled, rich, or necessarily even Venetian."

"We like you, and so you are fine!" Lynn finished.

Jordan laughed. "Well, thank you both so very
much. I admit to having been miserable, and now I
feel welcome, and so much better."

"Allora, we must go back," Anna Maria said. "Watch
as we leave; if you wish to come back to this café, you
will find it easily. It is not a tourist café; they will
not charge you an arm and a foot for an espresso or
cappuccino."

"An arm and a *leg*," Lynn corrected, laughing and
indicating the door.

"Andiamo," Anna Maria said.

As they walked, Lynn pointed out street names. "There!" she said. "That building, where you see the restoration store? In the fifteenth century, it housed the infamous mistress of a scandalous doge. The doges were elected, you know, but usually from the nobility, or most prestigious families. It is reputed to be haunted by her ghost; though it was not proven, supposedly he was stabbed in the midst of making love, for a dalliance with one of his ministers."

Jordan looked up at the building; almost every house and structure was old and unique, with incredible architecture. This one had charming balconies and the cornices were adorned with stone lions that seemed to stand as harsh sentinels, ready to protect those within.

Not looking where she was going, Jordan suddenly slammed into something.

Someone.

She was jostled and might have stumbled, but she was quickly righted by the hands of the person into whom she had crashed. Startled, she stared at a wall of black wool. A second later, she realized that she was looking at a man's chest, covered in a long, trim-fitting, excellently tailored Armani suit. She looked up. He was tall, a good six foot four, and very blond. *Rock star?* She thought at first. The feel of the hands straightening her and the size of the shoulders above his chest gave her cause for a second speculation. *World Wrestling Federation contender?*

His hair was past his shoulders, thick, neatly trimmed, not in the least unkempt or matted. His eyes were very blue; ice blue, a cool color that swept over her in a quick assessment.

"Are you all right?" he asked in English.

"Yes, fine—"

"You should look where you're going."

"Yes, of course, I am sorry—"

"Ragnor! Ciao!" Anna Maria said, interrupting.

"Anna Maria, ciao, bella," the man replied, his Italian sounding, to Jordan's untrained ear, as unaccented as his English. He broke into a rapid spate that left Jordan catching only a word or two as he kissed Anna Maria on both cheeks and she enthusiastically returned the greeting.

Lynn, in turn, greeted him, then indicated Jordan and suggested they switch to English.

"Ragnor, Miss Jordan Riley. Ragnor is a friend to all of us at the shop, and Venice. Jordan is new to Carnevale."

"Welcome, then," the man said. He greeted her in like fashion, taking her shoulders, stooping slightly to kiss both her cheeks. She had the strange feeling that he wasn't really all that pleased to welcome her; the lips that touched her cheek seemed cold and brusque. She was almost tempted to pull away. She didn't return the gesture.

She was American, after all; she wasn't expected to kiss in the European fashion.

"How do you do, and again, excuse me," she murmured.

Tall, very tall. As tall as the man with whom she had danced at the contessa's ball. The wolf who had been so courteous—and who had swept her from the bloody "performance" to send her from the palace. But this man didn't seem to know her. Not so much as a flicker of recognition touched his eyes.

How many people in Venice were this tall? Come to think of it, how many people anywhere were this tall?

More than one, she reminded herself dryly. And though Italians were often stereotyped as being small and dark, she had met many tall people here, and many with light eyes and hair.

"Were you at the contessa's ball last night?" she asked, deciding that a straightforward question might be the way to find out.

"No," he replied.

Did the slightest flicker cross his eyes then? Or was she as paranoid as Jared seemed to think she was?

"Ragnor wouldn't be at the contessa's," Lynn said, pleased. "He thinks she is obnoxious."

"Lynn," Anna Maria chastised wearily.

Ragnor was still staring at Jordan. With displeasure, she thought. *Paranoia?*

"It is what you said, Ragnor, isn't it, when we ran into her at the café?" Lynn persisted. She looked at Anna Maria. "I am not divulging secrets—I am trying to make Jordan feel better about not liking her."

"I never said that I didn't *like* her," Jordan murmured.

"I would not be on the contessa's guest list," Ragnor said simply. "You were going somewhere; I should not keep you."

"We're going back to the shop," Anna Maria said. "Our break has been too long. Were you coming to see me? You are going to the artist's ball tonight?"

"Yes, yes, of course. And I will be by." He again kissed Anna Maria and Lynn on both cheeks, and offered Jordan a hand—American style. "Nice to meet you, Miss Riley."

"Thank you; you too," she said. He hadn't been glad at all to meet her.

"You should come soon. We are trying to talk Jordan into vinyl for the fun tonight. You could give her a new perspective," Lynn said.

"Perhaps," he said politely, then indicated with a polite sweep of the hand that they should go on. They did so, Anna Maria and Lynn already into a discussion of what would be right for the artist's ball for a man of his height.

"Who is he?" Jordan asked as they walked, briskly now.

"Ragnor is . . . a businessman," Anna Maria explained.

"We have known him just a little time," Lynn explained.

"*You* have known everyone here just a little time," Anna Maria reminded her.

They had nearly reached the shop.

"He isn't Italian, is he?" Jordan persisted.

"No," Anna Maria said.

That should have been followed by, "*He is German, Austrian, American, or so on.*" But Anna Maria said no more.

"He reminds me of someone I met last night."

"That's quite impossible," Lynn said. "He is right; he would not be on the contessa's guest list. When what I call 'the old guard' are about, he is among them. That day, we were at the café . . . and the contessa arrived. They must have met elsewhere. When they were introduced, they were cordial, but you could see the hostility between them. He left. Do you know what I think?"

"I'm afraid we'll find out," Anna Maria said.

"I think that she is jealous of him. He has no title, no history here, but there is a rumor that he comes from an extraordinary family. He is not in the least showy or pretentious, but people want to be near him. He has a charisma, you know? Something compelling about him."

Anna Maria sighed. "He is a handsome man with a powerful appearance. And he is intelligent and interested in art and history—and Venice."

Lynn grinned. "And he's built like—as we say in America—a brick shithouse."

Anna Maria rolled her eyes. "Lynn speaks with such class in her expressions."

"I'm trying to teach you *real* English," Lynn said with a sigh. "I want you safe on the streets of Brooklyn, should you choose to go there on a trip to America."

"Oh, really?" Anna Maria said. She paused directly in front of the door to the shop. "What Lynn is trying to say is that she has the *hots* for this man *big time,* and that she would give an *arm and a leg* to *get it up with him.*"

"To get it *on* with him," Lynn said with a mock sigh. Her eyes flashed as she giggled. "He is the one who gets *it up.*"

Anna Maria gave a deep sigh. "Come, Jordan, and try your vinyl outfit on again. Raphael is going to insist that you wear it, and you should. It's terrific on you."

Despite the many people in the shop, Raphael saw her instantly and moved through the many groups of people looking at art pieces, masks, and costumes, to reach her. "Vinyl, yes! We'll dress you up one more time!"

"Sure, vinyl, why not?" she agreed. "And a really

good mask, Raphael, so no one knows me!'' She lowered her voice and smiled. ''They'll still be whispering about me enough!''

''Let them whisper—be outrageous!'' he said. ''Come, come.''

CHAPTER 3

Nari was tired, bored, hungry and restless. Last night, with the disaster at the party, she'd not been able to enjoy a thing.

She should be resting, and she should not be wandering through the streets so casually, even in a mask. She had a certain position to maintain. But she couldn't sleep, or even relax, and so she donned a mask and went out into the streets.

Um . . . she was definitely . . .

Hungry.

She needed to find someone with whom to dine.

Not to mention the fact that she didn't want to be home.

She didn't want to be caught resting by uninvited visitors. Because *he* would come. Of course. He'd been watching her, waiting. He thought that he'd come in, make demands, and force her to change her ways.

Ah, but he didn't know the half of it.

He didn't know who was in Venice now and with whom she had been keeping company.

Still . . . she had such a headache! She had no intention of coping with *him* today.

She was startled to feel a sudden sense of nostalgia, of loss. Of pain. It had been seeing him again. Remembering what had been. *Wanting* . . .

Once upon a time . . .

Once upon a time was over and gone.

And still . . .

How she hated Americans!

With a mental shake, she forced it all from her mind. The pain she was feeling was simply hunger.

She wandered around St. Mark's Square, listening to the band that was playing, watching for someone . . . alone, someone who might want to share some time with her.

She tapped her foot impatiently to the music. Such silly people came to Carnevale. Those with money who might spend an entire year planning a costume. Elegant costumes to be sure. Ridiculously uncomfortable. A group dressed as the moon and the stars walked by, and all with clothing that required tremendous wiring for the streaks of white and silver and gold that streamed from the stars. They couldn't possibly sit; they were entirely showpieces.

Many couples passed in traditional masks that covered the entire face of the wearer. Others passed without costumes. Many of these people had taken tour buses in from the poorer, often war-torn towns of eastern Europe. They were not so finely dressed. They came to gawk. Often, they had nowhere to stay except for their buses. They had little to eat. It was actually a kindness to befriend such a person. Their lives were so pathetic.

All men were born to live, suffer through life and then die. That was the way of it. With these poor people . . .

She watched, then noticed the American woman, Tiff Henley. She was not in costume. She was attractive—older, but attractive. She was a woman who moved, who saw, who took all that she wanted. If the way to acquire what she desired happened to be unpleasant, so be it. Nari had heard that the woman's last husband had been close to ninety—but had taken longer to die than Tiff had anticipated.

Tiff must be making up for it. She was staring into the window of one of the most expensive jewelry shops in the Square.

Nari smiled and started for her. Tiff would love to be invited to lunch.

But then, a stout man with graying hair came up behind Tiff, joined by two younger men in capes and bizarre masks. They all stared into the window, pointing, talking, arguing the qualities of the items displayed.

Another woman came up and joined them.

Nari sighed and shook her head.

There were too many people with Tiff Henley. Nari didn't mind charming a few of those beneath her status in her quest for company, but . . .

She was exhausted. Last night had been . . .

Draining. She really hadn't the energy to deal with such a group at the moment.

Still . . .

She really must have something. A little bite. She was so *hungry.*

Nari lifted the cowl of her own cape against the winter's breeze, turned and moved into the crowd.

It was still light.

She simply wasn't at her peak.

But the night would come.

"Molto, molto . . ." Raphael gestured wildly, then grinned. "Sexy!" he said.

She had dressed in her costume upstairs in a fitting room; he had brought her downstairs to be presented to Anna Maria and Lynn.

Nearly encased in blood-red vinyl, Jordan laughed ruefully, catching Anna Maria's eye. "I look like a hooker."

"No, no, no!" Raphael protested. He shook his head, surveying her from head to toe. "No, no, add the sweep of a cape, voilà, you look like a comic strip heroine! Now, the boots, the boots are the perfect addition."

"Give her a whip and chain," a deep voice said dryly, "and she can tame lions."

Startled, Jordan looked across the room. The tall blond man was in the shop, leaning laconically against the wall. She hadn't noticed him at first because of the row of marionettes hanging from the ceiling and the multitude of capes and costumes hung at various places around the shop. Now he stepped forward, studying her with the same thorough assessment as Raphael, yet somehow, his studious appraisal seemed different—*hostile.*

"Ragnor, it is terrific!" Anna Maria said.

"Terrific, yes," he agreed. The way he looked at her, she felt almost naked. "But I rather had the impression that Miss Riley didn't want to appear . . . *obvious* this evening." A slight smile curved his lips. "In this outfit, she will only be missed by the completely blind."

Jordan had indeed wanted to melt into the crowd. But this *stranger's* unsolicited and negative remarks caused her to be completely contrary in return. She felt her hackles rising at the nape of her neck.

She looked at Raphael. "I think you're right." She stared at the tall stranger. "It's definitely me. I'll take it."

"Molto bene!" Raphael said. He stared at Ragnor with a puzzled look.

Ragnor shrugged, idly running a hand over the black velvet cape hanging where he stood. "I merely hope that the police will be out in force. It is indeed sexy. Provocative, one might say." His fingers slid lightly along the velvet and then fell from it. "I trust that you will have a good evening, Miss Riley." He inclined his head toward her, kissed Anna Maria on the cheek, and left the shop.

"Strange!" Raphael said as the door closed.

"Maybe it is too . . ." Jordan murmured.

"It is too perfect!" Lynn announced. "This is Carnevale, Jordan, and you do not look too . . . anything. Except for terrific."

Jordan glanced at her watch, feeling guilty about Cindy. "I think I'd best get back to the hotel. But I will wear it."

"Nothing to fear," Anna Maria said, "we'll all be there, and we'll protect you from wayward wolves."

The comment was said jokingly, but it gave Jordan

a sense of unease. She shook it off. "Good, as long as I can be in the midst of you all, I'll be just fine. I'll just run and change."

"I'll walk you back," Raphael offered. "The Square will be crazy now, so crowded."

"I'll be all right—"

"I don't mind, and I have a costume to deliver to the Danieli."

"Thank you then."

In the dressing room, she wondered if she shouldn't have taken the tall blond man's advice.

"Hooker," she told her reflection in the mirror. "But a high-priced one, at that."

She changed into her street clothing. Downstairs, she found Raphael carrying a garment bag bigger than he was. "Andiamo!" he told her cheerfully.

"Have no fear; we'll find you right away!" Lynn called as she left the shop.

"Stay close behind me; we'll bulldog our way through!" Raphael said.

She smiled, following close behind. He did know how to move. "Scusi, scusi, scusi!" he said, creating a pathway through those still in streetwear, as well as the multitude of historical personages, monsters, creatures, suns, moons, and more. Following him, she again found herself amazed by the elaborate and intricate beauty of so many of the costumes, amused and awed by all that she saw, and once more in love with the city of Venice.

They passed the basilica, and crossed the bridge from the Doge's Palace to the Danieli, where they parted in the busy lobby. Raphael kissed her on the cheek. "You will outshine them all tonight," he promised.

"Grazie, ciao," she told him, and she wondered if
Jared was back at the hotel.

He gave her a thumbs up sign. "Good accent," he
said soberly, then grinned. "You will truly be splendid.
My work of art."

"I'll try to make you proud," she teased and started
up the stairs.

Ragnor arrived at the palazzo in a hired launch,
telling the boatman to wait, even if he were inside for
an hour.

He stepped carefully from the launch to the
contessa's dock, listening as the seawater lapped
against the piling. Long, determined strides brought
him quickly to the contessa's door. When his knock
wasn't immediately answered, he thrust the door open,
heedless of the groaning hinges and the snap as lock
and bolt gave. As he had expected, the contessa's
servants, a tall, skinny man of about sixty in black livery
and a sour-looking woman of the same age with iron
gray hair, were standing just inside. They had been
more than aware of his arrival, but why they had
ignored his knock he didn't know. They must have
expected him to enter, whether or not they opened
the door.

"Where is she?" Ragnor demanded.

"She is not at home," the man said, looking at
the door with disapproval. "And you have recklessly
broken into this palazzo, destroying the contessa's private property—"

"Call the police," Ragnor suggested. Ignoring the
pair, he started across the marble floor of the entry
to reach the landing. Halfway up the stairs, he swung

around. The servant had foolishly seized a sword from the arms display on the wall of the foyer and was attempting to lift the heavy metal in a wild swing. The fool. He'd have never reached Ragnor's neck, being nearly a foot shorter, down a number of steps, and absurdly out of his league.

He avoided the first hapless swing, ducking low and sweeping back up to catch the weapon at the hilt. He tossed it to the floor below, where the clatter against marble seemed to echo with a shattering recall. He pushed the fellow against the banister and continued up the stairs. Reaching the entrance to the contessa's bedchamber, he thrust it open.

Apparently, however, the servants had not lied. The contessa was not in. Ragnor strode into the room, throwing open the wardrobe. He stepped into the dressing room and bath, but there was no sign of his quarry.

In disgust, he turned, left her bedchamber, and strode down the hallway to the second-floor ballroom. His eyes swept the scene where her "merrymaking" had taken place the night before. They had scoured the scrubbed, gleaming marble flooring and columns, the grandly carved great hearth, and the stained glass doors to the terrace, now closed. He walked on into the room, eyes still sharp, senses keen. He knelt down to touch the floor. The heavy scents of bleach and disinfectant filled his nostrils.

He rose and turned in a sudden fluid motion. The disarmed servant had gone for backup. The two men now glaring at him from the ballroom entry were near his own height. Bulky as freighters.

And well armed. *Where had she found these two?*

He swept out a hand. "Gentlemen, come and get me." He glanced at his watch. "And do it quickly, please."

If the contessa wasn't here, where was she?

CHAPTER 4

Unlike the invitation-only party the contessa had thrown, the artist's ball was open to everyone, and it seemed that half the population of Venice had decided to attend. Just walking through the streets, Jordan felt the charged atmosphere of laughter and expectation. Groups of friends rambled through the streets, laughter was continuous, and those beings more reserved due to the character of their costumes and masks greeted one another with silent, polite bows and gestures.

Jordan had linked arms with Cindy on the way to the ball, ignoring Jared who continued to be obstinate. He had tried to dissuade her from coming. "Jordan, I don't think this is a good idea. After last night—"

"I'm not going to embarrass you in front of your friends."

"Jordan, you overreact—"

"Are you worried about me, Jared, or your own appearance?"

Despite the dottore mask he was wearing again, she knew he was scowling. "Does it matter? If you're going to go running out screaming about blood and monsters and cults—"

"Jared, guess what? I won't even be with you at the ball."

That seemed to disturb him. Poor Cindy was torn, at a loss with Jared's harsh manner, trying to be loyal to him and concerned about Jordan at the same time.

Jordan was sorry about what her argument with Jared was doing to Cindy.

She also wished Jared would jump in a canal.

"You're going to go walking around by yourself? In that costume? You think you were scared last night; you'll have every stray dog in Venice at your heels—"

"Thank you, Jared."

"Jared, stop it, she looks terrific, and it's a costume party—"

"She might as well have just painted her skin—"

"She can wear it! She looks beautiful, be proud of her!" Cindy insisted.

"Cindy—"

"Jared, we're already on *our* way," Cindy said.

"Yes, and you know what, Jared?" Jordan said, not wanting Cindy to have to fight her battle. "I think I'll move on ahead, and then you won't have to worry about me doing anything gauche or ridiculous—such as claiming that people are being murdered—in front of your friends."

That said, she hurried on ahead, and was surprised

when he came running up behind her. He put a hand on her shoulder. "Jordan! I'm sorry. Don't go running off alone."

She hesitated. She couldn't see his face, only his eyes. He looked like the old Jared.

"You know, Jared, one of the cops came into the costume shop today and said that I wasn't an idiot. Bad things can happen anywhere."

"But you went so wild against the contessa. You don't know who she is. You don't understand—"

"I understand who she is, Jared, and what she means to you."

"No," he said. For that moment, he sounded truly miserable. "No, you really don't understand. You don't know who she is . . ."

"I'm going to have fun, and I'm not going to think about your contessa. I'll avoid her all night."

"It's unlikely that she'd come to this," he said.

"Too common for her?"

"She doesn't like this much of a crowd."

"Well, then, we'll be fine, won't we?"

She was startled when he suddenly hugged her to him. "Yes, we'll be fine. But Jordan, please, please, for me . . ."

"I won't go around saying bad things about the contessa or her party. I'll simply tell people, if I'm asked, that I'm afraid it was a bit macabre for me."

He nodded, relieved. Cindy walked up, pleased to see them getting along so well. "We're almost there. The tent is in the square up ahead. Jordan, they had such great entertainment last year. The dancers . . . they're exquisite."

"Do they cut each other up?" she asked, then wished she could bite her tongue.

Cindy laughed—the sound just a little uneasy. "No . . . they're sexy. Erotic. They've practically nothing on and nearly perfect bodies . . . you'll see. Ah, there, look at the crowd."

They had arrived at the square. Dozens of people were in line, handing their tickets for the event to the jester waiting at the entrance. His face was painted black and white. Jordan stared at the man carefully. She'd never seen him before.

Within the large tent, there were tables set around a stage. At the moment, a group was playing Italian classics with a rock twist. Jared suggested they find a table while he went for drinks.

As they searched for empty spaces, they were approached by a masked queen in an elaborate velvet costume that shimmered with glittery iridescence.

"Hello, hello!"

"Raphael?" Jordan said incredulously.

He laughed with pleasure. "Si, si—come, we've a table over here. Cindy, ciao, bella, viene, yes?"

"Jared is coming," Cindy said. "He's getting drinks—"

"Fine, fine. We have wine for the table, too, and seats for you all."

Raphael slipped an arm through Jordan's leading them to the table. Anna Maria, stunning in a slinky Egyptian costume, complete with extraordinary head-gear and lifelike asp, jumped up to greet them. Lynn, apparently dressed as a biblical fig fantasy, rose as well, kissing Jordan on both cheeks, then greeting Cindy. There were others there from the shop, all greeting them, and a number of the shop's clients and merchandisers, including Justine, the cute young French girl who designed Jordan's boots, and a couple from Wales who dealt strictly in leather. It was difficult to talk over the music; and there were a wide array of languages being spoken. Before Jared even returned with their drinks, Jordan found herself out on the dance floor with a sixteenth-century cavalier.

As other couples passed them, she realized that she was being whispered about. She breathed a sigh of relief when a pretty young woman, obviously American, tapped her on the arm. "Excuse me, but that costume is fantastic! Where did you get it?"

Swinging beneath the cavalier's arm, Jordan was pleased to be able to tell her. "It's the most marvelous shop—"

"I'll be visiting them tomorrow."

A moment later, Raphael, heedless of the fact that he was an elegant queen, was cutting in on the cavalier. "Allora! Do I know my costumes! Everyone has asked about you, and the costume, and the shop. Now, are you pleased?"

"I am having a tremendous amount of fun."

"You'll have more fun if you come drink your champagne." He led her back to the table, producing a plastic flute for her. She had barely touched it when the band started playing an old Rolling Stones tune. "Come, come, salute! I love this song!"

She gulped the champagne, and found herself back on the dance floor.

An hour later, she had talked to dozens of people. She had walked around with Raphael to see some of the art displayed on the tent walls. She'd danced, she'd watched the first entertainment—a pianist with a delicately perfect woman on top of his baby grand, affixed to a tall glittering pole as if she were part of a music box. She was dressed in ruffly white and pink and carried a parasol, and her movements were as perfect as if she were indeed a wind-up doll. Jordan applauded strenuously, smiling as Raphael wolf-whistled by her side.

The master of ceremonies spoke, announcing the band again. Jared appeared, minus his mask now, asking Raphael if he could steal his cousin away for a minute. He seemed easy and relaxed, and Jordan smiled at him as the band switched to swing music. She had learned to dance to it from Jared and Cindy years ago, when they had first taken up ballroom dancing.

"Having fun?" he asked her.

"Yes, thank you, and you?"

His smile deepened. "Yeah, I am. A lot of fun. It's . . . just a good time."

"A very good time."

"I'm sorry, Jordan."

"And I'm sorry if I hurt you in any way, Jared. I won't say anything more, but . . . your contessa *is* weird."

"The contessa is—different."

"I won't say anything else unless a corpse lands at my feet."

"Jordan—"

"Jared." She frowned suddenly. "I know you think that I'm just . . . like gun-shy. But I do know—"

"Sh. Let's forget it. It's a party. And I'm sorry about insulting your costume. You're too sexy. As your older male relative, I'm supposed to object."

Before she could reply, Raphael cut in on them. He carried flutes of champagne for himself and Jordan. "I'm so sorry, you must go get your own and dance with your wife!'' he told Jared. The next song is a slow one—an Italian version of Elvis Presley!''

"Now I have to take orders from you?'' Jared teased.

"Yes, tonight I'm a *royal* queen. And I dance very well. You—you are so-so. The queen demands the lady in red vinyl. You get out of here!''

Jared winked at Jordan and went off in search of Cindy. Jordan watched him go, smiling, glad. He seemed to be the cousin she knew and loved again.

"Salute!'' Raphael said.

She swallowed the champagne as he did. Her head suddenly seemed to spin. "Whoa! How much of this have we had?''

"At the table?'' he inquired, then offered her a shrug, then a smile. "Molto, molto! This is a party! And are we driving home? No! That is the wonder of Venice.'' He began to sing along with the strangely accented version of the Presley tune. Then he suddenly broke away from her. "Vinyl! It feels as if you are a thousand degrees. Do you wish to sit?''

She hadn't realized it, but she was very hot. She gave him a smile of thanks. He led her back to the table as the master of ceremonies announced the next entertainment and the room went dark except for a spotlight in the middle of the floor.

Her chair faced the stage. She slipped off her mask, smoothing the dampness from her cheeks and fluffing her hair as she watched a beautiful and perfectly formed young woman walk out on the stage. Her costume was neon blue and almost completely sheer. Her hair was long and as dark as pitch. A nylon cord dangled suddenly from the roof. Slowly, sensually, the young woman approached the cord. She caught it and climbed higher with sleek agility. She wrapped the cord around an ankle, and to the soft music of flute and violin, she went into a series of poses that were nimble and all but impossible; she appeared as limber as a length of nylon herself, and her performance was spellbinding.

She held a pose, and the music darkened. A young man appeared on the stage, wearing a similar costume of neon gold. He too captured the cord, joined her, and created pose after pose on the wire, their bodies creating almost unearthly visions. Then they came down to the floor together and began a rhythmic, acrobatic dance. The music and the performance softened to a compelling sensuality. The performers' movements were kept from being graphic by their consummate grace and beauty. A spellbound hush fell over the audience. No napkins crumpled; no chairs shuffled.

Jordan found herself as transfixed at the others, yet somewhere in the entertainment, she became aware of a presence behind her, like a whisper in the darkness. She started to turn, and realized that Ragnor was now in the chair at her side. The chair was drawn close to her. His eyes were on the dancers, but he knew that she had noted his presence.

"Quite incredible, aren't they?" he murmured. He didn't seem to shift, yet he seemed to be even closer. She was sure that his words were heard only by her. He spoke softly; his tone seemed deep. A touch of warmth seemed to drift down her nape, as if she were caressed by his breath. "The capabilities of the human mind and body are amazing . . . when all avenues are explored."

His eyes were suddenly on hers. She found herself arguing for the sake of it. "They are extraordinary contortionists and dancers who have probably practiced dance and movement since they were little children," she whispered in return.

He smiled slowly. "Ah, there speaks the practical mind! But what they create with light and music . . . there's a touch of magic, wouldn't you say?"

The warmth he had evoked seemed to be spreading throughout her. "I'd say that they are excellent performers, and that the stage is well set, that the lighting and music are wonderful."

"So you feel no magic, no emotional pull?" He hadn't moved; again, he seemed even closer.

"Naturally, I feel that they are beautiful . . ."

"Can you actually *feel* beauty?"

"Perhaps you could play semantic games with someone else?" she suggested, but then found that she was giving him an answer. "Yes, you can *feel* beauty. Like the beauty within someone, the beauty of a gentle soul, a compassionate gesture—"

He was watching the performers again, a small smile still curving his lips.

She let out a soft sigh of aggravation.

"And what about magic?" he asked her suddenly.

"Do I feel magic? No," she murmured. Was it magic? No, it was discomfort, being so close, *feeling* his presence as if he touched her, watching the dancers, the eroticism of their every sinuous movement . . . the performance was arousing; it was meant to be arousing. She was suddenly aware of the fluttering of a few antique fans around the room. And a surge of whispering. Men's heads bowed to their wives. Or their lovers. Or the acquaintances they had made here, perhaps even strangers behind masks.

If he had touched her, instinct would have willed her to

*lean against him, to place a hand on his knee. She would
have liked his fingers at her nape, caressing her, the brush
of his knuckles against her cheek . . . no, more . . . his clothing
on the floor, her hands on his chest . . .*

The heat in the room was increasing. She reached
behind, groping for her champagne. She would have
liked a gallon of water; anything cold would do.

He procured the flute for her, barely seeming to
move again. The touch of his flesh as he passed the
glass to her felt as hot as blue fire. She gulped the
champagne in a swallow; her head started to spin
mercilessly. She was going to teeter against him, fall
right into his arms as he seemed, with all amusement,
to be expecting. His eyes were locked on hers, laughing, confident, uncanny . . . *yes!*

The lights came up; the room was suddenly alive
with a burst of applause.

Jordan was holding her empty champagne glass. His
chair wasn't all that close to hers. Around the table
people were talking and laughing, and Cindy was in
Jared's arms. His head was bent to hers, and he was
whispering something that brought a sparkle to her
eyes and the deepest smile to her lips.

Jordan bolted from her chair, startling Raphael, who
sat at her other side. "I see a friend," she lied quickly.
"Excuse me."

She hurried, intent on reaching a bar and getting
a big glass of water. Before she could make her way
through the tables at the stage's side, she was stopped
as a woman in Renaissance apparel suddenly rose,
taking her arm. She nearly shrieked aloud, but the
woman spoke quickly. "Jordan Riley! It's Tiff. Tiff
Henley! I thought that was you when I spied the cos-

tume, but you had your mask on earlier—smashing, really. I mean, absolutely smashing!"

"Tiff," Jordan murmured quickly. "Of course, hello, how are you? You look terrific yourself. Beautiful costume."

"Thanks, I had it made. It seems, however, quite ordinary next to yours. But then . . ." Behind her mask, Tiff quickly gave Jordan an up and down assessment. "Well, it seems made for you, and with vinyl, of course, it must be. Tell me, is it terribly hot?"

"Oh, yes. Extraordinarily so, at the moment."

"Maybe you need a breath of air . . . some water. Please . . . Roberto, per favore, acqua per Signorina Riley?"

Jordan glanced to the table. She should have noted the policeman, Roberto, right away. He rose at Tiff's bidding, quickly pouring Jordan a plastic flute of mineral water from the bottle sitting in the center of the table. He smiled at her, telling her, "Good evening," in English.

"Buona sera," she returned, accepting the glass, "and thank you."

"Perhaps you'd like to walk outside . . . ?" he inquired. "It's much colder."

"Cooler, Roberto," Tiff said, pleasantly inserting the right term.

"You needn't leave your party—" Jordan protested.

"I would like a walk," he told her.

"Go, go! Cool down!" Tiff advised, reaching for her own champagne flute. "We're on for coffee tomorrow, right?"

"Yes, certainly," Jordan agreed.

Roberto led her through the tables and out through the maze of low barricades that had been set up for crowd control just beyond the tent. The moon was high, and light shone from the tent, but the ancient buildings created a world of shadows beyond the spill from the party and the glow from the moon. Roberto seemed to understand the desire for light that sprang up within her, though, pausing casually by a cement bench in the center of the square, and lighting a cigarette. As he indicated, Jordan took a seat. He remained standing, but set a foot on the bench and leaned an elbow on his knee as he spoke to her.

"No further . . . difficulty?" he asked her.

She shook her head. "None at all."

"I'm happy. I love my city. Venice is beautiful. There is nowhere like it in the world."

"You've traveled a lot?"

"No," he admitted with a grimace. "But I have seen TV—and I read. And now . . . there is the Internet."

"It is a beautiful city," she assured him. "I love it."

Before he could reply, she heard him hailed from behind. He turned. Jordan was surprised to see another of the policemen from the other night, Alfredo Manetti. "Roberto, Miss Riley!"

The officer seemed to have forgotten his impatience with her. He lifted a hand, quickly indicating that she must not rise, and placed his hands on her shoulders before kissing her cheeks. She nodded warily to him, not returning the gesture.

He said something rapidly to Roberto, which she did not catch at all.

"Miss Riley is having a wonderful time," Roberto said carefully in English.

"I'm glad. You liked the entertainment?" he inquired.

"I did. No blood and guts."

"The Artist's Ball is quite different. Fun, beautiful
. . . for everyone. You know, though she would deny
it up and down, I think that the contessa is here—
she would not admit to having a good time with the
common rabble, but I saw a beautifully costumed Jeze-
bel in there this evening, and I think it was the
contessa—*slumming it*, as you might say in English."

"Everyone loves a party," Jordan said. She rose. "If
you'll excuse me, I think the party is winding down."

"Of course, of course," he said.

She turned to Roberto. "Thank you for the walk.
It was much cooler out here."

She didn't wait for his reply, but hurried back to
the tent. The ticket-taker had fallen asleep at the door.
She passed him, and excused herself as she walked by
the throng of people who were not leaving. Inside,
she was startled when she felt a hand on her arm.

It was Lynn Mallory. "Jordan, I picked up your mask.
Everyone was dancing, our table was bare. If you're
through with it for the night, I'll take it with me."

"Yes, thanks. You're leaving?"

"Um, we have a very long day tomorrow. Carnevale
goes on—and on."

Lynn looked tired, but happy. "Where is everyone—
still dancing?"

"I think. Jared and Cindy looked like newlyweds—
after watching the acrobatics! Thank God they brought
on a clown and juggler right after—for those of us
going home alone! Anna Maria . . . I think she has
gone, too. I last saw Raphael with another queen. They
were comparing costumes and jewels."

"Thanks, then. Good night."

"I'll see you tomorrow?"

"Sure. I'm having coffee at Tiff's palazzo, but I'll be by sometime in the afternoon."

Lynn gave her a cheerful wave and started out. Jordan was weaving her way through the tables when she felt a hand on her arm again.

"You ran away."

It was Ragnor. She noted that he had chosen to wear black again, a period costume from the era of the English reformation—black breeches, buckled black shoes, a black cotton shirt and quilted vest. His hair seemed very light against the darkness of his attire, but the ice blue shade of his eyes seemed almost to match in the muted light of the dance floor.

He was wearing a cape as well, a cowled cape that seemed to be a mainstay of apparel at Carnevale.

"You ran away," he repeated.

"I didn't run away. I was being baked alive in this. I needed to get outside."

As she spoke, she realized that he was leading her to the dance floor.

"It's late—"

"You want to run away again?"

She found herself being led into a spin; the band was now playing swing music. He seemed to know what to do with it.

"Actually, it's just late—"

"Actually, I think that you should run away. Go home."

"Well, *actually,* I'd like to get to the hotel—"

"I meant home. The United States. Your cozy little home in the South."

She arched a brow at him. For a moment, spinning once again beneath his lead, she had no breath to reply. When she faced him again, she said, "How incredibly rude."

"I'm afraid that you may be a cause for trouble here," he told her.

"*I* may be a cause for trouble? A woman with power and position stages a horrible scene and *I* may be a cause for trouble? Are you defending the contessa?"

"No. I don't defend her in the least. But I think that you should go. I can't imagine why you wound up being where you were when you were—"

"It was a party. I was invited."

He waved a hand in the air. "You'll notice that many others you know were not in that ballroom."

"How do you know where I was? You said you weren't there."

"The story is all over Venice."

"So I've heard. But it's in the past—"

"Is it? The police are watching you."

"Good. I didn't do anything wrong."

"But you've angered the contessa."

"You know, I really don't give a damn."

"You should."

"I'm an American. We don't grovel before European nobility."

He was swinging her out to the music; it might be the perfect moment to simply slip from his hold and keep going.

But there was no such thing as slipping from his hold. His hands were large, his fingers long. They held a startling strength, so much so that he seemed oblivious to the fact that she had meant to escape. She wondered when the song would end. Of course, she could be really rude and just stop dancing. Then he'd be forced to let her go.

"I was given the impression you disliked the contessa," she said. "But I suppose her opinion matters to you as much as it does to others."

"Not in the least."

"Then . . ."

"You should simply go home. You may have put yourself in danger."

"Why? Is the contessa some kind of a master criminal?"

"In my opinion? Yes."

"I'm sure I'm perfectly safe. As you noted, the police do seem to be where I am."

"I'm not at all sure you want to rely on the police."

"Are you saying that the police are criminals, too?"

"I would never say such a thing."

"Then just what are you saying?"

"That you're in danger; go home!"

"Why would I be in danger—"

"Because you are fragile."

She did stop dancing. She firmly stood her ground, not trying to pull away, but not moving. I'm not tall, granted, and I haven't a great deal of weight, but I assure you, I am far from fragile."

"It's my understanding that you are suffering from a recent loss—"

"Which has not unhinged my mind, sir. I was engaged to a cop, a good man, killed by flesh-and-blood criminals—people for whom he had empathy and regard. If he'd been a little less concerned for the value of any life, he wouldn't be dead now. He was a cop, not a seer, or a mystic. He was murdered. Therefore, I do know that very bad *people* do exist, that human beings can be monsters. I think that they are far too lax here, that there should be a far greater investigation into the contessa's *entertainments* than what I have seen. That does not make me fragile!"

"Your insistence that something has happened is what puts you in danger," he told her.

"So if something did really happen, I should just forget it?"

"You should just go home, on the first possible plane. You should let those who know what they're doing deal with matters here."

"So there are matters with which to be dealt?" she demanded.

He sighed deeply with aggravation, a sound that was almost a growl. "There is nothing that should concern you."

"Excuse me—"

"There is nothing you can do."

"Is there something *you* can do?" she queried.

"Trust me, Miss Riley, it would be best if you went home. You have lost someone recently—"

"It's been a year. I am not insane with grief."

"Perhaps you are susceptible to fears and nightmares."

"I am not!" *Or was she?*

The mannequin had stared at her through Steven's eyes . . .

"Just go home!" He said angrily. "You are causing a greater danger—"

"For whom?"

"Go home!"

She didn't need to pull away from him. The music had stopped. He dropped her hands and walked away without another word. Stunned—and furious with herself for staying with him on the dance floor as long as she had—she hurried back to the table where she and her party had been sitting.

She waited there for a minute as the master of ceremonies announced the last dance of the evening in several languages. She searched the dance floor from where she stood, but saw no sign of Jared or Cindy. She sat for a moment. Jared and Cindy would never just leave her. She drummed her fingers on the table. The sound of the last slow dance faded away.

Conversation and soft laughter could still be heard in the tent, but the band had stopped playing and even the die-hards were tiredly making for the exit. Jordan realized that Jared and Cindy must have thought that she had left, probably with the group from the Arte della Anna Maria shop, when they had seen that her mask had been picked up from the table. She was on her own.

She stood up, looking around for Tiff or Roberto, but the table where they had been sitting was empty as well.

Oh, well, she had walked here. She could walk back.

She joined the exciting crowd. Knowing the general direction from which they had come, she started that way, glad to see that most people seemed to be headed in the same direction. A knight in armor nearly plowed into her. He apologized profusely, nearly stumbling. She helped straighten him, reeling at the scent of whiskey on his breath.

"Wanna join us for a nightcap?" he slurred to her

"Thanks, but no thanks—early morning," she lied. And hurried ahead. Going beneath an archway between two fifteenth-century buildings, she quickened her pace until she could no longer hear the knight clanking along.

She came to a fork in the pathway, one walk leading over a bridge to another island, the other leading back inland. She paused, trying to remember how they had come, what landmarks she had seen.

Venice was historic, wonderful, beautiful. To the unobservant visitor, however, come the deep darkness, it all looked alike.

"Shit!" she swore aloud.

Something fluttered by her ear; not a bug, something bigger. She was aware of the flapping of wings.

A bat? She felt her skin begin to crawl.

The bridge. That would at least get her away from the old building to her right, a grand but derelict structure with a crumbling facade that apparently harbored bats.

She hurried over the bridge and along a path.

The stores were all closed for the evening. She peered into darkened windows, trying to decide if she had come this way or not. If she could just get back to St. Mark's Square, she would be able to find her way.

If she could just find *anyone* to point her in that direction, she'd be fine.

She saw a sign on a building ahead and hurried toward it. An arrow pointed to her left with the words "San Marco" printed above it. Of course, that could just mean the island, but at least, getting to the island would be a start. Once there, of course, she'd find winding pathways, piazzas and bridges as well, but hopefully, she'd see something familiar—or find another sign.

She followed the direction of the arrow through another archway between buildings. She looked back to assure herself she had come the right way. The buildings were casting deep shadows on the walkways beneath the light of the moon. The moon itself was now becoming a darkened blue orb in the night sky as clouds drifted below it. She started, stopping dead in her tracks, as the length of shadow seemed to stretch out from the buildings across the piazza she had just crossed.

Something flew by her again, close enough to tangle in her hair. She let out a startled gasp. Bats. This time touching her. She ran forward, shaking her head, feeling the first sense of real fear.

Nasty little creatures, bombarding her at night. But just *bats!*

She stopped again, shaking her head, inhaling deeply. Which way had she run? Ahead of her was another archway. Was it one she had already walked beneath? No.

Once again . . .

Wings . . .

Flying close, not touching her; she instinctively ducked.

This time, the wings seemed to whisper. Hisses, warnings, not formed into words, but sounds that seemed to echo and flutter with danger . . .

She ran, hurrying beneath the arch. She came upon another little bridge that traversed a small canal. She could see down the length of water to another bridge.

Someone was there. A figure . . . a man. In a dottore cape and mask.

"Jared!" she called out.

He stood there, waiting for her.

"Jared!" she called again. She had never been so glad to see anyone in her life, she thought as he made a sweeping gesture, indicating that she should come around.

Then he moved, crossing the bridge.

"Jared, wait, damn you!" she cried out.

She ran over the bridge, then tripped on the cobblestone landing. Despite her desperate effort to prevent a fall, she went down. Swearing, she cursed her high-heeled red leather boots and looked at her leg, feeling a pain in her knee but hoping she hadn't wrecked the rented vinyl costume. As she looked over her uninjured costume, she found herself staring at the ground. To her amazement, a shadow seemed to be sweeping toward her.

Heedless of her knee, she leaped to her feet and ran. She turned back. The shadow seemed to have risen from the ground, to have become a real form in the pathway. She kept running, trying to find the street that would lead around to the other bridge.

A flutter of wings suddenly seemed to surround her. Bats . . . shadows . . .

Again, the hissing sound. Fluttering. Speech that wasn't speech. Shadow whispers . . .

She ran faster, bursting out upon a lighted square. She could see the path to the other bridge. It was now empty.

"Jordan!"

She thought she heard her name being called. No, whispered, fluttered by bat wings. A breeze was picking up. She could hear it, whisking by her.

"Jordan!"

She looked ahead. A larger bridge loomed before her. He was there. Jared. Or a man, a figure, in a dottore costume.

"Jared, damn you!"

She heard the panic in her own voice.

She raced toward the bridge. Jared was already over it. It seemed he had gone down the darkest path before her.

"Damn you, Jared, wait!"

She started running again, telling herself not to look back.

She couldn't help but do so. Shadows seemed to be dancing, snaking around the facades of the buildings as well as the paths between them. Those shadows were encroaching, moving swiftly, as if they too ran, as if they would come and overtake her, and she would be swallowed into the darkness.

She nearly ran into a dead end, just barely stopping herself from plowing straight into a wall. She turned back. The shadows had her nearly cornered. She had to escape this dead end before the shadows covered it; somehow, she knew that, knew it in the naked fear that now ran rampant in her.

She shot across the space to the pathway she had strayed from, just barely making it before the stretch of shadow.

"Jordan!"

She thought she heard her name again. A fluttering, and now, a sound of laughter, deep husky laughter, neither male nor female, just . . .

Evil.

Fluttering, laughter, sounds, whispers.

She came to a halt. Shadows seemed to play and dance on the facades before her now. Graceful, a sweep of darkness, circling her. For a moment she stood transfixed, trying to tell herself, somewhere deep in the logic of her mind, that this could not be happening. Shadows were no more than an obstruction of light. The whispers, hissing, fluttering . . . the laughter, were no more than her imagination, night sounds taking on new meanings as she gave way to panic.

But the shadows did seem to take shape. Like dancers on the walls.

She felt a shove suddenly. And she was sure that she distinctly heard the word, "Go!"

Instinct moved her again. She ran—in the direction she had been pushed. A cacophony of whispers seemed to rise behind her. A fluttering, breathing, hissing.

She ran and ran.

A shadow rose before her.

She plowed right into it.

She heard fierce muttering in Italian. An old man rose, shaking his head, steadying her as she nearly tripped over him. He said something about "Carnevale" and something nasty about "turistas!"

Jordan could barely apologize—in any language. "Piazza San Marco!" she said. "Per favore!"

The old man pointed.

She nodded and thanked him. She ran again, then saw that she was on the path that led directly to the left of the Danieli—and that let out on the well-lit area that edged the Canale Santa Maria della Salute.

She burst into the light. There, on the broad walkway before the water, were other people. Not many. A couple ambling beneath the blue moon. A threesome waiting at a vaporetto stop. A restaurateur, sweeping up in front of his café.

She stopped running, doubled over, caught her breath. In seconds, in the light, she regained a sense of sanity.

She'd been lost and confused. A bat had gotten into

her hair. She'd panicked, and she'd run like an idiot, and hurt herself, but now she was safe.

She rose and felt a sharp pain in her side from the running, and she felt the soreness in her knee.

Damn Jared! He had waited for her, but not long enough for her to catch him! He hadn't been worried, she told herself. He probably hadn't realized that she was lost, or for that matter, afraid.

She stretched and looked back. If the old man was still out on the path, she'd give him a wave of thanks.

The old man was not there.

Her breath caught again.

In the moonlight, she saw a wolf. A huge silver wolf, sitting in the center of the path.

Yet even as she watched, the wolf rose to all fours. Strange glittering eyes seemed to stare back at her in the night.

Then the wolf turned and disappeared into the shadows.

CHAPTER 5

Entering the Danieli, Jordan saw that some night owls were still in the lobby bar. The tables in the handsome lobby and bar area were occupied by couples and small groups. At one of the period sofas that flanked a Persian rug, Jordan saw Jared and Cindy. On a coffee table in front of them were empty espresso cups. The two were tête-à-tête, apparently feeling both drowsy and romantic.

Jordan was about to accost Jared, telling him he should have stopped for her, when she gazed at his cup again. Empty. He leaned back in the sofa, his arm around his wife, his mask cast to the floor by the sofa.

"Jordan!" Cindy straightened, then stood. "I was starting to worry about you. We knew you left with the folks from Anna Maria's, but the party has been over now for quite a while."

"I didn't leave with the group from Anna Maria's," Jordan told them.

A waiter hovered nearby, smiling pleasantly.

"Last call, Jordan, if you want anything. They do have decaf espresso."

"Tea, thank you, something like an English Breakfast," Jordan said, sitting across from Cindy and Jared in a richly upholstered armchair.

Cindy sat again, staring at her. Jared leaned forward frowning.

"Where were you?" he asked.

"I knew we shouldn't have left. I thought you'd taken your mask and gone. As a matter of fact, I was angry with you for not telling us you were leaving."

"You left together?" Jordan asked.

"Of course," Cindy said.

"You've been back a while?"

"At least half an hour," Cindy told her.

"Were you all right?" Jared asked. He sounded anxious.

"I'm fine."

"But you weren't with the people from the art shop?" Cindy asked.

Jordan shook her head, watching them. "They thought I left with you; you thought I left with them."

"But where were you? You weren't in the tent when we left," Jared said.

"I ran into two of the cops."

Jared's frown deepened. Before he could say anything, Jordan added, "Don't worry. I made no accusations against anyone. I was charming and totally sane. We just talked about the artist's ball—and the beauty of Venice. And, of course, the heat of vinyl."

"You are smashing," Cindy said, smiling. Jordan

smiled back at her. Cindy was a wonderful friend. Sympathetic when she needed a defender and pleased with her every little accomplishment.

"Thanks."

"Smashing, but too provocative," Jared said, sounding distracted, a frown still furrowing his forehead. "You came alone? I mean, that's a definitely red costume, and I'm sure the streets were filled with wolves tonight."

"As a matter of fact, I thought I saw a wolf along the way."

I didn't see any wolf costumes tonight, did you Jared?" Cindy asked.

Jordan decided not to mention the fact that she thought she had seen a *real* wolf.

"No wolves," he agreed. "Believe it or not, I did see a giant ape. Jordan, I'm sorry. We'd have never left you. As Cindy said, I was kind of put out, worried, and angry—thinking you'd just walked off without telling us."

She shook her head. "I wouldn't have done that."

"But you made it home all right," Cindy said.

She lifted her hands. "I'm here." She smiled a thank you to the waiter as he brought her tea. Leaning forward to pour the tea, she told Jared, "As a matter of fact, I was ready to come in here and yell at you. I think it took me so long to get back because I was following the wrong dottore."

"What?" he asked.

"When I left, I did confuse the streets. Then I saw a dottore ahead. I thought it was you, and that you just weren't waiting for me."

"We've been right here—it couldn't have been Jared," Cindy said. "Jordan, the dottore costume is

one of the most common in the city. I'm so sorry . . .
I hope you weren't frightened."

"Oh, not at all," Jordan lied blithely.

A fire leaped and crackled in the fireplace. Low
conversation filled the lobby. A concierge remained
behind the long desk before the front door, and several receptionists were still on duty behind the perfectly polished check-in desk. The feeling of . . .
normalcy was so prevalent in the lobby—not just normalcy, but comfort and warmth—that it was easy to
believe that she was letting her own mind run riot.
Hadn't she seen Steven's face on a dummy today?

"So you had a good time?" Cindy asked.

"Yes, I did. The people from the Arte della Anna
Maria shop are wonderful."

"They are," Cindy agreed.

Both Jared and Cindy kept staring at her; Jared a
little skeptically, as if he doubted that she was really
relaxed and comfortable.

"We should never have left," he murmured.

"Hey, you're here, I'm here. And you should go
up to bed," Jordan said. She indicated their empty
demitasse cups. "Go on up to bed."

"We'll wait for you," Jared said.

She shook her head firmly. "I'm fine. I'll finish my
tea and come up. I have my own room, I'm over twenty-
one, I've caroused in the streets alone in the dark,
and I can surely make my way up the stairs to my
room."

"You don't need to drink your tea alone—" Cindy
began.

"Go!" Jordan said firmly. "I'd like to wind down a
little by myself."

Cindy rose; Jared joined her more slowly.

"Go!" Jordan repeated.

"You're sure you're all right?" Jared said.

She gave him a vast sigh of impatience. "Fine. I had a great time. I'm just going to drink my tea and go to bed."

Cindy gave her a kiss on the cheek and tugged on Jared's hand. He followed along behind her, still watching Jordan as he headed for the stairs behind the receptionist's desk.

When they were gone, Jordan leaned back in her chair. She was glad they had chosen seats near the hearth; despite the heat she had felt in her vinyl earlier, the excursion home had given her a chill. Now the natural warmth of the fire seemed to enwrap her, and it was comforting.

The waiter came by to clear away the cups. He cast Jordan a smile.

She smiled back, then leaned forward. "Scusi . . . are there any wolves in Venice?" she asked.

"Wolves?"

She searched her mind for the word in Italian. "Lupo?"

"Lupo, wolf, si, I understand, signorina." He smiled, shaking his head. "Big dogs, yes, people keep big dogs, even in little apartments. But wolves . . ." He shrugged. "No, signorina, no wolves. Why?"

"I thought I saw a wolf in the street."

He gave her a sage nod. "There are many wolves at Carnevale, signorina—out to howl when they can hide behind a mask, yes?"

She grinned, shaking her head. "Not the human kind. A real wolf."

"A big dog, signorina."

"Yes, probably."

"People down the calle . . . they have two huskies. And down by the fish restaurant, maybe a quarter of a mile over the bridge, there is a man who owns a malamute. A big, big dog that looks much like a wolf."

"Of course, thank you, that must be it."

He nodded, pleased that he had been of help.

She rose.

"Buona notte, signorina," he told her.

"Grazie, buona notte," she told him, and headed up the stairs. Once inside her room, she made a point of locking her door.

She walked across the room to the windows and saw that though they had been closed, the shutters opening to the walk and canal below had been left open. She opened the window, reaching for the shutters, but paused.

By day, she could look out and see the bustle of human traffic on the broad walk before the hotel; she could see the sweep of the canal and the majestic basilica beyond. Leaning far out, she could see the pillars before the Doge's Palace and the Piazza San Marco.

Now . . . the night was quiet.

It seemed that even the last of the revelers had gone to bed.

About to close the shutters, she hesitated, and took a seat in front of the window.

She loved her room here. The bed was set back in a section of the room that was divided from the sitting area by draperies held with gold cords. There was a window in the area with the bed, and the window here. A picture-perfect view was offered from either window. The room was furnished with well-kept antiques. Each night when she came in, there was a tray of fresh fruit and mineral water waiting for her.

She opened the water and walked back to the window. She sat in the chair there again and stared out, listening to the lulling lap of water against the docks beyond.

The tea had tasted good; the water was better.

She had drunk far too much champagne tonight.

Leaning back, she closed her eyes and let the cool breeze waft over her. Ragnor's suggestion as they danced passed through her mind. *Maybe she should go home.*

Steven Moore had joined the police force as a homicide investigator right when the city and the neighboring countryside had been plagued by a series of bizarre cult murders. The people of Charleston had been deeply concerned—it wasn't so much that her leading citizens were disappearing, but Charlestonians tended to be both old guard, as well as concerned with being progressive. The city was beautiful: the Battery area had its antebellum houses and courtyards, the public parks offered mature trees and gardens, and to the east lay the shimmering Atlantic. The city was rich with history, from Revolutionary to Civil War times, and yet it strove to move into the future. There were problems, yes. Moving into the future wasn't easy. The Deep South carried a great deal of baggage, as well as the traditional charm and hospitality. But such strange and bizarre happenings . . .

The countryside surrounding the city was also rich in ruins and marshes. First, the decomposed remains of a young woman were found in the basement of a condemned manor by the river; little more than bones

were found. Not a scrap of clothing was discovered
near the remains, no sign of cause of death. The medical examiner's office eventually sent the remains to
the FBI; the bones told her age and race—eighteen
to twenty-four, white. She'd had no dental work done
whatsoever and had died with perfect teeth.

Later, rumor started about Latour House, an abandoned Colonial mansion just outside the city. Lights
were seen, strange music was heard, and children from
neighboring farms swore they heard laughter and
chanting. The house was investigated; people had
indeed been living in it. Remnants of fires were found,
along with bottles, blankets, and cooking paraphernal-
ia—including a George Foreman grille. The homeless
had taken up residence, so it appeared. But then
another body was found. This one had not decayed
quite so thoroughly, and there were strange markings
found on the remaining flesh. This girl's teeth had
been riddled with cavities; her remains were traced
back to a missing persons report filed in Columbia six
months earlier. Steven had just taken his position with
the homicide department. He'd been among the officers to find the remains.

The next body was found in an abandoned mill.
This time, fingerprints on a beer bottle were traced
to a local high school tough guy who became a whim-
pering child in the hands of juvenile authorities. He
told bizarre stories of a devil-worshiping cult, of a
grand master who demanded that he and others lure
young women—preferably homeless girls and run-
aways—to designated places.

The boy swore he had no hand in the murders,
nor could he recognize the leaders of the cult. When

talking to the police, though, he suddenly clammed up. No amount of pressure could get him to talk.

He was found dead in his cell at the juvenile detention hall. He'd gotten hold of a straight razor, and slit his own throat.

Jordan had met Steven at a local restaurant. He'd immediately caught her attention with his deep concern for the young man who'd had such a checkered past, but was still a child. She'd started talking to him over coffee; she'd agreed to a date. His dedication to his work was admirable; his ability to keep his work and the rest of his life balanced was more so. He was often on call, but Jordan didn't mind. She always had work to do, a book to read, and Charleston was her city—she had friends, and loved the movies, plays, museums, and everything else the city offered. Her parents had left her a house near the Battery where she kept a canvas hammock beneath a giant magnolia. She would lie there, reading and waiting for him to come. She could still hear the grate of iron when the gate would open and he would slip into the garden, touch her hair, her cheek, and lie beside her. He'd asked her to marry him in that old hammock. She hadn't really known him that long, not even six months, but among his other attributes, he had been an incredible lover, and it had never occurred to her to refuse him, even though the speed of his question somewhat amused her.

Jared and Cindy had thrown them a wonderful engagement party, right before Christmas. They made their plans. They'd have a cat and a dog, maybe even a bird in the garden. One boy, one girl. They laughed as they talked about names, from the traditional to the odd. They teased one another about rethinking it all if they should have two boys, or two girls. If they couldn't use a name they loved for a child, they'd just have to get another pet.

Then, after Christmas, another body was found. In the marsh area, decomposition could set in amazingly fast; a body could be reduced to little more than bone in a few days. Animals and insects could see to that. This time, the medical examiners found slash marks on the vertebrae of the neck, and the police knew that the cult had not died away, but had just been lying low. The FBI was called in to assist in the continuing investigation.

Tire tracks were found near the marsh; the vehicle used to dump the body had been a new model truck. A knife found near the site was traced to a new Ford truck owner.

The man, however, and his truck, had disappeared. The search was on.

The last time Jordan saw Steven alive, he had stopped by the house to tell her he was hot on a lead, he'd be late, very late coming home. He worked long hours, but that had never bothered her because it was easy for her to adjust her work schedule. He had his own key to the house. He could come in and wake her whenever he chose.

But he didn't come back.

That night, there was a fire at an abandoned and tumbledown barn. Through the night, firefighters worked desperately to get the blaze under control, but it had been created through the work of a well-planned arsonist.

When the fire was finally out, eight bodies, hopelessly charred, were discovered.

Weeks later, forensic specialists had the remains

sorted. Steven's body was the first to be identified, his belt buckle hadn't burned completely and his badge had hardly been seared. Among the others were two backup officers, a twenty-three-year-old prostitute, the last victim of the cult, and five cult members. One of them was identified, through dental records, as the owner of the Ford truck. Piecing together the evidence, the police and FBI deduced that Steven and the others had hoped to surprise the cult members. A gunfight had taken place, and the kerosene, intended to destroy the murder scene, had ignited. Candles that had been set up around the victim had spurred on the flames, and the barn had gone up like a tinderbox.

In her grief, Jordan knew that Steven would have felt his life was a fair trade for having destroyed something so heinous as the cult that had taken so many young lives.

It hadn't changed the fact that he was dead.

The cool breeze coming in reminded her of the last winter they had spent together. She could almost hear the creak of the hammock in the garden, where she had so often bundled up and waited, regardless of the weather.

Soothing . . .

Jordan was never sure when she drifted from consciousness to sleep, or when memories twisted to become the substance of dreams.

She felt she was light as air. She was in the hammock, and it was winter; there was snow all around. But the snow wasn't cold; it was soft, and drifting, and not even wet to the touch. It wasn't snow, but clouds, she realized, and suddenly, he was walking through them.

Steven. Dark hair in a rakish mop, slightly tousled

as it so often was. He wore a sheepish grin, as if he were late, but had a good excuse, and knew that she would understand. She wanted to jump from the hammock and greet him, but she was far too lethargic to do so. He would come to her. He would arrive at the hammock, perhaps slip up behind her. She'd feel his breath at her nape, and his fingers slipping beneath the collar of her sweater.

He was there with her.

"Ye olde hammock," he murmured.

"Too cold, it's winter," she whispered. But his fingers were warm; hotter than vinyl, hotter than watching the acrobatic dancers . . .

"It's never cold, where you are," he told her.

She needed to talk. She wanted to tell him that she had seen his features on the face of a mannequin.

But he wasn't there anymore. He was ahead of her in the snow again. Not snow, clouds; he was walking and walking, coming through the clouds, but he didn't seem to be able to reach her.

"I love you, Jordan."

"I love you, too. I miss you."

"I'll get back to you, Jordan."

"You can't Steven," she whispered softly. She didn't say more; in the dream, it seemed far too rude to remind him that he was dead.

"I can, and I will."

She smiled, because he was stubborn, and this was a dream, so of course he could come to her.

"Steven . . ."

A dream, filled with clouds, and the memories of a slow-burning warmth that could destroy the very concept of winter. She smiled, reaching out.

The clouds seemed to swirl and stir.

She was staring into the strange, copper-penny shine of the eyes of a wolf.

The animal was enormous. It seemed to loom in the window frame. The animal snarled, lips pulling taut, canine teeth luminescent.

"Jordan, the damned wolf is in the way," Steven said.

"There are no wolves in Venice," she told him. "Only big dogs."

The clouds seemed to be streaming around both Steven and the wolf. It was snowing, and the snow was cold, blustering against her skin.

She woke with a start.

She nearly screamed aloud.

A man was standing above her. She was still seated by the window; the man was bowing low to her, he was nothing but a dark form . . .

"Jared!" she exclaimed.

He jerked up, giving himself a shake.

"Jared!" Jordan reached over and flicked on the lamp by the chair.

He was in long flannel pajama pants; his chest bare. For a moment, he looked disconcerted, as if he had been sleepwalking.

Then, he looked uncomfortable. He stared at the window and moved away. Frowning, Jordan glanced out.

It was snowing in Venice. Tiny crystaline snowflakes, drifting in the window.

She looked back at her cousin. "Jared, are you all right?"

"Yes," he said quickly. "I was worried about you."

"Why?"

"I tapped to make sure that you had come up and were okay. But you didn't answer."

She looked quickly around at her door. It was closed. She stared at Jared. "I locked the door," she told him.

He shrugged, edging back toward it. "It was open."

"I swear, I locked it."

"Slide the bolts." It seemed as if he didn't want to be near the window.

Of course not. It was actually snowing, in Venice. Something that didn't happen all that often.

Jared had a decent chest. He was tall and slim, had good shoulders and a wiry, athletic appearance. Now, there were goose bumps all over his flesh.

"It's a good thing I came in," he told her, sounding firm now that he had gotten away from the window. "You might have had pneumonia by morning! Lock those shutters, and close the window! And get under some blankets."

Because his commands made sense, she obeyed them, then stared back at him.

"Jared, I'm sure I locked the hallway door."

"Maybe you thought you locked it but didn't."

She nodded and shivered.

"Get in bed, Jordan, I've been really worried about you. Please don't come down with an awful flu or cold."

She smiled. "Jared," she told him, coming his way and setting her hands on his ice cold shoulders, "I'm fine. I am going to bed. I'm going to snuggle under the covers and sleep late." She gave him a kiss on the cheek. "I had a good time tonight."

He looked unhappy. "I'm glad."

She stepped back, frowning. "Why don't you look like you're glad?"

"Because . . . I shouldn't have let you come here. I shouldn't have brought you to the contessa's party . . . I shouldn't have . . ."

"I'm all right."

She wasn't all right. She was dreaming about her dead fiancé and wolves that stood in the shadows in streets.

No matter what happened, or what she imagined, she wasn't going to tell Jared about it.

"I'm fine, and I'm having a great time," she told him. She waved a hand in the air. "I m angry about the contessa's sense of entertainment, but when I see her again, I swear I'll be charming and cause no more trouble."

He shook his head, wetting his lips. "I'm sorry."

"Jared, quit, it's all right. Go back to bed."

"You don't understand. I'm really sorry."

"Jared, you're my cousin, my best friend, blood relation, all that. I love you. Now get out of my room and go to bed."

He studied her, nodded, and turned to leave. At the door, he hesitated, looking back. "Get over here and bolt the door."

"Yessir."

When he was gone, she carefully locked the door, making sure he heard the sound.

"Go back to your wife!" she said.

"Hey!" he whispered against the door. "Watch it, will you? Do you know what that sounded like?"

Jordan laughed. "Yes, and you must look great out there, too. Get to your room!"

"Goodnight."

When he was gone, Jordan found that she was wide awake. She flicked on the television, wondering if she could get anything this late at night. There was an Italian game show on. She couldn't understand the language of the enthusiastic contestants, but the game had to do with answering questions and losing pieces of clothing and then getting into a whipped cream fight.

She left the television on and crawled into bed.

The lamp was still on, dispelling the shadows.

She decided to sleep, for what remained of the night, with the light on.

Cindy Riley woke suddenly. She didn't know why. For a moment, she stared into the darkness of the room.

Instinctively, she reached across the bed.

Jared wasn't with her. Yet the moment she realized this, she saw that he was in the room. He had opened the window to the night, and stood there, despite the chill, staring out at Venice.

"Jared?"

"I woke you, I'm sorry," he said.

"No, no, you didn't wake me," she protested. She got out of bed and walked around to where he stood, laying her cheek against his back as she slipped her arms around him. "You're freezing!" she told him. "What are you doing, standing here like this?"

He was silent a moment, then said, "It's snowing. It doesn't snow that often in Venice."

"It's white wet stuff," Cindy said. "You've seen it before."

"Not in Venice."

"Jared . . . you're freezing."

"I know," he said, almost as if he were confused by that fact.

"Come back to bed, I'll warm you up."

He turned with a sudden fervor that startled her. "Will you? I am cold, so very, very cold."

There was something about him . . .

They'd been married for years. Good years, because they were good together. She loved him, liked him, enjoyed his company, and very much enjoyed their sex life. They had been together for years. Still, tonight . . .

His arms seemed stronger. The tension in him seemed to leap through his flesh, no matter how cold he seemed. The simple touch of his hands upon her shoulders felt erotic.

They'd made love that evening. Coming up from the espresso they had shared downstairs, they'd been warm and familiar and had fallen easily into bed, kissing, petting, slipping naturally into the act of love.

This . . . suddenly seemed almost illicit. Erotic, exciting . . . and it was just the feel of his body beneath her fingers, and the way his hands felt on her shoulders . . . and the way he looked at her, something in his eyes . . .

The window remained open. Cold air was sweeping in. He leaned down and kissed her with hard, wet, opened mouth, passion that belied the ice of his flesh. She felt his teeth graze hers, the length of his tongue seemed to sweep to her gullet, and it was like shooting a lightning rod straight down to every erotic zone in her body. A second later he was lifting her. When she hit the bed, her nightgown was already halfway ripped from her body.

Small loss . . .

His lips, his tongue were everywhere. Along her throat, her collarbone. Electric. She started shaking, not from the cold but from the eagerness aroused within her.

"My God, what were we drinking tonight?" she murmured.

He didn't reply. He was between her thighs. She went into spasms of ecstasy, trying to throw off everything around her, she was so on fire. She felt the graze of his teeth. He was growing too forceful . . . almost painful . . . in his ardor. She wanted to whisper a protest. She couldn't; her voice wouldn't come, and she was shaking violently as orgasms pounded through her system. He rose above her, and she could wrap her limbs around him quickly enough. Dimly, she wondered if the whole of the bed was shaking, if the people in the room beneath wouldn't waken, and think that the roof above them was about to fall in . . .

Later, she didn't know how much later—if the passion they shared had raged through the night or lasted no more than a few volatile minutes—she felt the cold again. By then, Jared was crashed to her side, still panting.

"The window," she murmured.

"Um."

"The window. It's freezing."

He still didn't move. She leaped up, stark naked, and rushed over to the window, drawing in the shutters first and securing them, then closing the heavy glass window. Shivering and bare, she wrapped her arms around herself, then decided to make a pit stop before flying back into the warmth of the bed. She closed herself into the bathroom—never being one to assume that such necessary things needed to be shared in marriage—and when she was done she washed her hands and doused her face with water. Looking into the mirror above the sink, she was startled to see thin scratches on her neck, and the slightest trickle of blood from one of her breasts. There was a streak of the stuff on one of her thighs as well.

She washed up quickly. The little cuts were nothing at all.

Turning off the light, she scampered across the room and flew back into the bed, wrapping the covers around her. She slipped her arms around her husband again. For a moment, he didn't move. He was lying on his back, staring up at the ceiling, or with his eyes closed, she wasn't even sure, it was so dark to her since she'd been in the bright light of the bathroom.

"Jared?"

At last he moved again, his fingers easing through her hair.

"Um."

"That was . . . wow."

"Well, you know, I try."

He sounded as if he were making an effort to speak lightly.

"Definitely different; I'm not sure I want to try it every night."

"Why not?"

"You bit me."

"Bit you?"

"Well, you know . . ."

"Love nibbles."

She didn't want to mention the fact that love nibbles didn't usually draw blood. After all, it had been . . .

Spectacular.

"Jared?"

"Hm?"

"I love you."

It seemed he was a long time answering. But then he turned, drawing her very close to him, holding her tenderly.

He was shaking.

"Jared, what's the matter?"

"Nothing . . . I'm just cold. Whoa, so cold!"

"Well, you silly man, you were standing in front of an open window watching *snow.*"

His lips brushed her forehead with a kiss. So different. Now, a touch as tender as a breath of sweet, warm air.

He was still shaking.

"I'm getting another blanket."

She got out of bed, stumbled over something in the dark, banged her toe against the bedstead, and swore.

"Jared . . . a light would be nice."

"Cindy, just come back to bed," he told her.

"I'm trying to get *you* a blanket," she informed him.

"Just come back to bed." He let out an impatient sigh. A second later, he was up, drawing her into his arms. "You're all the warmth I need."

She smiled, wondering if he could see at all in the darkness how he had touched her.

But when they were back in bed, huddled together as close as two peas in a pod, he was still shaking. She said no more, though; she just tried very hard to give him all her warmth.

She wished Jordan could see just how sweet he could be at times. He really was a beautiful man.

And to think . . .

There had been times lately when she had thought that she was becoming a monster herself.

A green-eyed monster.
She'd harbored such doubts!
But tonight . . . she was simply ashamed of herself.
He loved her. Completely, she thought.
Cindy slept with a smile curving her lips throughout the night.
Little cuts . . . a few drops of blood.
They meant nothing.
Nothing at all.

CHAPTER 6

Cindy and Jared were not at the breakfast table in the morning.

Jordan thought wryly of the way they had been the night before. Good for them.

Jared must have left her room and jumped his wife for the second time that evening. So much for romance fading with time and marriage!

At the rooftop restaurant, Jordan ordered coffee and a croissant, remembering that she was to head off to see Tiff's rented palazzo soon. She studied the advanced reading copy she had of the vampire book and jotted down notes on a few of the comments she wanted to make in her review. When she'd finished a second cup of coffee, it was still early. She headed back to her room, calculating the time in the States.

One in the morning.

Due to the fact that her work was heavily syndicated,

she got her assignments through an agent, rather than an editor. And Liz Schultz, her agent, was a night owl and a close friend. She had been the one to see a book review Jordan had written for a magazine and taken her into syndication. Liz had been new at her job; they had each taken a chance on the other. Their struggles, frustrations, rejections and triumphs had created a solid bond between them.

Liz wouldn't mind a call at home at this hour.

Jordan dialed the number through her phone card and was surprised when Liz answered almost immediately, sounding as if she were no more than a room away.

"Hey, Liz. It's Jordan."

"Jordan! Hey kid, it's great to hear from you. Wait, never mind. You're going to tell me that you're having too much fun, that you don't want to do any work."

Jordan laughed. "No, I wasn't going to say that at all. I was going to tell you that the director's vampire book is great. I'm going to fax the review to you soon, I've got all my notes. I'm just going to type 'em up this morning, and then the review will be there."

"Gory stuff, huh? But tell me, how is Venice?"

"Great. I'm having a wonderful time. I've always loved the city. This is different, though. You should see some of these costumes up close and personal. They're amazing."

"And the parties? Any good men?"

Jordan hesitated, thinking about the contessa's ball.

"Oh, Jordan, I'm sorry, maybe it's still too soon—"

"No, no, Liz, nothing like that. No, I was just thinking that having the vampire book with me was kind of strange—"

Liz let out a gasp. "I should never have given you that book!"

"Liz, no, wait, just listen. Do you remember me telling you that Jared was mainly concerned about one ball—"

"The one given by the princess or the duchess or whatever?"

"Contessa. Contessa della Trieste."

"I remember you telling me about it, yes. To Jared, it was like being invited to the White House or something. Was it spectacular?"

"No, it was horrible. And bizarre. I was in an upstairs ballroom, dancing, having a fine old time, then this storyteller started a tale about a horrible man who killed his wives. He grabbed people and they started falling . . . then all these other people in the room grabbed one another and where one woman fell, I saw this huge pool of blood."

"Oh, my God, Jordan!"

"Anyway, a wolf got me out of the ballroom—"

"A wolf?"

"A man in a wolf's costume. He put me in a boat and disappeared."

"Oh, my God! Did you get the police, what happened? I didn't read anything about it in the papers, and you know how many international newspapers I take—"

"As it happened, it was the contessa's idea of fun. And by the way, I did make the local papers."

"What?"

"I went to the police, the police went to the palazzo, they got the contessa, and Jared and Cindy, and they all explained to me that the entire thing was a show. Naturally, it was written up in the papers the next day

that an American woman had gone a little crazy over
the evening's entertainment."

"Entertainment?"

"I thought it was awful, but—"

"But she's a contessa, so whatever, is that the
thinking?"

"I guess. But the next morning, I read the vampire
book, and it was even more fascinating."

On the other end of the line, Liz hesitated. "I don't
know, Jordan. Maybe I was wrong, sending you that
particular book. Maybe you should come right home.
That book must have just made it all worse."

"No, Liz, honestly, I was glad to have the book. And
you'll like my review."

"I'm sure the author will be glad. Strange material
. . . but popular, it seems."

"Oh?"

"I've just gotten in another one, to be published
next October."

"On vampires?"

Liz hesitated. "Vampires, cults, Satanism, copycats,
rumors . . . there's a really interesting chapter on
defense against vampires. The author is a cop."

Jordan's fingers tightened on the wire as she felt a
spasm of pain. "A cop?"

"A fellow in New Orleans who has worked some
really bizarre cases. He doesn't say that vampires exist,
but he suggests ways of dealing with people who *think*
they're vampires. His book goes back into the ancient
legends and all as well—interesting reading."

"Send it to me."

"Jordan, all this reading may not be good for you
under the circumstances—"

"I am *not* a fragile person about to go over the edge.

If this book is by a police officer, I very much do want to read it. Send it by FedEx. The earliest delivery possible."

"You don't think that the contessa's entertainment . . ."

"Was real?" Jordan hesitated, remembering dancing with Ragnor—and his comments about the contessa.

Yes, he did think that the woman was a criminal. Dangerous . . .

"Liz, I'm keeping my nose clean, behaving rationally, I'm just a civilian visitor to a beautiful city, and especially because of Jared, I'm being as cool, collected and courteous as I can be. But I want that book."

"You want to get your ass on a plane. If that woman is dangerous—"

"Liz, I'm staying in one of the most beautiful hotels in the world, with my cousin and his wife just next door. I'm fine. And the police think I'm a little crazy, so they're keeping an eye on me. Send me the damned book. Please."

"All right. All right. But I'd better hear from you frequently."

"It's a promise."

They said their good-byes, and Jordan hung up. She glanced at her watch.

It was late enough for her to go down to the concierge and get instructions on how to walk to the palazzo that Tiff Henley had rented.

Sal D'Onofrio loved his work, and he loved Venice.

The mornings now tended to be quiet. Party-goers at Carnevale were usually late sleepers. But it was also a good time for work in Venice because there were so very many people here. And every human being with an ounce of romance in his or her soul was compelled to take a gondola ride.

He had already taken a couple of early-bird British women for a two-hour ride among many of the canals. They wanted to see the buildings of Venice, to go off the beaten track. He had taken them far, singing away.

They'd loved his singing.

They'd tipped him generously for his tunes.

But he didn't sing for money. He sang because it was fun. One of the British women had joked that a good singing voice must be a requirement for all gondoliers. He had told them that no—some gondoliers couldn't sing worth a single lira—they had just gotten lucky. He had told them, too, that not all gondoliers were exceptionally good looking—they had gotten lucky in that aspect as well. And few had his gift for languages. He'd never had much schooling, only what had been required; he had always known that, like his father before him, he would be a gondolier. He had a natural ear for languages and was fluent in French, Spanish, English, and Italian. He could converse somewhat in German and knew a smattering of Russian. He *was* good looking, and even the other gondoliers admitted grudgingly that he had the best singing voice. Italian, however, was a language made for singing. Those who came for rides usually wanted to hear Italian songs sung—after all, they were drifting through the beauty of Venice.

His British ladies were gone, but the morning had already been well worthwhile. He sang as he drifted along alone, thinking of heading back to the dock and waiting, but singing in hopes of luring some straying tourists.

They all loved, "O sole mio!"

Yet even as he sang, his pleasant tenor booming across the narrow canal he navigated, he noted something bobbing in the water ahead. He narrowed his eyes, still singing, but more absently, and quietly.

He used his pole expertly to slow his vessel.

His singing stopped abruptly mid-note as he narrowed his eyes and stared into the water.

No . . .

He hunched down and reached into the water, grabbing for the bobbing, ball-shaped object. His fingers wound into something.

Hair.

Even as the thought reached him, he saw the object, full front, just inches before his face.

He let out a hoarse cry of horror, dropping it as if it burned him.

The blood drained from his face. He felt the eggs he'd had for breakfast scrambling and scorching in his stomach.

He retched and plopped down into his boat, first using canal water to rinse his face, then remembering what he'd just found in the water, and retching again.

He breathed deeply and straightened his shoulders.

The . . . thing . . . was now bobbing in the water again, just a few feet away. He watched it, still breathing deeply.

After a moment, he knew what he had to do.

It was a pleasant, uneventful walk to Tiff Henley's palazzo.

Jordan crossed several bridges, but the directions she had been given were excellent, and she had no trouble finding the palazzo, a well-kept structure near the Accademia.

The entry was up a short flight of stairs, and Tiff herself answered when Jordan used the massive ring in a brass lion's mouth to knock.

"You made it!" Tiff said, pleased. She was dressed in faux leopard pants and a cashmere sweater with a fur-trimmed neckline that wasn't at all synthetic, Jordan was certain. Despite the weather, Tiff was wearing flashy sandals that clicked on the marble of her palazzo's entry.

"You'll see," Tiff said, leading her in, "This is nothing so fine as the contessa's ancestral home or whatever, but it's really quite adorable."

Jordan looked around with interest as Tiff took her coat. The foyer was small and cozy; the steps leading upward were narrow and winding, but the banister was really beautiful, marble with a blue tinge, and the steps themselves were covered in a plush, navy blue carpeting that made them seem warm and welcoming.

"This place was built during the Renaissance and it's still in the same family. The owner is a hoot. He said that they were the nobility of the lira! No titles in the family, but they made a mint importing and exporting."

"It's great—I like it much better than the contessa's," Jordan assured her.

"It's—cozier. But then," Tiff said with humor, "you'd like it better than the contessa's place if I'd rented a barn. Is there such a thing as a barn in Venice?" Tiff didn't wait for an answer. "Frankly, I'd stay in a barn just to be here; thankfully, I don't have to. Come on up, come on up! I ordered in Bellinis or whatever you call them from Harry's Bar—you have been there, right?"

"Yes."

Jordan loved the fabled Venetian establishment, once beloved of Hemingway. The prices were high, but the food was excellent. "Jared entertains at Harry's a great deal," she said.

"Well, of course, he would, wouldn't he?" Tiff said. "Actually, he could have told you how to get here— I rented this through your cousin and made all the arrangements for my stay through him. He's really quite good."

"Thanks. I rather like him myself."

"His wife is a sweetie, too. I should have invited them as well."

"Don't feel bad. They're sleeping in."

"I wanted to get to know you better anyway. Come up, come up, we're all set up on the patio on the second level."

Jordan followed Tiff up the stairs.

The landing on the second floor was large, with hallways going off to the left and right while directly in front there was a large expanse of marble flooring that led to columns, and beyond them, a plate glass window with a double doorway leading to a terrace that directly overlooked a charming canal.

"There are heat lamps out here; it will be warm enough," Tiff assured her, leading the way.

Jordan was barely seated with a famed Venetian Bellini in hand when Tiff leaned on the table across from her. "Okay, so I don't mean to be rude or crude or anything, but just what exactly is the sad history

behind your being so sensitive to things of a frightening nature."

"I'm not sensitive—"

"Your fiancé was killed."

Jordan sighed. "Tiff, I'm completely sane."

"Of course you are!" Tiff sounded almost angry, as
if it would be ridiculous for anyone to think anything
else. "It's just that I'm so, so sorry! How terrible. He
was a cop, right, killed in the line of duty? Hunting
down some terrible murderers—"

"Evidently, you have the story."

"Well, I have the story through one of the girls at
the art shop. And she, I believe, got what she knows
through Cindy. Not a long line of gossip, but you
do know how things change."

"You have it basically right."

"And you're still mourning this poor fellow? They
probably shouldn't have brought you here. I'm sure
they thought Venice! Carnevale! Such fun, that will
take her mind off things. And, of course, there are
masks worn everywhere and an abundance of handsome young men, only a few of whom don't speak
English. Hm. Maybe the not speaking English would
make a man more appealing." Tiff laughed softly.
"More Bellini?"

"I'm fine, thanks. This is a bit early for me, actually."

"Oh, these are just sissy drinks. And we're not driving anywhere! Oh, well, bottoms up, even if I'm drinking on my own."

Tiff finished her drink and poured another. "So—
are you still in mourning, and perhaps, just perhaps,
a bit oversensitive?"

"I loved him a great deal." She paused, eager to

change the subject. "You've been widowed, I've heard—"

"Several times," Tiff said. "As I'm sure you've heard."

"Yes. As to Steven . . . I miss him, still. I really loved him. But he's gone, and I know it. And I like going to parties; I enjoy meeting people—"

"And dancing."

"And dancing."

"I saw you last night, with Ragnor. You were beautiful together. I was jealous as all hell. Of course, he is a little young for me, but what the hell? I've always married old men, a younger fellow would be such a novelty!"

Jordan lifted her hands. "Go for it then!"

"Oh, but he's not interested in me. I watched him last night. He was watching *you* all night."

"I didn't even see him when I first arrived."

"But he was there. Watching you."

Jordan wasn't sure whether Tiff's observation disturbed her . . .

Or excited her.

She shrugged. "Tiff, you're most welcome to pursue him with all vigor. He was quite rude to me."

"Rude?" Tiff said, puzzled.

"Rude. He told me that I should go home, that . . . I don't know. That I caused trouble, or stirred trouble . . . that I could be putting myself in danger."

"Danger!" Tiff sounded delighted. "How . . . beguiling!"

"I'm not interested in Ragnor," Jordan said. She hesitated. She was lying. She *was* interested. Because he angered her.

That much was true . . .

But last night . . .

She felt an uneasy surge of warmth again. Last night, as they'd watched the acrobatic dancers, she'd felt . . . a stirring. That term was an understatement. She'd felt as hot as blue Sterno flame, dying to touch and be touched, as she hadn't felt since . . .

"Tiff, you must know what it's like when you lose someone: you learn to live with it and go on, but you never really get over the sudden loss—"

"I never had a sudden loss," Tiff said, helping herself to smoked fish. "In fact, I'm afraid, my last loss took far longer than I planned. But that, of course, makes me quite proud. I did marry an old fellow for his money—don't pass that honesty around to the rest of his heirs!—but the doctors had only given him six months to live. Thanks to me, he was a happy old cuss for almost a year and a half."

"That is—quite commendable," Jordan said, forced to smile.

"Yeah, I thought so," Tiff said proudly. "But now . . . let's get back to Ragnor. You know what I think?"

Jordan lifted her shoulders and arched her brows, waiting. She knew that Tiff needed no encouragement to go on.

"I think he's incognito here, that he's in some kind of hiding," Tiff said.

"In hiding? He walks around in the open."

"But no one really knows anything about him. He only showed up in Venice a while ago, although apparently, he's got lots of business dealings with some of the American businessmen who've been putting money into "restore Venice" funds and the like. He is popular with all the right people—except for the contessa, of course. I think he may be underworld."

"I don't think he's even Italian," Jordan said.

"No, no . . . but there are crime families all over Europe. Maybe he got into something horrible as a youth, maybe he is a criminal—"

"Maybe we should both stay away from him," Jordan said.

"Good Lord, no! That makes him all the more fascinating. Along with the fact that he seems *really* and *totally* repelled by the contessa!"

"That may be his one really admirable aspect," Jordan said dryly.

Tiff shrugged. "Well, no, I have to admit that I do love the nobility thing. I'm dying to get to know her better as well. Don't worry—I'll never invite you at the same time. Actually, I wish she'd invite me back to her palazzo."

Jordan decided not to mention the fact that the contessa had insisted she must come by again. "To use an American expression, Tiff, I'm afraid that I consider the contessa to be an absolute . . . slime bucket!"

Tiff laughed, pleased as punch again.

"Well, you tend to be so honest—I thought that I'd be honest, too," Jordan said.

Tiff smiled and went on. "Back to Ragnor—if I'm able to talk to him, and invite him over, may I use you as bait?"

The term Tiff used disturbed Jordan. "Bait?"

"Well, if I'm able to say I'm having a dinner—or a lunch, breakfast, or even drinks—and that *you're* coming, I can at least get him here, to my lair, you know. There's just something about him that's so . . . beguiling. If I get the chance, I'm just going to ply him with oysters and liquor. Did you know, oysters do have an effect?''

Jordan laughed out loud, setting down her glass. "Tiff—you're horrible!''

"Yes, I suppose so, but honest, at least, as you've said. May I use your name in my pursuit?''

"Sure.''

"Great! Thank you. I mean, I'll be careful—I won't plan anything too close to Anna Maria's ball or anything like that. Hey, I promised you a ghost tour. Want to hear my favorite story?''

"I'd love to.''

"Once, I think it was during the sixteen hundreds, the youngest daughter of the house, a beauty, fell in love with the wrong fellow. Her uncle had been elected doge at the time, and this fellow was the son of a rival politician.''

"Sounds like Romeo and Juliet.''

"You haven't heard the ending. The two fall in love, and there's a rumor that the family just won't have it. Anyway, such a young man can't just disappear, so you know what happens?''

"What?''

"He supposedly falls off the balcony and breaks his neck.''

"How terrible. So now he haunts the house?''

"Of course. Unfortunately,'' Tiff said with a sigh, "I've never seen him.''

"Too bad.''

"Now, of course, the daughter is certain her family caused the accident. So she decides to kill herself as well and jumps off the same balcony.''

"I guess that's why you never get to see him haunting

your bedroom. The two of them are haunting the place as a pair."

Tiff shook her head. "Nope! The daughter jumps off the balcony—but hits the canal. She means to drown, of course, but she's rescued by a young gondolier. She marries the fellow, and they move to Rome, and live happily ever after. Isn't that a happy ending?"

"Sure—except for the original young man the daughter was in love with."

"Oh, well, there can't be a happy ending for everyone!" Tiff said. "There's more; come on, we'll walk around the place and I'll give you more history."

The palazzo was beautiful, with the master bedchamber being exceptional. The original owner meant to make money renting the place. A large room had been converted into a bath with a marble Jacuzzi tub large enough to accommodate several people, a shower with multi-jet sprays, plush rugs, and massive double sinks. The bedroom itself had a sitting area, a breakfast table by a window, and a huge bed covered in rich maroon silk.

"Seductive, eh?" Tiff said, her smile gleeful. "Now . . . if I can only get the young blood in here that I want to seduce . . ."

"Well, then, I hope you get it," Jordan said and glanced at her watch. "Thanks for the breakfast, Tiff, and the tour. The place is really wonderful. It should definitely do."

"Thanks. I hope so. I mean, I'm doing all the right things. Of course, I have help here, but only every other morning. I'm actually quite a fine cook, and I've always been detailed, organized, and neat. Anal, even!" she admitted with a smile.

She went downstairs with Jordan, showing her out.

On the streets again, Jordan was surprised to realize that she laughed each time she thought about Tiff's brash honesty. Tiff was indeed something.

She'd enjoyed the morning, and walking back, she felt again just how much she loved Venice.

The city was uniquely charming.

And by day, there were no shadows.

Ragnor sat at an outside table in St. Mark's Square, watching.

The day was cool, and last night's snow had vanished as if it had never been. The sun was out, the bandstand was quiet for the moment, and he had a good view of the people coming and going from the Square.

As the day was bright, he wasn't the only person wearing dark glasses. He'd always been fond of shades anyway, ever since he'd gotten his first pair. They were great when you wished to see, but didn't want your thoughts seen in return.

He'd never been particularly fond of costumes and had no intention of wearing one by day. He sat in his long, black leather cape with a black turtleneck beneath it. Black boots kept his feet warm.

He was very fond of black.

It was the color of the night.

And the color of his coffee. It was good. He liked this particular café because they did brew large, strong cups of what they called American coffee, though he knew few Americans who drank their coffee quite so strong. Over the years, however, he'd acquired a taste for heavy, rich roasts, and this place brewed them well.

It was also an excellent vantage point. He could see from the Basilica to the newest part of the Square, the length erected by order of Napoleon Bonaparte, and gazing in the opposite direction, he could see those coming and going from St. Mark's and the Campanile, and even coming in from the pillars on the canal.

There were jugglers performing, and dotting the area, everywhere, were makeup artists, bartering for the privilege of securing clientele. Children loved the work; butterflies drawn on cheeks in vivid color, cat faces, kiss faces, diamonds, glitter, and sparkles. Adults weighed the value of makeup versus a mask.

The pigeons were everywhere. Vendors sold little bags of corn to be thrown to the birds, heedless of the fact that they tended to inhabit the Square for whatever tidbits of food could be found.

It was an interesting place for people-watching. As always, during Carnevale, those who were especially stunning, odd, or unusual paraded around in their costumes, posing by the pillars, faces bland as they met camera after camera. There were those who came only to watch, who oohed and aahed over a performer, then over a costume, then over a sparkling display in a shop window.

He shifted, sipped his coffee, and leaned back, certain, if he waited long enough, he would be able to accost Nari. She would pretend, of course, that she seldom wandered into the streets. Especially by day. He knew her better.

An American woman started screeching near him; he smiled, watching her. She and her husband had been attracting pigeons for their two young sons.

The pigeons had done what pigeons often do—on her arm.

Her husband did his best, running around, grabbing napkins.

Then he saw her.

Nari was across the road in a long dress, sweeping cape, and theatrical mask. He cast a pile of lire on the table and took off in pursuit.

She reached the walkway to the streets beyond the Square. He followed, making his way through the crowd. He walked down a length of shops, around the corner of a restaurant, closing in on her.

Back on a narrow canal, he nearly reached her. Then, suddenly, someone ran straight into him. Searching the crowd over the woman's head, he caught her shoulders, apologizing swiftly.

"Ragnor! Hello, ciao! It's me, Tiff Henley, fancy running into you."

He stared down into the woman's face, trying to remember her. Yes, Tiffany Henley, the very rich American, well-kept, attractive, widow of a man three times her age, a powder puff blond but not at all stupid. She'd used her assets and gotten where she'd wanted to go.

"Yes, Tiff, hello, how are you?"

He looked beyond her, his temper rising.

"I'm so pleased to run into you."

"I'm sorry to have collided, and I am awfully sorry, I've got to run—"

"Of course. But I would love to have you over for drinks tomorrow, before Anna Maria's ball—you are going, of course."

He barely heard her—he was still searching through the crowd ahead of him. Her hands were on his chest, stopping him from moving forward. He was tempted to shove her aside. There were crowds all around them. Seething at the interruption, he forced himself to hold his temper, and his anxiety, in check.

"Tiff—"

"The American girl will be there."

Distracted, he looked down at Tiff. "The American girl?" He knew exactly whom she meant, and also that she had meant to distract him.

"Jordan Riley. And her family . . . a few others."

Watching Tiff, he was certain that she was making up her guest list as she spoke.

"Will you come? Truly, I'd love to have you." She was still determinedly touching him, stopping him from moving on. "I mean, of course, you're welcome to come by any time at all. The palazzo is really quite charming—"

"I know."

"You've been there?"

"Years ago."

"Please, do come."

"Yes, of course, I'll try, but if you'll excuse me . . ."

He kept staring over her head. He meant to find Nari.

He was going to have to find her.

Dusk was closing in again.

CHAPTER 7

Though Jordan had intended to head straight back to the hotel, she found herself wandering instead, and looking into shop windows. She found a place with beautiful leather goods and bought a jacket that just happened to fit her perfectly.

On a roll, she found a pair of knee-high low-heeled boots in five and a half—an amazing find. Both shopkeepers were happy to have her purchases sent on to the Danieli, and so she wandered into a coffee shop for an espresso. It was while she was standing at the counter, idly noting the wood-framed mirror above the bar, that she saw the man in the dottore costume and mask—staring at her. She thought she saw the eyes within the mask—of course, she didn't, couldn't, he was too far away—but she knew that he was staring into the espresso bar, and that he was looking specifically at her.

She had the strangest sensation that this was the man she had followed last night, thinking he was Jared.

She sipped the last of her espresso, reminding herself that the dottore costume was one of the most popular in Venice. There was no reason whatever to assume that she was seeing the same man.

Nevertheless, she quickly left the bar, anxious to reach the street, and confront the man.

When she emerged, he was gone. She looked to her left. A small bridge crossed a narrow canal about a half block down. She saw the man in the black cape passing a couple in Victorian dress. She hurried that way.

Not at all sure what kept her footsteps so dogged, she followed the next passage along the canal.

Once again, ahead of her, she saw him turn the corner.

She passed by shops selling Versace, Dior, and Ralph Lauren, stores with handsome facades and fine goods within. The streets were crowded again; the party-goers of the night before had done their sleeping and were up and about, again some costumed, some not. She felt bold, not crazy, and not afraid; there were still a few hours of daylight left.

No matter how fast she walked, though, he seemed to remain ahead of her, always in front of several groups of people. She quickened her pace again and turned a corner. She passed under an archway between two buildings.

A balcony with gargoyles and stucco lions suddenly seemed familiar; she realized that she had walked this way the night before.

She paused, surveying her surroundings. As she did so, she looked ahead.

At the end of the pathway, off the busy and beaten track, there was another bridge. The black-cloaked figure stood upon it, looking back at her.

"Hey!" she called out. "Who are you!"

Apparently he didn't hear her. Once again, the man turned and started walking.

Onc more bridge, she decided. Then she was giving up this silly chase.

On the next bridge, she paused. She couldn't see the man anymore. Ahead, right after the bridge, was a piazza. At the far end of it was a beautiful old church. The walls were peeling; stained glass windows were broken and covered with boards. The structure, however, was very handsome, with marble steps; stone angels guarded the double doors of the entry, and the wooden doors themselves were carved, and apparently, at one time, gilded.

Jordan forgot the cloaked figure for a moment and approached the old church. Just as she crossed the bridge, she heard someone call to her.

"Signorina!"

She turned. A gondola was about to slip beneath the bridge. She recognized the handsome young gondolier she had seen two days earlier.

He'd said that his name was . . . Sal D'Onofrio, she remembered—and that she should come to him, of course, when she was ready for a gondola ride. He had sung so cheerfully the last time she had seen him near the Danieli. Now, he had no customers in his craft, and he looked grave and tired.

"Hello," she said, looking briefly back to the church, and surveying the corners of the piazza. The cloaked figure was gone. Following him had been foolish anyway. He probably hadn't even been looking at her. It was impossible to see a man's eyes through a mask like that at a distance.

The gondolier was shaking his head. "Beautiful lady, you should not be wandering here. This is not the area where there are people, not much to see."

"Haven't you heard? All tourists want to see what other tourists *don't* see!" she told him.

He didn't laugh; he didn't even smile.

He shook his head, maneuvering his pole to bring his gondola next to the low wall fronting the piazza. "Venice is wonderful. But now, you should be back with the crowds, by San Marco. You should feed the pigeons—all visitors must feed the pigeons."

"I'm not even sure where I am right now."

'I'll take you back."

"You know, I do intend to take a gondola ride, and I'm sure you're the best. But I was thinking more of a time near sunset—"

"No charge, signorina. I will bring you back to the Danieli."

"I'm sure I can find my way."

"Please. Allow me."

"There's no dock."

"You can jump the wall."

"Is that legal?"

"No. But please, this is not . . . this is not where people roam."

"I had thought to explore that church—"

"No," he said, shaking his head impatiently. "It is abandoned. Not a church anymore, you understand? Please, let me take you back."

Because he seemed so earnest, and so sincerely concerned for her, Jordan found herself relenting.

"Step on the wall," Sal encouraged her.

She did so. He had perfect coordination, and amazing agility, leaning to grasp her hand, then lifting her by the waist to set her into the gondola.

She teetered a little as the gondola listed from side to side, as the water lapped at the hull. He seemed relieved when she took her seat, and then he pushed off from the wall.

The gondola shot down the canal with startling speed as he wielded his pole.

They had entered a larger body of water when he turned to her. "Venice is a good place, a really good place. Little crime, but always, when you have so many people from so many places, people with money, jewelry . . . there will always be criminals who want what isn't theirs."

"Thank you for being concerned," she told him, studying him. She wondered suddenly if she was a total fool—if he could be among those criminals, planning to bring her down a deserted canal, lift her purse, bonk her on the head with his pole, and toss her into the water.

No. He was moving quickly, not singing, not pointing out the sights, bringing her bit by bit to more heavily traveled areas. Soon, she realized that they were back in the area behind St. Mark's Basilica. She knew these waters; they were lined with restaurants, hotels and shops.

"You're so serious today; is something wrong?" she asked him.

He hesitated, but smiled, shaking his head. "No. But you must be careful. There are so many people. All people are not good. There are thieves, maybe . . . worse."

"I am very careful."

"Be more so. Please. Stay with people you know."

He was so somber that she nodded, not at all tempted to tell him that she was independent and capable. Or that she had already been scared enough to make sure that she was doubly watchful in all that she did.

Like following a stranger in a cloak and mask? she mocked herself.

"I'll be more careful, Sal, really."

About to pass beneath a bridge, she noted that Ragnor was standing on the calle to her left side; she saw him immediately because he was taller than those around them, his light hair a beacon against the black leather of the cape he was wearing.

He wasn't alone, and he hadn't noticed her, or the gondola.

She smiled slightly. Tiff had found the object of her desire. The brash American woman had halted his travels; she was speaking to him earnestly, her hands on his chest.

"I'll be careful," she repeated, a strange sensation tingling at her nape. Ragnor had warned her about danger in Venice. Now Sal was doing the same, while Jared's belief was that she was losing her mind. *Maybe. She was seeing a dead man's face on a mannequin. Wolves in the shadows. She was hearing the whisper of wings in the night.*

She should just fly home. That would be the intelligent thing to do.

No . . .

She couldn't go home. *Something* was going on.

And though she had been afraid, she was also compelled, determined, and . . .

Beguiled?

That was the term Tiff had used earlier. As to her reason for staying, it seemed to fit perfectly. She would be careful, she told herself, as she had promised Sal. *And she knew for a certainty that bad things did happen. In a real world.*

"The Danieli," Sal said, sliding next to the side entry of the hotel. "Please, you will not be alone?"

A bellman waited to assist her from the gondola. As she stood to disembark, Jordan kissed Sal's cheek. "I promise, I'll stay close to friends. And thank you for being so sweet. You are the best gondolier."

He offered her a deep smile. "Grazie. Ciao, bella!"

"Ciao, bravo," she told him.

She thanked the bellman as well and entered into the lobby of the hotel. It was busy, filled with laughter, languages, costumes, and an air of camaraderie and warmth. She surveyed the lobby for a moment, smiling slowly.

People were so beautiful.

They were having so much fun.

She felt oddly protective of Venice. If something was happening here to mar the wonder of this city, it had to be stopped.

Sal D'Onofrio poled his gondola out of the narrow canal, heading around the vaporetto that waited at the dock in front of the Danieli. He passed the Square and the Doge's Palace, entering into the waters of the Grand Canal. He hadn't spoken of his discovery that morning to any of his friends, he had delivered his grisly find to Roberto Capo at the police station. And now . . .

He still did not feel like singing. He was going home.

Tomorrow, after a night's sleep, he would be himself again.

Gondolas were out in masses. He passed by one of the landings. Giuseppe Donati, a friend, waved at him; he had just picked up a young couple in full costume. He waved back. Giuseppe indicated a lone costumed figure on the dock, a man seeking a gondola.

Sal waved a thank-you to his friend. He had not really intended to pick up another costumer, but it might be a good thing to help shake off his unease. He slid to the bank, forcing himself to talk cheerfully to the man in English.

"Alone, signore? And you wish to ride?"

The masked man nodded gravely. He hopped into the gondola, needing no assistance. He spoke in a low voice; indicating the route he wanted to take. He spoke in English, with what accent, Sal couldn't tell. It didn't matter. He was glad—he'd drop this passenger near his own home, and then he'd be a little richer for the night he intended to remain home.

They moved along the busy canal, watching pedestrians, shopkeepers, children, dogs and dog-walkers.

They moved off the beaten path. Here and there, an old man shuffled along, headed for a bar or trattoria. A woman swathed in black hurried to a church service. A young housewife strolled with her baby in a carriage.

Another turn. They were far from the shops, into a mostly residential section of the city. Dusk was now falling. The lights that fell upon the canal were dim, coming from dwellings where fathers were returning from work, some to stay, some for a bite before returning to work to soak in the tourist dollars by night.

It was still Sal's city. Warm now in the glow of home and day-to-day living.

Ahead was a wide bridge, one that connected two islands of houses. They were not too far now from his own.

The gondola drifted beneath the bridge.

Sal barely heard the man in the dottore costume move.

He had just started to turn, not quite hearing but sensing the whispers . . .

He felt the hands on his shoulders, powerful in a vise that would soon break bone. The grip was agony, but even as he opened his mouth to scream, the noise was choked off in the sudden rampant flow of blood.

He wasn't even aware of the razor-honed piercing that seared into his neck, creating the bubble of blood in his throat . . .

Nari was in the center of the Square, masked, surrounded by revelers. She stood still, staring up at the sky, appreciating the dying of the day. Night . . . soon. She could hear the laughter around her, the talk, the languages. She could hear the music, playing at the bandstand. When she concentrated, she could hear more.

A pulse . . .

Thump, thump, sweet, delicious.

Breathing . . .

Life . . . essence . . .

Tonight. It might be tonight. She had a plan in place, and actually, missing out on her intent here and there wasn't so bad. It was rather like a game.

Cat and mouse. The chase creating an even sweeter scent of fear. And the taste of fear . . .

She started when she felt a grasp on her arm. She glanced up in horror.

Ragnor. He had found her. Here, in the open.

"It stops," he said.

She wanted to jerk away furiously. She knew that she could not.

"Really? What are you going to do with me to make it stop? *Kill* me?" she taunted.

"Put you away," he said quietly.

"That's your intent anyway, isn't it?" she said softly. She couldn't escape him. Why not enjoy the moment. She brushed her knuckles against his cheek.

"Ragnor . . ."

He took her hand, forcing her to drop it. She smiled slowly anyway. "Do you think that I ever forget?" she asked.

"Do you think that I ever forget?" he cross-queried harshly. "I'm telling you, Nari, that it stops. I'm warning you. Threatening you, if you like. You could have everything, you have a life here, a beautiful palazzo, a title, a position. You—"

"You forget yourself, don't you, Ragnor? I know the legends, that you think yourself so different, but in all honesty, are you so very above us all?"

"All? Many are living—"

"Henpecked. Locked into a world like a cage."

"Being rational and surviving. Nari, look around you—*you have everything!*"

She studied him for a moment. "No, I don't have everything. But I know what I am."

"There's so much more that you could be."

She rose on tiptoe to whisper in his ear. "I like what I am."

"Last time. Definitely a threat. I could—"

"You could what? Break me here and now? In front of all these people? They'd arrest you, throw you in jail. You could escape of course . . . but then, what about your face? You couldn't just wander around all these nice people, then, could you? Damn me and you damn yourself."

"We are already damned," he told her flatly.

"So you haven't!" she marveled. "The truth is what is, and you know it, though, you always thought *you* were different." He *was* different. She felt a spasm of hunger suddenly that was so violent she could barely contain it.

She wanted to touch him again. All these years . . . he was still Ragnor. Solid, never faltering. Beautiful. The rugged planes of his face, the wall of his chest. Old regrets died hard. Well, she had made her decisions and her choices. She had underestimated him. And now, looking into his eyes, she knew it was too late.

"There are laws—"

"*Their* laws? *Our* laws? *What* laws?" she taunted. "The world is in chaos, Ragnor—hadn't you noticed? And *we* will prevail. Foolish fellow! Don't you know—"

"I know that I can break you—and will."

"Will it be so very easy?" she whispered softly, moving against him.

"Like snapping my fingers."

She moved away. "It's that American girl."

"It's what you're doing."

"You're a liar. You've been watching that girl."

"If I have an interest in the American girl, Nari, you've created it."

Nari smiled. She had at least found his weakness.

"She doesn't like you, you know," she informed him. "She senses that you're not . . . well, you're just not right at all."

"Why was she among the . . . select guests at your party?"

Nari hesitated, then lied. "Can I help it if the foolish creature stumbled into the wrong place?" Was she being dishonest as well? Eventually, he would know the truth. The whole truth.

And that the girl was, indeed, select.

"What you're doing here, the horror you're creating, goes far beyond the American girl. And there are ways around it."

Nari shrugged. "Why? It's estimated that there are perhaps hundreds of serial killers all around the world today. The police continue to search for a majority of them."

"You will bring the fires of hell down upon us."

"On *you,* maybe. *We* are the fires of hell." She suddenly softened her voice, her words damp with a sweet whisper of breath. "Don't you ever . . . *crave* . . . old times? Remember what was, how it could be . . ." Again, she spread her fingers over the expanse of his chest.

Again, he removed her hand. She was startled by the fury of his rejection.

"What an ass you are. And as to the American . . . I, at least, am friendly with her family. As a matter of fact . . . I have plans with her this evening."

His grip tightened with such intensity that she was

afraid he would break a bone. She felt her cheeks paling, her power draining.

"If you so much as touch her—"

"And your interest is mere concern for the benefit of mankind?" Nari scoffed. "If *I* touch her?" Nari started to laugh. "Oh, Ragnor!"

Again, his grip tightened. She gasped with the pain, fighting, struggling to find her own sense of power. "If you think that I'm all that you have to deal with . . ."

"What? What the hell are you talking about?" he demanded.

"Ragnor, let go of me! You're hurting me," she cried out. Anyone in the crowd might have heard her. There were carabinieri in the Square. Still, he didn't let go of her; his eyes were a blue fire as he stared at her. She felt again the deep, bitter pain of loss. And a shooting agony of raw, furious, jealousy she'd thought could never touch her again . . .

"Tell me what's going on," he repeated. "What plans do you have? Where are you meeting her tonight? What is it you're talking about?"

"She'll be at Harry's!" Nari gasped out. She had to ease his grip; she couldn't afford to suffer any broken bones right now. "You'd have to kill me before I'd say more now. Yet if you kill me, you'll never know, you'll hunt forever, and your precious little midget of an American would be gone—"

"Don't try that, Nari. I told you that this all stops. It has nothing to do with one person—"

"Good." She relaxed into his hold. "Because if you hurt me now, I'll enjoy her myself! Every last . . . lick."

His grip had eased; he stared down at her, eyes still

the greatest threat he offered. "All right, Nari, tell me what you're talking about."

She swallowed hard. She forced herself from her fascination with simply being so close after so many years. *Once he'd been hers. Raw, lithe, supple, naked, moving. Raked with scars, torn with conflict, passionate and hungry, like lightning in the night . . .*

No. That time was gone. And she could give nothing away; he was destined to pay for being what he was. Bitterly, bitterly, she forced herself to remember only vengeance. Only life, as she knew it. The life she could have. Wild, free, abandoned, savage—a life with freedom to ease the torment inside her, fill the hunger . . .

She cursed him suddenly. She'd hit his weakness. He was worrying about the American girl. *Well, he'd best worry, because he didn't begin to understand the complexity of what was happening here.*

"All right, Ragnor. You'd best worry about *her.* Because guess what? *You're both going to die!*"

She saw the anger that tightened his features. *Now, here, in the Square—she had to escape him. Had to move, before he touched her again. She had been reckless; she had come so close to ruining everything. She had put him on guard . . .*

He would touch her again. And she couldn't allow it.

She found her strength. Stepping back, she turned into the crowd. She felt him reaching for her, felt the power exuding from him just a breath away. But there were so many people here. And she had her own strengths. Amid a jungle of capes, she disappeared into the coming night.

Her plans for the evening were ruined. And yet . . .

He couldn't follow her. He couldn't risk it. He had

threatened her, but she had warned him. And he did have his weaknesses, no matter how he denied it.

Now, he'd be afraid.

And always, he'd have to be on guard.

And while the cat was very, very busy, the mouse could play . . .

Upstairs in her room Jordan found a note from Cindy, slid under the door.

Hey, kid!
Where are you? Silly question, if you're reading this now, you're in this room! Missed you today; we're meeting at Harry's at 8:00—please be there, or call, or I'll be too worried to pig out on my favorite pasta!
Love,
Cindy

Smiling, Jordan set the note aside. Harry's was a short walk past the Doge's Palace and along the waterway. Crowded—very crowded at night. She liked Harry's and was in a mood for the crowd that would be there. The bar was always busy, and during Carnevale, she was certain that the wait would be very long, except that Jared would have made reservations, and he knew the people there well. She looked forward to a nice night with her cousin and his wife.

She glanced at her watch; she had plenty of time.

Walking into her bathroom, she filled the tub and added scented bath oil, making sure that the water was very hot.

Stripping down and slipping into a bathrobe, she called room service for a pot of hot tea.

She threw open the window as she waited, looking out to the bustling calle and canal. Venice was already coming alive for the night. Turning back into the room, she switched on her television and attempted to watch the news in Italian, trying to find out if there was anything going on in the city that might have upset Sal so much.

She saw a weather map and nothing more. A knock sounded on her door. She absently bade, "Come in!"

A cheerful waiter arrived with her tea. The tray was adorned with little cookies as well. She thanked the room service man, signed her bill, and made certain to lock her door when he left.

Cup of tea in hand, she went into the bathroom and slipped into the tub. She closed her eyes. The water was hot and wonderful. She thought about rising to look through the vampire book once again.

Why?

It would just get her going again. Tomorrow, with luck, Federal Express would find her and she'd have another book on the subject.

Eyes closed, steam misting around her, she relaxed. No costumes tonight. She was going to wear the wicked new heels she'd gotten in Charleston just before leaving, and the backless black cocktail dress. She was going to get a little buzzed, maybe. And like Cindy, pig out on pasta.

She was so relaxed that she didn't know what suddenly startled her.

She sat up in the tub, frowning, looking around, wondering what had so suddenly drawn her from her comfortable introspection.

Jordan listened.

Nothing . . .

She rose from the tub anyway, grabbing her robe. Leaving the bathroom, she walked into the bedroom and saw instantly that she had left the window open. The cool night air was drifting in, battling with the heater. Wind and whispers seemed to stir around her face and hair, chilling her.

She closed the window.

She was still cold.

Jordan gave herself a shake, walking around the room. She looked into the closet, then under the bed, and then felt like a fool. There was no one in the room. Yet she still felt the same sense of unease.

The bath was ruined.

She was definitely not getting back into it.

Nor did she feel comfortable in her room. She was suddenly eager to leave.

Too early to meet Jared and Cindy.

But never too early to take a walk over to Harry's and buy herself a drink.

She dressed quickly, barely touching up her makeup and brushing her hair with no more than a lick and a promise.

When the knocker sounded, Tiff was upstairs. Feeling pleased, she'd filled the Jacuzzi tub with scented crystals, and sank in. She hadn't been expecting anyone, and she considered staying in the tub. She was wonderfully relaxed. And the idea of getting up, toweling off, walking down the stairs and answering the door to *just anybody* was not pleasing.

The brass knocker sounded again.

It occurred to Tiff that it might just be *him*. Her latest obsession.

He'd been cordial enough in the street, even if he had seemed to be in a hurry.

Maybe, just maybe . . .

She jumped out of the tub and grabbed her robe. Since it was silk, it clung to her warm, damp flesh. Maybe that wasn't a bad thing. She still had a nice enough figure. Well, all right, it wasn't exactly hers . . . well, yes, it was. She'd paid for it; it was hers!

So thinking, she pulled the towel from her hair, shook it out, and went hurrying down the stairs.

Thank God for the plush carpet lining! Her damp feet would have gone sliding right off marble! She could have slid down the stairs, her obsession leading straight to her demise! Broken bones, broken neck, what a way to go!

"Hold your shorts on!" she called, rocketing to the door.

She should have looked out the little peephole, put in by the current owner, but by the time she reached the door, she was in far too much of a hurry.

She threw open the door . . . to a woman of medium height in costume, mask, and sweeping long cloak.

"Yes?" Tiff said, noting instantly that the clothing worn was expensive, that the mask was exquisite, lined with crystal, probably Swarovski.

"Tiff?"

She recognized the rich, cultured, slightly accented voice, even though her name had been the only word spoken.

"Contessa?" she said, too surprised to hide her incredulity.

"I was in the neighborhood. I heard you had taken this palazzo. It's so rude of me to come without warning, yet . . ."

"No, no!" Tiff said quickly, stepping aside. "I'm delighted to see you!"

"You were expecting someone."

"No . . . She laughed a little nervously. "I guess I was a little anxious. I wanted to reach the door before the knocking stopped. I'm so glad I reached the door before you went away."

The contessa smiled slightly.

"You must forgive my appearance," Tiff said. She shouldn't have gushed so much.

"But you are busy," the contessa said, indicating Tiff's robe and damp hair.

"I was pruning, ready to go out. Please, please, come in."

"Well, I won't stay long." The contessa stepped into the foyer, allowing her cowl to fall, and sliding off her mask.

"Here, let me take that for you," Tiff said, very carefully setting the mask on the carved oak stand by the door. "And your cape . . ."

The contessa surrendered her cape, and looked around the palazzo. "Quite nice. I've actually been here before . . . years ago. The work they've done is lovely."

"It's very comfortable. Far better than a hotel, though there are many lovely hotels here," Tiff said. She was trying not to babble. Here was the *contessa*, visiting her. This was almost as exciting as a visit from the *man* she had hoped to see. Of course, she was standing there in a robe, her hair damp, clinging to her face. She was hardly dressed for a contessa.

"If you give me just a minute, I can find something—"

The contessa waved her hand, her beautiful, ageless features curling into a smile. "No, no, do nothing! I'll be but a few minutes, and you can sink back into your tub. I would leave very unhappy if I ruined your bath!"

"Then I'll get some wine. We'll sit upstairs."

"Red wine, please. May I wander?"

"Yes, of course. The bar is upstairs—"

"Wonderful."

Still feeling awkward, stunned, and *complimented* beyond all measure, Tiff started up the stairs. The contessa followed her. But as Tiff went to the wine cabinet, the contessa did indeed wander. With two glasses of her very best wine poured, Tiff looked around and did not see the contessa. "Contessa?"

"In here!"

She had gone into the master bedroom. She turned as Tiff came into the room, smiling and accepted a glass of wine. "Magnifico!" she said. "They've done beautiful work. The room where the bath is now was a dowdy, closed-in place. Now . . . what a lovely . . . lair."

Tiff flushed, wondering if the contessa could be aware of her reasons for wanting such a sumptuous suite.

"I admit, I enjoy creature comforts."

"Something we share," the contessa said. She wandered to the long windows, which were open to the terrace beyond. "Quite wonderful. And this is my favorite time of day. When the colors of sunset fade away, day is gone, and night is with us! With all its shadows and secrets!

Standing there, she looked almost as if she were in rapture. Tiff walked over to the grand, silk-covered bed and sat, watching her.

"So much time is wasted sleeping," the contessa said. She walked over to where Tiff sat and sank down beside her, swallowing her wine. "Fruity, yet dry, rich and bold. A fine choice, thank you."

"May I get you some more?"

"No, no, just sit! Let me enjoy your company. I take my time when I savor a new taste," she said softly. "So! You fascinate me."

"*I* fascinate *you?*" Tiff said.

"Yes, I truly admire a woman such as you. It's a difficult world. Too many men, far too often, for too many years, have preyed upon women."

"Well, I'm not sure—"

"Ah! Think about it. The businessman with a young secretary who needs his approval to advance? The aging executive has an affair with the sweet, young thing while his trod-upon wife sits at home and can do little since her own life and livelihood depend on him. Movie stars ready to decay find young starlets for wives. While you, my smart and lovely and more mature woman, turned the tables. Here you are—a woman of substance! You needn't bow to anyone because you are your own master. And now, while you are still relatively young, you have the ways and means to do what you will, with whom you like!"

Tiff had to smile. "Well, there are those, including a few of my stepchildren, who have tended to think of me as a money-grubbing bitch. And I'm not so terribly young, I'm afraid."

She hadn't realized that she'd twisted, exposing the length of her legs, as she'd turned to the contessa on the bed so that they could converse. Now, she noticed the contessa looking at her exposed flesh. She felt the warmest flush envelop her. She started to close her robe, but the contessa's hand landed on her knee before she could do so.

"Young enough. Look how beautiful you are! You've kept yourself up, another point I admire very much."

The contessa's long fingers, covered with jewels, moved over Tiff's knee, slightly down her calf, slightly up her inner thigh.

Tiff didn't embarrass easily, but it seemed that her blood flooded her limbs, and she felt as hot as if it steamed. She should move, withdraw . . .

But now the contessa's eyes were on her, deep, languorous, sensual. Tiff found that she couldn't move; she could only stare into the contessa's eyes. The contessa smiled slowly as her fingers kept moving.

"Tell me, bella," she said, her voice a soft whisper that seemed to caress, "have you ever been with a woman?"

She should have said something witty, something in the way of denial for what was happening now, but all that came to Tiff's lips was one word, barely breathed out, "No."

The contessa shrugged, her supple fingers still just stroking. "Neither had I been for many years . . . many, many years. But when I discovered that men were deceitful . . . when they played about as they would . . . that it was possible to seduce beautiful young things myself. And I learned that women could be seductive, appealing . . . so appetizing."

Tiff managed to swallow. *No, she'd never been with a woman, but . . .*

"Poor Tiff! So many years with old men desperately

seeking their own pleasure! Oh, the things you must have done to bring them to the point of . . . possibility!''

The contessa seemed able to read her mind. Even as she spoke, Tiff felt the most ungodly surge of desire sweeping through her! God, yes! The things she'd done, the patience she had needed, the pleasure she had brought . . . while finding no satisfaction herself.

"I can show you pleasure," the contessa whispered.

Her lips seemed to be so much closer. Her words, her whispers, were like swathes of silk, sweeping over and around Tiff.

She wanted the contessa to do more. So much more. Bring those artful fingers higher and higher and higher, touch the intimate place that now seemed to be throbbing, crying out to be touched.

"Allow me . . ."

The contessa's hands were on her shoulder, a touch so delicate, and yet so forceful. Tiff fell back, the silk robe completely open, the belt lost somewhere, her legs splayed.

The contessa was still over her. Her fingers now stroked Tiff's throat and moved slowly down her torso.

"Such beautiful breasts . . ." The contessa's words were now no more than air, warm air that stirred and excited her until Tiff could barely stand it.

She'd never been with a woman . . . .

Why not?

This wasn't just any woman; this was the contessa . . .

And she couldn't stop now if she wanted. Those delicate, ring-laden fingers were on her breasts, tracing the tiny patterns of veins in them. Tiff's legs were spread. She felt liquid, unable to move.

"Beautiful, beautiful . . ."

"Lifted and enhanced," Tiff heard herself say.

The contessa's laughter was like the soft tinkle of bells. Tiff felt the wetness of her mouth. Tiny licks, like little drops of pure fire, darting as swiftly as the tongue of the snake, doing things as deliciously wicked . . .

The contessa's caress lowered against her. If she could have moved, Tiff would have seized the woman's head, and dragged it swiftly down between her thighs. She ached, throbbed, she could feel herself swelling . . .

Licks . . . traced her veins, touched her abdomen, trickled along her inner thigh, landed. Tiff nearly shot through the roof. Lord . . . what a climax! She was faint; she nearly blacked out. Dear God, but the codgers she had married had been . . . worthless. This was what the French called *le petit mort*. So good, it was like dying . . .

She'd never, ever, experienced anything like this, she hadn't believed it existed. She was drifting in the pleasure, her mind stunned, yet her thoughts racing, and the contessa didn't just leave it at that, she was moving lower, against her thighs, a slight stab of pain, the greatest pleasure, and again, the world fading in the ecstacy, the little death of the French . . .

Nari dined slowly, taking her time.

When she was sated, she sat back, surveying the shock white body of the woman on the bed.

Amused, she stood, still surveying the remains.

There was one woman who had died happy. There were so many excellent ways to enjoy the richness of a good meal. The veins at the throat were fine, but those in the thigh could be punctured in a way that let the blood flow smoothly.

She smoothed back Tiff's hair, fondly surveying the body that had provided such pleasure. She laughed aloud then, remembering Tiff's eagerness to greet her. "Poor Tiffany . . . you did rush down to your own demise, didn't you?"

She stretched, elated, as pleased as an alley cat that had just consumed an entire bowl of milk with no interruption, and without having to share a lick.

She walked to the window and looked out at the darkness that now shadowed the night. She felt completely invigorated, powerful, wonderful.

After such a delicious meal, Nari was surprised to feel a taste of bile rising in her throat. She clenched her teeth, hating him. She had come here because . . .

He'd left her . . . hungry, so hungry, but hungry in a way that she couldn't fill, no matter how sated she should have been, no matter how sweet the seduction of her prey . . .

She looked back at Tiff. Something now, must be done with the remains. What a bother.

She looked back to the street, frowning. The carabinieri were out in large numbers, she noticed. Why?

For a moment, she thought that *he* might be angry. Such a feast should have been shared. And perhaps she had not chosen the right victim . . .

He had his own agenda.

She tossed her head. Well, there were times when he forgot just who *she* was.

And now . . .

Now, tonight, she felt a terrible gnawing inside. Bitterness, hatred, vengeance. Well, she was moving toward her goal. And she was filled; she surely felt her own power.

She hadn't felt quite so deliciously strong in a very long time . . .

She closed the window.

The night was young.

CHAPTER 8

Harry's was busy, as always. Jam-packed.

People waited for tables, stood by the bar, huddled in the doorway.

Just within the door, Jordan hesitated. There was nowhere to sit, nowhere to go. She contemplated slipping back out and waiting outside, forgoing her drink, but the night was turning fairly raw. She hadn't wanted to stay in her room, but she didn't particularly want to stand outside shivering, either.

Even as she stood feeling a little lost and forlorn, she saw one of the doormen hurrying her way. She smiled, assuming he was bearing down on her to take her coat. Then she realized he was rushing to greet someone who had just come in behind her.

"Signore, welcome back."

She felt a hand on her shoulder. She started; as she turned, she saw that it was Ragnor, and that he was greeting the doorman. "Buona sera! The lady and I were hoping to have a drink," Ragnor said.

Though he was speaking pleasantly to the doorman, Jordan saw that he was watching a couple at the far end of the bar. The couple rose, leaving an empty space.

"Come, come!" the doorman said.

Jordan looked around, ready to refuse if there were people who had come in ahead of them.

"Come, come," the doorman insisted, ushering them along the bar. Tables for the others are almost ready."

A moment later, he had taken their coats, and she was seated on a bar stool. The bartender was instantly before them. She decided on a good old Southern Jack and Seven. Ragnor ordered Dewars on the rocks.

She swirled the swizzle stick in her drink, then turned to find that he was watching her.

"How did you do that?" she asked him.

"Do what?"

"Clear out the bar."

He shrugged. "People left; others are ready for dinner."

"Conveniently so."

"I know the doorman and the bartender, but don't worry, l respect a queue. There just happened to be an opening here. What did you think I might have done? Sleight of hand? Mind-controlling darts?"

He appeared amused. She felt a little ridiculous, and therefore, angry. And defensive.

"Were you following me?" she asked curtly. He had been so close behind her.

His answer took a moment. She felt the assessment

of his gaze. "You've got quite a bit of ego wrapped up in such a small package."

She felt her cheeks burn. "I was assuming you meant to tell me again to leave Venice." She stared ahead at the bar, turning her swizzle stick once again. She was aware that he kept watching her, also aware that her black cocktail dress was form-hugging and close to risqué. She was also aware that he was well dressed, his clothing was handsomely tailored. He had great hands, she noted as she had before. One rested against his drink, powerful there, the fingers long and tapered. He'd make it in a barbarian movie, just as he wore Armani with a smooth and cultivated flair.

"Are you leaving Venice?" he asked. He sat facing her on his stool. She felt the brush of his knees.

"Eventually."

"But you won't get on a plane and go right now."

"No."

She thought he would argue. He shrugged. "Maybe it's best."

"That I stay? How kind of you."

"How's the Danieli?" he asked, his tone casual.

"Fine. Have you stayed there?"

"Yes, but not in a while. I wonder if it's changed. Maybe I'll walk you back and see."

"You could have coffee or drinks in the lobby anytime," she told him.

A slight smile curved his lips. "You won't allow me to walk you home?"

"I'm meeting my cousin and his wife here."

"And Anna Maria, Raphael and Lynn, so it appears," Ragnor said.

From where he sat, facing her, he could see the door. She swirled around and saw that Jared and Cindy had arrived and that they were accompanied by the others.

Raphael's bright eyes widened as he saw Jordan. "Darling!"

He made a typically dramatic stride through the milling cocktail crowd to reach her. He kissed her on both cheeks, took her hands, and guided her down from the stool to turn her around before him as he admired her dress. "Simply scrumptious!" he said. "Delizioso! Ragnor, wouldn't you say?"

"I'm afraid so," Ragnor murmured. He rose from his bar stool as well, stretching out an arm as Anna Maria approached them, her smile broad. Lynn followed, delighted, and a round of double-cheeked kissing went around as everyone greeted everyone. Cindy seemed pleased to welcome Ragnor; only Jared appeared to be a little stiff. He spoke politely, and made no protest when Anna Maria suggested that Ragnor must join them for dinner. Jared seemed leery of the stranger among them, and curious—even suspicious—when his eyes met Jordan's.

She shrugged, trying to assure her cousin that she hadn't invited or encouraged the man to join them.

The doorman came, telling them that their table was ready. Jordan found Ragnor's hand on her back, guiding her through the crowd into one of the dining rooms. With his fingers against her naked back, she had to admit, again, that he had an effect on her. Like fire. An uncomfortable effect. At the bar, she had felt the urge to lean in against him, to feel the fabric of his suit against her cheek, to breathe in the clean, intoxicating scent of his shaven cheeks. Now, as she had last night, watching the dancers, she felt an intoxicating sensuality in proximity. Lynn would say that she wanted to jump his bones. She wouldn't be quite so crude—or honest. But her mind strayed during the simple act of walking from bar to table. His hands were unbelievably masculine. She wondered what it would be like to feel them moving along her arms.

And other places.

She wondered if his chest was as broad and compelling when naked.

She wondered what it would feel like if she were naked too, rubbing against the length of him. And if his chest was bare, his hips would be bare, and then she found herself wondering if he was powerful and lithe and large throughout . . .

He pulled out a chair for her at the table. She sat. Her face was lobster tinted, she was certain. From head to toe she felt a crimson flush. She wasn't even breathing normally.

Maybe he would sit somewhere else, other than beside her!

He didn't. He took the chair at her left. Lynn was already seated at her right.

A waiter set her half-finished drink in front of her. She reached for it, taking a long swallow. Menus appeared and Lynn reached over, pointing at items, telling her what she thought was especially good. She responded, nodding, saying something, she wasn't sure exactly what. Jared and Anna Maria were discussing a number of the people Jared had booked for her ball the following night; the seating had already been planned, there were several hundred guests coming, but it seemed that Anna Maria wanted to know more about those coming, so as to put people with similar interests together.

"So—where were you off to today?" Cindy suddenly asked Jordan.

"I went to have coffee with Tiff."

"Isn't the palazzo marvelous?" Raphael asked her.

"Yes, very nice."

"The marble in the foyer is supposed to have been salvaged from the ruins of a Roman palace," Anna Maria told her.

"You had coffee all day?" Jared asked. The question sounded a little grating to Jordan, and she wasn't pleased to realize that now everyone at the table was looking at her, as if they all waited for an answer.

"I had coffee, I shopped, I wandered," she said.

"I thought you might come by the shop," Lynn said.

"I knew you all would be very busy," Jordan told her.

"Tiff is something, eh?" Raphael said.

"In actuality, a very highly paid prostitute," Jared said.

"Jared!" Cindy remonstrated.

"Well! She marries old rich men for their money. Isn't that kind of the same thing?" Jared queried.

"What about old and middle-aged men who discard their wives of thirty years or so to go after shapely young things?" Jordan said in defense of her friend. "I like her."

"What do you think about Mrs. Tiffany Henley, Ragnor?" Cindy asked.

Ragnor arched a brow. "I suppose we all have our priorities. She is blunt, beyond a doubt."

Lynn giggled. "She has much more to say about you," she told him.

"She is fine; a bit much sometimes, but polite," Ragnor said with a shrug. "I don't know her very well."

"I saw you with her this afternoon," Jordan said.

His eyes suddenly turned full force on her.

"Oh? And where did you see me from?"

"A canal."

"What were you doing in the canal?" Cindy asked with a frown.

"I wasn't in the canal. I was in a gondola."

"You took a gondola ride all by yourself?" Jared said.

Again, she felt that he was asking questions like a disapproving parent.

"Are gondolas supposed to be dangerous?" she asked lightly.

"A gondola should be shared with a lover," Raphael said.

"Actually, I wound up on the gondola because of you," Jordan told Jared, wishing that she weren't so aware of Ragnor's eyes, always seeming to be on her.

"Me!"

"Um, I thought that I was following you home last night—but of course, it wasn't you. It was another man dressed in a dottore costume."

"Definitely a man?" Ragnor asked.

"Well, I assume."

"What does that have to do with you taking a gondola ride today because of me?" Jared asked, baffled.

"I thought I saw the man again. I followed him."

"You followed a stranger in a dottore costume?" Anna Maria queried.

"That was an idiotic thing to do," Jared said harshly.

"Everyone is in costume, Jared," Jordan said coolly. "And people follow people in costumes all day, snapping pictures."

"How did this man in the costume lead to the gondola?" Anna Maria asked quickly, trying to ease the tension.

"I saw a friend. And he gave me a ride home."

"Wait, wait, wait. What friend do you have who is a gondolier?" Jared demanded.

"Jared, you have lots of friends I don't know, and I have friends you don't know."

"In Venice?" he queried.

"Yes. In Venice."

"So . . . what was Tiff up to?" Raphael asked Ragnor. He might just as well have said, *"Hey, how about that game?"*

"Ah, well she asked me to the cocktail party she's having before Anna Maria's ball."

"Tiff Henley is having a cocktail party?" Cindy said.

"She assured me you were coming," Ragnor replied.

"I hadn't had a chance to tell you," Jordan told them quickly.

"You knew she was having a cocktail party?" Jared queried.

"I just learned about it this morning."

The wine steward, who had been standing nearby, cleared his throat. Jared quickly apologized in Italian, and a discussion regarding choices for dinner wine went around the table.

"I think you just found out about this cocktail party tonight."

Jordan started, Ragnor's whisper so close against her cheek, so softly spoken.

She smiled sweetly at him. "I think that big egos can come in very large packages as well."

His head remained lowered near hers, his eyes dark, intense, and strangely serious. "Do you dislike me, Miss Riley?"

"Yes," she whispered.

"Why?"

"Maybe because you insult me each time we meet."

"I wouldn't dream of insulting you."

"I think that you implied I looked like a real hooker in red vinyl."

A very slight smile curved his lips. "I could apologize, but that isn't really the answer, is it? So, why do you dislike me?"

"Maybe because you're a liar," she heard herself say.

"What lies have I told?" Ragnor inquired.

"You were at the contessa's ball. And you deny it."

He sat back. "We're not at all friends, I do assure you. That is no lie."

She would have believed him. Except at that moment, Raphael suddenly had a question for Ragnor.

"Ragnor. I saw you with the contessa in the Square today. At least, I'm quite certain that it was the contessa. She was wearing a mask, but . . . there's something in the way she moves, yes? Have you two decided that you are not such great enemies?" Raphael was full of his sense of fun. He lifted his wineglass. "You seemed quite close."

"Like the sun and the moon, my friend," Ragnor said evenly.

Everyone at the table was staring at him.

"Night and day," Anna Maria murmured.

Jordan excused herself suddenly, rising with a murmur about going to the ladies room and asking Lynn to order for her. She hurried off to the restroom and doused her face in cold water. She stared at her reflection.

"Go home, get out of this insanity!" she told herself. But the more it seemed she should do so, the more she longed to run, the more she felt impelled to stay.

Ragnor was a liar. He was with Tiff today, and with the contessa in the Square. It didn't change the fact that she was torn between hostility . . . and almost overwhelming desire.

"He's handsomely built," she told her reflection. "Good, rugged features, great hands. You've been alone; you lost a fiancé a year ago. You are human, and that is all."

She suddenly realized that another woman had come in and was staring at her. She had spoken aloud. "Scusi, scusi," the woman said.

"No, no, per favore, mi scusi," Jordan murmured quickly, slipping by the woman.

Great. As if the world didn't think that Americans were crazy enough.

She ran right into Ragnor. He had apparently followed her, and waited for her to emerge.

"I had to make you understand that I am not in any way the contessa's friend," he told her.

She shook her head. "Your friendships are completely your own business, Mister . . . Mister . . ." She threw up her hands. "I don't even know your last name."

"It's important that you believe me."

"Why?"

"It may be important that you trust me."

"I'm sorry, I try not to trust comparative strangers at the very best of times."

She started by him. He caught her hand.

"I shouldn't be such a stranger."

"Trust *me,*" she said, extricating her hand from his. "You are very strange, sir." She started by him again.

Somehow, and she wasn't at all sure how he managed it, he was in front of her again.

"Honestly, Jordan, I'm sorry I insulted your vinyl. I meant no offense. You were simply far too enticing."

"Thank you. Excuse me," she murmured, and this time, he didn't stop her.

"Jordan! I hope that I ordered well for you," Lynn said as she reached the table.

"I'm sure that you did," Jordan assured her, taking her seat.

She pointedly gave her attention to Lynn as Ragnor took his chair. "What am I having?"

"A great antipasto, there on the table now. Then rigatoni funghetti, delicious pasta with mushrooms in oil and garlic, and then seppia.

"And what is that?" Jordan asked.

"In English, cuttlefish. Like an octopus or squid. You've seen it here, surely. It's the special dish of Venice," Lynn told her.

Jordan's stomach instantly churned. Cuttlefish. Yep. She should have known. She'd seen it on menus, read about it in guidebooks. She was a seafood lover—of anything that didn't look too much like seafood. No whole fish with the eyes staring at her.

Or anything that was related to an octopus in any way, shape, or form. Octopus was very popular here, she knew. She'd never managed to enjoy a plate of anything with little octopi on it; seeing the tiny suckers on the little legs didn't do anything for her.

She hoped her smile didn't slip.

"Wonderful," she managed.

She turned her attention back to the general conversation at the table in time to hear Ragnor responding to something Cindy had said.

"Legends are always intriguing. Most interestingly, they correspond." He offered Cindy a rueful smile.

"Even the angels who were cast from heaven in Judaism and Christianity have much in common with say, the old Roman gods, Assyrian deities, and the Norse rulers of Valhalla."

"Angels align with the old gods and goddesses?" Cindy said skeptically. She paused to smile at the waiter as her pasta was served.

"Lucifer, the beautiful, the fallen. Satan was an angel."

"You're saying that God is a legend?" Anna Maria queried with a frown.

Ragnor shook his head. "Oh, no, I believe that there is a God. I'm saying that what we see as the pagan ways of the past are not so different. Knowledge is different, history is different, but there has always been a concept of good and evil and death has always been a great mystery. Different societies have tried to explain it in different ways, but worldwide and throughout history, there has been a belief in a hell, or an underworld. The Greeks crossed the River Styx. Hell has always been down, and heaven is always up."

"Just as people are really very much the same," Lynn commented. "Human nature does not change."

"We all love the glitter of gold!" Raphael put in.

"And we all fear monsters, and see the same creatures!" Anna Maria agreed. "The great hairy man, the missing link, is universal. Big Foot in the United States is Sasquatch in Canada and the Yeti in Asia."

"And darkness and shadows hide all evil!" Raphael announced. They all stared at him. He shrugged. "È vero! All over the world, children are afraid of the dark."

"The dark is what we can't see or understand. That's always frightening," Ragnor said.

Darkness and shadows, and things that seem to move within them, Jordan thought. She bit into her pasta. It was delicious. She would finish it, then move the cuttlefish around on her plate, and pretend that it was delicious, too.

"So, Ragnor—is there a Loch Ness monster?" Lynn asked.

"If so, I've never seen it," Ragnor said, bringing the soft sound of laughter around the table. "But who knows? There have been a lot of sightings—just no beached creatures for scientific proof."

"There is no such thing as a Loch Ness monster," Jared insisted.

The waiter arrived to take their pasta plates. Jared seemed to be scowling, irritated by the conversation that seemed to be fun for the others.

"But many legends have later been explained by science," Cindy said. "Sea monsters—we know that giant squid and other such things do exist. And blue whales! Larger than any dinosaurs! We accept them easily."

"We've seen blue whales—they've been seen since men first put to sea," Jared told her. "There's your proof."

"But I've never actually seen a blue whale," Cindy said. "Other people have seen blue whales, but other people have also said that they've seen the Loch Ness monster."

Jared groaned. "Cindy, it's not quite the same. You've seen pictures of great blue whales."

"I watch Discovery," Cindy said. "I've seen a few pictures of the Loch Ness monster."

"I think that the great blue whale has more documentation going for it," Lynn said, attempting a compromise.

The dinner plates had arrived. Jordan looked down at her plate, already forcing a smile for Lynn.

There was no cuttlefish in front of her. She was staring at a plate of chicken marsala. She glanced up and caught Ragnor's eye. He smiled.

The cuttlefish was before him.

"Lynn ordered it for me. You don't have to—" she whispered.

"It's all right. I've dined on far stranger creatures."

Lynn didn't notice the change. She was still talking about legends, faraway places, sea creatures. By the time she turned to Jordan, the plates had been subtly switched once again.

"How was it?"

"An adventure in taste."

"You didn't like it."

"I'm not certain I'd have it again, but—"

"You can say that you tried it," Lynn told her. "I'm sorry, I should have asked—"

"Oh, no. Thank you. My meal was delicious!" she said, and thankfully, she wasn't lying.

The evening went pleasantly. Lingering over espresso and dessert, they talked about the ball the coming night. Yes, Anna Maria assured them, they were all exhausted with the preparations, but pleased.

"So, do you think that the contessa will come?" Cindy asked Anna Maria.

"Oh, no. She does not have a ticket. She would not have one."

"But what if she is curious—she does put on costumes and walk around the streets, though she would never admit to it!" Raphael said.

"Raphael, we always know to whom we sell our tickets. And even those we give out through special friends with interests in Venice, like Jared are to people known to us because we are so careful to seat people where they will enjoy themselves. I have a list of everyone who is coming."

"But if she showed up at the door, would we let her in?" Lynn asked.

Anna Maria tossed back her beautiful, sleek hair. "The world is full of 'ifs.' I said that right in English, didn't I? I refuse to live by 'ifs.' And the contessa would not come to a party that I gave. It's late. We have a very long day tomorrow. We must get the check and get going. Signore, il conto, per favore," she called to the waiter.

The check had already been paid. "I crashed the dinner party. It seemed the thing to do, under the circumstances," Ragnor explained.

The others all thanked him and told him it wasn't necessary. Jordan looked at him curiously. "When did you manage to pay the check?" she asked him.

"When I 'followed' you to the ladies room," he told her.

"So you weren't really following me. You just happened to be there?"

"Not exactly. I was following you, too."

He pulled out her chair. Outside the restaurant, they went through a round of cheek kissing again. Anna Maria and her group were ready to take a vaporetto.

"Which way are you going?" Jared asked Ragnor.

"Actually, I've just taken a room at the Danieli," he said.

Jordan started.

"Great! We can walk back together," Cindy said. She slipped her arm through her husband's, leading them on ahead.

Jordan stared at Ragnor. "You're really at the Danieli?"

"Yes."

"Where have you been staying?"

"With friends."

"So why move into the Danieli?"

He shrugged. "I haven't stayed there in a while."

She started forward. He fell in step at her side, not touching her.

"Thank you for dinner."

"A pleasure."

She stopped walking. "Just what do you do for a living?"

He looked down at the street as he walked, a small smile on his lips. "You know, in many places in Europe, that might be considered a rude question."

"I'm an American. According to many Europeans, we tend to be rude."

"But you're not usually, are you?" he queried, looking at her.

She sighed with exasperation. "Why can't you just answer a straight question?"

He shrugged. "I dabble in antiques," he told her.

"Dabbling in antiques must be a prosperous vocation." She brushed his sleeve, indicating his dress. "Armani, Versace . . . rooms at the Danieli, constant travel, so it seems. And apparently, you speak a number of languages—well. That tends to imply quite an education."

"The world itself can be quite an education."

"Oh, I'm sure. But I think you've had a lot more."

"You are getting intensely personal, you know."

"I am intensely curious."

"Aren't you going to ask if I'm a drug smuggler?"

"No."

"All right. I have lots of that dreadful stuff known as family money."

"Where was this family from, originally?"

It seemed he still hesitated, then he shrugged. "Norway."

"Norway!"

He glanced at her, his head at a slight incline. "Yes. I shouldn't have thought that would be a tremendous surprise. I'm definitely Teutonic looking. Then there's my name—Ragnor. And my surname."

"I told you before—I don't know your surname."

He turned to look at her. "Wulfsson."

"*Wulf-son?*" she repeated. "Like . . . son of the *wolf?*"

"It's a fairly common name where I come from," he said dryly.

Wolf. Wolf's son.

A tall man in wolf's clothing, leaping from a balcony to a boat.

A wolf in the midst of the shadows.

A large dog. Right.

Jordan felt light-headed, uneasy.

They passed by a shop window. She glanced at it and started.

There was the mannequin again. The one she had passed earlier. An echo of Steven's face remained.

"What's wrong?" Ragnor asked. She hadn't realized that she had paused and was staring at the mannequin. Steven's face had passed through her mind's eye once again.

She shook her head.

It was a dummy; a mannequin. Well dressed, made of rubber or plastic, or whatever they used to make dummies.

"Nothing," she said.

She felt his hands on her shoulders, the intensity of his eyes on hers. "What did you see?" he demanded.

She shook her head. She wasn't sharing any more about Steven with anyone. "Nothing, really. I'm just tired."

He stared at the store window, then looked back at her. "I wish that you'd trust me," he said.

She lifted her hand. "It's a shop window, as you can see."

Jared and Cindy had paused ahead. Her cousin called back to them. "Hey, you two, are you coming?"

Jordan then heard Cindy's voice, though she hadn't intended her words to carry. "Jared, leave her alone! She's walking with a fascinating man after a year of mourning!"

Jordan was staring at Ragnor as they both heard Cindy's aggrieved whisper. She flushed.

"Let's go."

She turned; he followed. She walked briskly, passing Cindy and Jared. A moment later she turned back to the three who were a few feet behind her. "There's the hotel. Excuse me, will you, I'm going to hurry on ahead. I'm suddenly really, really tired. Excuse me, please."

She quickened her pace, nearly swinging the revolving door into a bellman as she hurried into the hotel. She apologized quickly and went to the concierge for her key. Before anyone could come up behind her, she raced up the stairs to her bedroom door.

Inside the room, she noted that the night maid had

been in. Her bed was turned down. The shutters had been thrown open. The window was almost closed; the night was very cool.

She remembered the uneasy sensation she'd had in the room before she'd left. She shook her head, wanting to sleep, hoping to not be plagued by ridiculous fears. Methodically, she went through her room, checking the bathroom, the divisions of the room, under the bed, even the television cabinet. She secured the shutters and closed the window.

She discarded her heels and black cocktail dress and got into a flannel Winnie the Pooh nightgown.

There was a knock on her door. She hesitated, peered through the peephole, and saw that Ragnor was out there.

She opened the door, glaring at him.

"What?" she demanded, anger, exasperation, and even a plea in her voice.

"I just wanted to make sure you were up here, safe, sound, locked in, all that."

"I was locked in—until you had me open the door."

"Mind if I look around?"

"Yes! It's the middle of the night."

"Deep midnight," he murmured.

"Well past midnight," she told him.

"I'll go away and stay away," he promised.

"Come in, come in, walk around, look around. Then please . . ."

He stepped past her and repeated the actions she had just taken. She watched him, arms crossed over her chest as she waited. She stood near the door. *He would leave. He had to leave. She couldn't believe it. She was tempted to ask him to stay. To just walk up to him and say 'I don't know a damned thing about you. I still think you're lying. You're evasive if not entirely mysterious. You could be a mass murderer for all I know. But, okay, I admit it, I'm no better than Tiff, I feel this incredible urge to touch you, to check out what's going on beneath the tailored clothing, lord, what a body, is it all that great? I'd really like to just hop into bed, turn out all the lights and have sex, the kind where you forget everything because you're so desperate for that moment . . .'*

"Looks good," he said, stepping before her.

"Gee, thanks. I thought so myself. You're not a drug smuggler. An antiques smuggler?"

"No."

"A criminal of any kind?"

At that, he seemed to hesitate.

"You *are* a criminal!"

"No. Not now."

"Oh, great! You're warning me to be careful, you're in my room—"

"I told you before—you seem to have created an . . . an atmosphere of tension."

"Get out," she told him.

To her amazement, he did so. The second he stepped out of the doorway, she was sorry. This was absolutely crazy. She had the most insane temptation to throw herself against him.

"When you feel like explaining things to me—telling me the truth about, just about anything—give me a call," she told him.

She closed the door, firmly locking it.

She leaned against the door for a moment, biting her lip. She didn't hear him leave. A moment later, she threw open the door again. The hallway was empty. She closed the door again, locking it carefully.

It took her a long time to get to sleep.

When she did, the dreams came again.

Steven was there. He was dressed as the mannequin in the window, but he was the man she had known, passionate, level, caring, noble . . . all the rest. He called her name, trying to reach her through a sea of fog, apologizing because he just couldn't come close enough.

"It's the wolf," he told her. "You've got to get rid of that wolf."

"There are no wolves in Venice," she told him. "I talked to the waiter. They just have very big dogs."

But the wolf was there again. Silver, huge, it sat a few feet away, much closer than it had been before. Steven, she saw, was beyond the window, walking in the fog.

The wolf was at the foot of the bed.

Steven kept coming. The wolf growled. She saw the great canine teeth.

"I've missed you so much," Steven said.

She had to explain the wolf. "The waiter really assured me. No wolves. I think it's just a malamute, Steven, see the eyes?"

The fog was rising all around her, swirling around the foot of the bed. There shouldn't be fog in the room. It had to be the maid's fault; she had left the window open.

"Jordan . . ."

It was Steven, calling her name.

"I miss you, too, so much, Steven." Guilt assailed her. She did miss him. He had been everything good in a man. A *cop.* He'd cared for victims; he'd wanted reforms; he done everything, given the final sacrifice of his life.

I miss you, but I'm dying to go to bed with another man now, Steven, she thought.

She didn't say the words aloud, but it was a dream. Could he read her mind in a dream? Was she speaking anyway? Even in the dream, she knew that a psychiatrist would have a heyday with her. This was all perfectly understandable. She'd been in love, deeply in love, engaged. She shouldn't forget so quickly. A year. Steven was dead, and she was not.

There was an explanation, yes, surely . . .

"I miss you, Steven!" she repeated.

"Love me more than the wolf!" he called to her.

"I do love you!"

"Bring me back in your mind, Jordan."

"You're always in my mind."

The wolf growled again.

The fog rose over the bed.

She awoke with a start.

Though the shutters were closed, little shafts of light streaked into the room. She could see the motes dancing in the air.

There was no fog in her room.

And there was no wolf.

And no sign of Steven, naturally.

Morning had come and dreams had broken.

CHAPTER 9

She awoke very late.

Despite the hour, Jordan went upstairs to the roof-top restaurant, desperately in search of coffee. One of the waiters, a pleasant man she was coming to know, greeted her with a smile, and the much needed cup of coffee.

"Buon giorno, Signorina Riley," he told her. "It's not morning, but then . . . it is Carnevale. I can get you eggs, if you wish."

"The coffee is wonderful, thank you so much. If it's already lunch—"

"An omelette. Formaggio, eh?"

"That would be lovely, thank you. Have you seen my cousin or his wife?"

"Signora Riley left not long ago."

"Thank you so much. Oh . . . by the way, have you seen a very tall man, light haired?"

"No, signorina, I haven't."

"Well, thank you."

At the next table, a woman was finishing a bowl of soup; her companion was reading an Italian paper.

"Even here in Venice," the man said in English.

"What is it, dear?" the woman asked.

"A head—a severed head was found in a canal."

"My God, how awful!" the woman said. Then she added "Just the head? No body?"

"Not yet—but I assume you've got to have a body to have a head."

"Yes, of course."

Jordan found herself rising, approaching the couple. "Excuse me, I'm sorry for being so rude. Did you say that a head had been found?"

The man lowered his paper, looking at her over the top. "Yes, I'm sorry to say. But you shouldn't worry. It was found far from here. This is a wonderfully safe city, young lady. It's likely that this was a personal vendetta."

"Oh? Did the man have enemies?"

The man cleared his throat. "Well, actually, right now, the man is an unidentified head. The authorities are trying to make an identification, checking missing persons reports and all. Here, would you like the paper?"

She shook her head, thanking him. "I'm afraid the amount of Italian I can read wouldn't give me much of the story."

"Well, as I said, it's not something you should worry about. Honestly. My wife, Alyssa—" He inclined his head toward his wife, and Jordan smiled at the attractive, silver-haired woman in acknowledgment, "—we've been coming here for nearly twenty years, every Carnevale. These are the most wonderful people in the world."

"Harold, the poor girl is white as a sheet. You shouldn't have been reading so loudly," Alyssa said.

"No, no, it's all right. I shouldn't have been eavesdropping. Um, does it say anything about how long the head might have been in the water?"

Harold shook his head. "I don't believe they know as yet. Unfortunately, when a head is in the sea . . ." He hesitated, clearing his throat. "Well, fish chew at it, you know."

"Harold! We're at lunch!" Alyssa admonished. "And this poor dear hasn't even been served yet."

"No, no, it's all right. I'm a pretty hardy soul," Jordan said. "I'm Jordan Riley, by the way."

"Alyssa and Harold Atwater," Alyssa said, extending a hand. "A pleasure. Where are you from?"

"Charleston, South Carolina."

"A fellow Southerner," Harold said, as if he had decided beforehand that there was something about her of which he approved.

"We're from Texas," Alyssa said.

"Oh, look, there's that tall fellow I told you about the other day!" Alyssa said to her husband. She grinned at Jordan. "I think he must be a European film star."

"Rocker, probably—look at that hair," Harold said.

"Rich rocker, Harold, look at the cut of his clothes," Alyssa rolled her eyes at Jordan.

Jordan turned, already aware that it had to be Ragnor Wulfsson coming into the restaurant. He carried a paper; his eyes were shielded behind very dark glasses. He was wearing black jeans, a tailored shirt, and a fitted black leather jacket, blond hair queued at his nape.

Jordan stiffened slightly and offered Alyssa a return smile.

"Antiques dealer," she told her.

"Oh, you know him!" Alyssa said, flushing. "We didn't mean anything . . . he's rather hard to miss, that's all."

"I agree," she said pleasantly, adding a soft, "I don't know him all that well."

"Big fellow," Harold said. "German?"

"Norwegian."

"He could be a bouncer. Or a tough guy."

"Oh, Harold!" Alyssa said softly, noting that Ragnor had seen them and was coming their way. "Don't be ridiculous! There is no such thing as a Norwegian mafia!"

"And this is Italy! Hush up about the mafia!" Harold warned.

"Good morning," Ragnor said, reaching the table. He nodded to Harold and Alyssa, and looked at Jordan. "You've just arrived."

"A few minutes ago. Ragnor, Harold and Alyssa Atwater. From Texas. Mr. and Mrs. Atwater, Ragnor Wulfsson—from Norway."

"Originally," Ragnor said, shaking Harold's hand, and inclining his head politely to Alyssa. "A pleasure to meet you. You must be familiar with Italy, Mr. Atwater; I see that you're reading an Italian paper."

"Oh, yes. I was in the service, stationed in Italy," he said. "Grisly thing, this, have you seen the headlines? Oh, do you read Italian?"

Ragnor arched a brow, accepting the paper. "Yes, I read Italian," he murmured.

"I tell you, Harold, the Europeans have it all over us! He's Norwegian, his English is perfect, and he reads Italian as well!"

"You speak Spanish nicely." Harold absently complimented his wife.

"Norwegian, Italian, English . . . and I'm sure Mr. Wulfsson speaks one or two other languages," Alyssa said.

Ragnor looked up from the paper long enough to offer her a smile. "A few," he agreed, and gave his attention back to the paper.

"There has been a severed head discovered in one of the canals," Jordan said.

"Yes, I see that."

Alyssa gasped suddenly. *Jordan Riley!* Why, you're the young lady who thought she was in the midst of mass murder at the contessa's party the other night."

Jordan felt her flesh warming uncomfortably. "Yes. Were you at the party?"

"I'm afraid we were."

"And you saw nothing . . ."

"We weren't in the upstairs ballroom, dear," Alyssa said. "Poor girl! No wonder Harold's words were so disturbing, and this story . . . but honestly, you mustn't worry. I mean—lord knows! This head might have floated over from Greece or Albania or . . . well, somewhere."

"I don't think a head would have made it quite that far," Harold said.

As he spoke, the waiter arrived with Jordan's omelette. It was decorated with greens and tomatoes. The plate was attractively arranged. But the eggs . . .

"Oh!" Alyssa murmured, appearing a little ashen. "Will you gentlemen please put that paper away!"

"Is everything all right?" the waiter asked anxiously. "Mr. Wulfsson, may I bring you coffee? Will you be joining Miss Riley?"

"Yes, thank you," Ragnor said.

Alyssa rose. "Go eat your omelette, while it's hot," she suggested to Jordan, glancing at the plate on the table as if it were the severed head itself. She shuddered. "Lovely to meet you. Harold, we have to leave."

"No we don't—"

"Yes, we do. Goodbye, we'll be seeing you." She had her hand on Harold's arm, he was up, a big man, ready to follow his slender wife.

"Keep the paper!" he said to Ragnor.

"Thanks. Thanks very much," Ragnor said.

When they had gone, Ragnor slid into a seat at Jordan's table. She took her chair opposite him.

"I don't remember asking you to join me for breakfast," she said.

"It isn't really breakfast," he murmured, eyes scanning the paper.

Jordan wished she could read Italian. "What does it say?"

"Not too much. A head was found in one of the smaller canals."

"Near the contessa's palazzo?" Jordan asked.

His eyes shot up at her. Not that she could really see his eyes. His Ray-Bans shot up at her.

He stared at her a while. "Yes."

"People were killed at her party. I'm convinced of it. If only someone else believed it."

He didn't contradict her. He translated from the paper instead. "Police will call in a forensic artist to try to re-create the face so that bulletins can be sent throughout Europe, as there are no reports of missing persons in the Venice area at this time."

She sat back, staring at him. "Can you take those off, please?" she asked, indicating his glasses.

"No," he said flatly.

"Wearing them at the table is extremely rude, something even an *American* wouldn't do."

"I see Americans wearing sunglasses at the table all the time," he replied absently.

She leaned forward, shoving the omelette aside. "You spend your time warning me that I'm in danger, that I create danger, then you tell me that a severed head means nothing in Venice."

"I didn't say that at all."

"What did you say?"

"That you can't go assuming that this severed head has anything to do with the contessa. And if you go to the police insisting again that the contessa's party was full of costumed creatures ripping up guests, they're just going to think that you're crazy again. Delusional, suffering from stress brought on by grief due to the loss of a loved one."

She started to rise; he caught her hand. "Why are you angry with me when I tell you the truth?"

"You're still not telling me the truth about anything."

"I'm telling you what you need to know."

"Well, at the moment, I have work to do. Will you excuse me?"

His face was expressionless, but he didn't release her hand. "Where are you going?"

"What on earth is that to you?"

"Where are you going?" he repeated.

"Down to the front desk—I was supposed to get some work by FedEx today. Then I'm going to my room to work."

"And then?"

"I'm going to bring the red vinyl costume back to Anna Maria's and pick up the outfit I'm wearing tonight."

"I'll be in the lobby. Make sure you stop by to get me before you go."

"What if I don't want you with me?"

"I'm hard to shake."

"Will you let go for now?"

"You haven't touched your food."

"I'm not hungry. And I am awake and aware, and it seems like a good time to get some work done."

He released her hand. His attention was back on the newspaper article.

Jordan took the elevator down to the lobby level and went straight to the front desk, asking if a package had arrived for her. To her surprise, it actually had; it had arrived in almost exactly twenty-four hours.

There was a note from her agent right on top. She scanned it and went straight to the manuscript. *Vampire Legend and the Criminal Mind.*

She started reading as she walked up the stairs. There was an introduction about the author, a cop named Sean Canady who lived in New Orleans. His record had been filled with commendations, and he had worked homicides for years.

The first section of the book centered on solved criminal cases involving occultism and vampirism, going back into history for centuries, and including cases involving cannibalism, all the way up to the murders perpetrated by Jeffrey Dahmer.

The book was absorbing. In her room, she flopped down on her bed and kept on reading until she realized that she hadn't locked her door.

Her reading material indicated that she really should do so.

She stood, rushed to the door, locked it, and stretched back out to read again. The manuscript was very well written: detailed without being graphic, to the point, and yet explanatory. There was a section on cases still under investigation, including the murder of several prostitutes in New Orleans, and the occult killings that had occurred in Charleston, South Carolina.

Steven was in the book, mentioned by name. She bit her lip while reading that section.

There was a chapter on the various psychologies involved in such murders, written in cooperation with one of the leading men from the FBI who worked on criminal profiles. The author stressed the fact that although serial killers were often white males between twenty and thirty-five—men who might have tortured animals as children, who held menial jobs, and were often married—there was also a breed of very organized killers with the ability to charm and get ahead in life, attractive and appealing men in appearance and manner, such as Ted Bundy.

Sometimes killers left their signatures. Sometimes they wanted to be caught. Sometimes they wanted the power trip that came with outwitting the police.

There were those who were truly ill.

And those who believed they were dealing with vampires.

Vampire lore had come into play in the capture of a 'vampire' killer in Colorado who thought he was a vampire. The scare had been so real in the small western town where the killings took place that many women had armed themselves with stakes and large crosses, kept vials of holy water by the door, and hung their windows and doorways with garlic. The killer, who selected his women by breaking into bedroom windows, had avoided these households, believing himself susceptible to the weapons of legend. The police knew of one victim who had saved herself through her efforts. The killer's footprints had been found in her garden and he later admitted to making an attempt to strike at her, but had seen the garlic, and knew that he would be falling prey to his own doom. There was a list of suggestions from the author on keeping safe. Most of them were common sense, but Jordan kept reading anyway.

- Avoid being alone in any dark or any potentially dangerous place.
- Always keep doors and windows locked.
- Keep a dog—barking is a deterrent to many would-be criminals.
- Never invite strangers in. *Never.*

There was a knock on her door.

She nearly jumped through the ceiling.

She glanced at her watch. Three o'clock. Hours had passed, and she hadn't even noticed.

She leaped up, then paused, and for some reason, decided to shove the manuscript under her pillow. Walking to the door, she looked out the peephole, expecting Jared or Cindy.

It was Ragnor.
Never invite a stranger in. Never.
But . . .
Last night, she had done so.

CHAPTER 10

The knocking sounded again.

Jordan squared her shoulders, giving herself a mental shake. Her reading material was beginning to have an effect on her. As he raised his hand to knock again, Jordan opened the door.

He stared at her expectantly and glanced at his watch. "Are you ready?" he queried.

"For what?"

"A walk to Anna Maria's to return the last costume—the vinyl. And pick up whatever delight Raphael planned for you for tonight."

She wanted to tell him no, to go away. She wasn't even sure she wanted to go to the ball that evening. Maybe her reading material was getting to her; she wanted to immerse herself in it.

Maybe she *was* simply and totally crazy. Ragnor had a . . . *presence.* He wasn't just striking, he was compelling. She liked the sound of his voice, the shape of his jaw . . .

As she had before, she felt the sudden temptation to fly into his arms, lay her head down, and believe that everyone was fine and normal, that he wasn't a man with a million dark secrets, that . . . that she could just bury herself in sensation. Turn off the lights, forget the shadows, have faith in the dark, and the feel of him.

She took a step back. She wasn't prey to true insanity.

And she was torn, longing to read more of the new book. She wanted to find out more about the author. She wanted to talk to him and tell him what she had seen . . .

And that a head had appeared in a Venetian canal.

But she knew she had to go to the ball. And she needed to return the one costume and get the other. And, of course, she had to go to Tiff's for drinks. She would ruin everything for Tiff if she didn't.

"Sure. Great. Let's go."

"Don't you need to get the vinyl costume?"

"Yes."

She walked back into the room to get the costume that was hanging by the window on a lamp stand. When she turned around, he was just inside her door.

She had invited him in last night.

Yes, and it was day, and she was alive and well.

She carried the costume, slipped her handbag over her arm.

A killer could be charming, attractive in appearance and manner . . .

Jordan hurried out into the hall, eager to reach the lobby and the flood of people there.

Tonight, the Danieli would hold its own ball in celebration of Carnevale.

She wished she were just staying here, attending this
ball instead of Anna Maria's.

Not fair.

Anna Maria had been wonderful to her; everyone
in the shop had been wonderful. They had sympathized with her when the rest of Venice had been
laughing at her. Lynn had promised good-humored,
beautiful entertainment. She had looked forward to
the ball, and she was going to enjoy it.

Even if her footsteps were dogged by this . . .

Stranger.

"Is there a fire?" he asked.

"What?"

She had breezed through the lobby; they were
already out on the street.

He took the costume from her, throwing it over his
shoulder. "You walk exceptionally fast, for such a small
person."

"You walk exceptionally slowly, for a giant."

"Why are you afraid of me?"

"Because you either lie or evade all my questions."

"I've answered your questions. My name is Ragnor
Wulfsson. I'm originally from Norway. I deal in antiques."

"And you loathe the contessa, but you were with
her in the Square. In a very friendly manner, according
to Raphael. What is it between you two?"

"There is nothing between us. I met her before—
and we are definitely antagonistic."

"Where did you meet her?"

"Scotland, years ago. We are natural enemies. Is
that enough?"

"No."

"It will have to do for now. And if you distrust me so very much, why are you with me?"

"Because I can't seem to shake you."

He didn't reply. His long strides were now passing hers, and she was puffing somewhat to keep up with him. They reached the Arte della Anna Maria shop. Lynn was outside, smoking.

"Buon giorno!" she cried happily, stamping out her cigarette and greeting them both with the customary kisses. "We were growing worried. Afraid you had decided not to come to the ball!"

"I'd never miss Anna Maria's ball," Jordan assured her.

"Come in, come in, both your costumes are ready!"

In the shop, Raphael left a slender woman to study a row of costumes and hurried to Jordan, his enthusiasm at seeing her very warming. He kissed her, fussed over her, greeted Ragnor, and relieved him of the vinyl costume. He had Jordan's costume ready for her, but ushered her into a corner to look at masks. "You heard about the head?" he asked.

She nodded. "Yes."

"In Venice! At Carnevale." He was indignant that such a crime should mar the beauty of his city, and the occasion. "But it must *not* worry you. No one knows where it might have come from—the police are on it. They are really very good here. We are hard on criminals. You have seen the officers with the automatic weapons, yes?"

"Yes, Raphael."

"You must still love Venice."

"I do."

Raphael sighed, smoothing the ostrich feather on

the mask. He glanced over his shoulder at Ragnor. "But you have found a good friend. Big! It is good to walk the streets with such a friend. Mucho macho. That's Spanish—"

"I know."

"For a very manly man."

Jordan laughed. "Or chauvinist," she mused.

"Perdoni?

"Nothing, Raphael, nothing. Hey, if I ever want to read the Italian paper, will you help me?"

"Of course. I will help you with anything. After today, our ball is over, we collapse, and then we are like free people again. I would love to spend time with you, help you read Italian."

"Thanks." She kissed him on the cheek. "What will you be tonight?"

He grinned. "Something very flamboyant. You'll have to wait and see."

Ragnor had been deep in conversation with Anna Maria. As Raphael walked Jordan to the entrance, apologizing that he must get to other customers, the door opened, and Cindy and Jared entered. Cindy looked tired. Wan.

"Hey!" Jordan greeted her cousin-in-law.

Cindy's face lit up with a smile. "Here you are. I was worried about you."

"You shouldn't have been."

Cindy glanced at Ragnor. "No, I guess not." She seemed pleased. Jared didn't. Anna Maria was coming forward to greet Cindy. Jared came over to Jordan, whispering to her.

"Aren't you spending too much time with this guy? We don't know anything about him."

"We were walking in the same direction," Jordan told him.

"Where have you been all day?"

"In my room, working."

That seemed to satisfy him. She wanted to believe that Jared was acting the part of the protective older brother today; she sensed it was more than that.

Anna Maria called to Jared, who stepped forward, dutifully kissing her cheeks, and responding with pleasure to something she said. Cindy stepped back to Jordan, smiling then with wicked delight. "You go, girl! He's a hunk. If it weren't for Jared, I'd be tempted. Oh, hell, I adore Jared, and I'm tempted!"

"Cindy, it's not—"

"His eyes are never off you!"

"How can you tell, behind those glasses?"

Cindy giggled. "I can tell."

"There's nothing going on—"

"There should be! Steven has been dead a long time now," she added softly.

"Tiff has a thing for him. That's why she planned that little cocktail party tonight."

"Are you sure we're invited?" Cindy asked. "I haven't heard a word from Tiff."

"We're all definitely invited, though I admit, I'm surprised she hasn't called."

"Girls, are you ready?" Jared asked, turning toward them.

"I didn't even get my costume," Cindy said.

"I have it," Jared told her, glancing at his watch. "If we're planning on getting to Tiff's and then the ball . . . it's time to make tracks."

"Yes, if we're to change and be ready," Cindy said.

"We'll see you at the ball. What are you going as, Anna Maria?"

"The hostess," Anna Maria said.

"I'll be someone you'll never expect," Lynn volunteered.

"Raphael?" Cindy asked.

He drew his finger to his lips, smiling mischievously.

"He'll be flamboyant," Jordan volunteered for him.

"Til later," Ragnor said, kissing Anna Maria goodbye. He started out the shop first. Jordan started to follow. Jared caught her arm.

"Why are you going with him?"

She pulled her arm back. "Honestly, Jared, we're going to the same place. And by the way, did you hear that they pulled a head out of the canal? Not a fish head, Jared, a human head."

He sighed with exasperation. "Yes, I heard. That must mean there are bodies by the truckload floating in the water, all from the contessa's."

"It means that someone was killed—and that his head was *severed.*"

"Hey, guys, you're blocking the door," Cindy warned.

Jordan moved ahead, catching up with Ragnor, who had both their costumes under his arm.

She slipped her hand around his free elbow. He looked down at her. She saw a brow arch behind his glasses, but an annoying smile was on his face, so she knew that he was aware she was merely irritated with her cousin.

"Be careful of him," Ragnor whispered.

"He's my cousin. I adore him. He's not a stranger."

"There can be no one stranger than a person you think you really know," Ragnor said.

"Oh, my God! Quit being so cryptic!" she implored.

He was silent as they walked along, several yards ahead of Cindy and Jared. Then, after a while. he startled her when he spoke.

"She doesn't look well."

"What?"

"Cindy. She looks very tired and pale."

"Naturally, she's tired. Everyone parties all night."

Again they walked in silence. Nearing the hotel, they went by the shop with the mannequin in the window that had twice seemed to look at her with Steven's face.

She hadn't realized that she had stopped, staring at it again. It was just a mannequin.

"What is it?" Ragnor queried.

"Nothing." She looked up at him. It was dark now, and he had shed his sunglasses at last. She was surprised by the intensity of his stare. "Nothing," she repeated. "Nothing at all. I like that outfit."

"And you say that I lie!" he told her softly.

"We have to hurry if we're to make Tiff's. Now, Mr. Wulfsson, *there's* a woman who is fond of you."

"She is a pleasant person."

Jordan smiled. She liked Tiff very much herself; there was just something about her. But she wasn't sure that "pleasant" was a word she'd use to describe her.

"I believe she finds you far more intriguing than merely pleasant."

He paused, gazing at her. "Perhaps the right person—under ninety—will come along for her. You knew absolutely nothing about her cocktail party tonight until I told you about it, did you?"

"I wasn't surprised. I told you, I saw you two together."

"We weren't together."

"She wants you to visit her palazzo."

"I've seen her palazzo."

"Okay, so she wants you to see her palazzo with her in it."

He didn't reply as they kept walking. Nearing the Danieli, he asked her, "And you have no interest in me . . . yourself?"

Jordan laughed, actually enjoying the conversation. *Yes, maybe once she could have been. If she had met him under different circumstances. If she didn't dream of Steven, if . . .*

"I don't trust you," she said.

"But you *have* to trust me."

"Then somewhere along the line, you'll have to give me a reason to do so."

They'd reached the hotel. Jordan went through the revolving door. As she asked for her key, Jared was close behind her. "We'll have to meet in the lobby in about thirty minutes. This thing at Tiff's is going to be a pain."

She turned and looked at him. "Jared, you don't have to go. I do. She's become a friend."

"Oh, good."

"Hey, she's been your client, throwing lots of money your way."

"She's still not the best social companion."

"She's blunt and honest and I like her. But I won't be angry if you don't go."

"Oh, no. Cindy and I will go." He glanced over his shoulder where Cindy and Ragnor were talking. She thought that his jaw clenched, and she realized that

Jared wasn't as concerned for her as he was hostile to Ragnor.

"Okay, the lobby in thirty minutes."

She took her costume from Ragnor, politely thanked him for carrying it, and hurried up the stairs. Apparently, Cindy, who did like Ragnor, was making sure that he also knew they were to meet in the lobby in thirty minutes.

Jordan barely had time to jump in and out of the shower and dress. But the fantasy costume was easy, and it came with a bejewelled tiara-like headpiece and mask. She ran a brush through her hair before donning it, touched her cheeks with glitter makeup, and was ready. She started for the door, then hesitated.

The maid had put her reading copy of the detective's vampire book on the desk, next to her laptop. She walked over to it and flipped to the copyright page. The book was being published by something called DeMac Publishing, New Orleans. There was an E-mail address for inquiries. Dropping her little jeweled purse, she pulled out her chair and typed out a quick E-mail to the author, introducing herself briefly and telling him she'd greatly appreciate a chance to talk to him, or chat over the Internet.

Satisfied, she sent the E-mail, then jumped up to meet the others in the lobby.

Ragnor was in a typical black cape and top hat; he was appearing in Edwardian fashion this evening. Cindy was gorgeous in an elaborate Elizabethan costume and Jared was once again in dottore adornment.

"I'm pretty sure I know the way," Jordan told the others. "But maybe I should get the directions again—"

"I know where her palazzo is," Ragnor said.

"Then you should lead the way," Cindy said and yawned. "My lord! All these parties! I'm sleeping half the day away, and I'm still exhausted."

It was good that despite being tired, Cindy seemed to be cheerful. Jared seemed tense; he kept his mask on as they walked. Ragnor was quiet, yet watchful, Jordan thought, and unerringly polite and courteous to Cindy.

They continued to talk, discussing the Bridge of Sighs and the prisoners who knew they were doomed once they crossed it, and famous residents of the prisons, such as Casanova.

Jordan kept on ahead, suddenly anxious to reach Tiff's. But when they arrived, and she tried the big brass knocker, no one answered.

Jared pounded on the door as well. They all stood awkwardly in the street.

"Well, great, she's invited us all over, and she isn't here. Are you sure this is the right time and the right night?" Jared said to Jordan.

"Before Anna Maria's party," Ragnor said. "That could be no other time or night."

Jared pounded again. They waited.

"Well this is ridiculous!" Jared said.

"I'm worried about her," Jordan said.

Worried about her!" Jared exclaimed. "She made us walk through half of Venice, and now she isn't here!"

"But don't you see, that's the point! She really wanted us over," Jordan argued. She pounded the door again, then stood back in the calle, looking upward. "Tiff!"

"Jordan, if she can't hear those brass knockers

pounding, she can't hear you calling," Jared said. He glanced at his watch. "We'll give her five minutes."

They remained awkwardly at the entry to the palazzo.

"I think we should call the police," Jordan said.

"The police!" Jared scoffed. "Because she forgot she invited us to a cocktail party?"

"She didn't forget; I know it," Jordan argued.

"Try the door," Cindy said.

Jared did so. "Locked. Bolted tight."

"I just know that she wouldn't have forgotten," Jordan said.

"But you said that you hadn't heard from her today," Cindy reminded her.

"And I arranged for a lot of the tickets for Anna Maria's party," Jared said. "I can't show up too late. If she hasn't even let us in yet . . ."

"Look," Ragnor said, "why don't you three go on ahead to Anna Maria's? I'll wait around here for a while and see if she does show up."

"I think I should stay, too," Jordan said.

Now, even Ragnor seemed impatient with her. "Go on, Jordan. I'll give Tiff a few minutes, then I'll be right behind you."

Jordan shrugged. Well, if Tiff did return in the next few minutes, she'd be elated to find Ragnor waiting there for her—alone.

She should happily walk off.

But something didn't *feel* right.

"I'll be here," Ragnor said firmly.

"All right," Jordan said at last.

She turned and started away with Jared and Cindy. Looking back, she saw that he did remain, a tall, caped figure, arms crossed over his chest, as if standing sentinel.

"Jordan, come on," Jared said.

She stumbled; he caught her arm. They headed through narrow streets to catch a vaporetto to Anna Maria's ball.

Ragnor watched them go.

He waited until he was certain they had rounded the corner. Then he tested the lock again. The doors were firmly bolted. He looked around the square.

Darkness, shadows. No amblers passing through.

Then he entered the palazzo.

The foyer was empty. There was no sign of a struggle. Marble floors gleamed. "Tiff!" he said, calling the woman's name.

He walked up the stairs, to the balcony, through the rooms. He came to the master suite. Nothing appeared to be amiss. The great bed was neatly made in its silken splendor. He turned and started to leave, but then, the faintest hint of an odor teased his senses.

Blood.

He came to the bed, stared at the silk.

There, the tiniest drop.

Perhaps Nari hadn't meant to, but she had left her calling card.

"Marisa, come on!"

Marisa Kosolovich turned her head to see that her friends, Josef, Ari and Lizabet, were waiting for her.

She tossed back the rich wealth of her auburn hair, impatiently. They'd been standing at the bar at the trattoria, and while her friends had spent some of their precious money on their own espressos, she had managed to get hers bought for her by the tall Italian man in the handsome suit. He wasn't young, but he wasn't old, somewhere between thirty and forty. He was very appealing, a businessman with bright hazel eyes and a quick smile. She'd chatted about her arrival with her friends—making it sound as if they had come by plane and were young people seeing the world, rather than a group from a war-torn nation on a bus that was now parked near the train station. They were nearly broke, sleeping on the bus that had brought them here. They were willing to come with no accommodations and food from home, just so that they might see the sights and sounds of Venice at Carnevale.

She sighed. The others seemed fine with their situation. She was not. She'd actually planned on finding some Americans—they usually had the most money to spend and were easily influenced by any foreign accent. She liked Americans, and she really wanted to get to America. When the soldiers had come to her village to dole out food, they had all been taken with her. She'd developed the plan then to marry and get away, but the troops hadn't stayed long enough for her to get to know any of the men. They had told her, though, that she was beautiful. They had said it with their eyes as well as their words.

And more than anything, she wanted to get away.

Carnevale was always full of foreigners—lots of them American. She had been certain that in the two nights the bus stayed in Venice she could find the right person.

She had chosen the trattoria for their splurge, and there hadn't been a single American in it. But the

Italian had been cute and kind, buying her an espresso and offering her something to eat. She'd accepted the espresso but demurred on the food, though God knew why, she was hungry enough. She didn't want to *look* hungry, that must be it. And she didn't want to look like a woman who would balloon into someone as round as a tomato in a few years.

Lizabet was at the door, looking stern. Ari just looked impatient. Josef was concerned.

They weren't together as couples, just friends. They came from the same village. Or what was left of it.

She lifted a finger, ready to swing back into conversation with the tall Italian businessman. But, to her disappointment, he had turned to his friends. Some sporting event had come on the television over the bar, and his back was actually to her.

"Marisa! The music starts in the square any minute!" Josef announced. Tall, skinny and awkward, Josef had gone the last few years without enough to eat.

She left the bar and came to the door. "Marisa, you mustn't just attach yourself to people like that. They will get the wrong idea."

Ari and Lizabet were already walking ahead. "And what would the wrong idea be, Josef?" she asked.

"That you are easy, that we are easy—that we are left with no pride, no sense of self-worth."

"That would be a *wrong* idea?" she queried.

"Our home has been through a great deal. We should have a stronger character," he admonished.

"Our home is a hellhole, and soldiers will come again and again. Bombs will fall."

Josef shook his head. "No, there is peace now. And we will rebuild."

"You will rebuild. I'm not going home."

Josef looked at her with surprise. "What do you mean?"

"I'm staying in Venice."

"You cannot stay in Venice. You don't have papers. You don't speak Italian!"

"I'll learn."

"And what will you do?"

"Get by."

"How?"

"I'll make friends."

"You'll be a prostitute."

"I'll make *friends,*" she hissed to him. "Look, Josef, you tell me all the time that I am beautiful. I will manage on that."

"To me you are beautiful. There are scores of beautiful young women. To me, you are special. To others . . ."

"To others—what?"

"You are . . . too loose."

"I'll be what I need to be!" she said angrily. "I am attractive only to you, eh?"

She walked on ahead, angrily. She passed Lizabet and Ari. "Hey!" Ari called, "now you're in such a hurry?"

She was dressed as a harem girl—the best outfit she could piece together from old scraps of clothing, but she was proud that she looked much better in rags than many of the rich tourists in Venice looked in their expensive hand-made or rented costumes.

"You intend to act like shy little refugee school-children!" she informed them. "I came to Venice to have fun."

"She came to stay," Josef called out in a sulky tone.

"She is going to meet a rich American, and he is going to take her away."

"Josef says that I am special only to him," she pouted.

"We are all only special to our friends!" Lizabet told her with a troubled frown. Lizabet was very religious. She had prayed on the floor of the bus for what had seemed like hours last night before finding her seat to sleep in cramped discomfort.

Marisa walked on ahead of her friends. Masked and costumed characters paused to bow to her; she bowed playfully in return. One man, tall and sleek, though he was costumed and in a mask that covered most of his face, did more than bow. He took her hand. Bent low over it, he kissed her. He spoke to her. In Italian. His voice was deep and pleasant.

"Beautiful," he said in English.

"Grazie!" she told him.

"And where are you going?"

"To the square, to listen to music."

"Ah, perhaps I will find you again, cara mia."

He walked by. Josef, Ari, and Lizabet reached her. "There, you see!" she told them.

"Can we please get to the music?" Lizabet asked. "We all know that you are beautiful, and you will go places."

"Or stay in Venice," Josef repeated acidly.

Josef felt more for her than she had realized, Marisa thought, but Josef had nothing and would go nowhere. If she was foolish enough to love Josef, she would have a child each year and grow as fat as a house and spend her life in her little village doing laundry and baking bread and washing dishes. She was sorry if she had hurt him, but she could see what he could not. There would always be war. Soldiers would come again, and men would go out and fight, and the villagers would be weak-willed and defenseless, able to do nothing as stronger enemies came and dragged them out, raped their wives, and burned their houses.

"I am sorry, Josef," she said, under her breath.

They hadn't gone much farther when Josef determined that they had made a wrong turn. The stream of human traffic was no longer with them. "We must go back."

"Do you have the map?" Ari asked.

As they pulled out the map, Marisa looked around the street. It was very dark here. The waters of the canal beyond them were black in the night. The few lights in the streets created blacker shadows against black streets and walls.

"This way," Ari said.

"No, I think, look here . . ." Lizabet told them.

Marisa wasn't paying attention. As her eyes adjusted to the shadows, she saw a man ahead, going up the steps of a building. He was wearing a cape and mask. She felt her heart pounding. Was it the same man who had kissed her hand?

As she stared at him, he turned. He drew a finger to his lips—well, as close to his lips as the mask would allow. Then he beckoned to her.

And disappeared behind a door.

"I'm going this way," she said.

"Marisa, stay with us!" Josef told her.

"I cannot stay with you; I will get nowhere!"

"Well," Ari said, "we are following that bridge, there, and going on to the square. When you get tired of the darkness, follow us!"

Even Josef turned his back on her. Marisa was glad.

The moment they started walking, she flew to the shadows against the wall and flattened herself there.

She waited until she could no longer hear the echo of their footsteps on the calle. Then she ran up the steps.

The door was ajar. She pushed it open. "Hello?"

It was shadowy and dark within, but the room was lit by candles here and there.

She stepped in, taking care to leave the door ajar, and started walking along a central aisle between pillars.

"Hello? Ciao?" she called, her voice softening as it seemed to ricochet around the room. She kept walking in.

It was a church, she thought, with a bit of awe. But a church like no other. There were no longer any pews in it, and as she neared the altar, she saw that there was no cross above it. There were paintings though. One very strange painting, of an angel ripping into and consuming lambs, was hung above the altar, where the cross should have been. She looked around. There were side chapels, as in most churches. They were dark and shadowy, some curtained, some open. She blinked. In the candlelight, dark shapes seemed to flit from chapel to chapel.

Was he playing games with her?

"I know you're here!" she called, walking to the left side, through chapel after chapel. Candles burned. Strange black cloth draped the altars.

She paused, thinking she heard whispers, or hisses. Wings, fluttering around her. Footfalls across the stone floor.

"I won't play forever, you know!" she said.

She crossed the nave and started along the right

wall of chapels, looked up at the last painting above the black-clad altar. A figure with a crown of thorns sat holding a handful of severed heads.

She was suddenly cold in her harem outfit.

A sound fluttered from across the room again.

"Hello, where are you?" she called. Her voice was stronger. Angry. And a bit too tremulous. "This isn't funny, if you want me to stay, show yourself."

Candles on the altar flickered and wavered. There was a sudden, sweeping hiss of movement near her, very near her. It seemed to brush her hair.

Slowly, she began to back away.

At first, she barely heard the creaking noise. It was the sound of a door. Moving slowly. The sound was somehow hideous in this shadowy, silent place. She turned, and the sound registered. It was indeed a door. The door to the strange church.

Closing.

Just as she started racing for it, it slammed with a vengeance.

She ran for the door, throwing herself against it. She pounded, slammed, swore, and pounded some more.

Finally, she exhausted herself.

She stared back at the altar. "This isn't funny at all. I will go to the police. The polizia, do you hear me!" Forcing her courage, she walked back toward the altar. "I am leaving here, now, do you understand? Do you understand!"

She called out, facing the altar.

Then . . .

It seemed as if ice touched her. As if a finger of cold stretched across the room, finding her nape, traced the line of her spine.

She spun around, and in surprise, she screamed aloud.

There he was. The figure in the dark cloak and the strange mask. She stared at him, her throat going dry.

For once, she had nothing to say.

He walked to her slowly. Very slowly. She could see his eyes. They were not so beautiful now, but she couldn't draw her gaze from him.

He reached her. He touched the front hooks on the bodice of her harem costume. She wanted to tell him no. She couldn't speak, and she couldn't draw her eyes from his. He slid his hands beneath the fabric on her shoulders, and the bodice fell to the floor with a strange whisper.

He stepped back.

"Beautiful," he acknowledged.

Then he lifted his hands, as if in supplication to heaven. "My children . . . I bring you beauty!" he said.

She still couldn't draw her eyes from his. She heard again the strange, whispered, rustling sound. A breeze, a hiss, blowing by her, lifting her hair . . .

And then the shadows moved.

And descended.

She was aware, in one split second, that she should have gone home. She should have married Josef, raised a dozen children, gotten fat, and baked bread.

She felt the first touch.

She started to scream . . .

And scream.

And as she was lifted to the altar, she realized that she had spoken the truth.

She was staying in Venice.

CHAPTER 11

By the time they reached the palazzo Anna Maria had rented for her ball, the festivities had already begun.

They were greeted at their water taxi by costumed hosts who helped them to the dock, as they neared the grand entrance, trumpets announced them.

They entered a spacious hall already crowded with guests in magnificent masks and costumes. People milled and talked, helping themselves to artistic little hors d'oeuvres at side tables, and Bellinis and champagne passed by servers in traditional black serving attire.

From the moment they came in, Jared was greeted by various business acquaintances. He made many introductions, then got into a conversation about arrangements for a group of grad school artists who wanted to come to Venice the following year.

Cindy suggested they move off and help themselves to hors d'oeuvres.

"Hey! Earth to Jordan. Shall we get something to munch on?"

"Um. I was looking for Tiff."

"She'll show up," Cindy said. "Jordan, honestly, I like Tiff. She's brash; she's had a past tarnished to pure rust, but she's fun. Still, Jared has made travel arrangements for her for years, and she changes her mind like the wind. Don't let her ruin your evening."

Jordan didn't respond to that. Cindy didn't understand that Ragnor Wulfsson was an object of desire to Tiff. But then, Ragnor had stayed behind, there wasn't anything she could do, and the party was fun and entertaining. On the dais at the foot of the double stairway, harem girls were dancing to flute music. Throughout the crowd, harlequins were practicing bits of magic. Everyone was dressed to the teeth; costumes were bejeweled as she'd never seen before, there were gladiators, wood nymphs, Edwardians, knights and damsels. On the tables, there were ice sculptures, flower arrangements, shining silver coffee urns. The beauty and activity were almost too much to take in.

"Those little pastry puffs are as good as they look," Cindy said between bites. "And I'm starving."

Jordan stared at Cindy. She was wearing a half mask, plumed hat, and Regency dress. With her sandy blond hair and tall stature, she was dazzling, but beneath the mask, she looked a little pale. She must really need to eat, Jordan thought.

"Lead me to the table," she said.

As they were sampling the food, they were suddenly approached by an elegant Southern belle with a

cinched waist, incredible spill of petticoats, and beautifully curled hair.

"Ciao!"

"Ciao!" Jordan replied, staring at the woman.

"Ciao," Cindy said politely.

They both waited expectantly. The belle burst into
pleased laughter. "It's me!"

"Raphael!" Jordan murmured.

He spun before them. "Am I not magnificent!"

"Lord, yes!" Cindy said.

He batted his lashes. Jordan wondered how he had
managed the false eyelashes without so much as a hint
of glue showing.

"You're gorgeous," Jordan told him.

"Grazie, grazie," Raphael demurred. "And you,
ladies! You're lovely."

"Thank you," Cindy said.

"Everyone here is spectacular," Jordan said. "Well,
few are anywhere near as spectacular as you," she
teased. "Raphael, have you seen Tiff Henley yet?"

"No, I have not seen her—not that I *know* of any
way. But if you had seen me and I hadn't spoken to
you, would you know that you had seen me?"

"Good point," Cindy said.

"She'll be along," Raphael said, and frowned.
"Were you to meet her here?"

"No, no, but she had invited us to a cocktail party
before the ball, and when we got there, she wasn't
home."

Raphael waved a hand in the air, indicating that
Tiff could be flighty. "She probably forgot that she
invited you."

Trumpets sounded again.

"Ah! There we are," Raphael said. "That is the announcement that we are to go up the stairs and take our places. Ladies?''

"You two go ahead," Cindy said. "I'm going to find my husband."

Raphael linked arms with Jordan, smiling at her. "The fantasy costume is just right! You are sparkling and glorious, like a mythical siren."

"Thanks. But, you totally outdo me."

He laughed with pleasure. "We shall be the most beautiful, together. I made sure that I am seated at your table. Anna Maria wanted to put you, Jared and Cindy with all his business people, but I could not do that to you."

"Thanks."

"I'm much more fun."

"I believe you."

"And I can dance. All the men will be trying to cut in on both of us. Depending on how cute they are, we'll let them cut in."

"Absolutely. Who else is at our table?"

"Lynn—she helped me convince Anna Maria that you could not be left with the chairman of the dental association's travel planner, or the agent for the American bankers group. His wife is . . . well, she would be like sitting with a battleship, you know? She is gray and solid. I've yet to see her smile. In fact, I think she came as Brunhilda."

"She could be a very nice lady."

He arched a brow with a secret smile. "I can still give up my place at the table."

"Never mind. Who else is with us?"

"There are ten at each table. At ours, Jared and Cindy, Lynn and I, a cookbook author and her husband, an English artist and his wife, and my friend, the policeman, Roberto Capo. You do like him, yes?"

She liked Roberto Capo just fine. He hadn't seemed to think that she was crazy.

And she could ask him about the head that had been found in a canal.

"What about Tiff?"

"Oh, she was seated with other friends long ago. But we'll look for her later, if that will make you happy."

"And Ragnor?"

"He speaks so many languages so well—he has been seated with a mix of German and Scandinavian couples. In the north," he explained, "most people do speak English. Where else can you go but Sweden to speak Swedish, eh? Still, Anna Maria tries very hard to see that everyone will have dinner companions with whom they can talk."

"Where will she be sitting?"

"Anna Maria does not sit—she flits!" Raphael explained. He rolled his eyes. She is the hostess, and so she moves about all night, and makes sure that everyone enjoys the ball—of course, she is a slave driver until we get here. But she asks nothing that she doesn't give. She is wonderful."

"Beyond a doubt," Jordan agreed.

At the top of the stairs, they were greeted by hosts dressed as Swiss Guards. They were led into one of the large ballrooms off the foyer. More buffet tables were filled with all manner of delicacies. At the end of the room, on a dais, a group played chamber music.

"Here we are!" Raphael said, indicating their table. Roberto Capo and two other couples were already seated. The men stood as Raphael made introductions. The English artist was Peter Smith; his wife was Sherry.

The American author of cookbooks was Mary Winston; her husband was Fred. They were both round and cheery, as if they truly enjoyed Mary's recipes. Jordan didn't remember her name; she hoped that if she had ever reviewed one of the woman's books, her words had been kind.

"And of course, Roberto," Raphael ended his introductions with a flourish.

"Of course, how are you?" Jordan asked.

"Delighted to see you," he said.

"Il piacere è mio," she told him, glad that, "the pleasure is mine" was one phrase she knew in Italian quite well.

He smiled; she took the seat next to his.

Lynn arrived then, as a matador, complete with dark mustache, red cape, and bull-slaying sword.

"Plastic, I'm afraid!" she explained, when it seemed her sword might pierce Mary Winston's Martha Washington skirts.

Jared and Cindy arrived, and the introductions went around the table again. Jordan admired Anna Maria's social talents as she saw how quickly and easily they all fell into conversation. At times, she thought, Roberto Capo wasn't quite following everything that was said, but Raphael paused now and then to make a quick explanation in Italian. Waiters arrived to fill their wineglasses and they all trooped to the buffet table. "My name was Astrella before I married," Mary Winston told Jordan as they stood in the line. "I do adore Italian food. My next book is on Tuscan cuisine. Perhaps you'd review it for your newspapers?"

"I'd be delighted."

"My publishing house is small," Mary said with a

sigh, "and your reviews are so popular in syndication, they've not dared send you anything yet. Thank you."

"Thank you. I didn't know I was so popular."

"Oh, have you tried this dish yet? In English, it's cuttlefish—"

"Thanks. I have tried it," Jordan said. "I think I'll have the swordfish."

As conversations took off at dinner, Jordan was grateful to be next to Roberto Capo. She spoke to him quietly. "I heard they found a severed head."

Roberto looked distressed. "You must not worry—"

"I'm not worrying."

"You . . . you think that you were right? That at the contessa's . . ."

"I'm not saying that. It's just curious. Have they found out who the head belonged to? Have they—" She broke off. He was looking at her, frowning. She realized that she was speaking too quickly.

But Raphael had heard her. He translated quietly, glancing at the others at the table, aware that Jordan wouldn't want Jared to know what they were talking about.

Roberto shook his head and replied in Italian to Raphael.

"The head is still with forensics. They haven't found the rest of the body, and they have no missing persons report with which to make a comparison. They will do an artist's reconstruction and send the picture around Europe."

Jordan was disappointed; she hadn't learned anything new.

"I understand your concern," Roberto said.

Jordan nodded. Jared was glancing her way suspiciously. As he turned his head she noticed that his features appeared lean and sharp. Maybe she had caused Jared a lot more trouble than she was willing to admit. Maybe that explained Cindy's pallor and fatigue.

Still, she hadn't been wrong. Either the contessa had hosted a group of murderous monsters, or her sense of humor and entertainment were warped beyond measure.

Dessert and coffee were served, and more activities for the guests were announced. On the ground floor, a rock band would be playing, while there would be ballroom dancing on the second floor. Tarot card readings were in the entry to the second floor ball-room. Palm readers would be there as well. Jugglers and magicians would travel to both levels. More coffee, sweets, and after-dinner liqueurs would be available at all the banquet tables. The 'Pleasure Palace,' for those who dared, would be in the back room of the second level.

"Shall we dance?" Raphael inquired immediately.

"I've never been asked by such a charming belle," Jordan assured him.

Raphael wanted the fast action on the ground floor, but as he started to lead her down, Jordan made him pause. "Where was Tiff supposed to be?"

"Table seven, in the room where they'll be setting up the Pleasure Palace. I think she wanted to make several trips," he said with a grin.

They walked over to table seven; it was already empty. It appeared, however, that someone had been seated at every chair.

Raphael shrugged. "You see why we don't worry so much about Tiff? Don't be angry; enjoy your night."

"Wait. Where was Ragnor supposed to be?"

"Table eighteen—the next flight up." He groaned. "Okay, we'll look."

But upstairs, the tables had emptied as well.

"Maybe they both decided to get lucky," Raphael said. "Give them no more thought."

Downstairs, they danced. As Raphael had expected, they were often cut in on. A dottore came and danced with Jordan. She was certain at first that it was Jared, but as she talked, and he failed to respond, she realized it wasn't he. He thanked her in Italian for the dance.

There had been something so familiar about him . . .

But as she was claimed by a short Julius Caesar, she noted that there were at least five dottores in the room. All of them seemed to be about the same height.

Around midnight, Raphael excused himself to dance with Anna Maria. This time, she was partnered by a handsome Basque jai alai player who had fun showing her the immense muscle in his right arm, and the smaller muscle in his left. She thought at first that he was explaining his costume, he wasn't. The game had given him two definitely different-sized arms.

As the dance ended, Jordan thanked him and hurried after Anna Maria and Raphael. Anna Maria, resplendent as Mary, Queen of Scots, kissed her cheeks. Jordan told her that the party was wonderful, then asked about Tiff.

She gave her the same reply Raphael had given earlier. "She must be very well costumed; I have not seen her." She frowned. "I believe all the tables wound up full, but then, though people are seated, many, many people here have known one another for years, and they . . ."

"Table hop," Raphael said.

"Table hop. Right."

"Let's have our cards read!" Raphael said.

"I don't know . . ." Jordan murmured.

But the next thing she knew, she was upstairs, watching as an Italian woman spread out her cards. She indicated that Jordan was to touch them. When she turned the cards over, she shook her head and shuffled them again. This time, Jordan gave close attention to what appeared. She saw the Grim Reaper before the woman could collect the cards.

"That was death, right?" Jordan insisted of Raphael.

"It can mean many things, she says."

The tarot reader spoke quickly and earnestly in Italian. She looked at Jordan as if she were about to whip out a cross and put it between them to ward her off.

"Raphael . . ."

"She says that you must watch out for the shadows. And take the gravest care at deep midnight."

"She is warning me of death."

"No, the card may mean many things."

"But death is one—"

"Jordan, watch out for the shadows. And deep midnight."

"What the hell is deep midnight?"

"The true dead of night. When all light has faded. When shadows fall even in darkness. Let's dance again. This was not good."

Downstairs, Roberto Capo was the first one to cut in on her. As they danced, he asked her if she was happy, if she was having fun.

"Yes, very much so."

"You look so worried."

"I went to a friend's house tonight and she wasn't

there. And she isn't here." She made certain to speak slowly. "Tiff Henley. Do you know her?"

He shook his head. "When did you see her . . . last time?"

"Yesterday."

"Then the head—it is not hers."

"Oh, no, of course not. I'm just worried."

"Let me know if you do not find her. And if you . . . if you find out anything else."

"About the contessa?"

He shrugged. "The contessa . . . this man who was there as well. The wolf?"

She wondered what expression she gave, or what movement she made that caused him to say next, "You have seen the man again?"

"No," she said. Was it a lie? She was certain that Ragnor . . .

"I am there. At the station. Come and see me if you are frightened. Worried. Concerned. If your friend does not appear."

"Thank you," Jordan said.

A moment later, Raphael was sweeping down on her again. "The Pleasure Palace! We must go do the Pleasure Palace."

"What exactly do they do?" she asked.

"They strip off your clothing, bathe you with oil and honey, and ravish you mercilessly!" he said.

"Maybe I'll skip it."

He sighed. "Don't be silly. They bathe your hands in hot oils and slip cold sweet grapes between your lips. It's fun; it's nice."

He wasn't going to let up. "If I wind up ravished mercilessly, I'll never forgive you," she told him.

"If they start to ravish me mercilessly, and you *stop*

them, *I'll* never forgive *you!*" he replied. "Come, come, we'll have fun."

Apparently, many people shared that view. The lines were long—one on either side of a brilliantly colored harem-like tent set up in the rear of the room. It appeared that they were mixing couples, taking one person at a time from each side of the line. A woman dressed as Marie Antoinette appeared with a man costumed as Julius Caesar. They were both laughing.

"Viene, viene! Come, come!" beckoned one of the girls in a harem costume. She held open the festooned flap to the tent.

Raphael gave Jordan a little push.

She stepped forward and into the tent.

The flap fell, and instantly, she felt as if she had stepped into a black pit.

For a moment, there was nothing. The darkness seemed overwhelming.

She closed her eyes for a moment, thinking that it would help her adjust to the total darkness. She had the strangest feeling of being pulled forward.

Come to me.

She wondered if she had heard the words, or imagined them. There was a scent in the tent; probably some kind of an incense, and yet . . .

Sandalwood, she thought. It reminded her of Steven. So much was reminding her of Steven lately. It was, she reflected ruefully, the intense attraction she was feeling for another man. Steven was gone, lost to her. It was all right to move on.

Come to me.

The words were so strongly set into her mind that she nearly walked forward. But she did not; the darkness was suddenly overwhelming. Fear bubbled in her, an almost uncontrollable panic. Something was going to jump out at her, rush her, sweep her into something horrible.

She could feel it, sense it, nearly taste it, touch it . . .

There was a very gentle touch on her hand. She almost screamed aloud. But she could see then, faintly. The harem girl was wearing something in her head-band that glowed in the dark.

The girl took her right hand. Another person reached for her left hand. She was drawn a step deeper into the tent, and then, though she didn't touch any-one, she was aware that she was standing in front of another person. She felt the rays of warmth that seemed to surround her.

Her fear subsided. The strangest sense of total well-being stilled her rising panic.

Her palms were brought upward. Warm oil was poured into them and rubbed gently into the flesh. Her hair was lifted. The warmth was rubbed into her nape. Something cool and exotic touched her lips.

A grape.

She obediently ate it.

She could hear the person opposite her breathing. A man, evidently; the figure was tall. The whisper of his breath held a sweet scent of wine. He exuded an aura of power, and that strength and masculinity apparently gave her the sense of calm and security that now enwrapped her.

Great! she thought briefly. This is someone's husband, for all I know!

The warmth he emitted touched her cheeks like a surge of sunlit air. A grape was pressed between her fingers, then she realized that they were being handed grapes to slip to one another. A grape touched her mouth again. She parted her lips and took it, marveling that the whole thing should have been rather silly, but that it wasn't. She brought her grape to her darkly shadowed partner's lips, and he too took in the fruit.

They were closer than they had been. She didn't remember being so close.

The oils that had been worked in at her nape and her palms seemed to grow hotter. A whisper of deepening heat seemed to work its way into her. A languor stole over her; she could easily lean forward, find the hands that touched her, will them to work their magic . . .

Fingers pressed into her shoulders in a kneading massage. She felt the tension slip away, felt the stranger's breath, and a stealing ray of lightning sweep through her. She closed her eyes. She could sleep, she could curl up with a total stranger, she could feel a sweet and slow-burning fire that somehow came with the languor, but defied it. Knuckles brushed her throat, caressing softly. Her hands were drawn to the stranger, to his cheek, to the lapel of his jacket, down the fabric of the breast. Something came to her lips again. Wine. Warm, rich, fruity. Delicious. Then fingers again, on her shoulders, stroking her cheeks . . .

A chime sounded, startling her from the reverie which had laid claim to her. The harem girl with the glow-in-the-dark headdress took her hand again, leading her to the exit.

She stepped through the flap and was startled, then angry, to find Ragnor right in front of her, waiting to help her down the steps. She had taken his hand before even seeing him. What an idiot. She should have known, should have recognized his scent, the size of him, the height!

"You planned that—"

"Excuse me, we were in opposite lines! And you walked into the Pleasure Palace of your own volition."

"Jordan!" Raphael called, ready to slip beneath the flap of the tent. "Were you wildly ravished?"

"No!"

"Damn!" he said, just as the harem girl slipped beneath the flap.

Ragnor was openly amused.

"That was very rude," Jordan said.

"Why? You're not supposed to know who you're getting."

"But you did, didn't you?"

"Be glad I was here."

"Why?"

"Someone else might have ravished you. You were putty."

"*What?*"

"Putty. Jelly. Molding clay."

"Oh, really? I do beg your pardon!"

"I needed to be there for you. You were just . . . compelled."

"Compelled! When I walked in, I was—"

"You were what?" he demanded, frowning.

"Scared," she admitted. She left him standing by the tent and started across the room; Raphael would have to fend for himself when he came out. After all, he was Italian, and this was his shop's party.

But then she paused, looking back. Ragnor had been following her at a leisurely pace.

"Did you see Tiff?" she asked him. "Was she home—had she not heard us? Or gone out? Did she come here with you?"

He shook his head, his eyes suddenly guarded. "I'm sorry. I waited. I didn't see her."

"And you haven't seen her at the party?"

"No."

Before Jordan could question him further, Raphael rushed up to them, his turn in the Pleasure Palace complete. He put an arm around Jordan's waist and buried his head against her shoulder. Ugh! You two . . . you two got each other! And me . . . allora!"

"What happened? Were you ravished?"

"Nearly eaten alive by a four-hundred-pound Amazon! She giggled insufferably and put her fingers where they were not supposed to be put!"

"You wanted to be ravished," Jordan reminded him politely.

"Yes, but . . . one wants to be ravished by the right people."

"You take your chances in the Pleasure Palace," Ragnor said, then added, "Excuse me." He left them, and started toward the one open balcony where the smokers, and those who just needed some air, had gathered.

Jordan watched him go, nonplused. She'd been so angry to discover that he had been the one with her. Because again, she had felt that intense . . . beguilement. After the fear. The very real and horrible fear she had experienced at first.

Just by standing there, he had done something that had lulled her. *Maybe she should have remained afraid.*

But now had walked away. She felt at a loss.

And cold again, as if his warmth were seeping away.

"Let's get back to dancing," Raphael said.

On their way back through the second floor ballroom, Jordan noticed Cindy and Jared waltzing together. When they reached the ground floor, they stopped for espressos laced with liqueur.

There were at least three dottores on the dance floor.

They had barely begun when Roberto Capo cut in on Jordan. "My friend never showed up," she told him, shouting over the music. "I'm worried about her."

"You are certain that she isn't here—somewhere?"

"I'm not certain of anything, but she wasn't at her palazzo tonight, which was strange, very strange. Having that little party meant a lot to her. I'm worried, and you're the only one who listens to me."

She was exasperated, and probably speaking too quickly for him, but he seemed to understand her. "Come tomorrow to the station. To see me. *Me*, you understand?"

She nodded her thanks, then quickly fell silent. Over his shoulder, she could see a dottore approaching.

The dottore cut in. Jared?

Unease welled within her. Because it might be Jared? Or because it might not?

CHAPTER 12

The dottore was a German with a good grasp of Italian and a little English. He was a pleasant man.

As they danced, she saw that Cindy had come down with Jared. At least, she thought it was Jared.

Her German dottore was fun, and a wild dancer. After three numbers, she was breathless, and begged herself off the dance floor. Downing a tall glass of mineral water, she saw that there were now at least four dottores in the room.

She wished that Jared had opted for something a little more original, at least chosen different costumes for each party.

A few moments later, she was pulled out to the floor by another dottore. She stared into his eyes the best she could while moving to the music.

No, not Jared.

During an excellent interpretation of an Elvis Presley

ballad, Ragnor cut in on the dottore. She thought about protesting, then wondered why. She was attracted to him. She liked being with him, even if her thoughts ran to the erotic. She was an adult; Steven had been gone now for a long time. She didn't deserve the guilt with which she seemed to be punishing herself.

She allowed herself to be drawn comfortably into his arms.

"Still no sign of Tiff?" she asked.

He shook his head. "No."

"There's something really wrong."

"She may still turn up," he murmured.

She didn't think that he believed that.

When the song broke, she told him that she was thirsty. A cold beer seemed the best thirst quencher, since there had been so much dancing that they had actually run out of bottled water.

For a moment, Jordan reflected on what she might be doing to her liver. Champagne, Bellinis, red wine, espresso with Kahlua, and now beer. But it was very cold and felt so good going down.

Ragnor wasn't wearing a mask or sunglasses. For once, she could see his eyes. He seemed to be searching for someone.

"Looking for Tiff?"

"What?" he asked, as if she had startled him. "Um. Excuse me for a moment, will you?"

Once again, he simply walked off.

Lynn found her by the table. "Hey, that's my favorite disco song. Want to dance with a matador?"

Jordan looked out to the floor. Guests had begun to depart, and the dancing had gotten down to a group of happy—partly sloshed—people wildly moving about. As usual at most such gatherings, the sex of a partner didn't matter anymore. People were just having fun.

"Sure."

"The costume may not have been such a great idea," Lynn admitted, shouting above the music as she gyrated. "No cute guys have hit on me! Actually, no guys have hit on me."

"I'm afraid it might be the mustache!" Jordan called back to her.

A moment later, another dottore popped in front of her. Lynn had turned around to dance with the gypsy sun god on her other side.

"So?"

Jordan raised her brows, looking at her companion.

"It's me, Jared. Are you having fun? What's the matter, too many Venetian friends? You don't talk to me anymore?"

She laughed. "Jared, I've tried conversations with a German and, I think, a Brazilian dottore. How was I suppose to know this one was you?"

"Because I'm tall and devastatingly handsome, even in a cloak and mask!" he told her.

"How silly of me! I forgot!" she teased. "Hey, have you seen Tiff yet?"

He shook his head. "But if I had—"

"Yeah, yeah, I know. You might not have recognized her."

"It would be like Tiff to purposely stand us all up, create an air of mystery, and then tell us tomorrow that she was the silver space alien or the woman in the Swarovski crystal cloak and mask. Did you see that costume? Man, it was spectacular."

"Everyone here is spectacular."

The music had taken a break; she realized that she

had shouted that last comment. A slow tune began again.

"Go find your wife!" Jordan told her cousin.

He nodded. "You're okay, right? Having a good time?"

"Absolutely."

He moved off. Jordan walked back to the buffet table where they were beginning to pack up what was left of the food. A waiter handed her another beer. She shrugged, thanked him, and accepted it. She watched the dancers and found herself approached by the sun god.

"Per piacere. Please?" he asked politely.

With a rueful shrug and a smile, she took a long swallow of the beer, set it down, and allowed him to lead her to the floor.

As they danced, he told her not to miss the Peggy Guggenheim museum. She assured him she had seen it several times.

"And the churches! So many, but you must try to see them. There are over two hundred." The sun god was an Italian with a good conversational knowledge of English. "When an address is 'Campo' something or the other, it means a square with a church. Pop into any of them; you'll be astonished at the art work you find, *especially* in some of the lesser known."

"I saw a great church the other day, but . . . oh, a friend stopped me. Maybe I can find it again."

"Make an effort to do so."

The band leader announced the last number of the night: another Elvis Presley song, slow and sweet.

"He likes Elvis," Jordan commented to her partner.

The sun god nodded. "That's my friend, Rico Andretti. He knows every song Elvis ever wrote. He loves this party; so many Americans. And he sounds like Elvis, yes?"

"Yes, he does, he's excellent."

The sun god was pleased with her comment. And he was a very decent dancer. When the number ended, he asked her if she needed a walk back to her hotel.

Over his shoulder, she saw a dottore at the door. Tall, dark-haired. And surely, *devastatingly handsome,* even in a mask.

"Thank you, but no. I came with family. They're just leaving."

Her partner graciously bowed aside.

The dottore slipped out the door.

Jordan followed, looking around as she did so. No sign of Lynn, Anna Maria, or even Raphael. They must be there somewhere; Jordan was certain that Anna Maria never left her own ball until the last guest had departed. But all she saw were the caterers cleaning up and a few people slipping out to the dock beyond.

She started across the floor, anxious to reach the dottore.

A hand caught her arm before she could cross the marble floor. She stopped, turning. Ragnor was there.

"I need to catch up with Jared," she told him.

"That's not Jared."

"How do you know?"

"He left a few minutes ago with Cindy. She wasn't feeling well."

"So he just left me?"

"He knows you have friends here."

"Oh?" she paused, staring at him. "I don't think that he likes you very much, and he doesn't trust you at all."

Ragnor shrugged. "That's natural. But you cannot go home alone."

"This is Venice. It's a very safe city."

"We're going to the same hotel."

"Then you're free to follow me."

The last of the vaporettos had left with most of the guests; they waited with a few stragglers—all going in different directions—for water taxis.

They wound up last in line.

"See, you're supposed to be grateful for me," Ragnor told her, as a group ahead of them boarded a water taxi.

"Oh?"

"There's no one left."

She inclined her head toward the Swiss Guard who was standing on the dock, ready to hail their taxi.

"He's a stranger."

"I don't think that anyone is stranger than you."

He shrugged. "That may be true."

"Why don't you talk more about yourself?"

"Why don't you trust what you feel?"

"Maybe I feel that you're a very dangerous character."

"Maybe I am—in a way."

She sighed. "We never get anywhere."

"We would, if you'd let us," he said very softly. A breeze stirred, and it felt as if there was a warmth to it, though the night was chill. His words were definitely a sexual innuendo. And to herself, there was no denying that it evoked a sexual response.

Yet even as she felt a growing excitement, a slow burn within, she thought she heard a hissing sound. Looking back toward the palazzo, it seemed that shadows swooped and fell around the entry. She looked up at the sky, wondering if the moon had been covered. A sense of fear and unease in the darkness again swept through her.

Yes, she was glad that he was there.

Inadvertently, she took a step closer to him.

She didn't protest when he slipped an arm around her shoulder.

The water taxi arrived. The Swiss Guard and driver helped her on; Ragnor followed closely.

The water taxi took off flying over the canals. She realized then that she'd definitely had far too much to drink. Her head was swimming.

She leaned against his shoulder. Fingers smoothed her hair beneath the fantasy headdress she was wearing. The touch was nice. She gave way to it.

A moment later, they'd reached the dock near the Danieli.

"What time is it?" she asked him, trying to steady herself to disembark.

"Almost three."

"My Lord, we did close that party."

'Deep midnight," he murmured.

She shook her head. That expression again. He hopped out of the water taxi, and she noted that he was careful to skirt any possibility of slipping into the seawater. He helped her out; she was more careless herself, and amused.

"Afraid of water?" she teased, as he steadied her on the dock.

"Trust me, that water is very, very cold."

He started leading her toward the hotel. As they reached the promenade, she looked back toward the dock.

Shadows, changing, shifting. She gave her head a

shake, thinking again that she heard whispers, and flutterings, like the sounds made by birds. Bats . . .

But there could be no bats near the docks.

Ragnor turned back. The sounds stopped. Were they real, or had she imagined them? Had he stopped them by merely looking that way?

"Come, let's get to the room. It is very late. And clouds are coming. The moon will be covered."

She leaned against him as they walked. "Are you afraid of the dark?"

"I love the dark."

As they neared the door to the hotel, she paused again, looking back. A shadow seemed to stretch nearly to the door; it shifted, receded. Fear stole into her. She could have sworn she heard whispering again.

If Ragnor was aware of it, he gave no sign. He urged her into the hotel. They stopped for their keys. She gave her room number; he gave his.

"So you really do have a room here," she murmured.

"Of course. What did you think?"

"I don't know," she told him honestly, then added softly, "Well, goodnight."

"I'll walk you to your room."

She nodded, not objecting.

When she opened her door, he entered first. She watched him, amused, as he went through the room, checking the bathroom, the bedroom area, the sitting area, and then beneath the bed.

"Are you expecting an evil chambermaid?" she asked him.

She leaned against the door. Her head continued to spin. She wondered wryly if she'd heard whispering, or the sloshing of alcohol in her own veins.

"Are you all right?" he asked, responding with a question rather than an answer.

"Perfectly," she said, but stumbled as she tried to cross the floor with dignity.

He laughed, coming to her aid, leading her to the foot of the bed. "Too much booze, eh?" he queried, sitting beside her. "Your fairy crown is on the side of your head." As he spoke, he reached for the headdress, removing the pins and untangling it from her hair. He cast it toward the armchair facing the shuttered window by the bed. Perfect aim. He hadn't even looked. His eyes were on hers. His fingers threaded into her hair, smoothing it. Knuckles grazed her cheek. Then he kissed her.

The heat that instantly pervaded her was electric. Like a shock, it traveled from her mouth to her torso and limbs; she trembled, instinctively curling her arms around his neck, holding on to something steady. He kissed like a practiced lover, parting her lips with a controlled, hot, wet passion. She tasted his lips, his tongue; the movement of it within her mouth seemed to be an invasion so intimate it elicited anticipation throughout her body. When his lips parted from hers, a bare breath away, she felt the moistness, the hint of slow, burning lava that remained. She felt the rising thunder of her heart; the pulse of blood, the fever of it. She inhaled with a deep shudder.

Should I leave?

Had he spoken the words, or like shadows and whispers in the night, had she imagined them?

"No," she whispered. His eyes were still on hers. She moistened her lips to speak again, silently praying first. *Dear God, don't let it be the alcohol!*

But it wasn't, and she knew it though the words she

spoke next were surely helped along by the flames of too many Bellinis. "Actually . . . I've been dying to see your chest."

"Really? he murmured softly, his whisper then against her forehead. "I'll show you mine . . . if you'll show me yours."

'That's a very old line."

"Not so old as you think."

She reached up, touched the planes of his face, and found his mouth again. His lips remained fused to hers, tongue entangled, as he struggled from the Edwardian coat and cravat and shirt. She broke from the kiss, breathless again, her palms against his chest. Muscle rippled there, almost as if he were a weight lifter. *Something else. He wore a medallion. A religious medallion. Beautiful, old, of a Celtic design. It appeared to be a finely crafted cross. She felt a strange relief flood through her. Surely this had to mean . . .*

That he liked jewelry?

She realized that she was just standing there, staring.

"Well? Did you just want to see my chest, or were you planning on doing something with it?"

She nuzzled against the supple plane of it, fingering the medallion, feeling a greater flood of longing. *It had to be okay . . .*

The intoxication of touching him was overwhelming. She forgot the medallion, and all her fears. "I always thought you had great hands, too."

"Ah, well, you know, I wouldn't want to seem loose or easy or anything, but lots of people have seen my hands. But not so many know what they can do."

"Is it that spectacular?"

"You can judge for yourself."

He scooped her to him, bearing her down to the

expanse of the bed, his mouth on hers, lingering on her throat, moving down to her collarbone, to the cleft in the fantasy costume. She wasn't sure how or when, and she must have been a participant, but the white and gold costume was off, and she was quickly aware of just how talented he was with his hands . . . and his mouth, and even the contours of his body. She'd wanted the shirt gone, in the stirrings of her mind, and wanted more gone, and in minutes, she wasn't thinking at all, and there were no ghosts to disturb her, no conscious thought at all. He was a wall of muscle, and dexterity, and he touched her with a searing hunger, a fierce passion that was tempered only by tenderness. She wanted to crawl within him, inside his very skin, come closer with each new wave of raw desire that assailed her. She would have been the one to forgo seduction and foreplay, so eager and desperate had she become, but he was the consummate lover. Yet, she thought, in a far distant corner of her mind, she had been seduced long ago.

Beguiled.

Yet, Lord, was it good . . .

His stroke brought her closer to ultimate intimacy, each touch of his lips was a caress against a new zone of her flesh, traveling, discovering, eliciting ever greater abandon. She buried herself against him, writhed, arched, felt the trail of touch and liquid fire burn over her limbs, her breasts, low against her belly. She felt like a ship caught in a storm, swept in a sea of sensation so acute and overwhelming that it left no room for conscious thought or movement. His flesh seemed to burn beneath her fingers, a bastion of sinew that aroused with each breath. He moved between her thighs. Sounds escaped her, words, cries . . . the storm and sea became a part of her, and though she could not crawl into his flesh, he at last rose above her, and even as he thrust into her, she felt as if the room became a burst of light as an orgasm shook through her with a force that seemed to stop the world. She soared on clouds of ethereal shadows, felt the power of his movement, and flew ever higher.

The night became a blur.

The night.

Deep midnight. Blues of a dark, moonlit sky, the blood-red colors of sunset. Hunger that became an agony of desire, moisture, lava, flying again, sensations of eroticism and fulfillment that left her shaken again and again. Fire and light, ash and shadows; cinders that sparked anew, again and again, to a blaze. She came so many times, she was intoxicated with the feelings, and then she was exhausted, so replete, and so glad to lie against him. And still, the darkness, just the feel of him beside her, and with it, no nightmares, no ghosts haunting her dreams, no wolves sitting at the foot of her bed. She slept, secure, ecstatic, warmed . . .

Safe.

Safe. The world mocked her as she fell into the depths of her sleep.

He remained a stranger. Stranger, by far, than a passerby on the street.

Strange . . .

Was she a total fool?

Totally . . .

Beguiled.

She woke with a pounding headache, groaning aloud, and bemoaning her mix of wine, beer, champagne, and after-dinner drinks. She glanced instantly to the side of her bed.

No one.

For a brief moment, she wondered if she might have enjoyed an alcoholic dream of bizarrely erotic proportions. She realized then that she was naked, and that the fantasy costume lay at the foot of her bed. A glance at the bedside clock told her that it was nearly three in the afternoon. She could hear movement in the hall beyond her door.

The maid, she thought, waiting patiently to get in.

That thought sent her flying out of bed, headache or no. If he had left, her door should be unlocked.

Yet, when she reached it, she found that it was securely bolted.

She stepped back, frowning.

How the hell had he managed that?

Had she imagined it all?

Lord, no, she couldn't have! There had to be an explanation. He had gotten someone to come, and lock the door from the outside. Surely.

She stared at the door, and her head pounded anew. She walked into the bathroom and quickly downed two Motrin. She turned the water on in the shower, hot and hard, and stood beneath it.

She leaned against the tile, just letting the water wash over her, praying that the Motrin would kick in, and her headache would fade.

She dressed quickly; she'd give her eyeteeth for coffee. She paused by her computer and saw the, "You've got mail!" announcement floating by. She quickly clicked in.

There was an amazing amount of spam, jokes from friends, a note from her agent and at the last, a quick note from the cop in New Orleans who had written the book. "I'd love to talk to you." He left an address and a phone number.

It was late in Italy; still early in the states. She E-mailed him back, saying that she'd call later, and thanking him for his response.

Armed with both books, she headed upstairs for coffee and something to eat. The American couple was there again, and they greeted her pleasantly. She looked around for Ragnor, but as yet, he hadn't put in an appearance.

She opened her book and read about a case that had occurred in an Old West mining town near San Francisco when the gold rush had been on. A saloon girl had taken sick after a mysterious miner had passed through town. She'd died; the town lamented her death, and buried her. Nights later, she began to appear to her old customers in their dreams. Three men were taken sick and eventually died. Then they, too, began to appear in dreams. The sheriff was a realistic, logical fellow, but he had still ordered his deputies out by day; the corpses of the "spirits" were exhumed, and their heads severed before they were burned to ash. Afterwards, there were no more appearances, and no more of the strange, fading sicknesses.

She flipped to a case of serial killings in the Midwest in the late fifties. The killer—a white male, thirty years old, married, with one child, and a blue collar job—had thought himself a vampire. His victims had been tortured, raped, and drained of blood. He had gained access through the sliding glass doors of victims' homes, selecting them because they lived alone in ground floor apartments surrounded by shrubbery.

He wrote letters to the police, warning that "voices"

had told him that he was a descendant of Vlad Dracul, and that he was forced to drink blood to survive. The police actually warned women living alone to line their sliding glass doors with garlic, wear large crosses, and keep vials of holy water at hand. When finally apprehended, the killer told police that indeed, several women had been spared because he hadn't been able to enter their apartments because of the garlic.

Jordan sat back, staring at the book. She wondered if Italian would-be vampires might consider themselves immune to garlic.

She found herself thinking about Ragnor. She never saw him in the early hours of the day. He had a strange habit of appearing when she expected him to be elsewhere, and disappearing when she was sure he had just been near. He would tell her nothing about his past.

She suddenly jumped up, thanked the waiter who was always so attentive and kind, and hurried back to her room.

She turned on every light and stood in front of the mirror. She studied her neck thoroughly. Not a pinprick. She felt foolish.

She looked at her E-mail. No return as of yet. She bundled her two vampire books into her bag and hurried out of the hotel, eager to reach the district station where Roberto Capo worked.

It was very much like any police station at home. There was an information officer at the front desk. There were a number of people there, all speaking among themselves in different languages. She didn't need to speak Italian to realize that two of the women being ushered in were being arrested for prostitution. A balding man ahead of her had lost his wallet in a gondola. The pretty Italian woman at her side was bringing her husband some lunch.

Jordan asked for Roberto Capo, apparently managing the question in Italian so well that the officer gave her a long reply—none of which she understood. But he read her baffled expression and smiled. "Roberto was in this morning and just left. He was not feeling well. The officer shrugged. "He had last night off. He'll be in tomorrow morning."

"Thank you so much. Does he usually work mornings, or nights?"

"Now, during Carnevale? He works all hours. Call if you like, before you come in. I'm Dominic Donatello. I'll be on days from nine to five for the next week. I'll find out his hours for you."

"Again, thank you so much."

"You are the American who was frightened at the contessa's party."

"Yes, that's me."

"I'm so sorry."

"Thanks one more time. Especially for not laughing at me."

He waved a hand in the air. "Women like the contessa . . . they don't realize that there is real crime in the world and one must not make fun of death and terror."

Jordan suddenly heard her name called. She turned; it was Alfredo Manetti.

"Miss Riley, how are you?"

"Very well, thank you."

"What are you doing here?" he asked politely. "Come, come, into my office."

A moment later, she was seated at the all too familiar desk where she had been made to feel a fool after the contessa's party. But this morning, Alfredo seemed to have no intention of making her feel foolish.

"You're still upset," he said.

She leaned forward, folding her hands on the desk. "I'm sure my cousin explained all this to you before. I was engaged to a homicide cop, and he was killed in the pursuit of cultists. I know that such people are out there. And now—you have a severed head."

Alfredo leaned forward then. "And I assure you, forensics are working studiously on discovering the identity of the man and the cause of his death."

"Well, I would say that the removal of a man's head is a good reason for death," she murmured.

He flushed; the tables were somewhat turned.

"What else?" he asked.

"A friend of mine is missing. Tiff Henley."

Alfredo threw up his hands. "Mrs. Henley comes and goes like the wind."

"Yes, but she had invited a group of us over, and she wasn't there. And she didn't show up at the party last night. I'd like you to find out what has happened to her."

"I will find out what I can about your friend," he said. "And as to the contessa . . . she has contributed huge sums of money for orphaned children through-out Italy. She helps finance large groups of poor Euro-peans, just so that they can see the wonder of Venice. She is generous to a fault."

"I'm accusing the contessa of nothing. I'm merely saying that I believe something bad is going on, and that if it doesn't stop, many people might die."

"I will take your words to heart," he told her.

She rose, wondering if he meant what he said, or if he was mocking her. She was determined to talk to

Roberto Capo, no matter how difficult it might be. It was aggravating to have to wait another day, but she didn't intend to say anything more to Alfredo Manetti.

She thanked him and left the station.

As she entered the lobby of the Danieli, the concierge called her to say that he'd received a message for her: Roberto Capo had called the hotel and wished to meet her. He had left an address for a trattoria where she could find him until seven-thirty or eight.

She glanced at her watch. It was just five, but she decided to leave right away.

The concierge brought out a map and showed her how to reach the address, suggesting that she might want to take a water taxi, since it was a bit of a walk. She didn't mind walking, and according to the map, she could take a side calle or two and stop by Tiff's, knock on the door, and see if by chance Tiff would respond today.

She thanked the concierge and headed back out.

Five o'clock, and it was already getting dark, she noted.

In front of the hotel, she stood still for a minute, listening. All she heard was the chatter, laughter and the occasional shout that rose on the promenade. A vaporetto had pulled in at the dock; there were plenty of people out and around.

She remained still for several more seconds and realized that she was listening for the sound of wings, for hisses and whispers on the air.

There were none.

At Tiff's, she pounded on the door and waited ten minutes, knocking again and again. Tiff made no appearance.

At last giving up, Jordan decided to start her walk to the trattoria.

At first, she ran into people here and there. The festivities for Carnevale were beginning to wind down; though some people still wore costumes, headed to private parties or events, more and more people were wearing street clothes, and seemed to be going about their daily business.

As she came closer to the area where she was to meet Roberto, she realized that she was encountering fewer and fewer people. Once again, as she followed the map, she crossed over one little bridge after another.

There were fewer shops.

Fewer lights.

She realized uneasily that it had grown very dark; the night came on quickly in Venice in the winter. The evening was chill, and clouds were passing over the moon.

"It may snow again," she told herself out loud, and realized that as she was speaking she was growing afraid.

She stared at the map again and started across another little bridge. Something looked familiar here.

She realized she was heading in the same direction she had come when she followed the dottore and ran into Salvatore D'Onofrio and saw the beautiful, but decrepit, old church.

Just then, she found herself halting in the center of the bridge. What there was of moonlight fell upon her here.

On either side of the bridge, the buildings seemed to melt into shadow. She swallowed hard, turning.

Down the narrow canal, she could see another

bridge. And standing in the center—just as she was standing—she could see the caped figure of a dottore. He seemed highlighted in moonlight, and all around him, the world seemed to be in shadow.

She wondered if she imagined the figure.

It beckoned to her. She felt her heart thundering. Instinct warned her that she should run along, but she stood still, just feeling the slam of her heart against her chest.

Then the dottore turned, and seemed to float across the bridge, cape flying behind him.

She did hurry then; she started to run. As she came across a shadowed walkway, a hissing sound seemed to surround her ears. She told herself that it was the sound of her own breathing.

She sensed the strangeness fluttering around her, as if a dozen birds flew by, close to her ears, twittering, whispering . . .

She tried to read her map while running. She burst from the shadowed walkway to a dark piazza with lights here and there.

Looking down an alley, cast in an eerie mist of shadow and light, she could see the old derelict church. Again, she stood still, afraid of the church, and yet tempted to walk toward it. More than tempted; she felt a pull . . .

She looked at the map. The trattoria was to her right.

She was going to come back to the church. But though she was impelled to go in that direction, something stronger bid her away.

She saw the lights of the small trattoria casting a glow upon the path ahead of her.

She started toward it, rounding the little angle in the street that would bring her to the entry.

In front of it was a medieval archway between very old buildings. Before she could reach the shadowed area below the archway, she saw Roberto Capo on the other side. He was shaking his head in a frenzy.

"Don't come! Don't come—go! To your left again as you head back, there's a vaporetto stop! Go!"

Suddenly, she was certain that she heard wings; a flurry of wings, alive with whispers and hisses. The shadows beneath the archway seemed to extend, like a black, viscous liquid, coming after her.

Shadows! she protested mentally. *Shadows, changing beneath the moon!*

But Roberto had told her to run.

The shadows were stretching in the other direction as well. Suddenly, they seemed to sweep over Roberto Capo, encompassing him as a giant wave of ink-black sea . . .

Or like the wingspan of a great ebony bird.

She turned and ran.

As she did so, she dropped her map. She didn't pause to pick it up. She didn't look back. She felt that the ink-black shadow wings were following, close on her heels, and she had to escape them before . . .

There was a feeling of glacial cold at her nape. As if an ice-encrusted finger of pure bone had thrust out from the darkness and touched her, as if it would creep around her throat like a vine, hold her, pull her back . . .

Heedless, half-crazed with fear, she turned left as he had suggested.

And then, like Lot's wife, she turned back.

A dottore stood there, in the calle where she had

been, between her and the archway where she had seen Roberto.

She stood still, startled, watching.

The dottore lifted his mask. His face remained in shadow. He reached into his pocket for something.

A knife? Was he a psychotic, hidden behind a mask, running through Venice, his cape flying behind him like some modern-day Jack the Ripper?

He did not draw out a knife. He'd reached into his pocket for cigarettes and a match. She stared, remotely thinking that she would see his face, that it would be important to do so, when he lit the match.

The match flared; he lit the cigarette. She could not see his face, for he bowed his head as he cupped his hands around the match.

No knife.

Yet somehow, he seemed more dangerous than if he had pulled out a machete. There was a carelessness in his movements. *He did not need a large weapon to torture, destroy, commit murder. She could run, and it would not matter, because he could catch her, no matter how fast she tried to flee . . .*

She pulled in a ragged breath, fighting for reason, for sanity, for movement.

She started to back away, then stopped dead.

There was a new menace.

Behind her.

She saw nothing, *felt* a second shadow approaching from behind. Around her, above her, in a strange cascade, darkness, deeper than night, seemed to be overtaking her. Terror, unlike anything she had ever known, assailed her. She was paralyzed where she stood, trembling violently, unable to do so much as open her mouth.

She saw the darkness soaring over her then.

She watched it, certain that the dottore saw it, too.

He did. He backed away, as if from her.

She heard, as if in echo of Roberto Capo's warning, *"Run!"*

She ran.

And as she did so, she mocked herself. She was running like an idiot *from shadows.*

No, from the dottore in the street, from a menace of evil stalking the streets of Venice, the innocent, the unwary.

She burst upon a broad calle; the vaporetto stop was right before her. People milled there. Families, tourists, business people. Dear God, she could hardly breathe! Her lungs were killing her, her calves felt as if knives were stuck in them. If her heart pounded any harder, she would go into cardiac arrest.

Because of a man in a dottore mask who had paused to light a cigarette!

He had just been a costumed reveler, a tourist in love with Carnevale, one of the dozens of people who chose the dottore costume for dress-up . . .

She could think rationally now as she paused, breathing hard, joining the group at the vaporetto stop. Everyone looked *normal.* Unafraid. They talked. A woman excused herself as she stepped around Jordan to rejoin her group. Jordan realized that she had shoved her way right into the center of the crowd.

Did fear create fear? Was she doing this in her own mind? What had she actually seen?

A man in a dottore costume, lighting a cigarette.

But what about Roberto Capo, shouting at her, warning her away?

A vaporetto arrived. She got on, realizing afterward

that she didn't have a ticket, and she didn't know where it was going.

Luckily, the vaporetto was crowded. No one asked her for a ticket. After it first stopped somewhere she couldn't begin to recognize, she asked a man in her faulty Italian if the boat went to the area of St. Mark.

"Si, si," the man told her. "A Hotel Danieli."

She thanked him. As the vaporetto made other stops, as people got on and off, she found that she was doubting her own sanity again. It was like going to a well-made horror movie. While the film was rolling, you were transfixed, caught in the fear. Then, when the credits rolled and the lights came on, the smell of popcorn and the sounds of conversation caused the fear to slip away. She almost wished that she could hold on to the feeling; perhaps then she could make some sense of it.

But she had seen Roberto Capo. And he had told her to run!

The vaporetto at last pulled up to the dock at the Danieli. She walked up to the hotel, then paused on the street. There were so many people out. They all seemed fine. Was she the only one in the entire city concerned about the fact that *a severed head* had been found floating in a canal?

She asked for her key, but before she could head to her room, she saw that Ragnor was sitting in the lobby, reading a newspaper. There was an empty coffee cup in front of him. It appeared that he had been there for some time.

He saw her and folded his paper, frowning and rising. As she walked over to him, he demanded, "Where the hell have you been?"

She arched a brow at his tone. "That's really none of your business."

"Your cousin has been worried sick."

A small twinge of guilt assailed her.

"They were sleeping. I went out."

"I was worried."

"I'm sorry. But I didn't see you either." She felt a flush of warmth spreading through her, being near him again. To her he had lost none of his attractiveness, even though last night dispelled any physical mystery they had between them. If anything, intimacy had made him more appealing.

But she hadn't elected anyone as her guardian, and as much as she liked being close to him, there were other mysteries still not solved. She didn't want him knowing that she had been to the police, nor did she want to share her strange experience of the night. She was a *wary* moth, drawn to the flame. So tempted, so impelled, and yet so aware of the fire.

"Have you had dinner?"

"I should check with Jared and Cindy."

"They ate and went up to bed."

"This early? When they were so worried about me?"

"I told Cindy that if you didn't appear soon, I'd go out and find you. But give their room a call. She'll want to know that you're back."

She left him and called. Cindy answered the phone; she sounded exhausted.

"What's wrong?"

"I don't know. A touch of the flu. I slept all morning, and I'm tired again. But you! We've been worried to death!"

"I went out. Remember, Venice is a really safe city. The cops carry big guns."

"Venice is a safe city, but still . . ." Cindy's voice trailed off. "I don't know. I just get scared when I don't know where you are."

"I'm fine."

"Great. Are you going to get something to eat with Ragnor?"

"Um . . . I guess."

"Well, have a nice night. And please, don't take off tomorrow without telling us that you're leaving, and where you're going, please?"

It was on the tip of her tongue to tell Cindy that she was well over twenty-one, and that she lived alone in Charleston, and that she knew a smattering of Italian—bad Italian, but enough to get around. But Cindy was earnestly concerned, and Jordan didn't want to hurt or worry her anymore.

"Are you sure *you're* all right? Maybe you should see a doctor."

"I will, if I don't start feeling a little bit better . . . well, it's not so much *better* . . . I don't really feel ill, just exhausted."

"If you don't perk up, you've got to see a doctor," Jordan insisted.

Cindy promised she would, then asked Jordan to hang on a minute, Jared was saying something.

She sighed when she came back to the phone. "He wants you to watch out for Ragnor. Don't trust him, and don't let him up to your room."

Jordan didn't tell them that that particular warning was too late.

"I'm going to dinner," she said simply. That wasn't a lie. How could she argue with her cousin when she wasn't sure what she felt herself?

"Dinner," Cindy said. Her voice dropped to a whisper. "Personally, I think he's the best in the world for you!"

"Thanks. Okay, get some sleep."

She rang off and came back to Ragnor. He was reading his paper again.

"All right. They've gone to bed."

"So you do want to go to dinner."

"Might as well. Give me a minute; I want to run up to my room."

He frowned slightly, as if not certain that she should. He started to fold the paper as if he'd go with her.

"I'll be right down," she promised, and headed for the stairs before he could stop her.

She hurried to her door and into her room. She quickly checked her E-mail. There was another note from the cop in New Orleans. It was simple, brief, and to the point.

Please call me anytime.

She considered putting through a phone call right then, but she didn't want to take too much time. She'd call him around noon tomorrow. That would be very early in the morning in the States but the cop's message had read *any time.*

And at noon, for some reason, everyone she knew tended to be sleeping.

She washed her face quickly, switched jackets, and opened the door. Ragnor was waiting for her in the hallway. "I was getting worried."

She sighed with exasperation. "Why is everyone worried about me all the time?"

"I've told you—I think you might have stirred up trouble."

He was quiet as they walked to the restaurant, a little place just a hundred feet away once they had left the hotel and crossed the bridge to their left. There were many people in the restaurant, and many people in the streets.

It felt very safe.

They ordered wine and joked with the waiter, a man who seemed to know Ragnor. Then they ordered their food. When the wine arrived, along with an antipasto, Ragnor drew the newspaper from the pocket of his black suede jacket. He opened it, smoothed it out, and pointed to a picture.

"Do you recognize that person?"

She stared at the face and at the headlines. The words meant nothing to her, except that she thought she recognized the word for death.

"I've never seen the man before. Why?"

"That's an artist's rendition of the man whose head was found in the canal."

She stared at the picture again. She shook her head slowly. "No, I've never seen him. I'm positive I've never seen him."

"They think he's Slavic."

"I don't know him. Do you?"

He shook his head. For once, she was certain he was telling the truth. "No," he said.

"Why do you think he was killed?"

"I don't know."

Now, she wasn't so certain he was telling the truth. But he leaned toward her then. "Don't go running out alone."

"Now wait a minute. You're telling me—"

"I'm telling you not to go running out alone."

"You don't ever explain anything."

"I can't explain."

"Oh—you have a hunch?"

"Something like that."

"We always talk in circles."

"So let's talk about something else."

"All right—let's talk about you."

"Let's talk about you."

Their pasta arrived. Jordan took a bite. It was delicious. Ragnor knew Venice, and he knew his restaurants.

She took a sip of her wine, studying him. "I'm an open book. I live in Charleston. I was born in Charleston. Jared and I both grew up with my grandmother, Granny Jay. We have her eyes. I'm short—he's tall. He started dating Cindy in high school. They adore one another."

"That's Jared and Cindy. What about you?"

"Well, I did leave Charleston to go to Brown. I majored in English and Comparative Literature. I write articles now and then, but mostly I do book reviews, fiction and nonfiction. I'm syndicated, and in the last few years I've done very well."

"And your personal life?"

She took another sip of wine. "I told you. I was engaged to a cop named Steven. He was killed. I'm sure you've heard the grisly details—that's why I supposedly went so out of my mind at the contessa's party, seeing real evil in her entertainment."

"And after his death?"

"I've been working. Don't you want to ask me about my life before Steven? There was a guy named Zachary my first year of college. He was cute—had great hair. Then there was Jimmy Adair. He wanted to move to the wilderness in Montana and rough it. Go back in time. Live in a cabin with no electricity and study wolves."

"You've got something against wolves."

"Nope—I'd love to visit him sometime. I just didn't want to live there. Oh—I love movies, too. Well, there you have it. Steven came along, and . . ."

"He was perfect."

"You're supposed to say you're sorry, or something like that."

He shrugged. "So . . . you've been in deep mourning."

"Something like that."

"I'm honored."

"Thanks," she murmured casually. "So—just *who* are you?"

"Ragnor. Wulfsson."

"Your real name?"

"It is my real name."

Their main course arrived. They smiled and talked to the waiter. He left.

"And you're really from Norway?"

"Yes. Originally."

"You've traveled a lot."

"Quite a bit."

"Doing?"

"Different things over the years. But mainly, spending family money. Parting with antiques here and there."

"And learning languages. You must be very bright."

"No more so than the next man. I travel, and I listen. And take the time," he murmured ruefully. "Time—time in a place helps a lot."

"So you knew the contessa before."

"I don't really care to go into that."

"But you think she's evil?" Jordan wiggled her brows, as if half teasing.

"I *know* she's evil," he said.

"You think the contessa caused that man to be murdered, don't you?"

"I have no proof."

"You should tell the police."

"Oh? And the police will arrest her because I *think* she caused a man's death?"

Jordan shrugged. "It would help if you went to the police. Then they might take me more seriously. Though I must say, Roberto Capo—" she broke off.

"Roberto Capo what?" he demanded.

"He doesn't think I'm crazy. You should tell him what you think. Maybe it will matter. Maybe they'll get someone in there to investigate the woman."

"It won't matter if they do."

"Why not?"

"Trust me, she covers her sins well."

Again, the waiter came by. It was time for coffee and dessert. They both decided just coffee, and it was then that Jordan remembered to ask, "Have you heard from Tiff?"

His expression became guarded. "No."

"Aren't you worried?"

"What would my being worried do?" he returned, sounding tired.

"We have to make someone look into the fact that she's missing."

"I believe the police are looking into her disappearance."

"What makes you think so?' "

He hesitated. "I called."

"Oh."

"Look, I'll go down there and insist they find out about Tiff tomorrow, all right?"

She nodded, pleased. Their waiter brought the check; Ragnor paid and they started out. The streets were quieter now, but with him, she saw no shadows.

And heard no whispers.

"You really insist they do something?" she asked as they walked.

"Yes."

When they returned to the hotel, he followed her to her room. She watched as he went through all the motions he had gone through the previous evening.

"You're more neurotic than I am."

"I've told you that I'm worried about you."

She was silent a moment as he watched her. Then she asked, "Are you staying?"

"Yes," he said softly.

She bolted the door.

A minute later, she was in his arms.

Later that night, hours later, she turned to him and asked, again, "Who are you—*really?*"

He was silent for a moment, stroking her hair. "I've told you the truth. I am from Norway; I have lived all over the world. And my name is Ragnor Wulfsson." He drew her against him, as if falling asleep.

But he wasn't asleep, she thought.

She pulled away slightly. It was very dark in the room, but she could see the planes of his face.

She traced them, thinking that his features were exceptionally fine, that he was an incredible lover, and that she liked him, liked being with him . . .

That she wanted to know him more, that she loved his touch . . .

That she had never felt as she did when she was with him.

Except that . . .

"Okay, then, *what* are you?" she asked very softly.

"A man," he murmured. "A man."

He didn't stir again.

Yet, she thought, he still wasn't sleeping.

CHAPTER 13

When he was a small child, he was unaware of the world of violence and cruelty into which he had been born, of the strange heritage due to come his way.

His village by the sea was productive and peaceful. Farmers tilled the earth; fishermen went to sea; shepherds tended their flocks. In spring and summer, the fields were rich, and the forests were filled with game. During the long, cold winters, men carved fine images from blocks of wood, and the storytellers entertained young and old alike with tales of the daring of the gods, the wars with the giants, the follies of all creatures upon the earth. There was law and order among his people; disputes were settled in the great central house, where his great-uncle had the final word. Sometimes, of course, a grievous complaint would be settled in battle, and the clash of arms was like a war among gods in which Odin blew the north wind and Thor, in his fury, sent down lightning and thunder. There was no dishonor in dying in such a battle, for Valhalla was open only to those who fought with the greatest courage and defied the realm of Hel, goddess of the underworld. Religion and storytelling were one and the same.

Despite the richness of his village and the customary peace and domesticity within it, he was, from an early age, taught the rudiments of battle. His father was nephew to the jarl and held a place of honor within this realm. His father was also greatly feared as one of the most powerful of the warriors; he was often gone, and his name was spoken softly and with a strange whisper of both awe and dread. As the seventh son of this incredible man, the boy was watched expectantly, and he knew, from the time he could talk and walk, he would one day go forth into the world, where he would be *required* to outdo other men with his prowess and courage. He would not be allowed to fail. This in itself was not in the least strange, for most young men of noble families were taught the virtues of strength and power. Despite the fine location and lush fields of his homeland, it would remain rich, and give plenty only if its sons went out upon the seas, settled new homelands, and brought back the wealth of others.

He always knew he would go a-Viking. It was a way of life. His brothers before him had gone, and they returned, sometimes years later, to boast of great conquests, to bring back foreign gold and art. They told about the monks who had inscribed the books they brought back, helpless fellows who cried to their one God but received no help from him as they battled the men they called demons who had come to their shores.

Often when his father was gone, his mother would speak of her husband, then lower her head and whisper a prayer to Freya. As he grew, he began to wonder whether she prayed that her husband would return, or that he would not.

As he neared his thirteenth birthday, he was already taller than most of the men, and they were a tall breed. He was also singularly adept in his training with arms.

Some of his first memories were of going to the docks to see the returning warriors, bold men, fierce men, berserkers among them, who had sailed the seas through wind and storm to strike the coastal towns of other peoples. There they sought gold and treasure, wreaked havoc, and sometimes returned not just with riches, but with a cargo of humanity as well, slaves to work for noble men's wives, to till the fields, gather the harvests. Theirs was an intriguing community, for dauntless valor and steadfast bravery were the greatest traits in a man, and a slave who proved his mettle might one day become one of them, and strike out upon the seas himself. When the warriors returned, the longhorns would sound, and the village would come out to welcome the returning heroes, to hear their stories of battle and conquest, and marvel at the goods from civilizations across the seas.

At thirteen, he was to sail with his oldest brother, Hagan. They would stop in the islands north of Scotland, held by Norse jarls, then head south and raid a village along the Hebrides where it was rumored that monks had come from France with reliquaries of gold fashioned by fine goldsmiths in Paris. The Norsemen had no interest in the fragile pieces of bone and ash so reverently contained in the gold vessels; they only wanted the precious metal.

Sailing was good; he loved it. He didn't mind the backbreaking labor of rowing the great dragon-pronged ship when there was no wind, and he loved a storm at sea. The wind sweeping the sky, the roiling gray, the black toss of the waves, all created a tempest that made him feel very alive, a warrior against the obstacles set forth by the gods.

The islands where his distant cousins ruled, slave-masters of many of the original inhabitants were intri-guing. He had never seen so many different peoples: many were short, dark-haired, and spoke a strange language that he found fascinating. There, on the isles, they were refitted for their travels; they practiced with arms, and held contests to win women, armor, weapons, and shields. All was going well until one of their hosts heard word of the treasure they had come to seize from farther south; the inhabitants of the isles felt that the treasure was more rightly theirs, and heated arguments arose, near to a drawing of swords and an all-out massacre between them. But rising from his seat around the huge fire in the jarl's circular hall, Hagan boasted that his brother had been born under a special sign, therefore he could best a man twice his height, and twice his size. His brother. seventh son of the seventh son, born beneath the black moon of deep midnight, would fight their strongest, most able man. They would fight to the death, and the men of the victor would be the warriors to seek the prize.

Ragnor was stunned—as stunned as those laughing at him—and though he could not humiliate his brother, he wasn't at all sure why it seemed his brother was intent on his murder. The jarl assessed him carefully. Ragnor informed him that this destined prowess of his had yet to be tested, but the jarl demanded that the fight should follow as Hagan had suggested. He called to one of his champions, a man called Olaf the Giant.

Olaf had been aptly named; he appeared as wide as he was tall, and his height was staggering, but there was nothing in the man run to fat or drink. His breadth was muscle. At thirteen, Ragnor was lean despite his customary work with heavy weapons and the monotonous labor of rowing. The gods expected courage when he stood before Olaf the Giant, but Ragnor could not meet his soon-to-be slayer without a look at his brother that indicated his feelings of betrayal. He knew, however, that it would be far better to fall to one of Olaf's massive blows than to act the coward and face the fury of his fellow Vikings. He stepped onto the dirt patch before the fire that was assigned as the fighting place. He was granted three shields and three weapons. He chose an axe, a mace and a sword.

He had barely stepped forward, barely hoisted his wooden shield, when Olaf bore down on him, vowing to give him a quick and painless death and allow him a "child's" place among the gods. Olaf's one simple swing of his battle-axe shattered Ragnor's shield into splinters. He retreated, taking up the next shield handed to him. The shield was barely in his grasp before Olaf was coming toward him again, raising his battle-axe.

This next time, Ragnor leaped aside; Olaf's swing missed, and his giant axe swung hard into the earthen flooring.

"Kill him now! It's your chance!" his brother roared.

But all he had known thus far was the role of student, and so Ragnor hesitated. Olaf brought his weapon from the ground and came at him, swinging again.

Ragnor ducked and circled around, to the great amusement of the onlookers. When Olaf shattered his second shield, Ragnor dropped the mace as well as the remnants of protective wood; he then picked up his sword.

When the giant came forward, laughing and drawing back his axe, Ragnor sped forward, striking instantly and with dead precision.

Ragnor caught him in the throat. Olaf, amazed, dropped his weapon and clasped his throat with both hands.

Blood gushed through the man's fingers. For seconds that seemed an eternity, Olaf stared at Ragnor.

Then he fell dead to the floor.

Men all around him cheered. His brother rushed forward and hoisted him on his shoulders. He should have felt the elation of his fellow men. He felt hollow instead.

That night, the jarl of the isles gave Ragnor a shield fronted with silver, an ancient bequest brought back from the ruins of an ancient Roman village on the mainland far to the south. The jarl awarded him two women as well, presents from a group who had gone a-Viking all the way to the lands of the yellow people.

He didn't mind the gift of the women at all. They taught him things he had never imagined. But despite the drink he consumed and the energy required from the women, he didn't sleep that night.

He should have died.

The next morning, he accosted his brother.

"You were quick to risk my life."

"I never risked your life."

"He was twice my size, brutal."

"But you are our father's seventh son."

"So I'm immortal? A child of the gods?" he scoffed.

Hagan put out a finger, touching him directly on the forehead. "The seventh son of the wolf, who is the seventh son of the wolf. And a child of deep midnight, conceived of the hour, born of the hour. You have the cunning of the wolf, and the hunger, and the loyalty."

"And that kept me alive?"

Hagan shrugged with a broad grin. "Well, I had heard that it would do so. And now I have proof."

"You risked my life!" Ragnor said again angrily.

"A Viking does not live forever. And his place in the halls of Valhalla is great only if he has performed great deeds on earth."

The following day, they left, striking out for the rich treasure they sought.

When they came ashore, Ragnor was sickened by the carnage. His brother's men set upon the little community of monks with a vengeance.

Men with tonsures, clad in brown wool, raced about screaming, dropping to their knees, crying for their One True God. Hagan laughed and ignored them, slicing them as he approached their place of worship.

Ragnor followed behind, trying to remind himself that he was a youth here, that they would call him a girl, weak as a woman, if he decried the violence.

But they had set him up to battle a giant; he had some say.

So he shouted with such force that he caused them

to halt and stare at him. "Leave them! Leave them be!" he demanded. And striding forward, he snatched the skinny man his brother was about to skewer from Hagan's hands.

"You've come for treasure. Take the treasure."

"Are you a coward?" Ulric, one of the fiercest warriors shouted. "The seventh son of the seventh son— a coward?" Ulric roared with laughter.

"I haven't such courage as you, to slice up men who are not even armed. The gods would mock you. A warrior! A man who slays men who are like sheep!"

There was silence among them.

"Get the treasure!" Ragnor insisted.

The monks were too stunned to protest; he thought later that many would have died to save their relics. One stood at the doorway to the monastery, a very tall man. "Take the silver and gold, leave what means nothing to you—the bone and the ash."

"The bone and the ash are the earth's!" Hagan ordered.

"Leave them their talismans," Ragnor said. "I have heard of the halls of Valhalla, and what I have heard is that the greatest warriors know when to give mercy."

The Vikings swore as they let the remaining monks house their precious relics in the stoneware dishes which were surely meant for their meals. But the precious relics were left behind. Before they left, the tall monk found Ragnor perched on a rock, waiting.

"I had visions that you would come," the monk told him.

Ragnor looked at him skeptically. The monk smiled.

"Don't bother me, or I'll let them slit your throat."

"A lad with fire," the monk murmured, "but a lad, still, nonetheless."

"Not anymore."

"It will be years before you are full grown. But I prayed years ago, knowing that the Viking ships were busy again. And God answered me in a dream, telling me not to fear. You would come to protect us."

"I came to steal silver."

The monk shrugged. He pulled a pendant from around his neck and held it out to Ragnor. Ragnor nearly hit him when he reached out to pull it over his head.

"Silver, not stolen, but given. It is set with jewels—and a relic said to come from the very body of John the Baptist."

"I don't believe—"

"You will. You are the seventh son of the seventh son, you know. But not the seventh son of your mother."

Ragnor frowned.

"Your father took her from these shores years ago. She was a healer, a pagan child, brought to the church. Your father was blessed—or cursed—with the way of power. Your mother knew the way of the earth."

"You're a fool, old man. How can you know all this?"

"To you, he is Odin. To the Romans, Jove. He is greater than they ever knew, but one and the same. And so I know."

The monk left him. Later that night, he asked Hagan about his father. Hagan, enjoying a fat leg of the holy men's sheep, shrugged. "Three wives. Maida, whom he loved as a child, my mother. Ingrid, whom he stole from the Danes. Elspeth, your mother, whom he seized from a raid just north of here, many years ago."

Later, as they sailed away, he saw the monk at the

stairs of the monastery again, watching them go. The monk lifted his hand.

Angry, Ragnor did not respond.

They did not return to Norway. News of their exploit with the monks traveled, and rather than making them appear weak, they found that their services were being sought by many nobles, of their own kind ruling the isles, of the various lords of the peoples of Scotland, and the rihts, or kings of Eire well. They even traveled down to Sicily. Hagan listened to those who would hire their services, and as was the right among Norsemen, the men were free to choose to fight or to refuse that particular battle.

Ragnor found himself returning again and again to the monastery they had first ravaged, intrigued by the abbot there, the books, and the many languages the monks could speak. He returned his share of the silver reliquaries they had taken.

"And what do you want for these?" the lean, sharp-nosed abbot asked him.

"Languages."

"What?"

"I want to learn languages, as you speak them. The Latin with which you write, the Gaelic I hear in the villages, the English of the lower countries. Then French and—"

"One by one, lad. One by one," the abbot told him.

And so, he became a regular visitor.

As time went by, Ragnor learned to join the fighting, and with each season that passed, he became more adept at the art of warfare. Among the Vikings, many came to him to ask him what he thought of a particular battle. "Dublin is a town founded by a Viking. Now the king asks us to fight against interlopers from the north. That is a good fight.''

He agreed it was a good fight. And he discovered, when he was convinced of the valor of a fight, he could be savage. There were times when he could take life with a vengeance, and yet, he always remembered the way he had felt when Olaf died, and he refused to allow wanton murder of peasants, women, children, and the aged in any place where he fought. Revenge, he had noted, could make murderers of those who had been downtrodden. It was amazing, he had discovered, when their force had won the day for a threatened people, just how quickly those people could turn, ready to cut out the hearts of their foes, once they had power.

They fought for the king of an isle off the western coast of Scotland, a battle they fought against a group of Danes, very much like their own.

The king of the isle rewarded them with a smaller island to call their own. They grew wealthy, and others joined them. The men took wives—some willing, and some coerced. They traveled home and brought riches with them, but Ragnor had no desire to stay. In the time he had been gone, his mother had died. His father had gone a-Viking a different way, and though he felt a deep loss at his mother's passing, he had not known his father well, and though respected and awed, he had not been in Ragnor's life enough for him to greatly miss his presence.

He was sorry forever, for the void he felt in many ways. There were so many questions he might have asked.

His uncle, however, was still the jarl. He assured Ragnor that his mother, though originally taken as a slave, had been among their people many years, and had been loved, and had been honored with the greatest of funerals; her byre had burned brightly on the fjord throughout a long, moonlit night.

"There is so much my parents might have told me," Ragnor said.

"Perhaps there is not as much to tell as there is to learn, and only time and life can be the teachers we really need," his uncle told him.

With little then to hold him to his old life, Ragnor returned with Hagan and their many men to their isle off the western coast of Scotland.

By his thirtieth year, he had his own home, cattle, sheep, and horses. He had not married, but neither was he lonely. There were many women in his life, strangers in faraway places, captives who were eager to please, and housemaids who were willing to serve. His brother and he had formed a bond of real friendship and led their large army of mercenaries together.

That year, they were called upon by the rich chieftain two days south of them, inward on the river. Ragnor traveled with Hagan to speak with the chieftain.

Their people were being taken and killed. Not far away, foreign enemies had come in and decimated a village. They were dark invaders, fierce, with small, slim, horses that disappeared into the night; darkness was when they wished to strike.

The people were terrified of them. They did not just come and kill. They could slip through the defenses at night, with no one knowing, and more of their children would be gone.

The mission appealed to Ragnor. But on their return trip, they stopped at the monastery from which they had first stolen the silver. Ragnor wasn't sure why, but

he was keen to talk to the old abbot he had so strangely
defended, a man whose name was Peter.

Peter seemed to be expecting them. He had soup
and bread ready, and he listened avidly to everything
Ragnor and Hagan said.

"The evil has come," Peter said.

"Bah!" Hagan told him. "They are foreigners—
cowards, as Ragnor would say, who only fight the
unarmed, the weak. They prey upon women."

"Are you telling us not to go?" Ragnor queried, for
his friend seemed so strange.

"No, you must go. And you must not just kill these
infidels. You must destroy them, utterly. They will use
any weapon: hands, fists, teeth. Yes, teeth, you must
beware in battle. They are an ancient enemy. I think
they are the lamia of the ancients in the East; they
bring not just death but infection. They are everything
against God."

"If your one great God were so powerful, he would
destroy them."

"God has created man with a heart and a soul. A
man may fight for good or for evil."

Hagan was aggravated. "A man's cause is good; his
enemy's cause is bad."

Peter ignored him. He stared at Ragnor. "Beware."

"We will destroy them," Hagan said confidently.
"We will return to our isle, gather our ships, and go
to the chieftain, and there, build and create his
defenses for him. Then we'll rout his enemies!"

Two weeks later, they had made the journey. Yet,
even as they steered their boats through the river pass,
they could see ahead. As they neared the village, where
so recently Hagan and Ragnor had been welcomed

and beseeched for help, they saw nothing but burned-out farmsteads and the rubble of homes.

They brought their longboats in, and the men all stared at the carnage in silence. Gudric, the Rune Sayer, shook his head. "Turn back!" he told Hagan.

Hagan would not be persuaded. "We go in. We see if any are living; we promised our aid, and we will see to the dead."

Even Ragnor felt a hesitance as they stepped ashore. He knew that his brother felt it, but Hagan didn't believe in allowing cowardice to rule a man's actions.

They had just gone ashore and seen the death, and the flies, when Eric, left behind to guard the ships, called out to them.

More ships were coming. To his amazement, Ragnor saw that a ship of monks was coming; Peter stood aft, tall and straight against the wind as the ship followed theirs.

The monks all carried swords.

Ragnor walked with Hagan to greet the monks as they arrived.

"You have given up God's way of peace and taken to the sword?" Hagan demanded.

"This is God's battle we wage. Against those who would steal the dead, not the living."

"Monk, you make no sense," Hagan said flatly.

Ragnor turned to start to the center of the village. The place held an eerie calm. It seemed that no creatures had been spared. Horses and dogs and farm animals lay about in the midst of slaughtered humans.

"There is something evil here," Gudric warned. Grudgingly, he indicated Peter. "As the monk says, the gods would fear to tread here."

The Norsemen continued forward. Hearing a hack-ing sound, Ragnor turned to see that Peter was industriously engaged in removing the head of a fallen man.

"Peter!" he remonstrated, more in amazement than in disgust or anger.

"We will cremate them with prayers," Peter said, as if that explained his actions.

"Let's look to the living," Hagan said.

They kept walking and came to the village church. As they stood there, the door creaked ajar. The brothers looked at one another. Hagan shrugged his shoulders. "Who wants to live forever?" he queried lightly.

"I'll go first," Ragnor said and shrugged as well. "I am the seventh son."

"We go together."

"It is just a church."

They took a step closer. The door burst open. A child came flying out; she buried herself in Hagan, who was so startled he nearly fell over.

A young man appeared, a mere boy with no more than a scruff of hair on his cheeks. "We ran to the church when they descended," he blurted out. "Oh, God, can you understand me? We are all that's left. They—they attacked the sheep and the cows. I saw my father . . ."

He said no more. He collapsed. The monks had come from behind. One of them helped the boy up.

"How many live?"

"Fifteen, twenty . . . all in the church."

"Start building a barricade!" Hagan roared to his men.

"You build your barricade," Peter said. "But I am telling you—you will be safe in the church."

"We must build defenses—" Ragnor said.

"Then you must," Peter told him. "And we must

do what we must do. Son," he asked the boy, "where are the others?"

"Coming out now that . . . that we see you."

At that moment, more people spilled out of the church. Those behind were so frenzied, they pushed those in front forward.

A woman catapulted into Ragnor's arms. She steadied herself against his chest and looked up at him with large dark eyes. Dark brown hair tumbled down her back. Her kirtle was ripped and torn, she was dusty, her cheek was bruised. She was beautiful.

"Thank God!" she whispered to him.

He stared at her.

"You're here, you've come. You didn't lie to my father, my chieftain."

"We've come too late."

"But you will keep the rest of us alive!"

"We will, or we will die with you," he promised.

"Alan—help the men find what remains of our tools. Mary, help me get together water, and what food we can find."

Her hands were still against him. "We will fight with you, or die!" she said softly.

He watched her as she drew her hands back and walked around him with a determined sway of her hips.

"Let's get going! Darkness comes quickly!"

"To the dead, my brothers," Peter said to his monks.

Ragnor shook his head, but the monks went to work with ferocious energy, collecting the animals and the people. A great crematory bonfire was lit.

The smell of the roasting flesh was ghastly.

Even to a Viking, Hagan told him woefully.

By nightfall, Peter insisted they all go into the

church. Hagan agreed. Norsemen did not fear the dark, he assured Peter, but his men were worn. The church afforded the best center of defense, with the spiked wall they had built circling around it.

Hours passed. The surviving women had gathered what food and water they could. The chieftain's daughter came to Ragnor's guard post by a window, standing by him as he looked out on the moonlit night.

"Hagan says another man will take watch. You are to eat," she told him. "Come, I have food for you."

She led him to a corner where the hard wooden benches had been drawn together, creating an awkward table.

He ate, wolfing down his food, then looking at her. "Have I taken your share?"

"If you had, you would have been welcome. I am in your service . . . though, of course, your kind take what you will."

He sat back. "My kind?"

She shrugged. "Vikings."

"Ah. Vikings."

She lowered her head for a moment, then stared at him again, smiling ruefully. "All right. Perhaps it is not just Vikings."

"Oh?"

"Men. Men always take what they will, and leave behind . . . devastation."

"Did you see these men, these dark enemies, come in the night?"

She looked away from him.

"I've seen nothing. I came here and hid under the altar, as my father said. We knew that they were coming, by darkness. Most of the men went out to fight.

You saw what befell them. Some of the women and children made it to the church. Most did not."

"I didn't see you when we met with your father and the others," he told her. "I didn't know the chieftain had a daughter. What is your name?"

She looked at him, hazel eyes brilliant.

"Nari," she told him. "My name is Nari." And she slid her hand into his hand, entwining her fingers with his.

CHAPTER 14

Cindy was sleeping soundly. It was a wonderful, dream-less sleep. She might have been dead to the world.

She was wakened by her husband's touch.

She groaned softly.

His whisper was against her ear. His hands were moving.

"Want me to stop?"

Yes! she almost screamed aloud.

But she didn't. She loved his attention; she was just so exhausted. But though she had been afraid to admit it, she had wondered about her husband's fidelity, and she had felt terribly jealous of the contessa, though she had determined all along that it wouldn't show. At first, of course, she had denied it to herself. She still tried to believe she was wrong. She had fallen in love with Jared as a teenager, and in all their years together, she had never lost the depth of her feelings for him. And lately . . .

It was almost as if they were kids again.

She gathered what energy she could, turning against him, stroking his cheek. "Never stop; I love you," she told him.

His energy seemed to mock her exhaustion. She told him softly, "I'm sorry, I'm just so, so tired . . ."

"That's all right." He sounded like the same old teasing Jared. "I've got the hots for two, babe."

He did. She didn't need to move. And he was so fevered and volatile she felt herself carried along.

But then he grew rough, which sometimes had been fine, but tonight . . .

He found what he needed; she would have to admit that she did too. But even as they drifted, he was kissing her again, a rough touch, teeth . . .

"Jared!" she found the anger and energy to stop him. "Jared, God I love you, but I don't understand this, you're *hurting* me."

A moment later, he was up. She saw him standing at the open window.

Now she was in pain and freezing.

"Jared, please!" she whispered.

He closed the window. She didn't feel him come back beside her.

It seemed to take every bit of energy she had to rise enough to reach the bedside lamp and turn it on.

Jared was gone.

Jordan slept so very well, deeply, dreamlessly, aware of the warmth and the touch of the man beside her. *This was probably one of the reasons people married these days,* she reflected, amused. Falling asleep beside someone this way. Resting and knowing he was beside you. A duo against the night, against the world. Someone to whom to say goodnight, and greet in the morning. This kind of feeling didn't come that often. And perhaps, it was the reason marriages fell apart, when the problems of the day intruded into the night, and there was no longer this wonderful feeling of just sleeping together.

As the night went on, she knew that he was there. Just before dawn, when the pale streaks of the sun were nothing more than a tease in the sky, he was still beside her.

Not much later, she turned for a more comfortable position. Now, the rays of dawn were just twisting their way through lattices and draperies, causing pastel whispers in the dark, and displaying the motes that danced within them.

Ragnor was no longer with her.

She rose, walking to the bathroom. "Ragnor?" she murmured, but there was no answer from him. Suddenly feeling a chill, she walked around the room, turning on all the lights. The room was empty. She checked the door. It was locked.

Perplexed, she sat at the foot of her bed. She should go back to sleep. It was ridiculously early.

She couldn't sleep, so she rose, and took a long shower. She dressed and noted her books on the desk. *She shouldn't read anymore; reading just gave her crazy thoughts.*

She went and picked up the book by the cop, plumped her pillows, and started to read again, flicking through sections she had read, noting the structure of the book. Things that had happened in history

came first, some of the examples of absolute intoler-
ance, such as the witchcraft burnings in Europe and
the hangings in Salem. There was a case of savage
murders that had occurred in France which had
received little attention due to the horror already prevalent as thousands went to the guillotine. However,
when one man, Comte d'Alargon, met his fate at the
blade, the murders, begun so suddenly and savagely,
just as quickly ceased.

The historical moved into the more modern, and
it was after a study of "modern" vampires and vampire
cults that the cop stressed the section on the psychol-
ogy of dealing with "vampires." Jordan chewed her
lip while reading that section, then suddenly flew out
of bed. She dropped the book, grabbed her key and
her purse, and left the hotel.

It was a bright, cool, but beautiful day. She wandered
along the rivas and calles she had walked the night
before. People were out and about; they walked dogs,
shopped, hurried here and there to work. At a café,
she paused for a café latte and a roll, then continued
down the street. She paused in a religious shop and
bought a number of crucifixes, small and large, and
splurged on a beautiful inlaid silver cross pendant,
and waited while the chain was adjusted for her. Her
next stop was a little shop where they sold blown glass
vials, and she went on to the first campo she could
find and the charming little church that sat within it.
Luckily, there were only a few tourists present; she still
couldn't help but look around her as she filled her
newly bought vials with holy water.

Her last shop was a pleasant open-air market where
she bought bananas, apples, grapes—and strings of
garlic.

Returning to her room, she decorated the windows with garlic. The maid had already been in, so for the day at least, her strange decoration would stand. She dripped some of the holy water on the window sills, praying. Perhaps they weren't really the usual prayers for what she was doing, for she whispered aloud, "Dear God, please don't let me be totally out of my mind."

She set the vials in clear view on her desk, grateful that this was a Roman Catholic country, and Italians were accustomed to rosaries and crosses, statues and more.

With all of that done, she went down to the concierge and asked him to call the police station for her.

Roberto Capo had yet to come in.

Next, she asked him to dial Tiff Henley, but though Tiff had left a personal message on the answering machine of her rented palazzo, Tiff herself did not come to the phone.

She thanked him, and would have taken coffee up to her room, but she saw Cindy then, sitting in the lobby.

To her amazement, Cindy, who eschewed sunglasses on the hottest days in South Carolina, had on a pair of dark glasses.

Jordan walked over to her cousin-in-law. "Cindy?"

"Jordan! Great. Want coffee?"

"Sure."

She sat down in the big, comfortable wing chair opposite the sofa where Cindy sat, staring at her.

"Something to eat?" Cindy said. "There's the nicest young waiter down here. He's earning money to spend a semester in the United States. He's an International Relations major."

"I had something earlier," Jordan said, "but coffee sounds great."

The waiter came by, a handsome young man with dark eyes and honey-colored hair. Cindy introduced them, and they talked for a few minutes about travel, the States, and where he was going in America. There were three places he really wanted to study: New York, L.A. and Miami. She suggested that he should visit Kansas as well, to get a better feel for the middle of the country.

A moment later, he brought their coffee. When he had left, Jordan leaned forward. "What's with the shades?"

"Oh!" Cindy took off her glasses. There were dark circles under her eyes. "I just—I just look like shit! So . . ."

"Cindy, you've got to see a doctor."

"We're due to go back to the States in a week—"

"They have excellent medical care in Venice. I don't know everything that Jared does, but I've read up on the place—"

"Oh, I know the doctors are good; I just really don't think that anything is wrong."

Jordan arched a brow.

Cindy shrugged. "Late hours. Really late hours."

Jordan sat back. "Jared is that much of an animal?"

Cindy flushed. "It's almost as if we're on some kind of a second honeymoon. I'm elated, of course. You know that I've loved Jared forever and ever—"

"He should let you get some sleep."

"Don't you dare say anything to him. I'll go back up in a few minutes and take a long hot bath, and then a nap."

"I'll try not to say anything," Jordan murmured.

"Doesn't he see the bags under your eyes?" she demanded.

"Jordan, if you say anything, I'll never forgive you. And watch it, please, he's coming."

Jared, in jeans and a casual jacket, came walking over to them from the entry. So her cousin had been up and about. Well, it wasn't that early anymore, she realized. It fact, it was well past noon.

He stopped by Jordan's chair and kissed her on the forehead, then sat down by his wife. Jordan watched him. He seemed to be attentive enough, taking her hand, kissing her cheek. He didn't seem to notice the circles under her eyes.

"Did you order me coffee?" he asked Cindy.

"I didn't know you were coming. I hadn't a clue as to where you were."

"You two forget; I work while I'm here."

"Just *who* do you work for, Jared?" Jordan asked.

"What?"

Cindy gave her such a frown that she amended her words. "Who were you working with?"

"Oh." He gave a wave of his hand. "Some people involved with the 'Save Venice' committee. They donate money to restore buildings, things like that." He glanced at his watch. "In fact, I have another meeting in a few minutes. And you—" He suddenly pointed a finger at Jordan. "The contessa has asked that you join us all for dinner at her palazzo tomorrow night. She is very concerned and wants to make up for the way she scared you."

"Jared, I don't want to have dinner with the contessa."

"Why not?"

"Several reasons. I don't want to go back to her

palazzo—ever. I can't imagine enjoying a dinner with her. I really dislike the woman."

He sighed deeply, stretching his hands out before him. "Jordan, I understand. But there are a lot of people I come across whom I find to be unpleasant. You don't realize what you're doing to me when you act like this. The contessa is big money. She influences lots of people who have big money."

"She's not the only woman in the world with money."

"Venice is my specialty—my love," Jared said.

He glanced at his watch again and rose. "I don't have time for coffee. Jordan, be a big kid for me, huh? You are screwing me royally here—I need you to come to dinner."

He kissed Cindy on the head again, assuming that he'd get an affirmative from Jordan on the dinner. "What are you up to today?" he asked Cindy.

"A nap."

Jared shrugged, a proud-as-a-peacock, macho look in his eyes. "Good," he whispered softly. "I'll be back by dinner."

"Love you," Cindy murmured as he started to walk away. But he paused, looking back at Jordan. "And you—what are you up to?"

She shrugged. "Maybe I can spread some more nasty rumors about the contessa."

"Jordan—"

"I'm going to return my costume. Maybe go shopping around the Rialto Bridge." She rose, giving a wave to Cindy. "I'll be in my room for a few minutes, if you need anything, Cindy."

As she walked by, Jared took her arm. "Jordan—"

"Lay off your wife!" she told him angrily and pulled free from his hold.

She was certain that he wanted to come after her; she was even certain that he wanted to haul off and strike her. But Cindy called him, and he turned back to her.

Jordan took advantage and ran up the stairs.

She didn't stay in her room as long as she had intended. She was really worried about Cindy, but as long as she intended to take a long bath and sleep, that was probably the best thing for her. Jordan picked up her latest costume to return, then, on a whim, brought the cop's book on vampires, and headed back down the stairs.

Neither Cindy nor Jared remained in the lobby.

Once again, she asked the concierge to call both Tiff and Roberto Capo for her. Tiff's answering machine came on, and Roberto Capo had yet to report to duty.

She left the Danieli and headed straight for the Arte della Anna Maria shop. After the usual greetings, everyone kissing everyone's cheeks, she lingered, admiring Lynn's latest puppets, and asking if they had all recovered from the hectic pace of the pre-party days.

"Si! All goes well," Anna Maria told her.

"We have time for coffee, a snack!" Raphael said with pleasure.

Anna Maria frowned. "All of us?"

"It's slow, not many people . . ." Raphael said hopefully. "Gina is upstairs; she can watch the shop." He slipped an arm around Anna Maria. "We'll take Jordan to the trattoria down at the corner; just for a quick break. They have spent a lot of money here, renting so many costumes!"

"Go call Gina!" Lynn told Raphael. "We'll be out waiting."

"You only want to light a cigarette. You just smoked."

"Lynn, you should wait, and catch up with us," Anna Maria said. She pointed out the window. "That lady is thinking about buying your latest harlequin. Talk to her—there is quite a price tag on the marionette, eh?"

As it happened, Lynn wound up talking to the woman interested in her art, Anna Maria went upstairs to talk to Gina, and Jordan and Raphael started walking to the trattoria. "How are you?" he asked her.

She looked at him. He seemed genuinely concerned.

"I'm not sure," she told him. "You know your friend, the policeman, Roberto Capo."

"Of course."

"Well, I went to meet him in a bar. I believe that he thinks something is going on as well, but though I don't understand the structure of the Venetian police, I think that Alfredo Manetti is his superior, and Manetti is convinced that I'm crazy."

"You met Roberto?"

"No, I went to meet him, I was almost where we were supposed to meet—then he told me to run."

"He told you to run?" Raphael was trying to make sure that he was understanding her English.

"I could see the place we were to meet, and I saw him . . . I'm sure it was him . . . and he suddenly told me to go, to run."

"Maybe he had stumbled upon a robbery or something. We're not like Rome, where the pickpockets are everywhere, but . . ."

"I don't know. I called the police station a couple of times, but he isn't in."

"That's strange. I'll call for you again from the trattoria."

They went through the line at the trattoria. Jordan liked the place very much; she could see all the food. No chance of winding up with seppia, or cuttlefish.

When they were seated, she showed Raphael the book she had carried with her. She sipped coffee, watching him. "I know that all of Venice is convinced I'm overreacting to everything because I was engaged to a cop who was killed. But this book . . . well, it stresses the fact that there are cults, and there are sick people, and that bad things do happen."

Before Raphael could reply, Anna Maria joined them, a plate of cold cuts and pasta on her tray.

Ah, at last!" she said sitting, then she glanced at the book. "What is this?"

"A book about killers who are vampires," Raphael said.

"Raphael!" Jordan protested. "It's about criminal cases in which people *thought* they were vampires, or monsters of some sort."

"You shouldn't be reading it," Anna Maria said, twirling her pasta. "You suffered enough with your fiancé."

"I know that Jared used my past as an explanation for my behavior, but I swear to you, I am completely sane," Jordan said. *Was she? Hadn't she spent the morning buying garlic and collecting holy water?*

Raphael flipped through the book. "You know, it wouldn't surprise me if the contessa was some horrid monster."

"Just because we don't like people doesn't make them monsters," Anna Maria said.

"But a severed head was found in a canal," Jordan said.

"And there have been other things," Raphael said. "Of course, in other places, they would not be so big. But here, in Italy, to desecrate a Catholic church . . ."

"What Catholic church?" Jordan demanded.

"It was no longer a Catholic church!" Anna Maria said. "The building had been *de*consecrated because of the danger in the structure."

"Still, it looked like a church, had been a church, and was still owned by the Church," Raphael said.

"What happened to it?"

"All manner of strange graffiti, that is all," Anna Maria said.

"Ancient strange graffiti," Raphael said. "Babylonian . . . Persian, something like that. The scholars never quite put it all together, or understood what was written. Much was in hieroglyphics."

"Egyptian?" Jordan murmured.

Raphael shrugged. "Rome did conquer Egypt!"

"Everywhere in the world, there is graffiti," Anna Maria said.

"Ciao!" Lynn cried, joining them at last with her tray. "I sold my marionette! Lunch is on me—oh, but you all have already paid, of course!"

"You can go buy us all some champagne," Rafael suggested.

"Not for me—no more alcohol," Jordan protested.

"And not for Raphael. He will be sending the clean costumes back to the cleaners, and attaching the wrong hats to the wrong costumes!" Anna Maria said.

But Raphael wasn't paying attention. He leaned forward. "Today's paper carried an interview with some poor young students bused in from a violent area in the former Yugoslavia. They had a wonderful time, but one of their friends did not get on the bus to go home. They seemed to think that she fell in love with Venice and intends to stay."

"If I had come from a war zone, I'd want to stay," Lynn said.

"She's probably attached herself to someone," Anna Maria commented. "Poor girl. Maybe she will find her dream."

Raphael stood up suddenly. "I'll call Roberto."

He left the table. Anna Maria shook her head. "Suppose, Jordan, that the contessa is an evil woman? We have no proof. You left her palazzo and went to the police. The police went to her palazzo. They found nothing. There has been graffiti in Venice. Tourists come in, and they don't want to leave. How can you prove anything there?"

"I can't," Jordan said. "But I believe that somehow the severed head in the canal got into the water because of the contessa."

Raphael slid back into his chair. He looked at Jordan. "Roberto called in sick today. I tried his home and got his answering machine." He passed a piece of paper to her across the table. "Here's his home number, if you wish to try later."

"Thank you. Thank you very much." She pocketed the paper in her jeans. "And!" She said suddenly, "Tiff Henley is still missing."

"Well, I'm afraid that will prove nothing," Anna Maria said. "Tiff has been known to swear she'll be at a function, and fly to Zurich the same day. I'm afraid that Tiff isn't at all dependable."

"The other cop I met, Alfredo Manetti, said that he would look into Tiff's disappearance," Jordan said.

"That's good," Anna Maria told her. "That will make you feel better, yes?"

Raphael was still flipping through the book. "I wonder how many disappearances happen without anyone knowing each year. In Venice, the government has long been concerned about the buses coming in. People sleep on them . . . they haven't enough to eat. When they leave, it is hard to have a real count of people. And some who come in . . . they are from very poor areas. They have no relatives, or their relatives are fighting to survive, and no money to spend on searching for those who may be lost. They must think that their family members have found rich Venetians, they are backpacking with other students. Maybe they have found an American, or a wealthy Japanese or German businessman."

"Raphael!" Anna Maria said with a sigh.

He looked up at her. "Remember when Carlotta stopped by for her costume? She told us that it was very strange around the church that had been so vandalized. She heard noises, and saw shadows at night."

"Shadows, in Venice, at night, imagine that!" Lynn teased.

Raphael made a face in her direction. He shook his head, staring at Jordan. "I work my fingers to the bone. *She* sells a marionette and makes a fortune!"

Jordan decided not to tell them that she saw shadows and heard noises.

"I think that you are all being far too . . ." He paused, searching for the word he wanted in English for Jordan's benefit. "Skeptical! That's it, skeptical! Jordan is right—there are bad people out there. And look how many people have seen ghosts. Or believe in spirits. And as Father Vesco once said at mass, if we believe in the power of God, or a force of good, there is also a force of evil. To the Chinese, yin and yang. Who is to say that someone has not believed himself a monster, and then gone about doing evil to people who would not be missed?"

"Raphael, you will get Jordan upset," Anna Maria protested again with a sigh.

"I'm not upset at all," Jordan said. "I'm glad that Raphael understands why I am so concerned—especially about Tiff."

Lynn looked at Anna Maria. "It is better that we admit things happen. Then Jordan doesn't feel like a fool."

"Maybe you are . . . putting egg in my face?" Anna Maria said.

"No, no—egging you on, I think," Lynn said.

Anna Maria nodded. "I do not like the contessa." She hesitated and gave a little shiver. "It is ridiculous, but I think . . ."

"Yes?" Jordan persisted.

"If evil is in people, then evil is in the contessa. Whatever money she gives, no matter that she is a benefactor of the arts."

As Jordan was listening to Anna Maria, amazed by her confession, she straightened. Where she sat at the table in the trattoria, she could see clearly out the glass door just behind the counter with the cash register.

She was sure that she saw Ragnor. Not many men were so tall, and though there were many light-haired Venetians and tourists, few were as blond as he.

She rose, kissing Anna Maria on the cheek. "You do have great instincts!" she told her. "The contessa *is evil,* I'm convinced, and I'm glad that others feel it. I think even Cindy knows it, she just pretends that it isn't true because of Jared. Excuse me, please, all of you. I think I just saw a friend."

Raphael started to protest, but she was already out of the trattoria. She rushed out to the street.

It was definitely Ragnor. He was in the calle, about a block before her. She started to follow, then stopped dead in her tracks.

A woman had joined him. A woman wearing a traditional, long, Venetian Carnevale cape. She wore a large hat that obscured her features, but no mask.

It was definitely the contessa.

She caught Ragnor by the arm. He turned to her. She said something earnestly. He lowered his head to listen.

As Jordan watched, he slipped an arm around the contessa, leading her down the next narrow alley.

For a moment Jordan stood very still, feeling the breeze against her cheeks.

Then she followed.

She reached the alley, but did not see them. She walked through the alley, coming upon the canal that stretched along the riva on the other side.

There was no sign of Ragnor or the contessa, but as she stood there, she was startled to hear slow music, and see that most of the people near her had paused, and now stood still by the canal.

A gondola was going by.

As well as being black, it was draped in black. There were bouquets of flowers strewn over the forward section.

Centered in the gondola was a coffin. Large, black, trimmed in gold. Drapings and flowers were over the coffin as well. A tall woman, dressed all in black, with a black veil, stood at the rear of the gondola, as if keeping guard over the coffin.

Behind the gondola followed others, all draped in black.

Jordan realized she was watching a Venetian funeral procession.

Next to her, a woman spoke softly in English, making the sign of the cross. "Poor Salvatore! Such a horrible end!"

"It's so sad. He was the very best. Such a handsome, charming and kind young man," replied her companion, a tall man with a German accent.

"They said it was an accident; he didn't duck for a bridge," the woman said.

The man made a guttural noise of doubt. "He was a gondolier for years! He knew every bridge in Venice. He finds a head in the water and gives it to the police . . . and then he dies."

Jordan stared at the couple next to her in amazement. "Excuse me, I'm so sorry for interrupting, but . . . is that a funeral for . . . Salvatore D'Onofrio?"

"Yes, terrible, isn't it?" the woman said. "I went on so many wonderful trips around the city with him."

"He has shown Venice to many, many foreigners," the man said.

"And he . . . he found the head in the canal."

"Yes, and brought it to the police."

"Then, the next day, he is killed by a severe blow to the head—and found in the canal himself. The body must have traveled." The woman swallowed, shaking her head. "I'm sorry, but . . . well, the body traveled. It was caught in the motor of some water vessel . . . and I'm afraid that Adriatic sharks had a way with him as well.''

"He was already dead when that came about," the German man said, consoling them both.

"Thank you, thank you for the information," Jordan said. She felt cold, cold beneath the shining warmth of the sun. As long as she lived, she would never forget the sight of the funerary gondola, draped in black, the flowers, the woman in her veil at the rear . . .

Salvatore. It was Salvatore, who had been so worried about her.

Who had found a severed human head in the water . . .

Kind, wonderful, gentle, handsome, his life ahead of him.

Salvatore D'Onofrio, a man who had known that there was danger in the shadows, a man who had warned her, taken her away, was dead.

As she stood there, the gondola passed under the archway of a pedestrian bridge.

Upon the bridge, watching as the funerary gondola poled by, was a man.

He wore the costume of the dottore.

Then, as the gondola passed, he looked straight at Jordan, stared for several minutes, raised a hand, and disappeared across the bridge.

CHAPTER 15

Jordan didn't notice the note at first. When she returned to the hotel and opened her door she was intent only on making sure that nothing had been changed.

Her garlic cloves still lined the windows. In fact, the room reeked of them.

Her vials of holy water remained where she had placed them, right on the desk. She fingered the large silver cross around her neck. It remained in place.

She went next to her computer, checking her E-mail. She was elated to see that she had received another note from the cop in New Orleans. "Please come and see us at the house, whenever you can." He left an address. She put through a call to him, but again, an answering machine picked up. She left a message. "Thank you so much, I would love to come see you."

She tried the number for Roberto Capo that
Raphael had given her. Again, she was frustrated when
an answering machine picked up. She left him a message. "Roberto, this is Jordan Riley. Please call me.
I'm worried about you. Also ... the gondolier who
died recently of a terrible accident was the man who
found the severed head in the canal. I knew him. He
warned me about danger." She hesitated. "There is
something going on here, and you seem to believe
me. Please, call me." She left the name of her hotel,
though he knew where she was staying, and her room
number as well.

She was about to call Tiff when she saw the envelope
that had been thrust beneath her door. She picked it
up and found a handwritten message in a hotel envelope. The operator had written out what she had
heard.

*Miss Henley called. Please meet her this afternoon, if you
are able.*

There was an address at the bottom of the paper.
It meant nothing to Jordan.

Once again, she made a quick survey of her room,
making sure it was properly protected. Not wanting
the night maid to come in and move anything—or
open a window—she was careful to leave the DO NOT
DISTURB notice on the door. Fingering her cross, and
putting one of the vials of holy water in her purse, she
hurried down the stairs.

At the concierge desk, she asked for directions.

"This is near the place you went the other night," he
told her. "You'll have no problems. On your map—"

"I'm so sorry. I lost the map you gave me the other
night."

"We have another. You wish to walk?"

It would soon be growing dark, but there was still daylight left. Jordan decided to walk, and to firmly retrace her footsteps. She wanted to know exactly where she was going, how to return, and also how to go back again, in case she needed to.

"Yes, I'll walk."

The concierge mapped out the best route for her and pointed out that if she were tired when it was time to return, there was a vaporetto stop nearby. She thanked him and left the hotel.

Along the way, she realized that she had left the cop's vampire book with Raphael at the table. She thought about ducking by the shop to get it back, then decided she could do that the next day. She wanted to find Tiff.

The sun was setting as she walked, and the wind was picking up, but she was still certain she could reach her objective before dark. She fingered her cross, saying a little prayer for Sal D'Onofrio. "What a good man!" she whispered out loud.

The walk was pleasant. The streets were filled with people, a few still in costume. On various corners, she saw artists and performers, including a man who did characterizations of tourists in their costumes, a woman who moved liked a robot, all dressed in silver and a dancer, on a pedestal, as if she were the figurine on a music box. On one corner, a violinist played.

Jordan stopped by each of them, leaving a few thousand lire in the hats they had set out to collect donations.

As she neared her destination, the streets grew quieter. She entered a mainly residential section of the city, with only a few tourist shops. She passed a fruit and vegetable market, campo after campo each with a beautiful church at its center, wells and statues, and even little garden areas. She wondered after a while just how many bridges she had crossed. She had meant to be so careful and determined, but she had been drawn to the charm of the entertainment for moments, even forgotten the heaviness that lay on her heart, having discovered that Sal D'Onofrio was dead.

At last, she came to a neighborhood she knew. She saw the archway under which she had last seen Roberto Capo and found the trattoria where they had been scheduled to meet. The host welcomed her, speaking English automatically, as if Jordan wore a sign that said, "I am an American, linguistically challenged."

"A table for one, signorina?"

"Not right now, thank you very much. I was to meet a friend here the other night. Roberto Capo. Do you know him?"

"Si, si. A good customer. A friend to me, too."

"Have you seen him today?"

"No, I'm afraid not. The other night . . . he was waiting for someone, yes. He had a . . . sneezes. A cold, as you say."

"So he is ill?"

"Oh, I think. He was anxious to see you. Perhaps he'll come in later. You may wait. Have a drink, on the house."

"Thank you, but I have to meet another friend. Oh, where is this address, please? I know that it is near." She showed him the map.

"Back down the calle. To your right. Somewhere there; I am not sure of this exact address, but you'll be close enough to find it."

"Thank you; grazie mille."

Outside, she realized that in the brief time she had

been in the trattoria, the sun had nearly set. There were shadows lining the streets once again.

She spoke to herself out loud to keep up her courage.

"If I don't find Tiff right away, I'll go back to the trattoria, and then straight to the vaporetto stop."

She followed the host's directions and found herself in a large campo surrounded by narrow little streets, or calles, that went off in several different directions. She looked for the address on the map, and it appeared that she was in the right place, but she didn't see anything except buildings that were old and beautiful, but were certainly not shops, restaurants, or any other kind of public place. Where the hell was Tiff?

She looked across the campo and saw the old church that had intrigued her before. It was boarded up, in great need of restoration.

Walking over to it, she saw that the boards covering many of the broken windows had fallen. Stone steps led to beautifully carved doors.

She stared at the church, tempted, then remembered how anxious she was to meet Tiff. She decided to walk down the street a way, and see if she couldn't find a resident or shopkeeper who might tell her exactly where she should be.

As she turned down one of the streets, she hesitated, looking back, remembering how Raphael had said that an old, deconsecrated church had been vandalized.

There was no graffiti on the walls, or on the boards that covered the broken windows, but it was a *de*consecrated church, she was certain. Sal D'Onofrio had told her so. It was definitely derelict. She looked around the campo, suddenly afraid that she would hear noises.

Whispers from the shadows; the flutter of wings;

hisses that seemed to sound right next to her ears, like words she couldn't quite comprehend.

The evening was quiet. The shadows were still.

She started down the street.

The sounds of her own footsteps seemed to snap and echo in the darkness.

She turned a corner and found an old woman sweeping her steps.

"Mi scusi, per piacere . . ." What was the proper tense for 'do you know where this is' when asking a stranger for help in finding a place?

"Sai dov'è questo numero?"

The woman understood that she needed help. She smoothed her graying hair and studied the map under the light from her front door.

"Si. La chiesa."

"La chiesa?" Jordan said. *Chiesa.* Church. "È vero?"

The woman sighed impatiently. She walked forward, showing Jordan the way, right around the next corner. "La chiesa."

"La chiesa," Jordan repeated and thanked her.

Jordan walked slowly back to the campo and stared at the church. She realized that there was light coming from within. Also, though she had thought that they were closed earlier, one of the carved doors was now slightly ajar.

"Tiff, if this is some kind of a joke, I'm going to throttle you myself!" Jordan muttered.

Tentatively, she approached the church.

Not about to have any tricks played on her, she opened the door fully.

It started to swing back. She gritted her teeth and looked around the campo. There was an old metal boot scraper next to the small fountain that stood in front of the circular path immediately before the steps to the church.

The fountain merely drizzled a trail of water escaping from the mouth of a big fish.

She swore at Tiff again as she went up to the boot scraper, a metal piece made of two fish facing one another.

"The damn thing is probably rooted into the street," she muttered, using such force in her attempt to pick it up that she nearly carcened backwards with the heavy weight.

"Well, I'm wrong." She gritted her teeth as she strained to carry the heavy weight up the steps, where she opened the door wider, and propped it open with the metal boot scraper. That done, she looked in.

"Tiff?"

There were candles burning in the church, most of them seeming to glow from an altar in front of the choir stalls, a distance that seemed far from the door.

"Tiff, damn you!"

She entered the church and started along the central aisle. She meant to move quickly.

Her footsteps were slow.

She saw the chapels on either sides of the nave of the church, secretive dens of shadow. There were altars in all of them and artwork hanging above the altars.

She curled her fingers about the cross that hung round her neck.

"Tiff?"

Fear was setting in. She glanced at the side chapels to make sure that the shadows weren't moving. She imagined she heard a fluttering of wings.

It was the sound of her own breath.

Get out of here, idiot!

Then she realized that the candles at the altar were set around something in a rectangular pattern. A long rectangular pattern.

A body.

For a moment she stood dead still; even her heart seemed to cease to beat.

"Tiff?"

She started walking again, forcing her footsteps along faster.

Yes, it was Tiff. She was stretched out on the altar in a long white garment, just like the innocent ingenue in a horror movie awaiting the menace of the villain.

"Tiff, damn you, this isn't funny! Get up."

Something swept past her head.

Then, the roof above her seemed to be alive with the flutter of wings.

"Bats!" She looked up at the ceiling.

Yes, bats.

"Dive bomb me again, and I'll come back with a lighter and a can of gasoline, and let them arrest me for burning down half of Venice!" she threatened, raising a hand to the roof.

"Damn you, Tiff . . . !"

She neared the altar, shaking she was so scared and angry, but not about to leave without Tiffany Henley, and not without telling her just what she thought of this cruel nonsense.

"Tiff, get up!"

She swore, brushing her sleeve on a candle as she reached out to shake Tiff.

It was definitely Tiff. Dressed in white . . .

Like a white shroud, winding all the way up to her neck. Any minute now, Tiff would open her eyes wide and go, "Boo!" She'd tell Jordan that she just couldn't help it, she had the money to play such an elaborate joke, and she just wanted Jordan to be able to laugh at what had happened at the contessa's palazzo.

But Tiff didn't move when Jordan shook her. Her arm was stone cold.

Jordan stared at her face. Her eyes were closed. Her color was ashen.

More than ashen. She looked as if her flesh had been bleached to white.

"Tiff . . . ?"

She shook the woman again. Tiff wasn't just cold; she was icy. Jordan swallowed, losing her breath.

"Tiff?" she whispered again, this time her voice a plea.

But she knew the truth.

Tiff was dead.

She lifted her newfound friend by the shoulders. Then she gasped in horror, dropping the body and stepping back.

Tiff's head had remained on the altar. It had been severed from her body. Only the white shroud had hidden the decapitation.

She found her breath and let out a bloodcurdling scream. For an instant, she was transfixed in horror; a second later, the human drive for self-preservation shot into her like lightning.

She turned to flee, even starting to run for the open doorway before she saw that it was blocked.

A man stood there.

In black pants and a black leather jacket.

Head shining golden in the candlelight.

Ragnor Wulfsson.

"Oh, you bastard!" she shrieked, stopping, looking madly about for a weapon, something to throw. A dusty hymnal lay on the ground; she plucked it up, throwing it.

"Jordan, no!" he called to her, but she was in a frenzy, beyond listening, far beyond hearing him or comprehending.

She raced back for a candle, reaching for it with such abandon that she scattered half the candles, and disrupted the body.

She was dimly aware of the awful sound as the head hit the floor.

She threw a candle, then another.

"Jordan!" he shouted again, striding down the aisle. "Jordan, damn you, watch out, come to me, run to me!"

But she was backing away.

She had to get around him.

"Jordan!" he shouted her name again.

And then, that was all she remembered. She felt the incredible sting of a sharp thud against the back of her head.

The shadows definitely moved.

They shot across her eyes.

They formed a solid wall of blackness.

And she careened into the dust-laden marble of the deconsecrated church.

CHAPTER 16

"Jordan, Jordan . . ."

At first, she was only dimly aware of her name being spoken. Then she felt the pounding in her head. The sound of her name penetrated through the layers of darkness and she opened her eyes.

Night.

She heard a trickle of water. She shifted her head slightly; skyrockets exploded. They cleared; she looked around and focused on the face peering down into her own.

Raphael.

"There you are. I don't own a cell phone. Stay still; I'll get help."

She stretched out a hand, grasping his arm. She was quickly gaining consciousness and memory. "No, don't leave me. Look in the church."

He stared at her, thinking that she was still under the spell of the conk on her head.

"Jordan, this was not a good place to meet. I don't know what you wanted, but—"

"The church, look in the church," she said desperately. She realized exactly where she was—just feet away from the steps to the church. She lay, half off, half on the silly little fountain. She touched her face; her cheeks were damp. Raphael must have used the water from the fountain to revive her.

He stood. "You need to go to the hospital—"

"No!" she said firmly. Was she crazy? She probably did need to go to the hospital. Her skull could be fractured, for all she knew. What had happened? She'd gotten there, gone into the church, seen the body . . .

And then Ragnor.

And then . . .

"Wait!" she cried suddenly. She didn't know how she had gotten outside the church, but Raphael shouldn't go in. There was something very wrong inside.

"What?"

"Tiff, Tiff. . . is dead. On the altar. Someone cut her head off."

He stared at her, then turned toward the church. "No, don't go in! You could be in danger, Raphael—"

But he ignored her. He was already heading toward the church. The door still stood open.

The boot scraper was back, next to the fountain, right where it had been. In fact, the way she lay, it might appear that she had tripped over it, fallen, and cracked her head.

Raphael was already going up the steps. She struggled to her feet, dizzy only for a moment. Her head

was clearing. She tested her skull. It seemed fine. Her
fingers were still upon her scalp as she hurried forward
after Raphael.

He stood just within the church. He hadn't gone in
far—there was so little light.

No candles burned now.

Down the stretch of the aisle, they could just make
out the altar. It appeared to be empty.

Every instinct in Jordan screamed that she shouldn't
enter the church again, but she couldn't believe her
eyes; astonishment made her travel down the aisle
quickly, determined to see the altar, and around it.

"Hey, Jordan, allora!" Raphael cried. "Stop! This
building has been closed down until repairs can be
made. It might be dangerous in here!"

She ignored him, proceeding to the altar.

There was no sign of Tiff. Not a speck of blood.

"She was here!" Jordan said.

"Who?" Raphael demanded.

"Tiff! I'm telling you, she was here, and her head
had been cut off."

Raphael walked down the aisle. He pulled out his
keys, flashing the mini-light attached to them around
the area.

"Jordan," he said very softly. "There is nothing
here."

"There was!" she insisted.

"Jordan, Anna Maria was right. I should not have
put things into your head—"

"Dammit!" Jordan raged. "I'm telling you, I came
here, and I saw her body on the altar. I thought Tiff
was playing a joke on me—she had left me a message
to meet her here. And there she was, on the altar. So
I walked up to it, yelling at her, telling her to quit

fooling around. Then I—I touched her, I tried to shake her by the shoulders. Her body came up; her head—her head stayed down. It wasn't attached. Then I saw Ragnor at the door, and then . . . someone hit me!''

Raphael was looking at her, trying not to appear skeptical.

"Do you think that you were so afraid for Tiff that you rushed here, tripped, hit your head . . . and imagined the rest?''

"No! I didn't take any trips to Oz!''

Raphael stared at her blankly.

"I'm telling you, I didn't imagine anything.''

Raphael flashed his mini-light around the corners of the church. There was nothing to be seen anywhere. Not even a rat scurried across the floor.

"You saw Ragnor.''

"Yes.''

"In front of you?''

"At the door.''

"And he walked up to you and hit you on the head?''

"I—no!'' she murmured, confused herself for a moment.

She had seen Ragnor, yes. He had been shouting at her, hadn't he? Telling her to come to him. And she had thrown something at him . . . a hymnal.

"I don't know.''

The church was very dark, and more deeply shadowed than ever with Raphael's little mini-light flashing around. He shivered.

"Let's get out of here.''

"Wait, one second!'' she whispered. She walked back to the altar, running her fingers over it. "Raphael, she was here! There's not a speck of dust on this altar.

Look at this place—if something hadn't been there, there would be dust!''

"We'll get the police," Raphael said.

Maybe Roberto Capo would be back in the station at last. Whether they mocked her or not, she had to tell them what she had seen.

"All right. But we're not leaving this area. Things—change around here, far too quickly."

He nodded, "We'll call from the public phone down the calle. But Jordan, please, let's get out of here."

They started down the aisle—two rational human beings, walking at a steady gait. She sped up a little to catch up with him. He hurried more; she sped up again. They were running by the time they reached the door and burst out upon the steps.

Jordan nearly tripped. She would have done so, and sprawled right down on to the fountain if Raphael hadn't been there to catch her.

He kept her arm as they came down the steps and studied her gravely.

"I didn't come running out and trip and wind up knocked out by the fountain," she told him firmly.

"Let me see your head," he told her, touching her temple.

"Not there! On the back of my head. How could I have stumbled *forward* and hit myself on the *back* of my head?" she demanded.

He shrugged. "We'll call the police."

"Make sure you get the right station, and ask for Roberto Capo."

They walked to the edge of the campo where there was an enclosed public phone. Raphael called the operator, then frowned.

"Which is the station you want?"

"Near the Danieli! I'm a tourist, I don't know the address. You should know!"

"I'm a law-abiding citizen. I never call the police."

"Roberto is your friend! You should know."

He swore softly in Italian. "Si, si, I have the number." He rattled off something to the operator; she put him through. He spoke for a minute, then covered the mouthpiece. "Capo won't be in today; he has a fever."

She could hear someone speaking into the phone. Raphael winced. "Alfredo Manetti is on the line."

Jordan threw up her hands. Convincing him of anything was impossible. She'd have to deliver her own head on a silver platter for him to believe that something was really wrong.

Raphael started speaking. He talked a long time.

He gave Jordan a number of sideways glances, and talked some more.

He hung up. "They are coming," he told her. "Come on, we'll get you a drink—"

"I don't want a drink; no alcohol."

"You may have a concussion, yet? Big bump, bruise on the bone. No alcohol; you're right. But a café or tè—we'll probably have a few minutes to wait. I told him that no, it wasn't exactly an emergency. No one is in danger at the moment."

Jordan wondered if that was true. Looking around the campo, she shivered. She heard no hisses, whispers or wings. The shadows stretched long in the night, but they weren't moving.

Still, she felt as if they were being watched. As if evil eyes looked out at them from the darkness.

"Coffee will be fine," she murmured.

They walked back to the trattoria. The same kind host met them. Before Jordan knew it, Raphael explained that she'd had an accident. The host's mother was there, and brought ice cubes and cold water and hot tea. She wanted Jordan's feet propped up. She was so kind and considerate that Jordan felt guilty.

It occurred to her to ask Raphael how he had come to be there. He seemed baffled. "You called."

"I called?"

"You called the shop and left me a message."

She shook her head. "I never called the shop."

"Well, someone did. I didn't take the call. Lynn answered and wrote down the message. I think she was jealous that you asked me to come, maybe, and not her."

"But I didn't call!"

A moment later, Alfredo Manetti arrived at the trattoria. He came over to the corner table where Jordan and Raphael sat, waiting. He pulled a chair out, straddled it and leaned on the back of it as he stared at the two of them.

"All right, now, Miss Riley. Tell me what happened."

She sat straight, pulling the ice bag from the back of her head and facing him squarely. "I received a note from Tiff Henley. Remember, I told you she was missing? And you promised to check on her."

Manetti nodded. "Go on."

"Her note left an address and asked me to meet her. The concierge gave me the directions. I followed them. I couldn't quite find the place, but a lady in the street told me it had to be the church. When I got there, there were candles burning. I saw something on the altar and walked up to it. What I saw was Tiff— playing a cruel joke on me, I thought. But I tried to get her to get up—and saw that she had been decapitated.''

Manetti was just staring at her. He studied her coldly. ''But the body has disappeared?'' he said.

''The body was there—have your men check. There isn't a speck of dust on the altar. And you know, if you do what I suggested before—use Luminal—that's l-u-m-i-n-a-l, in English—at least, you may find out that there are little spatters of blood around, undetectable to the naked eye, especially in the shadows of such a place.''

''Are you insulting the Italian police, Miss Riley?''

''No, I'm merely challenging your personal investigative techniques.''

He appeared a bit amused. But then he said, ''You're certain that you saw Tiffany Henley?''

''Absolutely.''

''Strange.''

''Why?''

''Well, because when I told you that I would investigate her disappearance, I did so. Mrs. Henley left Venice on an Alitalia flight to Paris Saturday at eleven A.M.''

Jordan felt as if a wave of ice water washed over her.

''That's impossible.''

''She purchased the ticket herself at the airport; the clerk remembers her.''

''Then she came back!'' Jordan whispered, but the words sounded false to her own ears. She leaned forward again. ''Will you please check out the church?''

He nodded gravely and stared at Raphael. ''What did you see?'' he asked sharply.

Raphael stuttered. He didn't want to let her down. ''Well, there was no body when I arrived.''

"And what were you doing at a boarded-up building?" Manetti asked him.

"Jordan called—"

"I didn't call."

"Someone claiming to be Jordan called me and asked me to meet her there."

Manetti nodded again. He seemed to be sympathetic.

Bull! Jordan thought

"So . . . you get a call, you arrive, and Miss Riley is unconscious by the fountain."

"Si," Raphael murmured unhappily.

"But you seem fine now, Miss Riley."

"There is a bump on the back of my head."

"Maybe we should get you to the hospital."

"No."

"But perhaps you have done injury to yourself, causing illusions."

"I am not having illusions."

"Come. We will retrace what happened."

They left the trattoria and walked back to the church. Manetti had brought other officers with him, and they were in the church. Large police lights now illuminated dark corners. The place did not appear sinister at all. Artwork was gone from the side chapels, and there was nothing above the main altar.

"There were other things here," Jordan murmured.

"They are gone now, too," Manetti said.

Jordan threw up her hands. "You have no intention of believing a thing I say, or really checking into the matter."

"On the contrary," Manetti said with a deep sigh. "You'll notice I have six officers in here. I made a point of going to the airport when I discovered that

Mrs. Henley was not at her palazzo. Now, we have looked and looked . . . but as you see, there is nothing but dust.''

Jordan strode angrily to the altar. She wiped her hands over it. "As you'll note, there is no dust here!''

"And the one thing my men did find was a crumb-filled food bag, Miss Riley. Someone has probably slept on the altar. With so many poor foreigners in Venice, this place was probably used as a shelter.''

At that moment, Jordan realized that there was nothing she could say or do that would convince this man that she had really seen Tiff Henley dead.

And decapitated.

"I nearly married a police officer—as you know. I would never play tricks on law enforcement officers,'' she told him angrily.

"I know that you would not.''

"Then—''

"I'm sorry. You hit your head, Miss Riley. I've put through a call to your hotel, but your cousin and his wife seem to be out.''

She needed help. Mental help. That's what he was trying to tell her.

"Whereas Carnevale is healthy fun for most people, perhaps it has not been the wisest time for you to visit,'' Manetti suggested softly.

She stared at him intently, but her mind was racing. *I don't trust my cousin at all anymore, sad but true. You doubt my every word. And now, the man who has made me feel secure has proven to be . . .*

What?

"I saw Ragnor Wulfsson after I saw the body. Find him and bring him in; then you'll have corroboration of what I'm telling you.''

"Fine. We'll watch for the man. Now, there is little else you can do here. I think you should go to the hospital, since we cannot reach your relatives—"

"No," she murmured. "I'm fine. No knot on my head. I'm sure I imagined my fall." She looked at him coldly. "I'll go back to my hotel, and stay in my room for a while." She was certain of what she had seen, and of what had happened. And that she was personally in danger here. "Please don't trouble yourselves too much, but if you are able to get hold of my cousin and his wife, please . . . please tell them that I'll meet them at Harry's between ten and eleven. That's usually a good time to get in without a reservation."

"Miss Riley, I'm sorry to say this, but I think it might be in your best interest to cut your visit to Venice short, and go home."

"Thank you. Maybe you're right," she told him. "I'll spend my time at the hotel looking into what arrangements can be made in the next few days."

"We'll see you to the hotel," Manetti said.

"I can walk Jordan back—" Raphael offered.

"We'll see her back," Manetti said firmly.

"That is kind of you, Officer Manetti," she said. "Especially since we must surely stop by the station first."

Manetti frowned. "The station?"

"I want to file a report. I mean, just in case any of this proves to be real in the future, surely you'll want what happened tonight in your records."

"Of course, of course," Manetti murmured.

"Raphael, I'd appreciate very much if you'd come as well." She stared at Manetti. She wanted her words recorded as she said them—she trusted Raphael to see that her account of what happened went down correctly on paper.

A police launch took them to the station. She sat with an unknown officer at a desk, ignoring his looks when his eyes fell upon her skeptically as he typed the words Raphael translated for her. Manetti looked on. As she was nearing the end of her story, there was a commotion at the front of the station. Manetti excused himself. Jordan finished, Raphael read the paper, nodded at her gravely, and she signed the typed police report.

"Let's go," she murmured to Raphael.

He nodded, but as they started to slip out the entry, they saw that Manetti was in deep conversation with a young woman who was very upset and insistent; Manetti was trying to calm her.

"What's going on?" Jordan asked.

"The woman . . . she is the sister of the gondolier who died. She is angry with Manetti, who is telling her what the autopsy report said—that her brother's body was mangled by the sea and sharks and other creatures, but that it still appeared he died from a blow to the head—slamming into the stonework of a low bridge. She says that he did not, that he was murdered."

"She's right—he was murdered," Jordan murmured.

Raphael stared at her.

"I know that she's right." Jordan sighed. "Doesn't Manetti think it's a little bit suspicious? The man finds a severed head—and all of a sudden he meets a grisly death himself?"

Raphael watched her for a moment, then whispered, "I don't think it will help right now if you bring that up."

Maybe, maybe not. Jordan couldn't help herself. She walked up to the two, apologizing to the woman in Italian, then telling Manetti. "Here I go again, insulting you. Listen to her! What kind of an ass are you? Look into Sal's death, do some investigating!"

Before Manetti could reply—and she began to fear that his reply might be an arrest and a one-way ticket to an Italian institution for the insane—she swung around, grabbed Raphael's arm, and left the station.

"I'll stay with you until we can find Cindy or Jared—" he told her, but she shook her head firmly. "I'll be okay, Raphael, honestly. In fact, I need to be alone. And you—I want you to take care of yourself. Manetti thinks I'm crazy, but something very bad is going on here. Please, Raphael stay close to other people. And wear a cross. You've been friendly with me, and I may have put you in danger."

"Jordan—"

"Sal D'Onofrio gave me a ride back to the hotel from the area of that church before he died," Jordan told him. "Please, please, Raphael, just take care of yourself."

"And what are you going to do?"

"Please don't worry. I'm going back to the hotel. I'll be locked in—"

"You said that you would go to Harry's—"

"Later, that's hours from now, and I'll walk by the front, across the main path, and there will be many people around me all the time."

He walked with her back to the hotel, kissed her on both cheeks. She promised to see him the next day; it was a lie, but she would call the shop when she could and assure him that she was fine.

When he left her, she hurried up to her room and

moved as swiftly as she could. She didn't intend to be caught there.

Ragnor had an uncanny habit of appearing when she did.

First, she went on the Internet and found that she could still get out of Venice that night. She could get a flight to Paris that would connect her directly to New Orleans. If she hurried. If she could get out of the hotel and get a water taxi to the airport quickly enough.

She paused suddenly, feeling as though a breeze had picked up in the room, when there could be no breeze. She looked around the room, an uneasy feeling seeping deep into her bones. She jumped up and searched the sitting area, then burst into the bathroom, her heart pounding. The door was still locked. She returned to her laptop, desperate to move quickly.

She booked the flight, praying that her credit card, overextended in her travels, wouldn't be rejected. She had grown overly anxious but took the time to E-mail the cop in New Orleans, telling him her flight arrangements and her time of arrival. She was going backwards, in time. If she made the nine o'clock flight out of Venice and connected with the overseas plane in Paris, her arrival time in New Orleans would be just after midnight.

She packed up her laptop, underwear, and an overnight bag, leaving the rest of her clothing and belongings in the room, carelessly shutting her bag. Terrified that some force was going to stop her, she was running as she left the room, and had to force herself to go back and lock the door.

She didn't check out, nor did she take a water taxi from the Danieli. She hurried to the hotel across Saint

Mark's Square and took a taxi from there to the airport.

After presenting her passport, she was the last person to run aboard the plane. She watched Venice disappear, feeling a strange sorrow as the plane rose in the night sky, She loved the city like few other places in the world.

But she would be back.

Gino Meroni walked into the second-floor ballroom of the palazzo.

He was alone in the room, dressed in the dottore costume. He liked to be known as the dottore. Oh, yes, he'd said. He liked to cure people of all their ills.

Gino was accustomed to the eeriness of costumes at Carnevale, and the strangeness of his employers, as well. He had shamed himself, he knew. But he had also done well in his efforts to make up for his errors, and he hadn't expected to be afraid tonight.

But he was.

A fire crackled in the great hearth. That was the only light in the room. The dottore sat in a huge wing chair by the fire, but he was a large man, and did not at all appear dwarfed by the chair; in fact, his power seemed enhanced by it. He was angry. Things tonight—things with which Gino had *not* been involved —had not gone well. He knew that the contessa was not even here, she had been wounded so badly. And the dottore . . .

He had escaped with little injury, but the contessa and others had taken a sad toll for his deliverance.

That night, Gino had done well at all his tasks.

Still, the light from the flames burning in the hearth

seemed to dance upon the room in shades of blood red. The dottore sat so still, his knuckles white on the arms of the chair as he clutched them tightly. The room was very quiet. It was an ominous silence. The dottore made Gino stand in that silence for a very long time, nervously shifting from foot to foot.

"Well?" the dottore said at last.

"I went as directed," he said. "I was able to clear our place, but I could do nothing about the woman for she wasn't alone." He didn't say that he had been clearing away the last of the refuse when the man had entered the church with the woman. He told the dottore instead that "The police came. Many of them. But it was all right. I saw to it that nothing was left behind."

"But the girl walked away with the police?"

"It doesn't matter. The police think that she's crazy." Gino then put a note of trial and exhaustion into his voice. "There was quite a mess you left behind; I was scarcely able to manage for your safety."

The dottore nodded gravely.

"So much would not have been necessary—if you had not been careless with your duties. There is still a wealth of trouble to be dealt with due to your inability to dispose of our refuse with efficiency."

He'd lost the head. That one head! He cleaned up so much for these people, and he'd lost one head . . .

"I work well for you," Gino said. "I ask no questions. I risk myself."

"You didn't bring the girl."

"I couldn't." Gino lifted his hands. "What is so special about this one girl? I can bring you dozens of girls."

"Miss Riley is my concern," the dottore said coldly. "You have failed me."

"I didn't create the problem at the church—"

"You have failed me."

"I defended you! The girl will still be available. You will have her eventually. Your game will just go on a little longer. And as to the other . . . I made one error. One mistake."

The dottore leaned forward. "There are *no* mistakes in my employ, Gino."

"The contessa said that—" Gino began, sweat breaking out on his flesh. Odd. He was sweating, yet felt cold inside, cold down to his shoes.

"The contessa does not matter in this anymore. You have failed *me*."

Since he'd been an adult, Gino had dealt in death and danger. Entering a world of crime, he had always known what the consequences could be.

He had always thought that he would know, and accept, when his time came.

The dread and fear he felt then were horrible. He was afraid that he would begin to shake, that he would lose control of his bowels, humiliate himself completely.

Perhaps the dottore was bluffing, warning him with such a threat.

There were no mistakes.

And the dottore didn't bluff.

"So, after all my service, you will . . . you will sate your bloodlust on me," he said, and he tried to sound as if he would die with honor.

"Me? I would be sickened by you, Gino," the dottore said.

"Then . . ."

"There are others who are hungry."

The dottore lifted his hand.

From the far corners and shadows of the room, Gino heard a scurrying sound.

Hisses . . .

Laughter.

Whispers.

He wasn't going to scream, he wasn't going to . . .

The first pain seared into him. Horror began its crawl over him.

He began to choke on horror. And his own blood.

The crimson tongues of flame that had glowed over the room had been but a taste of what was to come. And as red death descended upon him, he lost all resolve.

His screams echoed with bloodcurdling agony throughout the palazzo . . .

And into the night.

Though her first flight went like clockwork, Jordan was once again the last person to board the plane when she came running along the walkway to her gate at Orly.

This time, her late arrival was good; she wound up being placed in business class with a comfortable seat and plenty of amenities. She was exhausted but tense when she sat and buckled on her seat belt. A glass of champagne seemed a good thing. Wine with dinner might help give her a few hours of sleep before she arrived in New Orleans. Dinner was good. She tried to watch a movie. The seat next to her was empty. Perfect.

But after the first few hours into the flight, she knew

that she would be missed at the hotel. Manetti would have gotten hold of Jared and Cindy by now; they'd realize that she wasn't going to show up at dinner.

If Manetti had really traced Tiff Henley's departure from Venice, he could do the same with hers. She was going to visit a man she didn't know, who could be an insane and corrupt human being, and it was beginning to seem possible that she was losing her mind.

Or else she wasn't.

She found herself looking around the plane. Again, she had the uneasy feeling she had experienced in her room.

Someone was there.

Of course someone was there. It was a full plane.

People were settling in, reading, playing with the controls at their seats. No one was watching her.

But she couldn't help it. She experienced the sense of being . . .

Followed?

The flight attendants looked suspicious, as if they were watching her. She could swear that the pinched-looking woman in the seat across the aisle was watching as well. She was skeletal looking. Jordan could swear she could see the outline of her teeth beneath her thin skin.

That is crazy! she told herself.

She forced herself to close her eyes, to try to sleep. The champagne, wine, and long hours she had been keeping all seemed to kick in. She slept.

There was a noise. A terrible hissing sound. Whispers . . .

The flutter of wings.

She opened her eyes. The flight attendants had gathered to stare at her. The skinny woman was

between them. They all stared, and smiled, then
opened their mouths.

*They had far more than teeth . . . they had fangs, canine
fangs, huge, glistening, white, seeming to drip a slimy green
liquid. No, no, not dog fangs, snake fangs, long, sharp,
glistening, and they were laughing because she was here, on
the plane, cornered, and there were monsters in the world.*

*She turned, trying to back away into the next seat. She
was wearing a cross; she carried holy water . . .*

*But she couldn't reach her purse. She couldn't crawl into
the next seat because someone was there. Ragnor. And he
was laughing, and the plane was alive with flying creatures—bats. Their wings fluttered everywhere. And she whispered to Ragnor, "Help me, please, help me!" But, of course,
he would not, because he had taken her for a fool, and his
mouth was opening then, and he had the longest fangs of
all, dripping, sparkling, like razors caught in the light, but
it was midnight, deep midnight, and she could almost feel
the pain of his touch . . .*

"Miss Riley!"

She awoke with a start.

A young Frenchwoman, a flight attendant who
spoke English perfectly, was standing over her. She
had been gently touching her shoulder.

She had no fangs.

No bats flew about the plane.

"I'm afraid you were dreaming—a nightmare," the
woman told her gently, and with an awkward smile.
"You screamed," she added, indicating an irate man
standing in back of her. "It's really . . . well, we really
try not to allow our passengers to scream on overseas
flights. Other passengers think that something is
wrong. Really wrong."

"Oh, I am so sorry!" Jordan said.

The woman gave her a smile. "It's all right. None of us can help our nightmares, I guess. If you could just try to stay awake . . ."

"Yes, of course," Jordan said apologetically.

"Um . . . I mean, please, really, I know it might be hard, but you really might want to stay awake."

"Yes, of course, again, I am so sorry!" Jordan said.

"I'm sorry, too, but—it was a loud scream. They heard you in the back row."

"I'll stay awake."

She felt her cheeks reddening. She tried to apologize to the man behind her. He wasn't mollified.

Stay awake . . .

She was losing her mind.

Making everyone around her a monster.

No . . .

She wasn't losing her mind. She'd had a nightmare; she knew she'd had a nightmare.

But what had happened at the church had been real.

She glanced at her watch.

And prayed for the time to pass quickly as the plane continued over the Atlantic.

She had been dreaming . . .

And still, she had the bone-deep feeling that something wasn't right. That she was being stalked by forces unseen.

Hunted.

CHAPTER 17

Ragnor faced his brother, his own flesh and blood, and so, it seemed, a horde of demons.

And it was Nari who had led him to this point. Nari, who through his efforts to save her, had brought about the deaths of so many men. Nari, who had shared his new savage passions and hungers, and the hope that he had found a way to exist.

She didn't intend to take part in the carnage; not willing to risk injury to herself, she stood back, keeping her distance.

"So you survived," Ragnor told Hagan, buying time and trying to decide if there was a way to reach his sword.

"Survived, yes, brother. With a power greater than yours. The seventh son of the seventh son. The miraculous seventh child of the wolf! You refused to accept the gift of your birth, brother. *I* would have known what to do with such strengths and abilities. For years I lived in your shadow, knowing that our father's power lived in you, while I was the greater warrior. Now I have a power even greater than what you knew at birth. And do you know what, little brother? I don't wish to share this new strength. I know how to use this gift and rule with it. I will not let you hunt down the chosen of my kind, *our* kind, with your would-be holy but so fragile monks!'' Hagan paused to spit on the floor. ''There can be but one of us, brother. And the one who remains, who rules, will be me.''

A strange fear, deeper than that for his own exis-tence, wound into Ragnor. 'What have you done with Peter?'' he demanded.

Hagan leaned casually upon his sword. ''Well, brother, what do you think? The blood of a holy man . . . it was really quite delicious. And when we were done, we roasted the flesh. There is a singular lack of game in these parts, if you haven't noticed. The blood is the life, but I must say. there remains a tremendous joy in a well-prepared meal. And in our earlier rovings we learned that nothing of the hunt should be wasted.''

Rage filled him.

With all the supposed power of his birth, and the disease that now raged within whatever his existence might be, he should have had a sense of reason. At that moment, he did not. He lunged for his brother.

Hagan's creatures moved forward.

Ragnor managed to dive beneath the enemies and roll upon the pallet, making it to the end of the floor. He seized his sword, and turned, swinging. Blood sprayed as his weapon sliced into those creatures who had so recently glutted themselves on the weak and the holy; yet blood sprayed from his own flesh as well. He felt the pain, and felt the loss, but knew that he must not go down.

A dark man emerged from the front, and he lunged low, bringing his sword up through the creature's gullet; he was aware of the man at his rear, and more aware than anything else that he could endure injury, but not to his throat and neck.

He had to keep his head. Figuratively—literally.

A sword shot into his back. He stiffened in his agony, and spun, catching the creature right at the neck. The enemy fell, hands at his throat.

Another flew forward, lifted from the ground, sank.

Easy target. He had not for nothing learned his battle techniques at the hands of Viking masters.

More came, more went down.

But there were too many.

In the end, he bled from a hundred wounds. And in the end, he fell, and he knew that his brother, the unknown but bitter rival from the minute of his birth, would triumph.

Hagan stood over him.

"You should thank me," Hagan said. "I have let you die engaged in fierce battle. You will rise to the halls of Valhalla and drink and be merry throughout eternity."

"You will live in the darkness of the world ruled by Hel."

"No, in life I lived in darkness. Now, I live in the power and light of . . . Hagan!" He roared with laughter. "And now little brother . . ."

Ragnor clenched his teeth but kept his eyes open as he watched his brother's biceps bulge when he lifted his mighty battle sword.

But when the steel came down, it landed in the dirt by his side.

"Kill him, be done with it!" Nari hissed at his side. "He is tortured. beaten; you have proven yourself. Don't let him come back!"

Hagan roared out his wrath, and brought his sword down again. And as he hacked and hacked in fury, the others joined him, but though the blades pierced his flesh, they fell to the earth each time, short in their pursuit of his decapitation.

"It's the chain about his neck, the silver chain!" Nari cried.

"Take it!" Hagan commanded her.

He could do nothing when Nari fell to his side. She didn't so much as glance into his eyes. She reached for the silver chain, the relic the monk had placed around his neck so many years ago. But as she touched it, she screamed, backing away in pains, her fingers burning. She sizzled, smoke rising into the air, and she jumped back, astonished and in pain.

Hagan let out another great roar. He grasped the chain until the burning seemed to snake up his arms. He let it go.

"Get a stake; we'll pin it through his heart and bury him beneath the ash and stone of his precious church!" Hagan roared out.

By the time they dragged him into the night, Ragnor could feel nothing. He wasn't even aware of the shafts of wood being plunged into him.

He could not open his eyes; he couldn't feel. Darkness descended, a black void, nothingness . . .

So that, he thought, was death.

* * *

Death then was painless . . .

Life, or *existence,* was agony.

As little as he had been unaware of the damage done to him, he knew acutely the moment he came from the void; he felt the removal of each stake with an agony that brought screams tearing from his lungs and throat.

"There, look! There is something about this one!" someone cried.

Ragnor had vision. He looked up at a blond man, tall, looming over him in the decaying remnants of what had once been a village. How long he had slept, or died in his world of darkness, he did not know. Trees and vines overgrew the ashen timbers of the old church. Time had passed, days, months . . . perhaps years. The man who stood over him appeared to be one of his own kind; a Viking, one with an amused grin, a massive sword upon which he leaned, and curious blue eyes.

Another man moved into his vision, both of them towering over him.

The second man hunkered down. He was darker, and different in appearance. He wore a tunic with the woven colors of the Scots brooched over his shoulder.

"What have we here?" the fellow demanded.

"Think it's him?" the blond man asked.

"Rumor had it that we'd find him, and so it appears he is here," the Scotsman said. "Are you known as the son of the wolf?"

Ragnor studied the strange men who seemed to have dug him up with purpose. "Who are you?"

"Ah, now, I asked the question first! There has been a rumor about that the one man who might help us stand against the scourge of the isles and his blood-thirsty mistress had been buried amid the remains of the church within an old abbey. I ask you again—are you the son of the Wolf?"

"The seventh son," Ragnor agreed. "And who in damnation are you?"

"I am damnation," the man replied. "But damnation with a set of rules, a vengeance of my own, and a will to survive." He rose, stretching a hand to Ragnor. He took the hand, wincing as he tried to stand. Every wound he had received before the darkness came to life. He could scarce make it to his feet, despite the power of the man helping him up.

"He needs sleep; time to heal," the blond man said.

"Aye, and there's time," the other man said. "I am Lucian, self-proclaimed power of what we are, if you will. A monster, perhaps. But there are rules to survival, and I have my reasons for doing so—as do you. I maintain the hungers and lusts of the others, but there is a law, as well, far more ancient than my own meager existence, and those who do not accept that law will doom us all. Do you join us with your strange power, or do we pack you back in a tomb of stone and ash and the crisscross of swords where you should have perished long ago?"

Ragnor leaned on him, gritting his teeth. It was night, he realized. The light had seemed so great after the darkness of his entombment that he had thought it day. Now he looked around, and saw that these two were accompanied by something of an army. They were Viking, they were Scot, they were Irish . . . they were from the continent as well, he thought.

He looked back at the one called Lucian. "You're not monks," he murmured.

"Far from it, I'm afraid," Lucian told him. "But we like to think that we are men—or monsters—of a certain enlightenment."

"We are the rule," the other offered, and stepped forward, clapping a hand on Ragnor's back that nearly sent him sprawling once again. "I'm Wulfgar. Do you join us?"

"Why did you come for me? How did you know I was here?"

"In the worst of havoc, rumors fly. There is one who acknowledges no rule; yet there are those who say that he lives in his own world of fear as well, knowing that his brother might arise.

"We thought you should arise," Wulfgar said.

Ragnor stared at the one called Lucian. "I have free rein to destroy my brother?"

"We are counting on your knowledge of him."

"He must be destroyed, completely," Ragnor said.

Lucian shook his head. "Entombed, as you were. But for eternity. We do not destroy our own. Nor do we create more than two per century, lest we create the unbalance in the world that has occurred now."

"Now?"

"How long has he slept, Wulfgar?" Lucian asked.

"Near to a hundred years, if rumor is right."

"A hundred years . . ." Ragnor said.

"High time to wake," Lucian said, watching him. "Ah, catch him, there, Wulfgar—he's about to go down again. He needs sustenance, and proper rest."

"I need to find Hagan—and Nari."

"A time to heal, my friend," Wulfgar said.

"And then a time to fight," Lucian told him.

Night deepened, but due to the monk's insistence, they were all within the church, and the door was barricaded with rough hewn pews.

Ragnor had eaten. With the woman Nari at his side, he rested near the door to the church, back against the wall, eyes closed. He had learned to sleep in nearly any position and to wake at the first whisper of sound.

It wasn't a whisper, however, that woke him. There was a terrible noise, like a burst of thunder, a roaring, that went on beyond the church.

He stood, drawing his sword. Around him, others awoke, and leaped to their feet. The noise faded; then a slow, steady sound grew. A shrill sound, like the call of a hundred birds, or a fluttering of a thousand pairs of wings.

Ulric strode across the church floor, staring at the door. "What in the name of Thor . . . ?"

Brother Peter was at the altar, on his knees.

Ragnor strode over to him.

"What is it?" he demanded, interrupting the monk's prayer. Calmly, Peter lifted a hand, stopping the interruption. Ragnor waited, knowing that he could not sway Peter from commune with his God even if he were to put his sword to his throat.

Peter rose after a moment. "It is evil, but we will persevere this night."

"If it's evil, we will fight it!" Hagan roared.

"You cannot fight this evil with your simple methods of brutal violence," Peter said with a sigh.

"And you can fight it?" Hagan mocked.

"Yes, for I know the face of this evil."

"I will know its face if I go forth and see it!" Hagan said angrily.

Peter shook his head. "My faith in my God is stronger than the evil."

"I don't believe in your god."

"Then pray to your Odin, and if you listen well, he, too, will tell you not to venture forth from these walls."

Abruptly as the noise had come, it faded.

Peter stood still for a long time, listening. "For tonight it is over. But it will come again."

"And what do we do?" Ulric demanded, "Cower within these walls night after night? It is not our way, priest."

"I am not a priest; I am a brother," Peter said calmly. "No. They have power by day, but not the strength they have at night. They do not turn to ash in the sunlight. They are weakened by it, though, and God knows, there is little enough strength in the sun here in winter. By light, we hunt them out. We find their lair. We hunt them as we would hunt wolves, and we destroy them."

Ulric and the others voiced their disapproval, but there was a strange sound in their tones for men such as they were; there was fear among them.

They rested.

By morning, the brother had them cutting trees and preparing pikes, or stakes. Such weapons would bring the evil ones down; then they must be burned or decapitated, or they would heal themselves of the injury, and come back.

While Ragnor was in the woods, the woman, Nari, brought him water and food. After he had eaten, she sat with him, and told him that she believed the words of the brother, for she had seen the fate of the village.

She seemed different from the others, and he told

her then that he hadn't known that the chieftain, so recently among the deceased, had had a daughter.

"They are good people here. He took me in. I was orphaned when my parents came north to attack the Scots. My father was from Normandy. My mother from the south." She laughed then and told him, "My poor father! He worried, wanting a good marriage for me and fearing that I was far too hot-blooded. He knew little about women, for his wife died soon after he married, and he spent his days defending his clan from other chieftains nearby, and from the likes of men such as you. He had no idea that although we may bow our heads and pray, we long for the same excitement that stirs the souls of men."

The suggestion in her tone was obvious. They were fighting a strange and unknown enemy, and might never live to see another sun. He had not dreamed that they would make love that afternoon. They coupled in the forest; she was wild, passionate.

Later, when the midday sun rose in the sky, they rode out, searching the surrounding countryside. But that day, they found nothing, and by night, the sounds came again, violent as a storm beyond the church that they stayed in. Hagan walked around swearing; Peter prayed. The noises ceased, but later, deep into the night, the howling began.

Hagan raced for the door to the church in a fury. Peter cried for him to stop; Ragnor and Ulric fought to pull his brother back, and it took half the power of the Viking forces to bring him down.

"There is the attack," Peter said, "which these walls, however fragile they may seem to men such as you, will withstand. Then there is the temptation, the cry in the night, the seduction. These walls cannot defend you from that. You must defend yourselves within your own souls.''

Hagan was persuaded to remain within the church.

The next day, they started out again.

Still, no luck.

That night, in the church, the noises came and departed. Ragnor slept deeply until something startled him awake.

He realized that he lay against the wall alone, that Nari was no longer with him.

He swore violently, rising. The pews had been dragged away from the door. He went to the entrance and found that his brother and a few of the men were ahead of them. ''They've gotten in!'' Hagan told Peter angrily when the monk would have detained them.

''They have not gotten in!'' Peter said. ''Nari has fallen to the temptation.''

''Where was your God?'' Hagan demanded angrily.

''Not in Nari's soul,'' Peter said.

Ragnor listened, but ignored them. He was sliding his great battle sword into its sheath at his waist and preparing to ride. ''Give me what weapons you will, Peter. I am going after them. Give me your crosses, what you call holy, and we will go.''

''You fools! Don't you understand? The cross will aid you only if you believe in its power, just as the creatures cannot come in here, because they have a bloodthirst in their souls.''

''Then give me no aid. I am going,'' Ragnor said.

Peter ran after them when they departed the church, but to no avail. They rode out, a Viking party of twenty hardened warriors with shields, swords, battle-axes, maces and spikes as their weapons. In the deep of the night, it was hard to find the trail. Ulric found the human footprints, followed by those of a four-footed creature with padded paws and long claws.

"Bah, what monsters!" Hagan cried. "We are tormented by a pack of wolves."

And he would have spurred his horse to race forward in fury if Ragnor hadn't stopped him. "Wolves don't make fluttering sounds, like the wings that we have heard."

"There are wolves ahead now, and we will stop them."

"And take care as we go."

"It is your woman they have taken," Hagan said.

"And I will get her back. But we ride with care."

Through the darkness, they continued, the moon and the torches they carried gave a little illumination against the night. In time they came to a high tor, and in the forest surrounding it, the entrance to a cave, or shelter.

Hagan dismounted.

"Brother, take care!" Ragnor warned.

But Hagan shouted back, "I am not the seventh son of the seventh son, but I am a child of the great warrior wolf of our people, and I will not fear a fight! Men who would dine in Valhalla, follow me!"

They drew their weapons and headed for the cave. Gunther, known as a berserker in battle, strode ahead, and before the others even reached the dark shadows of the entry, he had let out a cry like a man meeting a hundred swords with bare flesh and bone.

They came upon them then, the enemy. They were men, and they were not. They had the darker skins of the Mediterraneans and the lighter skins of the Northern peoples. They were not so many—perhaps a dozen, and there were women among them. They didn't seem to need to stand on solid ground, but could move in the blink of an eye, rise to the air, disappear into smoke, or vapor, or air.

Ragnor rushed forward in defense of the men. The enemy did not fight with weapons, but with their bare hands.

And teeth.

They were wolves, or could appear as wolves, men one minute, creatures the next. He came into the fray, slashing. Then he remembered the monk's warning, and he went after the creatures with his sword swinging with a direct purpose, that of beheading the enemy. Two went down, three, but he found that he was fighting ever more alone because the Vikings were so quickly torn asunder by their foes. Four, five, six . . . and he stood alone, swinging in every direction, sword in his hand. He saw them coming together, forming a circle around him. Lean, thin, dark-skinned fighters in animal furs, then a tall man with the look of the North, a woman who might have come from somewhere in the East . . .

They weren't speaking, but they were communicating somehow. Closing the circle. He hefted his sword in a tremendous sweeping arc, trying to bring down as many as he could . . .

Then they were upon them. He felt the agony as his flesh ripped. Blood seemed to rush before his eyes . . .

And then darkness.

He came into consciousness late the next day. He was on the ground, and his first thought was amazement that he could be alive. Then he felt a tremendous pain, and an agony of thirst. Gritting his teeth, he sat up and looked around. His men lay all around him.

Mostly in pieces.

He staggered to his feet.

He felt some strength. If only he had water, he could pick up his dead. He could burn the remains. He could . . .

Water. He needed water.

He looked to the cave, and he looked to the sky. The winter's frail sun now seemed to be merciless. He staggered to the cave, forgetting the enemy, determined to escape the sun. Inside, he found that the enemy was gone. Slumped against the wall he found Nari. She appeared dead, but she had not been torn apart. He looked at her more closely; she wasn't quite dead.

He looked for water. For himself, and to revive her. There was none.

A rat raced by him. He stunned himself, reaching out with lightning speed, catching the rat, biting into it like a madman . . . draining it. He looked at the carcass with horror and threw it across the cave. But his strength and will to live had overcome his disgust. He rose and left the cave to gather wood. As he started to build a fire for a mass funeral pyre, he heard the sounds of hoofbeats, and when he stood, waiting, his sword at the ready against whatever enemy came, he saw that the monks were grimly riding to the scene.

Peter didn't seem surprised to see him standing.

"The others?" he asked.

"They are as you see."

"Burn them."

"As I was doing."

"Did you find Nari?"

"She is in the cave."

"I will see to her."

Peter's words disturbed Ragnor. "You will leave her be!" he thundered.

"She must be destroyed."

"They did not kill her. Perhaps she was taken to draw us out."

Peter ignored him. Ragnor went after the monk, catching him by the arm, flinging him around to face him. An overwhelming desire to tear into the monk, rip him apart with teeth and bare hands, seized him. He gritted his teeth hard, in agony to stop himself from such brutality. "Leave her be!" he commanded. "We will burn the dead."

With the help of the monks, the fire was quickly built. A deep sorrow seized him as he dragged the body of the great berserker Gunther into the flames. Torsos, limbs and heads were gathered. He could think of no words as the bodies went into the flames. The monks chanted prayers in Latin. He hoped that their supplications would bring the Norse to their own Valhalla. Yet as they smelled the burning flesh and watched the flames snap and crackle and rise to the sky, Ragnor suddenly grabbed Peter's arm. "My brother. I did not bring his body to the flame. Did you see him? He must receive this funeral rite as the others . . ."

"The brothers collected all the bodies," Peter told him. "Except that of the woman, Nari."

Ragnor nodded, and when it was done, he went back into the cave for Nari. She stirred, and awakened, and looked at him gravely, shaking as she stretched her arms out to him. "I was so afraid."

"You're all right now."

"I'm so frightened . . ."

He cradled her in his arms. "I thought you were dead. You were nearly thrown into the flames," he told her.

"But you saved me," she said, and smiled. "Ah, Ragnor, in my father's defense, you have lost everything. But we will build a world between us."

He set her upon his horse as they rode back to the church by the sea. Nari wanted to remain in the sun, though it was growing dark by the time they returned.

She could remember nothing of the night before. She could tell them nothing of their enemies.

Peter sat with Ragnor, having him relive the battle over and over again.

The monks brought food, fowl they had killed in the forest. Ragnor was ravenous; the meal did not end the hunger that seemed to be tearing into him. He knew that Peter was watching him, and as he eyed the monk in return, he again found himself seized with the desire to consume the monk.

They had been in the church; he stood abruptly and went outside. And to his horror, he found Nari down by the water, seated on a rock, the body of one of the brothers dragged over her lap, his throat torn open. Nari looked up at him. Her lips were coated in blood.

He wanted to lash out at her in horror, put her to death himself at that moment. But more than that . . .

He wanted a share of the blood. The scent of it was a power unlike anything he had ever known. He rushed forward and pushed her away; he began to ravage the body himself.

Covered in the good man's blood, he staggered to his feet.

Nari smiled at him. "There is another world out there. A world of pure power. Greater power than even you have ever known."

He jerked her to her feet.

"No. We will not live like this."

She pulled away from him. "You think you're so strong. You're weak! You don't begin to understand the gift you've been given."

"Gift?" he said incredulously. "We are cursed!"

She came close to him, leaning against him. "Help me, then. Help me."

"There has to be a way . . ." he murmured, then he shook his head. "Come." He drew his sword from its sheath and brought it back to the church.

Nari cowered at the entrance. "I can't . . . I can't go in."

"Then wait here."

"You intend to destroy us."

"I intend to give us Valhalla."

He entered the church, taking his sword and throwing it at Peter's feet. "Do it!" he demanded, shaking, his voice a roar. "Take my head, and see that I am burned to ash, and cast to the sea. Damn you, do it now! And Nari . . . you must see to Nari as well. Then set a flame on a dragon boat, and send our remains, together, out to sea."

Peter ignored the sword at his feet.

"I cannot," he said.

"Peter, don't you understand, you fool. I just *ate* one of your holy men!"

Peter shook his head. "Look where you are standing. In God's holy place. I have seen you with the desire to ravage my neck throughout the day; when we found you, I knew that you were no longer one of us. But you are who you are, and even changed, you still have the power to fight evil."

"You idiot, I *am* evil!"

"You could not be here, not in my God's house, if you were."

Ragnor let out a cry of rage and strode from the church, determined to show Peter the truth. He meant to take Nari, but she was not there.

The stupid monk! He would not believe, he could not comprehend the agony, the hunger, that tore at him. He strode straight amid the monks who worked calmly at their tasks, stoking a fire, chopping more wood. He let out a roar, a cry, a howl, ready to tear into one of them just to prove his own menace. But the monks stared back at him, unshaken.

He turned and strode into the forest, then ran . . .

And as he ran something happened. He was hunched, he was down, he was a beast, racing through brush and forest and trees. Then he slowed.

There was a buck ahead of him in a lea. He crouched lower and began a slow, stalking movement through the grass. He attacked the creature.

His hands had no fingers, just claws. He reveled in the fury of his attack, in the taste of blood.

And later . . .

The moon was full again. He rose, and he was himself, and he clutched his head in his hands, and wept. Tears did not come. His body shook with the violence of his agony, and in the end, he sat, and watched as the sun fell, and he felt a surge of power coming into him.

Peter found him there, came to him, not afraid of the night, or of Ragnor.

"You must destroy me," he told Peter. "Look what I have done."

"You've eaten a deer," Peter said with a trace of humor. "I am fond of the meat myself"

Ragnor shook his head. "I am one of them, one of the monsters."

"You must come with me."

"Where?"

"Back to the church."

Ragnor looked at him with amazement and then aggravation. "So that I can consume another monk?"

Peter merely started walking. Ragnor swore and followed him, staying on the monk's heels, as if in warning that at any moment, he might rip into him. But never once did Peter so much as look back.

The area of the village and the church smelled of burning flesh. The brothers had cremated their own.

In the church, Peter took Ragnor's hands. "You will swear a vow tonight to answer to a higher power."

"I don't believe in your God."

"I think that you do. But it doesn't matter if you swear to the One True God, or to the Allah of the Arabs, to Thor, or even the earth goddess of the pagans who came to this place before us. It is the nature of men, and of the world. There are forces. That no one denies. There is thunder, and there is calm. The earth quakes, and is still. Men fight, and they find peace. There are the innocent, and the evil. You will swear as I tell you, because I need you, and because you must exist, because for every force, there is a counterforce. My God would have no use for you if not for the free will of men, and the compassion within them."

"You are a madman."

"Then treat me as one. Do as I ask."

Ragnor repeated the words the monk demanded.

When he had done so, he realized that the monks had come into the church and were on their knees.

That night, he lay in the church in misery. The night sounds did not come. Yet long after midnight, in the darkness of deep midnight, he felt the craving to escape.

He stood by the doors to the church, and Peter came beside him.

"What is it you want of me?" Ragnor cried to him.

"You will learn. You will learn to harness the pain."

Ragnor did not believe him.

At dusk the next day, Nari returned. She came to him with bowed head, tears tremulous in her eyes. "Help me, they want to hunt me down, destroy me."

"We should be destroyed."

"No . . . they will not harm you. Please, let me stay with you. If there is a way . . . I must be with you, I beg of you."

He had never felt so alone, or so enraged, and above it all, so helpless. She knew what he felt. And she had discovered the agony within, and the only way to appease it. There was a way. She would stay with him, she would learn.

The monks built them a place to live while they stayed on at the church. In time, Ragnor discovered that the anguish could be appeased.

The forest was nearly depleted of deer.

The most savage boar could be quickly tamed.

It was a strange living; the monks ever watching, and riding on their own by day. Ragnor at last asked Peter why it was that he stayed, and what he hoped he would find when he rode. The attacks that had come so forcefully had ceased; the creatures had moved on.

"I will stay as long as you need me," Peter told him, and Ragnor was surprised, because he was certain that the monks would be much safer elsewhere.

But Peter would not elaborate.

In those days, it didn't matter. There were discoveries he made on his own. The ability to think, and to be. The strange and awesome power of the mind, and the senses. And then there were the nights, with Nari.

They had formed a bond. Greater than the horror they shared at what they had become, greater than the knowledge, the acceptance of what they were. She seemed to understand him. At night they ran, felt the wind, the darkness, the power. They feasted on blood; they made love as wildly and savagely as they hunted and hungered.

At the first light, they slept, and rested.

The monks watched, and waited.

In a year's time, Ragnor grew restless. He talked to Peter and told him that he wanted to go home, or to the isle he had called home for so many years.

Peter studied him carefully. "You're ready."

"I know that I am."

"And Nari?" Peter asked.

"She listens to me."

Peter was quiet. "Then go home. But remember, we are here."

"Why? Why don't you just go home as well?"

"Because it isn't over."

Ragnor didn't believe him. There had been no more disturbances. The few villagers who had survived were rebuilding. In time, the earth would replenish, and the population would grow. Others would come, and the cycle of life would go on.

"Return when you feel you should," Peter told Ragnor.

He sailed the next day with Nari. They returned to the isle where he had settled with so many of their followers. He created a great story regarding his brother's death in battle, every warrior deserved such a saga.

He lived with Nari, and again, sailed the seas with his men. There were wars to fight that were right, and he fought them with a vengeance.

He feasted on the violence that ruled such savage fighting. Nari was like a Viking queen, awaiting his return, and sharing with him the secret of his ever-greater strength.

Then, again, after months had passed, he felt the urge to return to the church where Peter stood guard against the evil he was so certain would come again. Nari chose to remain behind, telling him that there was a reason she must stay. A rune-sayer cast the stones, and said that it was fate that she should do so.

Ragnor returned to the village with a nagging worry that something was wrong. Yet when he arrived, the village was thriving, though the people still slept in the church by night. The fields were rich, the game plentiful, and others had found the village by the sea.

Ragnor slept alone in the small wooden shelter that had been made for him. He spent days with Peter, talking, arguing, learning.

Then, at dusk one night, Ragnor found Peter standing on the steps of the church, staring out at the coming of night.

"What is it?" Ragnor asked.

Peter looked at him strangely. "You don't know? You don't feel it?"

"No."

"There is something . . ."

"What?"

"They've come back."

"They?"

"They're out there. Wanting something. Watching. Waiting."

"Then stay inside. There is nothing else they can do."

But the next day, the church caught fire.

The blaze began at dusk, and all the desperate measures to keep it standing were useless. By nightfall, it burned still, and the people were left to huddle around the fire in fear.

Ragnor stood guard, aware now, of the proximity of something . . . someone. . .

A whisper of evil on the air.

Then they came.

They came in a flock, like wings of blackness. They shrilled the night air with their cries and the sounds of something beating against the air. They were nothing but shadows, and then they were real. Darkness and sensation, then a blinding vision of light in the flames.

The monks fought them with swords, strange warriors in brown robes and tonsured heads, battling the demons from above and around. They knew to go for the heads, and the enemy fell all around them. Some fell as flesh and bone, and others decayed before their eyes, and were like so much ash from the fire.

Yet when it was over, though the enemy lay all around them, so did their own. And in the darkness of the night, fire raged again as they cremated all the remains.

By light, Ragnor had to sleep. The monks and villagers set desperately to work; they built a church again, a sad structure, and the monks prayed and begged that their church be sanctified.

Ragnor awoke to find that he was not alone. Nari had come to him.

"I heard the call," she told him and touched him gently on the cheek. She curled next to him, soothing his brow, then moving against him with an ever greater need until he came fully awake in a storm of hunger to be appeased only by the volatile passion she offered. Yet then, she did not remain beside him.

She moved suddenly, and he saw what she had done.

His sword lay across the earthen floor. They surrounded the foot of the pallet that was his bed. Their leader stepped forward into the room, his sword drawn, a snarl of a mocking smile curling his lips. Ragnor rose upon his elbows with amazement. "By all the gods . . . you!"

"Time to die, seventh son of the seventh son."

Nari slipped around the other man. "I'm so sorry, Ragnor. But we are not meant to consume the vile blood of rats and boars. You might have been the greatest power among us, but . . ."

Her voice trailed away.

She had set him up for destruction; she had planned it well.

"I'm sorry, Ragnor. In Valhalla, think to forgive me."

The man with the sword stepped forward and Ragnor jumped up, naked, unarmed, but desperate to fight however long he could.

"Who wants to live forever?"

The sword made a strange silver slash against the twilight shadows haunting the room.

CHAPTER 18

When she left the plane and cleared customs, Jordan was intent only on reaching the car rental desk.

As she walked, she tried to shake the feeling that she had been surrounded by beasts on the plane—and that anyone who glanced her way was a monster, intent on her destruction.

She had just signed her rental agreement when a woman came up to her. She was tall, lean, and attractive, with green eyes, auburn hair and a quick smile. She extended a hand. "Miss Riley, my name is Jade DeVeau. I'm here to meet you."

Jordan took the woman's hand, but as she did so, she felt that someone was behind her again. After her.

Paranoia!

But she had come this far. She smiled at the woman, but was afraid. How would this woman have known to meet her? Who was she? The cop who had written the book was named Canady.

She was probably a friend, a co-worker, someone sent to meet her . . .

She had no intention of taking such a chance.

"How do you do," Jordan murmured. She looked around. The airport was not very crowded. She felt a terrible unease. She wasn't going anywhere with this woman.

"My car is in the lot, through the parking garage—" the woman began.

"Great" Jordan interrupted. "If you'll excuse me just a moment?" Jordan indicated the ladies room.

"Of course!" the other woman said.

Jordan pretended to head for the bathroom door.

The woman had taken a chair in the waiting area. Jordan just kept walking. She raced outside the airport, breathing heavily with the weight of her laptop and overnight bag. For once in her life, her prayers were answered—there was a taxi waiting. She didn't dare look for the bus that would take her to the car rental agency.

Once in the taxi, she sat back, relieved. Then she stiffened, trying to get a look at the driver in the rearview mirror. He was a dignified-looking, middle-aged black man. She still felt a sense of fear snaking into her. Then she saw the rosaries hanging from his mirror. Did that mean he was . . . safe? She had to hope so; she needed to reach her car.

Trust only yourself!

The driver took her to the rental agency. She was a wreck as she got into the Honda and checked the map they had given her. She had been to New Orleans before, and she loved the city. But she wasn't that familiar with the streets.

And I'm not thinking clearly! I'm exhausted, and I'm frightened, and I may, after all, be really, truly, crazy.

She forced herself to concentrate on the road. She had already taken a wrong turn somewhere. She was on the outskirts of the French Quarter, but she needed to find the road to the old plantations.

She couldn't drive and read the map; she had to pull over. She tried to find the inside light switch, but could not. She stared around, then realized that she was outside the gates of one of the city's famed old cemeteries. Looking through the wrought iron, she could see winged angels, crosses, and the glowing shapes of a half dozen mausoleums. Fog was settling around the ground. Swirling, creating strange, eerie shapes.

She had to get out of here.

She opened the driver's door just a hair, and the lights popped on. As she looked at the map, she was startled and then panicked by a knock at her window.

"Hey, lady, you got a dollar? Maybe you got a twenty? A five?"

The man holding on to her door was filthy. He was a white man with a thick beard, a horrendous scent, and so much dirt on him that he was the color of an islander. "Hey, lady, I know I smell. Hey, just cause there's whiskey on my breath now, doesn't mean I'm going to go buy more booze. Okay, you got some change?"

She saw his teeth. Or what he had of them. They were green and slimy. She had a vision of him changing into something else, with salivating fangs, right before her.

She screamed. Her scream startled him.

He screamed and stepped back. She gunned the car. The automobile burst out on to the road with a shriek of tires.

She didn't know which direction she was going in. She just drove.

Rudy Trenton stood on the street, watching the little red Honda drive off into the night. He shook his head, then removed his baseball cap, and scratched his head.

"Okay, lady, so I do want to buy more whiskey!" he muttered. He shook his head. "Crazy. What the hell is this world coming to? Maybe I shouldn't have asked for the twenty. Some folks just don't know about inflation."

He stretched, thinking it was time to hop the fence and find himself a nice little nook in one of the mausoleums. Lots of them were locked, but some of them were really old, and the decaying corpses inside had no living relatives left in the vicinity, so it was easy enough to crawl in and get some shelter from the night.

He grinned. Folks were scared of cemeteries. Dumb. Weren't no people less dangerous than dead folk. Hell, no, dead folks couldn't hurt you any.

Rudy turned. To his amazement, there was a man coming out of the cemetery. Or was he a man? How could he have come out of the cemetery? The gates were still locked; he hadn't jumped over the fence, as Rudy intended to do.

"Hey, buddy, you got a twenty, a five, a one, a quarter? I need some food, man. "All right, so I need a drink."

The man smiled, as if amused by Rudy's request. Rudy smiled back. He was going to get lucky. This fellow looked as if he understood a fellow's need for a drink now and then.

"Yeah, I really need a drink," Rudy said.

The fellow laughed out loud.

"So do I," he told Rudy.

Rudy started to grin.

He was still grinning when the man gripped his shoulders. He didn't stop grinning until he felt something . . . pain. Agony. The bones in his shoulders breaking . . .

He started to scream, but the sound was broken off almost immediately as his jugular was slit and the sound was drowned out by the flow of his own blood.

Jordan reached the house at last. At least she thought it was the house. It was a mansion, a beautiful old plantation, kept in top-notch shape. The porch was expansive with traditional columns, and a welcoming, white-painted swing. She glanced at the address she had written down, and at the number on the house again.

Yes, this was it.

She got out of the car, fingering the cross at her neck, patting her purse to assure herself she had her vial of holy water handy.

If this cop is legit, he's going to think I'm crazy!

Still, she had come this far.

Resolutely, she slammed the door of the Honda, strode across the lawn and up the steps, and knocked on the door.

It was immediately opened by the woman who had been at the airport. "Thank God!" she said earnestly.

Jordan felt herself blush as she stood there awkwardly. "I'm sorry; I've just had so many strange things occurring lately—"

"Yes, of course, I understand. We were still worried. Come in, come in."

Even then, Jordan hesitated. But she heard the reassuring cry of a young child in the background and she stepped over the threshold of the house. A tall, dark-haired man shook her hand as she came in.

"Mr. Canady?" she murmured.

"No, I'm Lucian DeVeau," he told her. "Jade's husband." He turned, indicating a woman behind him who was holding the toddler. "This is Maggie Canady, and Sean is right through there in the office. I was about to go out and try to find you. Jade has been very upset since she lost you at the airport."

"Again, I'm very sorry."

"You're here—it's all completely understandable. Come on in, we can all talk."

As she stepped through the foyer, she noted the historic beauty of the house. A grand stairway rose from the entry, and at the landing, there was an exquisite painting of a beautiful woman in mid-nineteenth-century dress.

"Lovely house," she murmured.

"Thank you," Maggie said. "I'm just going to put this one to bed; I'll be right with you all. You must be exhausted . . . tired, hungry, thirsty. But Jade can get you anything you need."

"Thank you."

This was very strange. All these people seemed to have been expecting her, and they all seemed to think it was quite normal that she should be here; in fact, they seemed more than relieved that she had come.

"This way," Lucian said.

"This is very rude, of course," Jordan murmured. "But . . ."

"I'm the publisher of Sean's book," Jade said. "And Lucian . . ."

"Let her meet Sean," Lucian suggested. "And then we can begin the explanations that she isn't going to believe."

She had been expecting to tell a story that no one was going to believe.

Lucian led the way across the room to a library with double doors. As she walked in, she saw a man leaning against a mantel, a drink in his hand, as he spoke to someone across the room.

"Sean, she's arrived. I didn't have to look for her," Lucian said.

"So you're Jordan Riley," Sean Canady said. He was about forty, fit and handsome, with fine, serious eyes. She started across the room, ready to shake his hand.

Then she saw the man to whom he had been speaking.

She froze where she stood; Ragnor Wulfsson was standing just across the room from where Canady leaned against the mantel.

"Jordan," Ragnor began, walking toward her.

God! This was it! She had traveled through the night, only across the expanse of the Atlantic, to find herself facing the same terror.

There would be no escape here, she thought. She had run from a place with friends and family, and she was here alone and he was here.

No escape . . .

She pictured Tiff's ashen body, saw her shoulders pull free from her head.

She turned and ran.

Ignoring the startled cries of Jade DeVeau, she shoved the woman out of her way and fled from the house, bursting through the front door, racing down the steps. She hopped into the Honda and gunned the motor, realizing that she could mire the car in the unpaved driveway if she didn't calm down and use some sense. She didn't even know where she was driving. She peeled out, and shot along the lonely strip of road.

Suddenly, she slammed on her brakes. There was something in the road ahead of her. A shadow. A shape . . .

A man. Her lights focused on a *man* standing in her path. Ragnor.

She hit the button for her window.

"Move out of the way. I swear, I'll run you over."

"Jordan, stop it, you're in danger—"

"From you!"

"No, damn you, not from me. Will you come back to the house and talk? We will do our best to explain."

"Explain that you're monsters, and that you kill people, and that Sean Canady writes about vampires with such knowledge *because he is one?*"

"Sean isn't a vampire."

"But—you are?"

"Jordan, I have to explain—"

She didn't let him finish. She floored the car, sickened that she was going to hit him, but so panicked that she could do nothing else. Yet as the car sped across the highway, Ragnor seemed to fade into the darkness.

She slowed when she came to a crossroad, peering through the window, trying desperately to decide which way to go to get back to people—lots of people. Normal people.

Then she let out a scream of terror. Ragnor was at her window. "Jordan, you've got to listen to me—"

Once again, she hit the gas pedal, shot out into the intersection. A car was coming from the left. He blared his horn.

Jordan swerved and lost control. The car spun. The next thing she knew, she was flying into the foliage at the side of the road. The car came to a violent halt as she hit a tree stump. She'd neglected to wear a seat belt in her haste to escape. She only kept herself in the car and in one piece with the death grip she had on the steering wheel.

"Jordan!" She heard his deep voice as he called to her. In panic she pushed open the door and started to run into the night.

"Jordan!"

The next thing she knew, he was behind her, his hands on her shoulders. She turned, screaming, kicking, fighting. In her effort to free herself from his grasp, she stumbled backward in a pile of weeds and fell flat, bringing him down with her.

He braced his hands against her shoulders, sprawled halfway over her. "Jordan, stop it, for the love of God, stop it! You have to listen—"

He broke off so suddenly that she ceased to fight. She stared at him and realized that he was listening to something that she didn't hear. It had taken his attention from her. If she chose just the right moment . . .

But then she heard it, too. Wings . . .

Wings in the night.

A whisper, a hiss, a warning . . .

She didn't need to escape him; he was no longer touching her. As she stared into the darkness, she saw a shadow form just feet away. Ragnor leaped to his feet, turning to face the shadow. The darkness took shape. A man, a man in a large black coat. From beneath it, he drew a long and glistening sword.

Ragnor walked toward the man on the roadway. Jordan lay stunned, watching him. Then, as she saw Ragnor draw some kind of a weapon from his jacket, she got to her feet.

She watched the two men approaching one another. The sword was swung by the stranger, a man with a face she'd never seen before. Ragnor ducked the swing of the blade, and the sword whistled through the night air.

Jordan found the strength to move. Her car was useless. She moved carefully, silently across the road, standing opposite the two men edging back toward the way she had come.

Then she saw Ragnor strike. He had only a long bladed knife, while the other man wielded a sword, but the stranger had lost his balance. Ragnor sprang forward with a sure, true aim, catching the fellow dead center in his throat.

Jordan screamed.

The man dropped his sword, clutching his throat. Blood was spilling from his wound. Ragnor went in mercilessly for the kill.

She screamed again as the man's head flopped to his side, and still, Ragnor did not cease. He struck out again, and again, until the man's head fell from his body, and into the foliage. A second later, the body—

which had wobbled even after it had lost its head—went crashing into the bushes after it.

She had never felt such pure hysteria. She simply stood, screaming and screaming, and then she saw Ragnor stare at her, and she backed away, and she wanted to run, but she couldn't, she could only stare at him as if she could preserve her own life by keeping him locked in front of her with her eyes.

"Jordan!"

Once again, she started backing away, shaking her head in disbelief and horror.

"Jordan, he was sent to— kill you. Or stop you, bring you down. I still don't completely understand—"

"Stop!" she raised a hand before her, still backing away. She hit soft dirt. Her heel sank, and again, she stumbled backward.

A second later, he was towering over her.

"Do it!" she shrieked. "Kill me, cut off my head, do . . . do . . ."

He reached a hand down to her. "Get up, scream again if you need to, and then get logical and listen to me!"

"Logical!" she said, her voice rising again.

He had a grip on her arm; he pulled her to her feet.

The headlights of a car suddenly pinned them both in brilliant light. Jordan looked to the road for help.

Sean Canady was driving the car.

Her heart sank.

"Jordan, let's go," Ragnor said curtly.

He drew her to the car. Canady opened the door; Ragnor ushered her in, then took a seat in the back.

The car made a quick U-turn.

"What are you going to do with me?" Jordan asked.

"Give you some clean clothes, by the looks of it," Canady said lightly. "Then a good stiff drink."

She caught Ragnor's eyes in the rearview mirror. They were hard blue, cold as ice.

"Imagine being a cop and having to come to grips with all of this," Canady said lightly.

"A cop—but not a vampire?" Jordan said.

"Yeah. Almost . . . but never really," Canady explained.

She fell silent, thinking that she must be dreaming, as she had been dreaming on the plane. But she wasn't dreaming. She could feel a pain pulsing in her ankle and her knee hurt. And her back. And catching sight of herself in a dim reflection on the windshield of the car, she saw that twigs and bracken were in her hair.

The car pulled up to the house. Before she had a chance to move, Ragnor left the rear seat and opened her door. He drew her out, none too gently. "Could we have a discussion now, in the house, please?"

She shook off his touch and walked up the front steps. Both the women were waiting for her there.

"Lucian?" Ragnor asked.

"He went looking for you, too," Jade said. "He was afraid you might have met with trouble."

"I did."

"Did you know him?" she asked.

He shook his head. "They've been creating their own little army. They're novices, and can't fight worth a damn."

"Come into the office, please!" Maggie said. Evidently, she had gotten her child to bed in the midst of all this.

Without looking back at Ragnor, Jordan took a seat on the edge of the antique sofa that faced the mantel.

There was a fire burning in the hearth. At least that brought a warmth to her that she found she desperately needed.

They flocked around her, Maggie on one side, Jade on the other, Sean in front of the mantel on one side, and Ragnor—who had just sawed off someone's head on the other side. He was in a leather jacket, breathing easily for a man who had just engaged in such strenuous exercise; his long blond hair somewhat tousled but his clothing still amazingly, in place. She wanted to run to him; she wanted to run away from him.

Now she knew why.

"Jordan, first of all, I swear, none of us means to hurt you in any way," Sean Canady said.

"We're trying to protect you," Maggie explained.

Jordan stared at her. "Are you a vampire?"

"No . . . but I was. That's a very long story, and I'm not exactly sure what forces gave me a cure."

"I am a vampire," Jade said softly. "By choice."

Jordan swung around to stare at her. "As is Lucian," Jade explained.

"So, you see, we know what we're talking about," Sean said.

She just stared at them, all of them, one by one.

Then she looked at Ragnor. "Great. Just great."

"There are more than you might realize," Maggie said.

"I think she needs that good stiff drink," Sean said.

"Perhaps you'd better get it," Ragnor said. "I'm sure she'll think I'm trying to poison her."

Sean brought her something in a glass. Her fingers wound around it, shaking so badly that she could hardly hold the glass. She decided to down the drink in a single swallow. How could she make things worse?

"I'll try to explain things to you in a nutshell," Sean said. "Vampires do exist. They have for centuries. They've survived, usually, by keeping a low profile."

"A low profile," Jordan repeated woodenly, extending the glass. "I think I'll have another."

Ragnor hunkered down before her. "In ancient times, it was easy. There were wars, feuds, deaths . . . everywhere."

"And no mass media," Jade said.

"And no forensic detective work," Sean continued.

"But there are legends," Ragnor said. "Some of them true, some of them exaggerated, some entirely made up."

"I existed for years, never hurting anyone," Maggie said. "But there is . . . an instinct. A hunger. And that hunger creates a disregard for human life."

"Which has been shared by many 'normal' men throughout history. There has always been a despot somewhere, a tyrant, a king, a dictator, willing to dispose of hundreds and thousands of people," Ragnor continued, his eyes hard on hers. "The Romans conquered and killed throughout Europe and beyond. The barbarians swept down on Imperial Rome. England sent armies time and time again to Scotland and Ireland; they were at war with France for years. Peter the Great did a lot for Russia, but he was a ruthless ruler. The Europeans came to America and practically wiped out the native populations. Thousands died in the slave trade. Then we entered into the modern world. Hitler attempted to decimate entire populations. Japan savaged China. There has never been a time when wanton and senseless slaughter hasn't taken place. There's always been a way for death to take place without being noticed."

"And then there have been cases of 'strange' murders throughout history," Jade said. "And of course, some have occurred through the sickness of men."

"And others through the curse of hunger," Lucian said.

"But it's a disease . . . a very strange disease," Maggie explained quickly. "And everyone who is a vampire isn't necessarily a . . . a killer."

"But those who are, of course, are exceptionally dangerous and lethal, because of their power," Jade told her.

"Most of us have done a great deal of which we are not proud," a voice said from the doorway.

Jordan turned to see that Lucian DeVeau had returned.

"That was the past," Jade said softly. And she looked at Ragnor with a shrug and an affectionate grin.

"I really need that second drink," Jordan said.

This time, Maggie jumped to her feet.

"In a nutshell," Sean continued as his wife went to refill Jordan's glass, "There was a time when there was just an order—and rules. Lucian rose to a point where he was . . ."

"King," Maggie supplied.

Jordan was glad of the drink slipped into her hands.

"King of the vampires," she echoed.

"There was an order," Lucian explained. "Things that we could do, and things we could not, passed on throughout the ages. I was guided by another, who died. Usually, when someone is turned, there is a certain force that can be felt. From time immemorial, there were laws. For survival. Vampires could not create more than two of their own kind in a century. A form of population control, you might say. We were not to destroy our own kind. We were to dispose of our victims, and not bring attention, and mass destruction, down upon ourselves. Those were the rules, for years and years.''

"There were always those who rebelled," Maggie said. "Those who would kill indiscriminately, wantonly, cruelly."

"And those who don't accept the fact that we are in the twenty-first century, and there are alternatives, so many alternatives!" Sean said.

"Sean wrote the book, Jordan, and Jade, who has a small publishing company, will get it out in the market. Because there is a danger, and has always been a danger. Only in the last few years, because of science and the media, has a clearer line been drawn between those of us who see ourselves merely as predators, and those of us who long for simple survival," Lucian said.

After two drinks, large portions of straight whiskey, Jordan didn't know whether to laugh or cry. *This* had to be a masquerade, a charade, an entertainment. Here she was in New Orleans with a cop and his publisher and God knew exactly *who* else and *what* else. *Even after all she had seen, all she knew . . .*

"So, you are the king," she said, looking at Lucian. She stared at Ragnor. "Then what exactly is your role in all this?"

"Ragnor is the enforcer," Lucian said softly. "He was born the seventh son of the seventh son, and his father had a tremendous strength and power, passed down."

"And your father, then, was the wolf, which made you Wolf's son?"

"I enforce the decisions we make," he said.

"The enforcer," she repeated, then grew angry with

herself. She was beginning to sound like a parrot. "It was you," she said coldly, "at the contessa's ball. The wolf."

"You shouldn't have been there."

"You've been the fucking wolf I've seen, in the streets at night."

"It's a matter of thought, and what's in the mind," he said. "It's what is seen by the eyes, a trick of light, or matter. Yes, I've been there. Guarding your room by the window, before you invited me in."

"So you do have to invite a vampire in?"

"I thought you'd read the book," Sean said.

"The contessa was after you—in a personal vendetta," Ragnor explained. "I had been watching her, through the city. I knew that she and her followers intended to strike the night of her ball . . . I just hadn't realized quite how large her cult had grown, what she had done. What *they* had done."

"They?"

"Nari is never alone," Lucian said. "Throughout time, she has searched out the most depraved companions."

"You shouldn't have been there, not in the section of the ball where you were," Ragnor told her. "Even with the belief that she's a predator, and like a lioness, entitled to the hunt and kill for the simple reason of her being, she's not usually stupid. She likes a fine and elegant lifestyle, and that can only be achieved when you're accepted in your chosen community. So to hunt, for her feasts of this type, she seeks out foreigners without relatives in the country. The poor, the lost, prostitutes, known crooks, drug dealers, murderers, and more. The disappearance of a bad seed is seldom researched too diligently; a dead prostitute merely brings about a belief that she asked for what she got."

"So you decided to save me from the carnage," Jordan murmured. "How lucky for me."

"I went back," he told her coldly.

"You knew it was going to happen; you let all those people die."

He shook his head. "I didn't know exactly what was going to happen. I had just discovered that she had escaped, and I was afraid that she was with someone in Venice, someone with a greater power than her own."

"Escaped—from where?"

Ragnor glanced at Lucian, who replied, "She had been entombed in a lead coffin at the bottom of the Adriatic for two hundred years. Somehow, she escaped."

"If she's a horrible creature," Jordan said, "Why don't you stop her—and then stop the others?"

Ragnor shook his head. "Nari herself is being used—yes, she's a horrible creature. But without her, we'll lose the power behind her."

"Why didn't you tell me—"

"You would have believed all this?"

"I *saw* all this!"

He shook his head. "I couldn't just walk into an office of the Venetian police and convince them that Nari was a vampire. I have the ability to kill Nari, yes—"

"Except that it's against the ancient rules," Jordan interrupted. "But I just saw you attack a man, sever his head—"

"He attacked me," Ragnor said, glancing at Lucian and shrugging. "Our old order has fallen into a certain chaos. So we have changed the rules. But at first, I thought that you had wandered into the wrong place at the wrong time. I was afraid that you would put yourself into continued danger by insisting that something be done. But that wasn't the case at all. You were meant to be there; it was planned that you should be there. Either way, I had to try to follow Nari until I found out who was really behind what was going on."

"What do you mean, it was planned that I should be there?"

"Your cousin Jared set you up. Why, I don't know. But he is under Nari's infuence."

She felt a chill. "Jared is my closest living relative. He wouldn't hurt me."

"Normally, no. But that's not the case now," Ragnor told her.

She stared into his eyes. "Why should I believe you? Why should I trust you now, when you lied to me. When you let . . . Tiff is dead. I did see her body. Then I saw you."

He shook his head with aggravation "You, you saw me, I've spent days dogging your path, trying to follow without others knowing I was there. You must understand—Nari never works alone. There's someone more powerful behind her, and strong enough now that I haven't been able to find out who. Between them, they've created a powerful network."

"So, you were using me as bait," she said.

"At first, yes," he admitted.

She sat back, having expected him to deny the words. "How can you be here? Can you travel the Atlantic by 'thought'?"

"I was on your plane."

"How did you manage that?"

"I was in your room when you pulled up reservations on the Internet."

"And you think that Jared is evil, but so far, you haven't destroyed him?"

The silence that followed startled her, and scared her deeply. Maggie cleared her throat and tried to explain. "There are different things that can happen," she murmured. "If a person is drained of their blood and dies, they'll turn—unless the body is decapitated or destroyed right away. Then there's a blood . . . taking. Bit by bit. Sometimes the infection, or whatever you would call it, can be cured then. Blood transfusions can save lives; other factors may enter in. When a vampire chooses to have obedience from a victim, blood is taken very slowly. Then the victim belongs to the vampire, perhaps doing things he might not do normally. Like Jared."

"Jared has been bleeding Cindy," Ragnor said matter-of-factly. "And surely, you know that I'm telling you the truth."

"You're not going to destroy my cousin," Jordan told Ragnor. "I read a great deal of Sean's book. I'll destroy you before I'll let you get anywhere near Jared."

"As long as Jared lives, there is a possibility that he can be wrested from Nari," Maggie said, causing both men to stare at her.

"You will not harm my cousin. I—I have holy water," she warned. Of course, she didn't really. Not now. Her purse was back in the rental car. She hadn't thought to go back after watching Ragnor take the head of the shadow creature.

Her threat didn't seem to faze anyone.

She turned on Ragnor again. "You let Tiff die!" she accused him.

He shook his head. "I had no idea Nari would go after Tiff," he said softly. "I was busy watching you."

"What about Roberto Capo?"

"Roberto Capo is fine. Or he was fine, when I left. I hadn't realized I'd be leaving Venice so abruptly."

"Why did you follow me, since you knew I was coming here?"

"I knew they'd be following you as well."

"How?"

"It's the computer age," Ragnor said, aggravated. "And there are those throughout the world who are with us—and those who are not. Don't you understand? All it would take would be one E-mail, and a killer could be waiting for you at the airport. A killer *was* waiting for you at the airport. Everything has changed in the last few years. Sides have been drawn. Nari and her group have defied all the ancient rules; they have been creating their own followers. They are weak, and foolish, and they haven't taken the time to learn anything. They die easily. But Nari doesn't care about that—her creations are all expendable. That doesn't mean they aren't dangerous."

"I saw him—I saw him that night under the arches."

"Yes, and he knew something was wrong, so he was warning you the best he could. Nari, and her most recent companion, have created a following in Venice. Like the fellow I killed on the road. I stayed behind long enough to see that Capo was safe, then came following after you as quickly as I could. Capo is really sick—he has a terrible flu."

She kept staring at him. "If all of this is going on,

and the rest of you are really such good people, why weren't you in Venice?"

"Nari isn't the only danger out there," Lucian said.

"If it had been Nari alone, I could have dealt with her the night of her ball," Ragnor said. "What's important here is that you've been targeted. Why and by whom, we have yet to understand. We need your help."

'I don't know any vampires," she told him angrily. "I've never had people ripped up in front of me before."

"You do know about vampires, at the least," Sean said.

She stared at him. "When you E-mailed me, I looked up the case in Charleston. Cultist activity was taking place."

She inhaled on a long ragged breath. "And you think that . . . that they weren't just cultists, that they were . . . real."

"Your fiancé was killed, right?"

She nodded. "She—this Nari—might relate to his death?" she asked.

"First thing tomorrow morning, I'll go in and look at all the police files again," Sean said.

"Jordan, it's important that you tell us anything you can," Lucian said. "We need to know what we're up against," Lucian said.

"I know that a man was horribly killed by a group of cultists. I didn't work with Steven; I listened to him after a day's work. I don't have names, or faces. I'm a book critic—he was the cop," Jordan said.

"Please, try to think of anything. You've got to understand. We can all be destroyed ourselves," Lucian told Jordan. "In the past, when our kind have stepped beyond the limits that might bring about mass destruction, we've found a way to imprison them, be it in a form of containment, or through physically wounding. Now, as we've told you, things have changed. There are two sides out there. And we're on yours."

She started to stand, then blinked. The whiskey, the time change, and sheer exhaustion had gotten to her.

Before she knew it, she was sliding back to the sofa. She tried to stand again and speak, but the effort needed seemed too great.

She didn't black out.

She simply faded away . . .

CHAPTER 19

The time to heal took place on a tiny island in the Irish Sea called the Isle of the Dead.

Both the Scots and the Norse, still debating ownership of many of the islands scattered south of the Hebrides — and often deciding the matter by arms — kept clear of the little island.

Unless, of course, they had business with the inhabitants there.

It was not so difficult in those days for the common people to accept the 'different.' Many worshiped in church by day, and left offerings to Mother Earth by night, baked bread for the "little people," and accepted that there was surely a god, one God, but creatures as well, not thoroughly known by man. There were enough of those "different" who were known in life; the midget, the giant, the blind man who could create incredible work in gold, the hermit in the Highlands who had lived well past a century. There were berserkers who could bring down twenty men who were double their own size, and holy men who could touch a man, and cure his ills and woes.

The folk on the Isle of the Dead were different, to be avoided . . . unless they were needed.

Sometimes, it was the spurned who came there— dwarfs who had lost favor with the noblemen they had entertained, wiccans, cursed in their homelands for supposedly bringing about famine, disease, or death. There were others there as well—those considered to be touched by the full moon, who ran in the darkness, who howled in the night. Each country claimed that some creature of their legend and lore existed upon the Isle of the Dead, from the Irish selkies, banshees, and wee people to the pixies of the Scots, the fallen gods and mischief-makers of the Norse, and even the lamia of the Middle East. Shape-shifters, ghosts, and demons, all were said to live on the Isle of the Dead. Among them as well were the simple farmers and tradesmen, those who did not fear their neighbors, for in their service they were safe from the savage attacks that came with the fierce struggles between Danes and Norse and the tribes ruling their various sectors of the British Isles.

Life, and death, were easy in those days, for wars and feuds were constant, and bloodshed was a way of existence. Men of all ilk chose their sides, and barbarism was the rule of war.

When there were no battles, there were herds of shaggy cows and sheep to tend, their populations always kept at a maximum by the natural inhabitants of the isle.

There were years in which Ragnor healed, and years

in which he learned, for one of the greatest oddities of this damned habitat was the number of holy men who came seeking help in quests for vengeance as well as for peace. Ragnor discovered early on that Lucian had his own demons to destroy, and that he intended to keep a sharp control on the world in which they existed. In his first years among the damned, he was often attended by a strange and beautiful young woman who continually appeared and disappeared, a cursed creature, but unlike themselves, damned to a life in which she must continually return to the sea.

She was Lucian's wife, from what had become a distant time and world to them. She never explained herself, or asked for explanations in return.

In time even the scars from the multitude of sword slashes that had covered his body disappeared, and it was soon after that complete healing that Ragnor awoke with the dusk to a strange feeling of unrest. Rising, he realized that he had dreamed of Nari, coming to him, whispering that she was afraid, that she needed him. She had cried, tears of shame and horror and fear. She had begged his forgiveness.

He rose and came to the wooden structure much like a longhouse where Lucian slept and entertained their guests. There, he found that an exhausted warrior, the remnants of a steel chain about his neck, had come to the isle, telling a tale about a terrible battle that had taken place in the south of England.

"The Normans arrived upon the coast of England. Our Saxon king was ready to meet them, and England should not have fallen, but in the terrible clash that took place, King Harold was killed. The Norman lord makes his way north. Comets ride the sky, and the people think that the world is coming to an end," the man told them. He was dirty and unkempt, his hair long in the Saxon manner, a scraggly beard covering his face.

"If the Saxon king has been killed, and a Norman will take the throne of England, bringing with him his own nobility, the world as they know it will come to an end," Ragnor said.

The man turned to him, startled. He then lowered his head. "Aye, the world as we have known it is indeed over, and the freedoms we have known are gone with it. But that is not why I have come." He looked back at Lucian. "As the Norman army moves north, there is death and destruction."

"That is the way of it, when one people conquer another," Lucian said. He lifted a hand. "We were not a part of this war, and were not asked to be."

"It isn't war that brings me here, though the death and devastation are pitiable and tragic. Wars are fought and won and lost. And in this battle, there were those who believed that Harold himself thought that God stood against him, and so a new reign will come to England. But much of the Norman horde was made up of mercenary troops. And it is doubtful that even the great Norman lord knew from where they all came. He came to seize the throne; men such as he seldom count the cost."

"Why are you here, if you see that this battle has been fought—and lost?" Lucian demanded.

"I don't fear death," the man said. "My name is Edgar, and I was a thane of the low country, taken, as you see—" he paused, indicating the steel collar around his throat, "—in battle, to become a serf, a slave to their feudal system. I escaped my captors when they ceased to guard us so vigilantly. Death itself is nothing. Not when a man's soul falls to God's hands. But in the wake of the Norman army . . . there came a terrible sickness. So many of the invaders were left behind to hold the countryside, to subdue the people in the towns and villages surrounding the battle. And then . . . peasants, farmers, artists, warriors, the injured, and the innocent, all began to fall prey to this illness . . . it is like a plague. A plague of demons!'' Edgar continued, red-rimmed eyes wild. He was worn, exhausted, and probably starving, but he spoke with conviction and a dignity that belied his shabby appearance. He had a straight posture, dark hair and eyes, and the courage to speak his mind. "God knows if any of the poor souls will be left alive in the south when I return. I told you, I managed my escape because the Norman invaders are afraid themselves; they stay behind walls in confinement, fearing only for themselves. It is a strange evil, seizing victims voraciously. Evil, in a sweep of shadows. They come by the day's end; the victims don't even sicken, they fall dead by morning. And there are hauntings where they return to their loved ones, and by morning, the sister, the brother, the mother has fallen dead as well, and the sickness goes on and on.''

"Perhaps it *is* black death," Lucian said, watching the man. "A man touches his wife, and her illness is his. A mother tends to her dying child, and loses her life as well.''

Edgar shook his head. "Not that kind of a plague— unless the plague can take on human form, and laugh as the priests pray over the dead and dying.''

"There is no plague, Lucian; we both know it," Ragnor said, striding up to the man. "The evil you speak of takes human form, you say. And you have seen this. Shadows, forming into solid shapes. Men— or women?"

"A woman came upon me as I helped a priest tend to a dying man before St. Mary's, near the battlefield at Hastings. She stood beside me, draped in black, as if she were a mourner. But then she laughed, and told me that the Normans had opened the door to the damned. And—"

The man suddenly broke off.

"And?" Ragnor said.

"The man whom I prayed over, dying even as I spoke the words, walked the next day. Walked with her when the dusk was falling, and stepped among the others on the field before the church . . . dying as well."

"Why do you come to us?" Lucian asked.

"Because it is rumored that you are shape-shifters as well," Edgar replied after a moment.

"And you're not afraid of us?" Ragnor inquired.

"Yes, I am."

"But you come anyway?" Lucian queried. "When your country lies in devastation?"

"Wars are won, and wars are lost, but the souls of men are eternal. Aye, I'm afraid. I was afraid on the battlefield. But not as I am now. They say that others have come here. That you can be as brutal as any conquering army . . . but when you are done, there is the order of life and death, and even the fallen can pray for salvation."

"That's quite a reputation," Lucian murmured.

"We'll come with you, south to England," Ragnor said.

"I am safe among you." Edgar said the words strongly, and yet, Ragnor thought, they were a question.

"Oh, aye," Lucian said gravely.

Wulfgar, who had been silent, laughed softly. "We drink the blood of the conquered and the holy on holidays sacred only to our kind."

The man paled, but didn't falter. "Would there be a church on this island?"

"Aye, that there is," Wulfgar told him.

The man started out. Then, in front of Ragnor, he paused. He reached out and touched the silver pendant around Ragnor's neck. He drew his hand back quickly, but studied Ragnor. "You were meant to be a great ruler; a champion of God."

"If so," Ragnor said smoothly, "perhaps God changed his mind."

"Just as evil comes in shadow, so justice can be found in evil," Edgar said, and went on.

"Saxons!" Wulfgar muttered, "they do enjoy speaking in riddles, in seeking answers where there are none."

"The answer is the balance," Ragnor said, and when they stared at him, he shrugged. "We are all three savage in battle; were before, are now. And there is little guilt, because we were all born into a world where it was right to fight and be savage against equally barbaric enemies. So it remains among men. The Normans came to seize the crown, and they will keep killing to gain it—and the Norman lord will proclaim that God is on his side, the side of right. The Saxons will fight, and they will kill, and be killed. We all believe we are right when it is our enemies we kill. All the different tribes and people fought within England in times past, and now they must fight for it. The Normans won't slay the populace indiscriminately, or there will be none to till the fields, to herd the livestock, to prepare their meals, make their clothes. It is always the same. The greatest destroyer knows that he will have gained nothing if he has not won those to serve him. As the Saxon has said—he understands battle, dominion, and death. But he believes in a death in which the souls of men will go to their God. Perhaps we are damned ourselves, but we do know that there is balance on the earth, and without it, we all perish."

"Quite a speech," Lucian told him skeptically. "So we will go out—as champions of the dead."

"We will go out because I know that Nari and my brother are most certainly to blame. And vengeance is the greatest of my concerns. I have healed, and I am ready to meet them again."

"So be it, then. We'll sail south with the Saxon."

"And pray that our ships don't sink!' Wulfgar muttered.

They sailed south, around the coast of Cornwall, then rode the distance inland. Along the way, they came upon houses etched with the sign of the cross. Bodies had been burned in great piles in the fields. At each dwelling and farmstead, they halted, and destroyed the remains of any they found within houses and home, for there were areas where no one remained to see to the dead. They rode mostly by night, and when they stopped, they prowled through the churchyards as well, where Edgar seemed to turn a shade a green as they ripped through the shrouds of the freshly buried, dismembering the bodies, or setting them on great pyres.

Never, however, did Edgar protest.

At last they came to the village known as Twickham, where Edgar's overlord had once ruled. There, the Saxon earl of the region had ruled from the power of a fortress of wood and earth, built high upon a motte.

As they approached, by moonlight, Edgar begged them to halt. "The gates were kept securely locked by night when I left. Now, they stand open."

"Wait here," Lucian told Edgar.

"I'd rather take my chances with you," Edgar said.

"Better to let him enter in flesh, while we take shadow," Ragnor said.

"I will be bait?" Edgar asked.

"We'll be with you," Ragnor assured him.

And so they left the horses behind, and concealed themselves in shadow, following as Edgar rode slowly.

Torches burned from sconces set into the walls once they breeched the main gate. And within, men in armor lay here and there upon the earth, among slaughtered animals, dung, and refuse. Edgar's horse shied, and would go no further, and so the man dismounted. He walked along, heading for the manor house, and they followed. At one point, the Saxon warrior let out a gutteral cry of fear as a body moved, a mail-clad arm reaching out for his ankle. Ragnor took form, and reached for the newly fallen man. The arm was cold as ice; stone dead. Edgar turned away as Ragnor disposed of the fresh remains of the once mighty Norman knight, removing the head with a powerful twist.

"Keep moving," Ragnor murmured, from darkness. Edgar walked on.

The door to the manor stood open as well.

Within, Hagan sat at the main table before the fire, fur-booted feet upon the rough-hewn table, hands laced behind his head as he eased in a carved oak chair. Before him, a fire burned at the hearth. Throughout the hall, the dead and dying lay at odd angles while his fellows bent over them here and there, seeking the living among the dead, hot blood which had not yet turned cold. Nari sat at the end of the table, hands folded in her lap, lips pouting as she stared at Hagan. Ragnor saw the cause of her anger; Hagan had taken one of the Norman slave collars and set it around the throat of a young, light-haired woman dressed in a tunic of fine dyed linen. She was leashed and on her knees by his chair, her eyes downcast.

"Be done with it, Hagan," Nari said angrily. "We are finished here. The others search for scraps! You claimed that you would follow the conquerors, that we could gain position and wealth, as well as a feast of the fallen."

Hagan appeared to ignore her at first, drawing on the chain that held his captive to him, catching a strand of the young woman's hair, twirling it in his fingers. Then he looked up at Nari. "I am amused by this one's courage. I think she should join us."

"I think she should not."

"You're jealous, and how silly of you, dear Nari!"

Nari sighed. "I am weary of you!"

"You're a coward. You were afraid one of those stalwart fellows so quick to slice the throats of peasants would manage to sever your pretty head. You want to run away and hide. No, that's not it, is it? You're such a liar, Nari. And such a cheat. You want to go back to Scotland and dig up my dear brother. Leash your hunger, as I have leashed this slave, and enter the world of sotted fools! Why, you're afraid of me."

"You're an idiot. You forget who I am."

"Do I? Never. You were not the chieftain's daughter, Nari, but a child adopted from a raid in the East. You had your village completely fooled—the poor naive idiots never knew that it was you, the adored child taken in by a powerful man, who brought hell on earth down upon them! But you never imagined that you would take a warrior with a greater thirst than your own, and so you have found a companion such as you never imagined! But you do still hunger for my brother, so you will allow me play with my captives."

Listening, Ragnor nearly lost his concentration and his grip on the shadow world. He had never known . . . would have never known. Brother Peter had not known that they had harbored the lamia who had started it all.

She had come to him in dreams, as if afraid, repelled by the existence she had chosen. And perhaps he had hoped that what he had seen in dreams had been true. He had never suspected that she had been the initial evil to seize upon them all.

And still . . .

Hagan's followers, dark and light, Scot, Norse, and Easterner, had gone still. Hagan himself fell silent.

They had seen Edgar, standing at the door.

"Well, well," Hagan muttered, standing. He smiled slowly. "What have we here? A strayed and beaten Saxon thane, seeking to return to his home! Well, sir Saxon, you should be pleased to see this all—before you perish, of course. There, you see, about the floor, your enemy! Aren't you pleased to see that those who thrashed you so soundly have fallen as well?"

"I see only that you are a greater destroyer than any on earth," Edgar said. "And I have come to stop you." He pulled out his sword.

Nari stood as well, backing away from the table, her eyes narrowed. Once again, she wanted no part of danger.

Hagan started to laugh. He lifted his chin. Two of his undead followers strode forward.

Edgar was no coward; he went to strike one, but the other rose, attempting to fly at him. Ragnor swept forward, hurling his weight against the creature who would seize upon Edgar's throat, and they hurtled across the room.

As Hagan became aware that Edgar had not come alone, he reached for his own weapon, striding forward in a fury, roaring out a challenge. "This is my domain! I honor no law of the ancients and will destroy anyone— living or dead—who challenges my conquest here!"

Edgar, in desperation for his life, fought with no thought of squeamishness—swinging with learned swordplay meant to sever heads as more of the demons rushed forward. But by then, Ragnor and the others had thrown off the cloaks of shadow they wore, and the room was pitched into an instant battlefield.

And while the others dealt with the dark army of Hagan's making, Ragnor stepped forward to face his brother.

"You! I should have known!" Hagan shouted, and seemed glad of the challenge. "Little brother, how many times will I be forced to put you into hell?"

"This time, Hagan, you have no edge of treachery

or surprise to serve you, and you are the one who will
lie in hell.''

Their swords clashed. Steel locked with steel, and
their eyes met as each struggled for the upper hand.
Hagan rushed at Ragnor; he ducked low, butting his
brother hard in the midriff, and casting him off with
such ferocity that he flew across the room and crashed
against the mantel, sending tongs and pokers flying
into the blaze, and sparks flying across the room.

Hagan immediately rose, howling as bits of flame
seared his flesh. Enraged, he stared from his scorched
and burning arm to his brother, and once again
came across the room, a cry like thunder on his lips.
Ragnor was ready—stepping aside of the charge,
and bringing his sword down on his brother's shoulders as he raged past. As Hagan fell, Nari suddenly
came to life, flying at Ragnor, and catching his arm.
''Ragnor, he's your brother, and one of . . . us. You
must stop, you can't—''

''I can't what, Nari? Both of you took swings at my
neck, if you'll recall.''

''But you can't do this, I know you, and I need your
forgiveness, and—''

Nari was suddenly drawn from him. Wulfgar was
there, shrugging. 'No, no, my dear. The two of them
must settle this alone.'' Wulfgar had one of the iron
collars the Normans had used on their slaves. He
chained it around her neck, dragging her back to
attach her to the heavy grate by the fire, even as
another man snarled, showing fangs, and leaped for
him. Wulfgar was adept, shaking off the fellow until
he had secured Nari, grabbing a log from the fire,
and spinning with it before the man could attack again.

But then, Hagan had stumbled back to his feet,

bleeding like a sieve, since he had glutted so heavily upon so many victims in the last weeks. Still, he smiled, seeing his brother. "Who wants to live forever, brother? I do." And he came at Ragnor again, finding an incredible strength and lifting his heavy berserker sword with a vengeance.

Ragnor dropped his own weapon, ducking under the unstoppable crush of his brother's sword so that it pinned Hagan to the ground as it fell. As his brother struggled to retrieve the weapon, he caught him from the rear and threw him once again.

This time, Hagan flew straight into the fire.

The logs crackled and then roared, and fire spewed everywhere, as if a burning comet had dropped from the heavens.

Ragnor stared at the rush of flame.

A hand fell on his back. Lucian.

"Out! We've got to get out!"

Wulfgar was there as well, taking his other arm, leading him toward the door.

Edgar the Saxon was standing by the door. "Wait!" he shouted. "The girl—the prisoner!"

He rushed back in. The manor was ablaze then in every direction. Ragnor swore, breaking free of Lucian and Wulfgar to rush after Edgar. Where the room was not alight with fire, he was misted with smoke. He knocked against the table, found the woman by touch, dragged her to her feet, threw her over his shoulder, and rushed from the flames.

They burst out into the night.

As they did so, the roof caved in with a sound of thunder in the night.

They looked back to an inferno.

"Ragnor!"

It was Nari's voice.

He looked down. He had not found the Saxon girl.
He had saved Nari.

CHAPTER 20

Jordan dreamed. This time, it was Jared standing over her in his dottore costume. "Sorry, Jordan, I'm sorry, so sorry . . ."

He pulled off the mask. The sight of him, eyes glowing a strange red, teeth glinting, glimmering, dripping, as if he was half creature from an *Alien* sequel. She watched the teeth, coming closer and closer . . .

"No, Jared, no! They'll kill you, don't you understand, they'll kill you!"

The teeth were almost on her.

She must have screamed then because she was being shaken awake. She opened her eyes. Ragnor was there. Ragnor. A creature of the night. She'd been having a passionate relationship with the undead. She nearly screamed again.

"Jordan, there is no danger. You're dreaming again."

She sat up, blinking. He was beside her, sitting on the edge of the bed. She must be upstairs in the grand old mansion. There were windows that opened to a wraparound balcony.

They were closed, secured.

The bed was set in a cherry wood frame. There were matching dressers, a rocker by the windows, a hearth in which a fire burned, the embers low. Someone had given her a flannel nightgown. She didn't remember changing, and she didn't remember coming to the bedroom.

And now, as Ragnor touched her, she drew away, staring at him. He let go of her immediately. "I grew up with my grandmother," she murmured. "She warned me about wild guys on motorcycles and dope addicts and married men. She never thought to warn me about vampires."

He ignored that.

"It's important that you help us."

"Of course. I'm bait."

"It isn't like that."

"You said that you followed me, to find out what the contessa was up to."

"At first."

"Um. Then you fell head over heels."

"I liked you," he said. "I liked the fight in you. And . . ." A small smile curled his lips. "I warned you about the vinyl. You were incredibly attractive."

"And you needed to be close to me."

"I was close to you. I became desperate to save your life."

"Why is it so hard to believe you?" she demanded. *And why did all this hurt so badly? She'd known all along that something wasn't quite right. And though she had known that, she'd still wanted him. And still did.*

"I see, because *then* you fell for me, head over heels."

"Something like that."

"But you're an enforcer. And the seventh son of the seventh son. A good bloodsucker. You know, I asked you again just who exactly you were—*what* exactly. And you told me that you were a man."

He lifted his hands. "I am a man. What exactly else? I don't know. When I was young, there was an awe and mystique about the fact that I was the seventh son of the seventh son. That supposedly meant that I had a power. Maybe it was just a power for survival. A monk I met seemed to think that meant that I was innately bound to be merciful—a strange state of being for a Viking."

"So you were a Viking—who never pillaged, ravaged, or fought?"

"I fought." He studied his hands for a moment. "I have shed blood, yes. But there was . . . that other power the monk claimed I had. When we tried to defend the last of a village against the vampires, it took many of their number to bring me down. When I thought the monk would end it all for me, he forced me to heal. And to take a vow."

"A vow?"

He lifted a hand in the air. "To defend the persecuted and the hunted; never to shed innocent blood . . . that type of thing. I swore to Odin and to the Christian God . . . so what am I? In a thousand years of existence, I haven't quite figured that out. And now, I've told you the truth. I've admitted to you that I watched you at first because I had to know who was standing behind Nari. I know her, yes, I know her well.

She's a follower. The dottore is the man behind her. But I haven't been able to get close enough to him yet to know who he is. There was a time when the rule was so strong that we could sense what was going on—"

"Lucian being the rule?"

Ragnor shrugged. "Lucian is still incredibly powerful. But . . . in the past, more violence, more crimes against humanity were acceptable. Lucian was called the king, for lack of a better description, but he had his days of extreme violence as well. Maggie . . . Maggie was always different. She denied her fate from the beginning . . . and she's much younger."

"Five, six-hundred years old?"

"Around three hundred. Maggie has always been exceptional. And even if you accept all this, don't ever deceive yourself that either Lucian or I were ever as pure in spirit as Maggie. We both have blood on our hands. But even in the old days, Lucian kept order, for preservation, for balance. No one man among us can stop all violence or the natural hunger of predators, any more than a pope could make all Catholics good people who regularly go to church. Before . . . the lines were not nearly as clear. So there was a greater order. There were always rebellions, those who defied the rules. But things had to change. And in the last few years, those who jeopardize the entire society that has moved into the twentieth-first century, who have learned new ways of existence other than in terrifying a human populace and killing indiscriminately, have gotten bolder. They want to overthrow the entire order. But it will destroy us all if they succeed."

"But if so many of your kind are capable of existing without killing, why don't you come out in the open?"

He stared at her as if she were crazy. "Many of us remember the burning days—when totally innocent people were burned at the stake. If you were told that vampires—the real thing—were living in your neighborhood, would you just say, 'Oh, how nice'? That would be like living by a lake or canal with an alligator in it. Maybe we aren't man-eating reptiles, but how many people would calmly accept such beasts in their neighborhood?"

"So you could turn into a man-eating beast?" she inquired.

"I told you—I've done my share of damage."

"You should have told me," she said.

"Oh, yeah."

"Before . . ."

"Um. That's always a great, intimate opener. Want to be with me? I don't have any sexual diseases, but I am a vampire. Honest, I promise I won't suck any blood while we're at it?"

He stood up suddenly. "You should get some more sleep." He walked out of the room then, and closed the door behind him.

She was tempted to call him back. She wanted to forget all the confessions she had heard here. She wanted the strange man who had checked out her room at the Danieli; then held her through the night.

No strange sexual diseases.

He was just a thousand or so years old, and was a vampire.

And she wasn't sure that it mattered at all. She just wanted him.

She lay back down. For once, she needed to be intelligent and logical. And keep her safe distance. She curled back into the bed. In time, she slept.

When she woke the next morning, she found that her purse and overnight bag had been brought into the room. She showered quickly, dressed, and started out the door.

From the staircase landing, she could hear them talking in the kitchen, and she paused, certain it was in her best interest to hear what they were saying before they were aware of her presence. From the long conversation last night, she could recognize the individual voices.

"I think that Jared Riley has gotten dangerous." That—from Ragnor.

"Maybe not," came a reply. Maggie.

"We're going to have to make arrangements to get to Venice," Lucian said.

"Let's let Sean get back and see what he's discovered about Charleston."

"I'm willing to bet I know what happened in Charleston," Ragnor said. "We'll have to check it out."

Ragnor's words about Venice disturbed her. They were menacing. He didn't trust Jared. He thought he should be . . .

Destroyed.

Biting her lip, she moved back up the stairway. In her room, she found her purse and dug out her phone book.

Under ordinary circumstances, she'd never make an overseas call from a house where she was a guest, but these weren't ordinary circumstances.

She dialed the Danieli, and after a moment, she was put through to Jared's room. The phone rang and rang. She felt a deepening sense of dread.

Then Cindy answered the phone.

"Cindy? It's Jordan."

She was greeted by silence. Then suddenly Cindy lashed out at her.

"You bitch! You rotten little bitch! We spent half the night looking for you. We finally traced you to the airlines and New Orleans. And by then, Jared was sick, so sick they had to take him to the hospital. I'm going there now. What the hell is the matter with you, taking off without a word like that, telling the cops to say you'd meet us at Harry's?"

"Cindy, I had to get out of there. Tiff Henley was murdered. I saw her body."

"Tiff Henley is in Paris. The cops said so. And Jared said so, too."

"Jared lied to you, Cindy."

"Don't you understand me? He's in the hospital—sick. He may be dying!"

"Cindy, I love Jared, you know that—"

"Like hell! Your mind is twisted. You went unhinged when Steven died, and now you're crazy. You're simply crazy, and you've hurt him . . ."

Cindy's voice dissolved into a torrent of tears.

"I have to go. I just came to get some things to stay with him at the hospital. If you give a damn about him, you'll get your ungrateful ass back here!"

The phone went dead in Jordan's hands. She felt someone at the door. Great. Good thing she'd never decided to be either a criminal or a cop. She'd left the door open to make her secret call.

Ragnor was standing there.

"I have to go back to Venice. Immediately. You may not have to destroy Jared. Cindy says he may be dying."

"We'll go back to Venice," he said, eyeing her coldly. "But you shouldn't have called. Phone calls can be traced."

"They already knew I was in New Orleans."

"And now they'll know we're warned about Jared." He paused. "There's another stop we have to make first."

"Where?"

"Charleston."

"Why?"

"Sean has spent the day tracing your Steven Moore. He made a really sudden appearance in Charleston. He'd also disappeared from his last job in New York. Supposedly, he'd been injured and suffered amnesia on his way to recovery. Oddly enough, his family died at the same time. A close friend on the New York force met with a serious accident. No one remembered him very well."

"What are you saying?"

"I'm saying that your fiancé might have been a rather cunning vampire."

She shook her head. "No—that's impossible. You didn't know him. He was the kindest man, the most compassionate—"

"And maybe a damned good actor. Make yourself a cop. It's amazing how that could keep a lot of evidence from being found. And amazing how easy it would be to get rid of people who were getting too nosy. And how easy to restrain people when they were trying to escape."

"You're wrong!"

"I'll be happy for you to prove me wrong."

"How?"

He turned and started out of the room. She ran after him, grabbing his arm. She let it go quickly, having forgotten in the last few hours just how much power lay in his biceps.

"What are you planning?" she asked.

"We have to exhume Steven Moore."

She gasped, backing away. "He was burned! And you can't just dig him up—an exhumation order could take days . . . weeks. More. And I have to get to Venice—"

"We'll be on a plane by midnight," he told her.

"Then—"

"We'll be in Charleston in a matter of hours. And as soon as it's dusk—"

"You're going to dig him up yourself?" she asked incredulously. "No, no, we can't. I'm telling you, he was burned. He's been buried a year. He's deep in the ground, in a sealed coffin."

"I'm willing to bet your coffin is empty."

"Steven was never evil! We'll be wasting time. You'll see—he's going to be in his coffin."

"You're right; we'll see."

"You won't be able to get him out of the ground—"

"I'll have help. Lucian and Sean will be with us."

"And the three of you are going to sneak into a cemetery at night and dig up his coffin?"

"The four of us," he said. "You're coming too. I don't intend to let you out of my sight."

* * *

They had entered a new age.

Maggie Canady arranged for their flight tickets on the way to the airport via her phone and when they arrived at the airport, they arranged for their transportation from Charleston to Rome and on to Venice. He never left Maggie alone with their toddler and their infant.

While waiting for last-minute arrangements to be made, Jordan had a few minutes alone with the two women.

'You still look shell-shocked,'' Maggie told her.

"I am still shell-shocked. I read your husband's book. I knew something was going on, that strange things were happening, but I was looking for logical explanations. I thought there were killers loose—"

"There are killers loose," Jade commented.

"But in legend and lore, all vampires are killers," Jordan insisted.

"And most of us have killed," Maggie murmured.

"But you're not a vampire anymore. I've never heard of a vampire being cured, in any legend, television show, movie, book, what have you."

"There is a very old legend that if the tie between a mortal and a vampire is deep enough, a bloodletting can bring back mortality. In my instance . . . this is too long and confusing a story to tell quickly. When I met Sean . . . well, I think he lived before. We became involved here, in New Orleans, because an old enemy of mine was active and Sean was the cop on the case. I don't have all the answers; for us it worked."

"Okay, you were a vampire, but now you're human. And Jade, you were human, but now you're a vampire. So you weren't Lucian's long-lost soul mate."

Jade looked at Maggie. "She sounds so skeptical. Doesn't this all sound perfectly normal to you?"

"I remember when you thought we were all insane," Maggie said.

Jade shrugged. "I came across a group of terrorists in Scotland, chewing up tourists. They tried to finish off the survivors one by one, and there I met Lucian. I think he believes I lived before; I don't."

"But you say that you are now a vampire," Jordan reminded her.

"I was caught in the final episode with the creatures terrorizing the vaults and crypts of Scotland. With the depths of the tainting I received . . . well, it doesn't matter. Lucian had no desire to become mortal; he was well aware that the upheaval was happening, and he felt responsible to see that . . . that the world changed. He was responsible for his own kind, and to keep a balance and . . ."

"And to protect people," Maggie said flatly. "Jordan, the world is black and white and all shades of gray. But you have to believe us; maybe we're all trying to make amends now. Maybe all vampires want to believe even they can get to heaven one day. I don't know. It's just that in the last year or so, many of the stricken—the cursed, or the blessed, as you would have it—have formed something of a coalition. They lead fairly ordinary lives, and when such an upheaval occurs, they fight it together. Anyway, here they are . . . coming for you. Take care; trust us, please trust us!"

Maggie gave her a hug as Ragnor came for her. "Hurry—we'll just make the plane."

He led her into the airport as Sean and Lucian said

good-bye to their wives. He was all business, in a hurry to make sure they didn't miss their flight.

She was seated next to him on the short hop from New Orleans to Charleston. She was still worn to a frazzle, and he seemed in no mood for conversation. When the plane landed, they immediately searched for a car rental place.

"What about the car I wrecked yesterday?" she asked Ragnor at the desk.

"Sean took care of it."

"But—"

"He's a cop. He took care of it," Ragnor said again.

A few minutes later, they had their car. It wasn't quite dark.

"We can go to my house, if you want," Jordan suggested.

"No . . . I'm not sure that's such a good idea."

"Hey, I know a great restaurant in the area," Sean suggested. "Southern fried cooking, but then, those two don't have to worry about high cholesterol."

Jordan tried to smile at the joke.

She knew the place where they stopped. It was an old converted house on the outskirts of town, very near the cemetery.

Both Sean and Lucian ordered fried chicken, potatoes, succotash, salads and desserts. They ordered wine with dinner.

She decided that since she was going to dig up the grave of a man she had loved, she needed a large glass of wine as well.

"And to think," she murmured, halfway through the meal, "legend has it that vampires don't need normal sustenance, only blood."

Ragnor looked at her seriously. "We do like our meat rare."

"How have you managed . . . the—er—kind of sustenance you do need?" she asked awkwardly.

"We often pay visits to the local blood banks," Lucian said. "And animal blood will suffice."

"Human is better," Ragnor said flatly.

"Are you trying to make me more nervous?" she asked him.

He leaned close to her. "If I intended to take your blood, Jordan, I could have done so many times before now."

"She's not a very trusting soul, is she?" Lucian inquired.

"Oh, and I should be?"

Ragnor shrugged. "Left corner table," he said to Lucian and Sean.

Jordan started to move her chair back. "No," Ragnor warned her softly.

"What are you telling them?" she demanded.

"We're just keeping an eye out."

"For—"

"Hey!" Sean said. "I'm a cop. My eyes are always open."

None of them explained any further. Lucian asked for the check and paid it. It was time to leave.

When they reached the cemetery, Sean drove the rental car deep into a grove of trees by the side of the very old burial ground.

"We'll have the gate open in a minute," Ragnor told them. He and Lucian started walking toward the entry. They disappeared into the darkness. A moment later, Sean and Jordan heard the creaking of the old gate.

Sean carried a duffel bag with him as they started in.

"What if the Charleston cops show up here?" Jordan demanded.

"We'll be done before anyone shows," Sean assured her. "Let's go."

Inside the now open ten foot gates, Ragnor and Lucian were waiting for them. As so often occurred at night in the outlands of Charleston, fog sat low on the ground. For a moment, Jordan closed her eyes, thinking of the insanity of what she was doing. On a dark and foggy night, she was wandering around a cemetery with a very strange cop and two self-proclaimed vampires.

Fog drifted around sculpted burial figures. Cherubs rose above many graves; Madonnas, heads bowed in prayer over folded hands, graced others.

The fog seemed to swirl with a life of its own. Jordan tripped over a broken old stone as they hurried off the path. Ragnor caught her arm, righting her.

"Steven is—just ahead," she told them.

He was buried in an open area between two pre-Civil War private mausoleums. She pointed out the grave.

The stone was black marble, making it hard to read the inscription in the darkness, but Lucian and Ragnor seemed to have no problem with night vision.

They paused for just a moment. Jordan remembered the day when she had stood here and listened to the prayers as Steven had been interred.

It had rained.

The sky had been a leaden gray. She had felt as if they were burying her heart.

Now she was allowing people to dig him up.

There would be no way to stop them, she knew.

Sean carried three spades in the duffel bag. He took them out, and the three men started digging. Jordan watched, standing just a few feet back, amazed at the spced with which the men could move the dirt.

She swallowed hard, feeling the mist swirl around her. She closed her eyes, imagining them bringing up the coffin. It was sealed in lead. She didn't know what device Sean had brought for that, or how he'd managed to get this luggage on the plane, but she was sure it had to do with the 'last-minute arrangements' they had made at the airport.

Soon they would reach the coffin. She was afraid it would be like the old Hammer films she watched on the Movie Channel. They would open it up; there would be a horrible creaking sound. And there would be Steven, restored to health and splendor, sleeping with his arms crossed over his chest. And he would open his eyes, but she wouldn't see Steven's eyes, she would see the red glowing orbs of a demon . . .

"We're down to the vault," Ragnor said to Sean.

Sean crawled out of the hole and saw Jordan's pale face. "It's almost over."

He had some kind of a battery-operated welding gun in the bag. He grabbed it and dropped back into the hole. Jordan heard the hoot of an owl and clenched her teeth, looking around the graveyard.

She stared back at the hole, seeing the sparks that created an eerie red glow within. Then, as she watched and listened to the drone of the gun, she had the feeling that someone was behind her.

She turned. There *was* someone there. A young man in tattered jeans and a worn Grateful Dead T-shirt.

His hair was long and greasy; he looked as if he'd been on his way to a street fight.

She didn't scream; she just stared at him in surprise.

Then he smiled. She saw the fangs of her dreams. In life, the youth hadn't kept up his teeth. They were marred and yellowed, and even the glistening fangs seemed almost green.

She opened her mouth. At first, no sound came. Then she managed to scream while reaching into her purse for the holy water.

She threw it at him, doubting her ability to do harm.

To her amazement, he screamed, louder than she. It might have been acid that she had thrown at him, the way he clutched his face, backing away. She heard a sizzling sound . . . saw flesh on his face began to decompose . . .

He wasn't alone. A foul-looking young woman with spiked hair came running up from behind him, as if she were a frenzied animal. Jordan tossed more water from her Venetian vial. It was not enough, for the girl was still coming.

Before she could reach Jordan, a black shadow seemed to fall before her. Jordan saw Ragnor's bulk take shape. He swung a fist, knocking the girl from her intent, sending her flying back against a tree. The youth remained on the ground, rolling in pain. The girl sat stunned, slumped against the tree for one moment; then she rose again, as insanely as a rabid dog, and came running forward.

By then, Ragnor had taken up a discarded spade. He swung as she ran. Jordan cried out with a sick sound as she heard the spade strike against the girl's throat. She turned away, knowing that the head was flying free from the body.

Lucian, too, had come from the grave. He walked over to the rolling youth. Jordan turned away, not wanting to see the end.

"There's one more coming," Lucian said, walking back to Ragnor.

"The businessman from the restaurant," Ragnor said. He inclined his head toward Jordan. "I think that Buffy the Vampire Slayer here is out of holy water."

Sean nodded, taking a stance by the grave. The other two slipped back in. A moment later, she heard a groaning, like nails pulling hard against a board. They had the leaden sarcophagus off. Then she heard the wrenching of wood.

Then . . .

Silence.

"What is it?" Jordan demanded tersely.

Sean Canady walked around the grave, leading her carefully. Ragnor had a flashlight in the hole.

He shone it into the coffin.

Jordan nearly retched. There was a body in the coffin. Burned and decomposed. Hair gone; features hardly recognizable as human.

"I told you!" she breathed. "I told you!" She backed away. "Put the cover back; fix the lead shield. For the love of God, let him rest in peace!" She turned, ready to walk away from the coffin. She stopped instantly.

There was a man in front of her now, in a business suit. Pleasant looking. Dusty blond hair, nice eyes, easy smile.

Except that he smiled with long teeth. "Come!" he said softly.

Ragnor rose from the grave; floated from it, as if he were on an invisible elevator platform. Jordan realized she was suddenly more afraid of him than of the strange businessman.

"Come with me," the man beckoned again. "This man doesn't know what a woman is for. I can show you."

Ragnor stepped forward. Jordan turned away, covered her ears with her hands. Sean came to her, holding her against his chest.

"A lot to take in, huh?" he asked her.

"Please . . . let's finish and get out of here."

Later, in the car on the way to the airport, she asked, "What about the people we've now left in the graveyard? And the freshly dug earth around Steven's remains?"

"The police will have a bad time with that," Sean mused.

"That's it . . . ?" Jordan said.

"There was nothing else we could do tonight," Ragnor said.

Jordan had chosen not to sit by him. She was in the front with Sean, who drove. "What do you make of our visitors?" Lucian asked Ragnor.

"Rank amateurs," Ragnor murmured.

"I agree."

"I think they were sent to delay us, no more. Or make us believe we weren't up against much power or strength."

"Those young people were someone's children," Jordan said.

"They had lost their children already," Sean told her quietly. He looked her way. "Maybe that will help you understand. This has to be stopped."

Ragnor touched her shoulder. "You are handy with a vial of holy water. And it will work against enemies such as those. But you should know as well, seawater is deadly."

"Seawater?"

"Seawater. It's absolutely deadly. To all of us. And Venice is full of canals. Remember that, if . . ."

The 'if' scared her. As traumatized as she had been, she realized that she was suddenly afraid *for* him rather than *of* him.

At a gas station outside the airport, they cleaned up. They arrived in plenty of time to board early, and Jordan realized that whoever had put out the money for the tickets must have some real income.

Last minute, first class tickets. The plane was a 777. Jordan felt almost as unreal boarding the plane calmly with them as she had felt standing in the cemetery.

She found herself taking the seat beside Ragnor. She indulged in champagne.

He read a magazine. *U.S. News and World Report.*

Somewhere over the Atlantic, she knew that she was tired enough to sleep. But before she extended her nearly horizontal seat, she turned to him, studying his features again.

"Do you believe that I lived before?" she asked him.

"I never gave it any thought. Why?"

She shook her head. "Just curious. Maggie thought she had met Sean before. That—that he had been the great love in her life, or something like that, years and years ago. And she told me that Lucian was convinced, when he met Jade, that she had been someone else."

He turned back to his magazine. "I've known many people throughout the years."

"Ah. But there wasn't a great love of your life?"

He stared at her again. "I'm sorry; if there ever was one . . ."

"Yes?"

"A long, long time ago, it was Nari."

"Oh."

She turned away from him, stunned, feeling like a fool.

Later, she thought she felt his fingers, smoothing her hair. She did. She heard his soft whisper. "Sad, huh?"

"What?"

"That I once knew Nari so well."

"You still saw her in Venice."

He shook his head. "Only to demand answers."

"I thought for sure that you—I don't know. That you were one of her . . . kind. Well, you are one of her kind. That you were with her. I mean, part of her . . . following."

He had leaned toward her, but he didn't press his point.

"I will destroy her," he told her softly.

"Can you, really?"

"Without blinking. Someday soon, I'll tell you why."

She wasn't going to get any more out of him than that. She twisted in her comfortable chair, trying to sleep.

He pulled her little pillow against his shoulder.

She slept until the cabin lights came on, and the flight attendant offered breakfast before landing in Rome.

They transferred to their last flight.

And it was mid-morning when they at last reached Venice again.

They walked to the dock where the water taxis

waited. Jordan didn't have to remind Ragnor why they were back. He asked the driver to take them to the hospital as quickly as possible.

Seawater! She remembered.

Seawater could destroy the beasts.

CHAPTER 21

For years, Nari was the perfect companion. She so nearly perished that night; whether he had chosen to obey the ancient rules or not, Edgar had survived the carnage, and he would have gladly taken a sword to Nari's throat. But she had cried so pathetically, begged forgiveness, and pleaded in such a way that even Lucian and Wulfgar had shrugged, saying that by their law, they could not simply take her head, or throw her with premeditation into the flames, or cut out her heart.

And so she had lived. And spent the next weeks, months, years, decades, trying to prove that she had learned loyalty, control, and moderation. Ragnor preferred to spend his time in the very far north; she seemed, for those years, to want nothing more than to be with him.

Wars came and wars ended. The world was ruled by

the sane and merciful, and by the cruel. Every rebellion from a new lord brought about another new lord much the same.

But when King Philip of France sent out his call to arms in a great Crusade, Ragnor decided to leave the northern isle they had called home for so many years and ride to battle. Nari encouraged him and came with him on the Holy Crusade. The journey fascinated him; he loved the different places they went—France, Spain, and Italy—on the way to meet the Infidels. Italy especially fascinated him; the Romans had left behind such magnificent masterpieces in sculpture and architecture. It often amazed him that the ancient civilization had come so far, only to perish in the wealth of excess, with, of course, a little help from barbarian tribes. Nari was amused by his wonder at everything they saw. She was familiar with Italy and the days of the Roman Empire. It was as they traveled that she told him that it was a homecoming for her, in a way, since she had come from the East as a child, and lived in Italy for many years.

The Infidels were intriguing as well; they were exceptionally learned, and as dedicated to their Allah as the Christians were to their one true God.

But the desert sands were hot, the fighting was fierce, and in such a world, sides must be taken. There were gains, and there were losses, and Ragnor fought with as great an ardor as any man, and he killed, as death was the duty of a knight in battle. A man such as he needed enemies.

There were times as well when the enemies negotiated, and he was often with the leaders of the great Crusade when they met with the representatives of the great Arab leader Saladin. The tents of the enemy were exotic and rich, the fabrics of the draperies were exceptionally fine. During one such meeting, he met a man he quickly recognized as one of his own kind. When the talks had finished on a discordant note, he met with the swarthy fellow outside. "Your Christians will perish here," he told Ragnor, as they stood by their horses, ready to mount. "I am eager for this battle; there is nothing like the taste of a holy warrior who is in the midst of an effort to seize the homeland of my people."

"There is nothing like the taste of a man who believes his god will honor him for the death and destruction of others," Ragnor replied.

The Arab shrugged, a grin on his strong, swarthy, face. "Indeed, for the two of us, there is simply the love of the taste of battle, and what better excuse than a war for ideals?"

"There will always be wars over ideals."

"Indeed. Thank both Allah and your God for that!" said the Arab.

His name was Ali Eban, and in the battles to come, he excelled, and was noted by the Christian warriors with great respect. And as even the leaders of men, King Richard of England among them, were excessive in their slaughter. whatever rampant tastes he allowed himself went unnoticed.

One night, returning to the scene of a battle with Nari, Ragnor found that he was not the only man to slip back to the battlefield. The Arab Ali Eban was there, ripping into the injured with a wanton and careless abandon. He and Ragnor came face to face, and when Ali realized that he was not up against an easily taken opponent, he backed away, sharply reminding Ragnor of the law of the ancients.

"Seize upon your own dying then, and leave those who will walk again," Ragnor told him.

Ali motioned to him, indicating that he would bow to that term. Nari stood at Ragnor's side and was with him when they parted. She feasted upon those who were near to death, speaking gently, easing them on to their Heaven. She returned with Ragnor to the Christian camp that night, and she was more exotic and passionate than ever in her lovemaking.

In the morning, she was gone.

He hunted her through the months that followed. And when he came upon her and Ali again in the aftermath of a cataclysmic battle, he stole her back.

When she cried that time, he wrapped her in a shroud with a stake in her heart, found one of the oldest churches in the ancient town, and paid a somehow knowing priest to see that she was encased in stone, and buried deeply.

Nari would always be a child of her nature. On her own, she did not practice the wanton excesses that would see them all destroyed. But she would always betray him when she saw another pack with which to run.

Ragnor saw Nari once again in later years.

He was dividing his time between England and France in those days, having taken up company with a young French countess who had determined to help her countrymen escape the excess of the machine invented by Dr. Guillotine. The French royalty had certainly shown disdain for the masses, but the machine of the revolution rolled into a heinous persecution of so many innocents, it was impossible to stop the flow of cruelty.

Ragnor was glad of the challenge of stealing the

innocent from the jails, and seeing the consternation of the powerful when their victims disappeared by night.

He had slipped into the Bastille one night to take the keys from the jailors and to take enough blood from the guards to leave them unconscious. He entered a cell to find that his old lover was among the broken and fallen on the floor. He hadn't recognized her at first, but one of the other prisoners—a girl huddled against a wall as far as possible from her—told him that the woman was Countess Arabella—and that she was going to the guillotine for her abuse of her servants.

"Abuse?"

"She was married to the Lord d'Argentin. He was rumored to be a monster of a man, but he was killed when the father of a peasant girl he had taken went mad and sliced him to ribbons with a sickle. That did not stop the countess; she was the wife of royalty and protected by the crown. The law pretended that she did not entertain herself with the deaths of her servants," the girl told him. "I beg of you! Save me. I have been in terror here! The guillotine would be a blessing over having her awaken in this cell and find me! As yet, she has not harmed me, for she was sorely injured when she was seized. If you must save her, then, good sir, leave me, for I would die happily rather than live with her near."

Ragnor paused there for a very long time. He had heard rumors about the Lord d'Argentin and the Countess Arabella, the nobleman's lady who had caused the disappearance of many young maids and servant boys.

Hundreds of years had passed. He still felt something of an old pain.

Still, he turned away. He knew that it would be right for Nari to go to the guillotine.

"Come, we head for England tonight," he told the girl.

He reached for the young girl, and left the cell.

In the days ahead, he waited, certain that he would know, that he would feel something when the time came, when the blade fell, and Nari's existence was at last ended forever.

The feeling never came.

Then, years and years later . . .

He awoke. And he knew.

She was back.

CHAPTER 22

Ragnor asked the questions at the desk when they arrived, explaining that Jordan was Jared Riley's closest living relative.

He didn't, however, come up with her. He said that he and Lucian had to start moving, but that she shouldn't be worried; Sean would be there with her. He fingered the cross she wore around her neck, smiling.

"It doesn't work against you," she murmured.

He smiled. "I'm partial to nice pieces like this."

"Does it mean anything to you?"

"Yes, actually, it does. One of the best friends I ever had was an abbot, and he taught me the safety of a church—and his faith. But keep it on, at all costs. It can help to keep you safe."

"Will it stop someone like Nari?"

"At the least, it would delay her."

"Is there anything else I should know?"

"Yes. Someone like Nari *cannot* enter a building that is consecrated. If you're ever in trouble in the streets, get into a church. Thankfully, in Venice, remember, there are over two hundred."

She smiled. "I'll remember."

Sean took her hand in support as they went up to Jared's room. He told her he'd be just outside, waiting, if she needed him.

She gave a little cry at the door when she looked in at Jared. He was beyond ashen. IVs pumped blood into him through a needle in his arm. He looked as if he was dead already.

"You're back."

She started, turning to see that Cindy was slumped into a chair at the rear of the room.

She didn't look much better than Jared. She had almost no coloring; her beautiful hair had taken on a lusterless hue. Her sweater was buttoned wrong.

"I'm here." She came over to Cindy, wondering if her cousin-in-law was going to throw off her touch when she tried to hug her.

But Cindy's malice hadn't remained. She broke into a flood of tears. "I love him so much!" She looked at Jared with wild eyes. "I thought that . . . oh, God, Jordan! I was . . . no, I am . . . certain that he was having an affair with that woman. The contessa. But . . . I love him." She gripped Jordan's arm, and her pupils seemed large and distorted.

She was on a tranquilizer, Jordan realized.

"It's that woman. That's why he's dying."

"He's not going to die," Jordan said, wishing that she was certain.

"I've called the police. They're going to come and

talk to me. I've hated to leave him . . . but you're here now. You—if I'm out of the room, and he takes a turn . . . you'll come get me."

"Of course."

Jordan gently disentangled herself from Cindy's frantic hold and went to sit by her cousin's side.

He had been dead still. He moved his head then, from side to side. His lips started moving. She leaned low. "Jared, it's going to be all right," she said firmly. Tears rushed to her eyes. "Jared, they're giving you blood. It's going to make you live. It's going to cure you."

She was amazed when he suddenly gripped her wrist. His eyes opened on her. "Jordan!" He gave her a weak smile. "Forgive me. Cindy . . . never forgive me. Police, no, the police, too late, God, no . . . God can't forgive me."

She smoothed his brow. "Jared, it's going to be all right."

"No . . . dying."

"Not anymore. You're not going to die."

Cindy had heard him and had risen. Jordan shifted aside so that she could reach him. She was crying again. "Jared, don't you dare die, I love you, I forgive you, I'll see that she dies, that evil, evil woman . . ."

Jordan watched as she leaned over Jared, holding him tight. He had stopped speaking. For a moment, it felt to Jordan as if her own heart stopped. Then she looked at the machines that were monitoring him. His pulse was slow, but steady.

He was still breathing.

There was a soft tap at the door. She looked to it. Roberto Capo was standing there. She gasped with surprise and pleasure, and walked out. He was alive and well. On second thought, not too well. He looked thin and pinched, and before she could hug him, he lifted a hand, warning her away, and sneezed.

She ignored the hand and gave him a hug. "You're all right."

"Non troppo bene!" he said. *"Not all right,* but hopefully . . . soon. I'm so sorry you were worried."

She saw that Sean was there, just as he had said he would be. "Sean, I'd like you to meet—" she began.

But Sean stopped her. "We've introduced ourselves."

"American cop," Roberto said sagely, indicating Sean.

"Yes," she said and smiled.

"We will find out the truth behind the contessa, eh?" Roberto said.

"Yes."

He held both of her hands for a minute, then sighed. "I have come to talk to Cindy. She called . . . very upset. She doesn't know how, but she thinks the contessa made Signore Jared sick. I have come so that she can talk to me."

"Thank God it's you, and not Alfredo," Jordan murmured.

Roberto shrugged. "Alfredo is here, too. In the waiting room."

Cindy wasn't up to handling such a skeptic at the moment, Jordan thought. She looked at Sean. "Perhaps you could go introduce yourself to another Italian. And explain . . ."

Sean arched a brow to her.

"Explain about some of the murders in America."

"Sure. Except that—"

"Alfredo speaks English perfectly."

Sean nodded with relief. "Sure."

"Thank you!" Jordan whispered. He walked down the hall to the waiting room.

"Roberto, maybe you could talk to Cindy here, away from Alfredo. She's . . . she's on medication, I'm sure. And not making much sense."

"Of course."

Jordan went back into the room. "Cindy, Roberto is here."

Cindy jumped up. "I'm going to tell him. They have to arrest that woman."

Cindy went out of the room with Roberto, and Jordan took a seat next to Jared again. She watched the machines. She looked at his face again, stroked his cheek. *Don't die, don't die! I know that you're not evil, and you might have been under the influence of a monster, but in truth, you're not one yourself, you can't become one yourself!*

Was his color just a little bit better?

The door suddenly opened again. It was Roberto. "She's . . . crazy," he said. "She ran out—I will follow."

Jordan looked at Jared, then shook her head. Sean was still here, just down the hall with Alfredo.

She ran out, after Roberto, down the hall, and to the elevators. He watched the numbers, then started for the stairs. Jordan ran after him. They reached the bottom of the stairs after the elevator, despite the speed with which they had descended. "She was so . . . wild. I'm afraid . . ."

"That she'll hurt herself?" Jordan queried. *Why in hell had Cindy run out of the hospital?*

"There . . . there's . . . Cindy."

She was hurrying for the docks. Hailing a water taxi.

"Stop!" Roberto shouted.

Too late; Cindy had hopped in.

"We have to follow her!" Jordan said, grabbing his hand. They ran to the docks. Tourists strolled into the line right ahead of them.

"No!" Jordan whispered.

Roberto pulled out his badge. "Polizia!" he said firmly, and this time, he took Jordan's hand, dragging her along.

They hopped on to the next water taxi that came along. Roberto spoke to the driver.

They sped over the open water, then slowed as they followed the taxi ahead through various narrow canals.

"Where is she going?" Jordan murmured.

"I know this place . . . it's near the trattoria. She's going to the church," Roberto said.

She glanced at him, and suddenly something stirred in her mind.

Mistrust!

The water taxi came to the dock. While Roberto spoke with the driver in Italian, Jordan made a run for it. Skirting one piazza, she raced down a narrow alley, studying the buildings around her. She saw an arrow directing a left turn with the words *Campo di Fratelli.* Campo . . . it meant a square with a church. She followed the sign and sighed with relief when she saw a notice board in front, listing the times for Mass. She started for it, passing an outdoor café where a few people were sharing drinks.

There was a wine decanter on a table right by the street. She deftly swept it from the table, and poured out the wine as she raced for the church, praying that no one had seen her.

She ran into the church. There were a number of

people in it, their heads bowed in prayer. One or two looked up.

She looked around for an urn of holy water, found it, and filled her carafe. As she was doing so, she saw that a frowning priest was walking toward her. She flipped out her cross as she filled the carafe. "Catholic, father. Honestly. I swear to you!"

With her carafe half full, she started to run out of the church—and ran straight into a man. As she started to apologize, she gave a nervous laugh instead.

She had crashed straight into Raphael.

"Jordan!" he said with pleasure. "I had heard that you left Italy. I heard that your cousin is sick as well, I'm so sorry—"

"It's all right. But you have to help me. Cindy is in danger."

She grabbed his arm. "Raphael, there are vampires, and I'm not crazy. The contessa is part of an awful group of—of—bloodsuckers, and I'm afraid that even the cops may be in on it. Come on!"

"Come on?" He tugged back a little as she dragged him, "Where?"

"The deconsecrated church. Please, help me!"

He let out a deep sigh, but allowed her to drag him along.

"This street is shorter," he told her.

"No . . . I need . . . first . . ."

"What? What?"

She saw a small trash can just outside the door to an office building. It would do. "I need water, canal water."

"Jordan, please. Let me buy you a drink—"

"I need canal water. Hold this!" She handed him

the holy water, dumped the trash, and filled the can with water from the canal.

It wasn't as easy to run with the trash can, but Jordan moved as quickly as she could. Raphael followed.

When they reached the church, she hesitated at the door. Shadows seemed to be all around the church. She felt a strange, very cold, breeze. She closed her eyes, and imagined the sounds of whispers . . .

Wings in the night.

Cindy was in there; she was certain.

She went up the steps, Raphael behind her.

There were no candles lit within the church. There was no light.

Suddenly, light flashed from behind her, illuminating the aisle. "You carry buckets of icy cold water. I am the one really prepared, with something useful— like a flashlight," Raphael said.

"Good, shine it up ahead."

He did so.

Jordan started for the coffin that stood in front of the altar. She reached it, knelt down, and looked.

Cindy was within it.

She was afraid. She would touch Cindy and see that her head was no longer attached . . .

"She's breathing."

"We've got to get her out of here."

But before either of them could move, there was a voice from the entry.

"There you are!"

Roberto Capo. And he sounded angry.

Jordan snatched the holy water from Raphael. As Roberto came striding toward her, she tossed a portion of the water at him.

It splashed against his face. He stopped, stunned,

and wiped his face. He swore in Italian, something that ended with, *"Americana!"*

"Roberto, I'm so sorry! I thought that—"

She broke off, suddenly chilled to the bone. Someone . . . *something* elsc was here. She turned slowly to look at Raphael. He was staring at her.

She tossed some of the water at him.

"Jordan!" he said indignantly, wiping his face as well.

"This is crazy, and must—stop!" Roberto said firmly. He reached into his pocket; for a moment, Jordan thought he was going for a gun.

He pulled out a cell phone.

"I am calling headquarters. You are all—"

"Look, will you? Cindy is in a coffin!" Jordan said.

"I am calling headquarters," Roberto repeated, flipping the phone open.

But before he could dial, they were all startled by a sudden flurry of wings, a cacophony of sound that grew louder and louder. Shadows seemed to loom over them, even in the darkness.

"Bats!" Roberto murmured, looking at the phone again.

A shadow descended.

The phone seemed to fly from his hand.

He spun around, facing the cntry.

Nari Contessa della Trieste was walking down the aisle toward them, wearing a black Carnevale cape, her hair flowing free behind her, a smile of pure amusement on her face. She stopped several feet in front of them.

"Silly, silly, man! As if you can call the police against *me!*" When she reached Roberto, she swatted him, as if he were a fly.

That simple touch was enough to send him flying far across the church and smashing into one of the pillars.

"You, you, you . . ." Raphael sputtered.

"Cat got your tongue? Or just your tongue in English?" Nari teased.

Raphael looked petrified. He reached toward Jordan, wanting the holy water. She let him have it. He was so nervous that the carafe fell.

And spilled against the floor.

Again, the contessa laughed.

"How kind of you!" she said, and another step brought her to Raphael. With the barest effort, she flicked him aside.

He crashed to the floor, hard. Jordan watched as he tried to lift his head, groaned, and fell back to the floor again.

"And dear, dear, Jordan! Here we are at last! A day of reckoning after all this time."

"What a bitch you are! " Jordan said. She still had her final weapon—the can of seawater.

Nari shrugged. "I am Diana, goddess of the hunt!" she said. "And you, dear girl, are the hunted."

She lifted her arms, stretching them to the rafters.

The flurry of wings began again.

Then a dozen shadows descended. They came to the floor and slowly took shape, encircling Jordan.

The figures wore masks and capes. Carnevale masks. Some, the expressionless theater faces of Venice. Some, creations that were more like Halloween masks . . . wolves, aliens, monsters, among them.

As Jordan spun around, looking at them all, the circle tightened.

They came closer . . .

She waited, then picked up the trash can with its seawater. She tossed it out.

To her amazement, the monster-faced creature she hit started to scream. It stopped, swirling around in horror.

It began to fall, to melt . . . with a sizzling sound. She stared.

They all stared as the creature kept melting, and melting, spilling out over the ground in a black ooze.

The eyes of the monsters, and the contessa, moved from the black ooze to Jordan's face. She saw the amazement in them, and then the anger.

"Take her," the contessa said softly.

The group hesitated.

"Take her!" the contessa screamed.

Jordan began tossing the water again, but there wasn't enough. The creatures screamed and beat at themselves where the water touched them, but they came on.

As they moved in on her, they pulled off their masks.

They were people. Old, young, male, female. No. Not people. They were smiling at her now, smiling angrily, snarling . . . growling, moving in.

She threw the last of the water. Another creature went down.

But the rest were upon her.

She screamed as rough hands reached for her. She waited to feel the pain as the gleaming fangs sank in.

But none of them broke her skin. She was lifted, struggling frantically, and thrown upon the altar. She kept screaming, kicking, shouting, flailing, as she found herself tied down. Then, to her amazement, the creatures moved away.

She was to be the contessa's supper! she thought.

But Nari merely came near the altar, standing in front of the coffin where Cindy lay in her deep, deep sleep, oblivious to it all.

Then, twisting her head, Jordan saw him.

The dottore.

The man who had appeared all around Venice. The man she had followed.

The man who had followed her.

He walked slowly toward her along the aisle, and as he came, she felt a fetid coldness unlike anything she had ever known before, a fear that went beneath her skin, a terror that was far deeper than any dread of death.

He came, closer and closer . . .

And with him, the feel of darkness. A haunting of the grave. Cold, black . . .

Evil.

He moved Nari aside and came to Jordan. He reached out gloved hands, and stroked her face, and she shrank inside, horrified. She would have screamed with revulsion and the deepest horror in her soul, but the sound would not come . . .

"Hello, Jordan!" he said softly.

And he pulled off the dottore mask.

She gasped, so stunned that for a moment, the fear left her.

"Steven!" she whispered.

Yes, Steven, and not Steven. Steven had laughed; he'd been kind, his features had been touched with life and color and . . .

His eyes now seemed to glow red, and his face was taut; his mouth, so prone to a smile, was caustic and cruel.

"In the—flesh, shall we say."

"It's impossible. I—we—they—"

"You dug up my grave, and there I was. Jordan! Come now! Another corpse, burned to a total crisp, easily passed as mine."

"I . . . no!" she whispered. "You were . . . a cop! You were compassionate—"

"Good?" he inquired. "Not at all. I was bored, and I was afraid that my wanderings in Europe—since my release—might be noticed. I didn't want to be noticed. Not then. Oh, there was a Steven Moore. And he was a right decent fellow, as they might say. I enjoyed him—and his very moral and righteous family—very much. Then I took his name and came to New Orleans. And met you. You really were incredible. So much passion and love of life and humanity all rolled into such a perfect little package. Of course, you turned out to be more of a pain than I had imagined but . . . well, all's well that ends well, right?"

"How does it end, Steven?" she asked coldly. She realized then that he had been the end; she had been shocked beyond belief. And now . . .

She couldn't fight him.

Only hate him.

"Well, the only way possible, of course. You will join us. *Us!* The true strength within our kind. You'll become a hunter. Stronger, better, than you ever were before. You'll join me now. Ah, Jordan, remember what was? It will be better. You little fool! Falling for my wretched, pathetic enemies! They are nothing, nothing against the kind of feast, and satiation, and thrill that you can know. We are the masters. The predators. And you will join me. They had me imprisoned in a steel vault in Yugoslavia for the longest time. Then there was an earthquake. The kindest people came to rescue me. I was starving. My rescuers provided the most delicious meal. I wandered, met up with dear Nari again . . . and found you. It seemed so easy. Nari got to Jared. Jared has nearly killed Cindy. And though you eluded me at the party—and in your room, and through the streets—you'll not elude me this time. I have missed you, my love, and now . . . now we'll be together."

He started to lean toward her, as tender a lover as he had ever been.

But his mouth opened. His fangs dripped, oozed with saliva. They were immense, longer, ridiculously long, and sharp. She watched them. She closed her eyes, clenching her teeth, waiting, praying . . .

He gave out a startled sound, ripped back from her. Jordan's eyes flew open.

Another shadow had descended, a shadow so large, winged and menacing, it seemed to cover all the church.

Ragnor.

He had drawn Steven from her but now the two faced one another.

"Get away from her," Ragnor said.

"It is Steven," Jordan got out. "You were right."

"Steven, yes, and no. Hagan, get the hell away from her."

Steven laughed. "You really didn't know it was me? I've gotten good. You couldn't get into my mind. You thought I was still deeply buried from the last time we warred. No, I've been drinking blood—so much of it! I have a power even you can't imagine now."

"I'm telling you one last time—get away from her."

"No, brother, this one is mine. I've always been able to take your women."

"Brother?" Jordan whispered, working furiously at

the knots binding her to the altar as the two men stared one another down.

"Half brother," Ragnor said. "I should have known. He has spent the last thousand years trying to destroy me."

"She has no interest in you, brother. I'm telling you—I've always had the ability to take your woman."

"You mean Nari? Well, she didn't prove to be such a treasure. But this woman, Hagan? No, you'll never take her."

Ragnor smiled at her. She felt something flood within her at the sign of assurance, and of faith. With a shrug, he extended his wry grin to the man he called Hagan—the man she had known as Steven.

"You've spent your existence being jealous of me. This time, it's going to send you on. Not to Valhalla, but to the Hel, or Hell, or whichever in truth you care to call it, after all these years."

"I don't think so."

"I do. The old rules have been broken too many times. This time, you will die your second death, and it will be over."

Jordan shrieked in both pain and surprise as Hagan reached for her, his grip so strong that it broke the ropes tied around her wrists and ankles, burning her flesh, nearly breaking bone. He drew her to stand before him. He lifted her hair. She felt the heat of his breath. His teeth were lowering. "Watch brother," he whispered. "As I take her . . . for eternity."

She saw, just below her, a small puddle of the holy water that had fallen before. It had pooled between two tiles in the ancient floor.

She slammed her elbow back into his ribs and ducked for the water. Not enough! Still, as he roared, ready to restrain her again, she splashed the little droplets into his eyes.

He roared with pain.

She was free.

She raced forward, straight into Ragnor's arms. He caught her shoulders, met her eyes. He moved her carefully aside.

Ragnor walked toward Hagan. He sensed the movement, and went flying upward toward the ceiling, landing on the rafters. Ragnor followed him. With a sudden, fierce shriek Nari went flying after Ragnor.

He threw her back down. She landed hard on the floor. A massive wave seemed to move across the ceiling as Hagan cried out to the others. "Seize him, kill him, take him, you fools! I am half blinded."

Before the others could rise, Ragnor had returned to the floor. As Hagan's followers came after him, he caught them one by one. He took them by their heads and shoulders . . .

Twisted.

Dropped the pieces.

Someone came flying out from a side altar after him, brandishing a sword. The creature never reached Ragnor.

Lucian slipped down from the rafters, seized the attacker by the neck, took the sword, and ended him quickly.

Others suddenly began to appear. Jordan ducked down, for it seemed as if the ancient church was filled with bats.

Bats, wings, noises . . . a chattering, soft at first, then growing in a crescendo.

The door to the church was suddenly flung open.

Sean Canady came in, vials strapped to his chest, a sword at his waist, and buckets in both hands.

He threw water in a swinging, upward, arc.

Screams of agony echoed so loudly that Jordan covered her ears, praying. She looked up just in time to see a shadow forming, coming for her . . .

She turned and fled toward Sean, ripping one of the vials from the holder on his chest. She tossed the holy water at her would-be attacker. She watched, still amazed, as he shrieked . . .

And decomposed.

The noise suddenly died away.

The floor was littered.

With freshly dead . . .

And decaying bones. Then a massive flutter, like wings, seemed to vibrate the entire structure. She looked up. The massive shadows of Ragnor and his brother met again and again. Sean started to move forward.

Lucian was suddenly at his side, holding his arm.

"No. Ragnor must finish this himself."

The shadows came back to the ground.

The two men stared at one another in fury.

"Who wants to live forever?" Ragnor inquired quietly.

Hagan let out a roar and rushed him. It was a mistake. Ragnor was ready. He bowed his frame and caught his brother by the head as he would have butted him into the wall.

There was a twisting sound. Sickening. Horrible.

Then all that Ragnor held was bone that fell from his hands to the floor, becoming dust. He stared at his hands.

There was a sudden motion at the side of the church.

Jordan turned to see Nari, ready to slip away. She raced to the door, breathing heavily, ready to face the woman.

She realized she had no weapons.

Ragnor had come down the aisle. Nari turned to him. "Ragnor! How can you forget what we were?"

"Time, my dear, has had a wonderful effect on that. Then again, there was the fact that you betrayed me—with my brother—trapped me, and tried to kill me."

"Ragnor—"

"Throughout history, Nari, every time you've escaped . . ."

"But Ragnor, you can't!" she whispered. She walked to him, placing her hands on his chest, looking up into his eyes. "Ragnor . . ."

He lifted his arm and wrapped it around her. Like the others in the room, he had worn a Carnevale cape.

It covered Nari as he cradled her to him.

Then he dropped his arm.

A great pile of dust fell to the floor.

Ragnor turned to Lucian. "It is over," he said softly.

Lucian nodded.

"I'll deal with the local law enforcement," Sean said, indicating Roberto where he lay on the floor, just coming to.

Ragnor inclined his head in agreement. He kept walking down the aisle. He reached out a hand to Jordan, just far enough away so that she would have to take a step forward to accept.

"You are different, you know."

"Oh?"

"A thousand years worth of different," he said softly. "Take my hand?"

"Where will we go?"

"We'll have to see," he told her. "You've wanted the truth. Confessions. There are lots of them I can give you now."

She inclined her head. "At the least, it must be interesting listening."

"I didn't intend to talk all night."

She smiled and reached for his hand, then hesitated. "Cindy!"

"I'll get her back to the hospital," Lucian assured her.

"And Raphael, he may be hurt—"

"We'll all go to the hospital," Lucian said with a shrug.

"Well?" Ragnor offered his hand again.

She took his hand and smiled.

"Just so long as you *don't* talk all night . . .

They left together.

He could talk . . . and talk. And she wanted explanations. Lots of them.

But . . .

Only time would really tell

For a sneak preview
of Shannon Drake's next
novel in this series
coming from Zebra Books
in October, 2002,
just turn the page . . .

The gloom in the crypt was overwhelming. Despite the many portable lamps hung around the vault deep in the earth, the corners were cast into gloomy shadows, shadows that moved in a macabre dance, bringing to life an eerie profusion of angels, saints, gargoyles, and demonic statues.

"Dig carefully!" Professor Dubois admonished.

Carefully! They could barely see.

"Carefully, carefully!" he repeated.

The man was distraught. But then, to Jean-Luc, Dubois always appeared on the edge of a frenzy, as if his explorations in the crypt were world-shattering and his findings would change the shape of the globe.

Down in the ground, in the area of deconsecrated ruins of the old St. Michael's recently rediscovered foundations, the workmen were tired. Jean-Luc Beauvoir stared at the professor with his coke-bottle glasses and wild gray hair and bit his lip to keep silent. He and the American, Brent Malone, had been working tirelessly for hours, slowly, slowly digging away the age-old rot around the coffins. Professor Dubois was expecting an incredible archeological find. He was certain he was going to unearth not only the dead, but worldwide recognition, honors and awards, and naturally, the fortune to be made from the book he would write, and the lectures and speeches he would give. The professor gave little thought to the fact that most learned men thought he was a raving lunatic, or that he had bought his way into the excavation by bribery—or a large donation to the current St. Michael's. Little money had been left to pay for the highly trained archeological staff Dubois had wanted, and so the professor constantly shouted orders and ridicule at the two-man team of laborers he had managed to obtain. The American seemed able to silence the professor with a single stare from his strange, gold-tinted hazel eyes, but the professor would merely start all over again.

The St. Michael's now standing in the little village just outside Paris dated back to the sixteenth century; the crypt in the old ruins they now worked so laboriously to probe and restore predated the new church by three or four hundred years. The work was treacherous, but they had shored up the area enough to allow for tourists to pay extra francs to come and view the dig in process. Now, to add to the aggravation of the professor leaning over their shoulders, directing the tedious and backbreaking labor, there were the curious tourists stopping to ask questions every other minute. The Americans were easy to ignore; he pretended he spoke no English. The French were more annoying because the professor would pause to speak with them, then shout at his laborers again that they were working too roughly; they might damage coffins that had survived for centuries.

Jean-Luc stared over at Brent and rolled his eyes as a young woman began a conversation with the professor. Not just a young woman. A beautiful one, with a smooth cultured voice and a knowledge of the area and the church. Her accent was definitely American. Her comments were knowledgable, and there was a curious charm to the sound of her voice. It was not lost on the professor. The old man was not without a lascivious nature; he would hold the young woman to balance her over the opening so that she could see better, and so that he could get his bony hands upon her young flesh.

Brent didn't seem to catch Jean Luc's look. He was distracted, not noting the young woman talking to the professor, either. He was studying the area where they worked, which connected to the underbelly of the new church through a maze of vaults and corridors, many of which had housed the bones of the noble dead. This area, some distance from the new foundations, was different in its style and decor. Typical Gothic arches created both support and architectural features, but the walls and crypts were decorated with a strange combination of the customary and the bizarre. Large crosses, in various metals, surrounded the grave sites, but they were joined by demonic gargoyles and other such creatures.

In the pit where they now dug, they had just come to an obstruction. Brent knew it, and the American knew it. As the professor chatted with the young woman in French, Brent at last gave Jean-Luc his undivided attention. He gave a little shake of his head, indicating that they should not tell the professor just what point they had reached.

Jean-Luc grinned. The American was smart. The corpse they were about to exhume might be laden with precious jewels and adorned in gold. Let the professor have his accolades. They would take the riches.

But the American frowned, and Jean-Luc frowned as well. What was Brent planning?

The young woman was lingering, speaking with the professor, but watching the American as he worked in the crypt. Why not? Jean-Luc thought with a shrug. The woman was young. Pretty. She had blond hair and smooth skin. Professor Dubois was as wrinkled as a prune and as wild looking as an electrocuted Pekinese. The American was tall and wiry with an easy grace of movement and finely honed muscles that seemed to swell and tighten each time he used a tool. His features marked him as somewhere between twenty-five and thirty-five years in age, while his eyes were that strange green gold color and his hair, neatly long, almost to his shoulders, frequently queued, was a dark sable. Rich, probably tempting to a young woman. The world didn't change. Women might marry a man with intelligence and riches, but when it came to man with whom to find pleasure, they tended to hunt out a man with physical power. Animal instinct. The American, however, wasn't giving the pretty woman the least notice. He was pretending to dig deeper now, but making no real moves to disclose whatever treasure they might have come upon.

Jean Luc had simply paused; now he wondered if it was the American, or the grave, to which the young lady was giving her sharp attention while casually making conversation with the professor.

"Professor," Brent said suddenly and impatiently, interrupting the conversation and leaning on his shovel.

"What is it?" Dubois demanded.

The American looked at his watch. "It's late. We have to begin again in the morning."

"Not so late. We shouldn't stop. I have studied the old records. We must be nearly upon the grave."

"And if you are upon the grave you seek, you'll want experts in here to move the final layers of dirt and sand, and you will not get the professionals you will need at this time. As of now, we have nothing here, nothing to bring in grave robbers by night. If we start again by morning, you will have ample time to do your discovery justice. It is nearly seven. We have already worked hours overtime. The church is closed. We must get this young lady out, and close down for the evening."

"Oh, I have overstayed!" The young woman exclaimed. "I simply find it all so fascinating. Forgive me."

"Forgive you? Not at all, my dear," Dubois said, drawing Jean-Luc's greater attention to the woman. She wore jeans and a sweater and handsome black loafers, now covered with the dust from this realm of the dead. Simple clothing, but worn very well, hugging the form that had so drawn the professor's intrigue. Her hair was drawn back in a smooth, sleek ponytail that heightened the fine sculpture of her features. Her eyes, deepened by the murky light and shadow, appeared to be almost turquoise, the color of the sea off the coast of France. They were never going to get the professor to let this morsel go . . . Jean Luc could almost understand the aging man's desire to hold on to something so simple as conversation, just as long as he could.

"Shall I see our guest out?" Brent asked bluntly. He stared coolly at the woman. "She needs to be *out*."

"Yes, of course, she must be seen safely out, but you

must finish up. I will see the young lady out," Dubois said. "My dear, if you will?"

"Oh, please, don't worry, I can make my way," she said pleasantly. "I am simply so intrigued. I'll be back, if I may?"

"Please, you are so very welcome, Miss . . ." Dubois said.

"Marceau. Genevieve Marceau, professor. And thank you, you've been so kind."

"A French name. But you're an American."

"Of French descent. And I'm familiar with such vaults—"

"But still! Alor! You must not go alone. The flooring is tricky. And despite the lights . . . well, it gets late, and though we are underground, it seems even darker once the night has come."

"I am absolutely fine. I will see you then, professor. Thank you so very much."

She shook the professor's hand; he was loath to let go of it. She managed to retrieve her fingers, and repeated, "I'm fine, please!" She started out then, quickly, determined to exit on her own. The professor looked after her for a long while. When she was gone at last, he stared with narrowed eyes at the American. "Make sure that the tomb is secured when you leave. Totally secured."

"Of course."

The professor glanced at his watch. "You're right. I must make calls . . . find the right people. And you! Jean Luc! Keep your heavy hand off the work from now on. You hack away as if you were plowing weed-strewn fields. This is great work going on here."

Without another word, the professor turned and started from the tomb.

Brent looked at Jean Luc. "I have to open this tomb tonight," he said.

"Yes, yes, of course. We have done the work. The professor will take everything; we are nothing to him but muscle. He is like a slave driver. But what will we do? If we rob the tomb, he will know. The government will be called in."

"No, no, pay attention to me," Brent said impatiently. "We will open it carefully, and reseal it."

"And rob it first, of course."

"No."

"But—"

"There will be a trinket, something you can take. But we are not robbing the tomb."

"Then . . ."

"There will be a reward for you, and Dubois will never know. All right? Help me with the last of the dirt. Quickly."

They both went to work. The dirt was easy to shift but the sarcophagus was covered by a huge stone slab.

"We will never shift this," Jean Luc muttered.

"Take the side."

Jean Luc hefted his huge frame against the slab, grunting and groaning, sweat immediately popping out on his brow. The American set to the task with him. The stone shifted and Brent shouted that they must be careful; they didn't want it crashing to the floor and breaking. The stone settled. They could see the coffin itself.

It was black. Crosses abounded over and around it. Brent immediately set to work removing them; Jean Luc joined in. "There is strange writing on the coffin. Look, how odd, I cannot make it out completely, but the words speak of the devil while the coffin is covered in signs of the Lord! Sacré bleu, how very strange!''

Brent had picked up a crowbar.

"I don't think it will work. It appears as if the coffin has somehow been sealed with some kind of adherent . . . like a soddering.''

"I will open it.''

Brent shoved the crowbar against the coffin. The creaking sound it gave out caused even such a man as Jean Luc to feel a prickle of fear at his nape. The silence that followed the creaking was deep and complete.

So deep, in fact, that they were both startled to hear a sound . . . a furtive, rustling sound, coming from the exit to the vault. One of the portable lamps suddenly burned to an end; in the wall sconce at their side, a popping sounded, and the area went dark. And still, they could hear something . . . footsteps, stealthy, careful, coming from the exit to the vault.

"It's the woman, surely,'' Brent said, and swore impatiently. "I'll get rid of her. Touch nothing, nothing, do you hear me, nothing, while I am gone.''

"Of course!'' Jean Luc said. But as he watched the American silently disappear into shadows that seemed to close around him, he felt the birth of resentment in his soul. The American wanted to rob the tomb without getting caught—but Brent wanted the finest riches in the coffin to be for himself.

Jean Luc looked toward the stygian darkness of the exit vaults. Brent was not returning, yet.

He edged his way around the coffin to the side where his work partner had stood. He could not resist. He lifted the lid of the coffin, hearing again the blood-chilling creaking as the hinges, hundreds of years old, gave way. He steeled himself against the ghastly look of the ancient dead; he had become quite accustomed to skulls; to open jaws that appeared to have been captured in a victim's last scream against death. Decayed flesh, withered flesh, gray and moldy, fragments of clothes, boots, with bits of bone poking through . . . this would be nothing new.

Yet he gasped as he stared into the tomb. Their was no scent of decay; no bone to be seen. What he stared upon was . . .

Eyes.

Eyes wide open, black as pitch, but open. Staring, staring straight into Jean Luc's own. As if the corpse had never died in truth, but slept, and waited . . .

And then . . .

The corpse moved.

Moved . . . for Jean Luc.

He let out a shrill, bloodcurdling scream that might have wakened all the dead not only in Paris, but in all of France . . .

Darkness, wavering light, filled the tomb as the lamps suddenly swung. The black of the grave, the white of the flickering light . . .

The brilliant crimson color of blood . . .

All filled the tomb.

Standing in the vault, about to accost their unwelcome visitor, Brent heard the scream.

And he swore, damning himself. And damning *her*.

"My God!" she cried.

The woman had been returning to the vault. Sliding along the vaults with their smell of rot and decay, she had been returning to the site of the dig. *Why? Who the hell was she? What was she doing . . . at this site, here, and now?*

She forgot to hide as they heard Jean Luc's scream tear through the corridors of the vault like the haunted shrieking of the damned.

And so she cried out herself. Cried out, and . . .

She saw Brent, saw his eyes . . .

Her scream echoed Jean Luc's.

She turned to run.

Too late . . .

Oh, yes, by God.

Far too late . . .